PROPHECY
AND CHANGE

PROPHECY
AND CHANGE

Edited by Marco Palmieri

Based upon STAR TREK®,
created by Gene Roddenberry,
and STAR TREK: DEEP SPACE NINE,
created by Rick Berman and Michael Piller

POCKET BOOKS
New York London Toronto Sydney Singapore The Promenade

POCKET BOOKS, a division of Simon & Schuster, Inc.
1230 Avenue of the Americas, New York, NY 10020

This book is published by Pocket Books,
a division of Simon & Schuster, Inc.,
under exclusive license from Paramount Pictures.

ISBN: 0-7434-7073-7

First Pocket Books trade paperback edition September 2003

10 9 8 7 6 5 4 3 2 1

Cover art by Cliff Nielsen

Manufactured in the United States of America

For information regarding special discounts for bulk purchases,
please contact Simon & Schuster Special Sales at 1-800-456-6798
or business@simonandschuster.com.

Contents

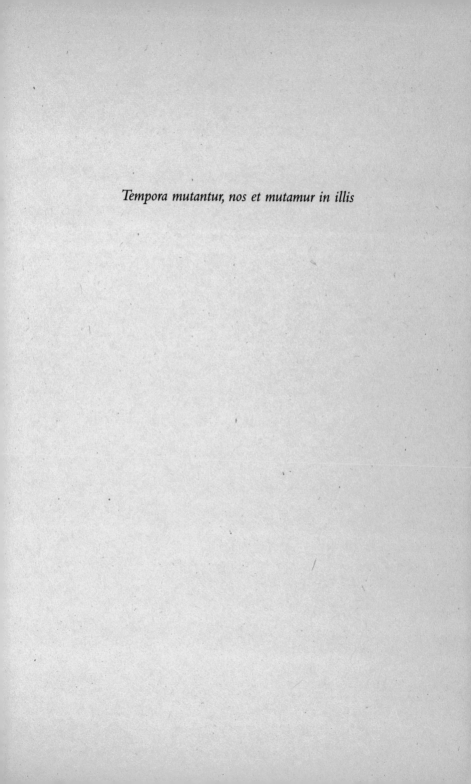

Tempora mutantur, nos et mutamur in illis

PROPHECY
AND CHANGE

Introduction:
"What We Left Behind"

When *Star Trek: Deep Space Nine* debuted in 1993, we had no idea how big a part of our lives it would become. For seven years, we ate, drank, and slept *Deep Space Nine,* gathering the details that one day would appear within our book, the *Star Trek: Deep Space Nine Companion.* Watching those 176 hours of television over and over again could have become an onerous chore. But it never did, thanks to the largely unsung efforts of the brilliant writers, the phenomenal actors, and all those behind-the-scenes people whose names, we suspect, too few viewers remember. The show kept getting better and better, with storylines that grew ever richer and more complex. The primary characters came to feel like friends, completely capturing our hearts. And not since Shakespeare has a more fascinating group of spear-carriers supported the ranks.

When the series completed its seven-season run, the two of us would have gone into serious withdrawal if we hadn't had our temporary crutch. For nearly a year after the series ended, we continued to be absorbed in completing the work on that doorstop of a tome mentioned above. During those months, we could almost imagine that the characters were still around. While we were writing, Kira commanded a daily portion of our lives. Odo insinuated his way into every conversation. Garak skulked about in our heads as we reviewed the galleys.

Then we finished the *Companion,* and our connection to those characters was severed. Marco Palmieri and the other fine folks at Pocket Books launched a series of wonderful novels that move the characters forward, exploring their lives after the close of the Dominion War, after Sisko had joined the Prophets, after Odo had gone home. But still we missed that seven-year period when they all were together on the station, living their day-to-day lives. When O'Brien could count on meeting Bashir at Quark's for an evening round of darts. When Jake and Nog could hang out together, their legs dangling above the Promenade. When the characters were learning as much about one another as we were learning about them.

Now, thanks to this book, we have brand-new stories from that extraordinary period that bring our friends back to us, exactly as they were.

Some of these stories convey the moments that must have taken place for the characters, either between scenes or between episodes, but that we didn't get to see on-screen: The triumphant moment when Nog makes a decision that will change the course of his life; The bittersweet moment when Jadzia opens her mind to the prospect of a future of hope, rather than numbing sorrow.

Some of the stories take the characters into new adventures that would have made wonderful episodes of their own: A visit from the former chief of security on Deep Space 9 draws Odo into a compelling mystery; Romance leads Quark to a not-so-pleasant realization about his true nature; Garak sends a fascinating communication to Doctor Bashir . . . but would you expect anything *less* than fascinating from the likes of Garak? Particularly in a story written by the plain, simple tailor's alter ego, Andy Robinson?

As Vic Fontaine once observed, "Nothing lasts forever." But on the pages that follow, you'll find everything it takes to get you back into the "zone" (as O'Brien might have put it), at least for a while.

Depends how fast you read, pallie.

Terry J. Erdmann and Paula M. Block
Los Angeles,
March 2003

Revisited
Part One

Anonymous

The author gratefully acknowledges the work of Michael Taylor, upon whose *Star Trek: Deep Space Nine* script, "The Visitor," this story is based.

It was raining in the bayou that night.

Softly pelting the window pane, the droplets merged and ran together over the glass, weaving a veil of streaming silver, the rivulets becoming incandescent against occasional flashes of distant lightning. In those instances, fleeting glimpses of dense greenery outside the old house became possible, but then vanished just as quickly, leaving only the delayed echo of the lightning to fill the void beyond the rain.

Jake Sisko treasured such nights; the storm had come as a pleasant surprise. He hadn't expected it, although he should have. Such things were foreseeable, after all—had been for centuries. But even now, in his advanced years, Jake found he still cherished his uncertainty of what the next day, the next hour, the next moment, would bring, especially when looking back over a life in which past, present, and future so often seemed to merge and run together.

Almost without thinking, Jake reached for the baseball on his desk, gnarled fingers brushing its old worn hide, tracing the path of its stitching before his hand closed around it. It felt good against his palm, as it always did; a simple pleasure in his old age. Playfully, he tossed it in the air, his hand staying open to catch it when gravity called it back.

As the ball reached the apex of its short flight, the door chimed.

Jake caught the baseball and half-turned toward the sound, wondering who would be calling at such a late hour, and on such a night. He returned the baseball to its pedestal, got up, and crossed the living room to the door.

There was a face framed in the diamond window—a young woman, by the look of her, and soaked to the bone. Jake *tsk*ed to himself as he hit the touchpad on the wall, and the double doors parted.

"May I help you?" Jake asked.

The young woman stared fixedly at him, her big round eyes conveying both optimism and awkwardness. She'd draped a shawl of some kind over her head—futile protection from the plump, heavy rain. "Sorry to bother you. It's just that . . . I've been . . ."

Jake noticed a nasty cut on her forehead. He ushered her inside and the doors closed. "You're hurt," he said, relieving her of the drenched shawl.

The young woman touched her forehead, saw the blood on her fingertips. "Yeah, I must have scraped myself on a branch."

"Ah, that's what happens when you go tromping around the bayou in the middle of the night," Jake said good-naturedly, guiding her toward the fireplace and laying the wet shawl over the back of the couch. "Come, warm yourself by the fire. I have a first aid kit around here somewhere. Now, where is it . . . ?" Spotting the kit across the room on a high shelf, Jake went to retrieve it. "So what are you doing out here, anyway?"

His guest drew back some stray wet locks of blond hair behind her ears and tried to sound confident. "I'm a writer," she said. Then, reconsidering her statement, she admitted, "At least, I want to be. And the truth is . . . I was looking for you."

"Oh?"

"You *are* Jake Sisko . . . the writer?"

"Yes."

"I can't believe I'm really here. Talking to you. You're my favorite author of all time."

Jake smiled wryly as he took out the dermal regenerator and activated it over her wound. "You should read more."

"I mean it. Your books—they're so insightful . . ."

"I'm glad you like them." Jake withdrew the device and returned it to the kit. "There. Good as new."

"Thank you."

Jake wondered if she had any idea how eager she sounded. Probably not. But it was flattering, nonetheless. "You certainly have gone to a lot of trouble to tell me what you think of my books."

She blushed. "A friend of mine recommended *Anslem* to me and I read it straight through, twice in one night."

Jake blinked. "Twice? In one night?" His first novel, written decades ago when he was still a teenager, under what he considered to be disturbing circumstances at best, had almost never seen the light of day. It was years before he'd come to terms with what had happened and accepted the idea that *Anslem* was, in fact, wholly his own, despite the taint of Onaya.

"It made me want to read everything you'd ever written," she went on. "And I did! Your novels, your short stories, your plays, your poetry, your essays . . ."

Jake brought over a blanket and draped it across her shoulders. "You don't look worse for the wear."

"You're joking, I know that. But I want *you* to know, you've given me so much joy. You've made me *think*. I don't know how else to explain it . . ."

Jake held up a hand. "That's all right. I appreciate the sentiment. There's no higher praise you could offer me. What's your name?"

She looked embarrassed. "Oh, God, I'm sorry. It's Melanie."

"Well, Melanie, I'm gonna get us some tea. Make yourself at home," he told her, and went into the kitchen.

Minutes later, he returned with the tea tray to find Melanie studying his bookshelf. "See anything you haven't read?" he asked as he set the tray down.

She turned to him and shook her head. "No, I own every one of these. Although," she added with a hint of wistfulness, her gaze returning to the gold-embossed spines, "just seeing the titles brings back memories of reading them for the first time."

"And there's only one first time for everything, isn't there? I hope you like Tarkalean," he said as he poured. "An old friend of mine was quite fond of it."

Melanie joined him on the couch. "Thank you," she said as she accepted the cup. She took a sip and smiled. "It's wonderful."

He lifted his cup and nodded. "Just what the doctor ordered." Jake sipped his tea and regarded her. She shifted nervously. *So eager. Was I ever that young?*

"I read a biography about you," she said at length. "It said you started writing when you were a boy."

"Is that what you came to find out?" Jake asked.

Melanie hesitated, then looked down and shook her head. "Not really." Silence settled between them. Jake waited. Then she said, "Can I ask you something?"

Jake nodded.

"In all your writings, you never talk about the station where you grew up. About Deep Space 9. Why not?"

"Oh, that," he chuckled, shrugging dismissively. "Well, really, what would be the point? There's so much out there already. The declassified logs of the crew alone . . ."

"That's the official record," Melanie said. "And you're right, everyone knows that stuff, it's well documented. I just thought you'd have something to add. I mean, you of all people . . ."

"Now, what could *I* possibly add to the official record?"

"Only everything it doesn't have!" She laughed, sounding incredulous. "All the writing you did during your years there and since—I'm just amazed that none of it was about those people, those times. . . . It seems like it must have been a formative chapter of your life, and yet you never write about it."

Jake sighed and set down his cup, leaning forward with his elbows resting on his knees. "Every chapter of our lives is formative. You realize that when you get to be my age. You look back on your life with the idea of trying to pin down the single most crucial moment, the one that set your life on its path, and brought you to where you are . . . and you suddenly realize that they were all crucial. Each moment affects every one that follows it, like a drop of water hitting a window, or a baseball thrown at a batter. . . ." Jake drifted off, lost in memory.

Melanie was watching him carefully. "There's more to it, isn't there?" she asked. "There's so much more to those days than is generally known."

Jake looked back at her and shrugged. "Maybe a little."

"Tell me," she said. "Please?"

Jake leaned back, considering the unexpected request, and the stranger who was making it. "So you came for a story," he said, nodding in approval. "And here I am, thinking after all these years that maybe it's time I shared with someone those things that only a few people know about, the stories that happened between the stories, and those that came after."

Jake reached for the kettle and refilled her cup. Then he settled back into the couch, and with his visitor listening, he began his tales.

Ha'mara

Kevin G. Summers

Historian's note: This story is set a few days after the events of "Emissary," the pilot episode of *Star Trek: Deep Space Nine.*

Kevin G. Summers

Kevin G. Summers is the author of the critically acclaimed short story "Isolation Ward 4," which appeared in the *Star Trek: Strange New Worlds IV* anthology. Outside of DS9, Kevin's obsessions include *Moby Dick*, the works of Kurt Vonnegut, Cherry Coke®, and rare steak. In the alternate universe, he works as a graphic artist. Acknowledgments go to The Lost Sea in Sweetwater, Tennessee, for their advice on elements of this story. Kevin would also like to thank his mom and dad, Sandy, Nell, Katherine, his sister Anne, and, of course, Marco. Kevin lives in Leesburg, Virginia, with his beautiful wife, Rachel, and a moderately well-behaved dog named Fistandantilus.

It was a time to sing.

Alone in her chambers, Kai Opaka stood at the narrow window, her eyes closed against the breeze. She smiled slightly as she listened to the distant voices of the gathering multitude united in song. Opening her eyes, she looked out over the domes and spires and verdant gardens of Ashalla, watching as the people below flocked to the foot of the steps leading up to the ancient monastery. The meek and the strong, peacemakers and freedom fighters, farmers and politicians—from every village, from every province they had come to hear what she had to say.

The sound of a bell rang softly behind her. Without turning, she called out and bade her visitor to enter.

She heard the door open and close again. "Eminence," a voice said.

Opaka smiled, still watching the crowd. "How often must I remind you that I have never cared for that title, Tanin? Especially from you."

"I ask your forgiveness, Kai. My old mind is not what it once was."

She almost laughed. "I think, old friend, that you have probably forgotten more than I can remember, and remember far more that I will ever know."

"Indeed. Then perhaps you can mention that to my wife when you see her next."

Opaka did laugh then, but she never took her eyes from her people. Their voices continued to float up to her.

"The day is finally upon us," she said after a moment.

"So it would appear."

"You have doubts?"

"Not of what has happened . . ."

"But . . .?"

Tanin hesitated. He had served Opaka as her teacher, her advisor, her supporter and her friend for decades. To find himself suddenly conflicted by her judgment could not have been easy for him.

But then, she reflected, *these are uneasy times.*

"The prophecies aren't always clear," Tanin admitted. "The path of Prophets even less so . . ."

"Which is why faith is faith, and not mathematics," Opaka said.

" . . . But what you are about to tell them will put that faith to the test in ways not even the prophecies have foretold."

"Is that what concerns you? That our faith may not endure this test?"

"Sulan," Tanin said softly. Opaka turned away from the window to look at him. He seldom used her given name anymore, not since she became kai. "Are you sure about this? He is an alien. A nonbeliever . . ."

Opaka smiled again and lowered her eyes. She went to him and took his hand, lifting it slowly to her exposed left ear. Surprised by the gesture of intimacy, Tanin's hand actually trembled as he pinched her lobe between his thumb and forefinger. He closed his eyes as her *pagh* opened to him.

Opaka watched his face, his sharp intake of breath, then felt his fingers relax. His eyes opened and focused again as he released her.

"This is a strange path," Tanin whispered.

The kai took her old friend's arm and smiled up at him. "But we need not walk it alone."

Major Kira Nerys stood among the faithful, her eyes fixed on the man standing nearby.

She had returned to Bajor—together with Terok Nor's new

Starfleet administrator, Commander Benjamin Sisko, Sisko's young son Jake, and the space station's CMO, Dr. Julian Bashir. They had come to show support for Kai Opaka's call for global unity. Much of Bajor was still split into squabbling factions in the wake of the Cardassian withdrawal, and the provisional government was having a hard time holding the shattered pieces of the planet together. From the border disputes between Paqu and Navot, to conflicting reconstruction and resource priorities, to the divisions created by the government's decision to petition for membership in the Federation—a decision Kira herself had opposed vehemently—Bajor was dangerously close to civil war. Kira had been convinced, as she had told Sisko not long after his arrival, that Opaka's intercession was the only hope Bajor had of getting through this turbulent time.

So Sisko had gone to ask Opaka for her help. And while Kira still had no knowledge of what had passed between them, the kai had remained in seclusion. And the commander . . .

Sisko had returned to the station—renamed Deep Space 9 by Starfleet as if it made a damn bit of difference to the people who had suffered and died there during the last twenty-odd years. He brought with him the Orb of Prophecy and Change.

Kira still couldn't believe it. She hadn't even known that any of the Orbs had been saved from the Cardassians. When she learned Sisko was in possession of the last one on Bajor, her first thought was that he must have taken it forcibly from the kai, claiming it for his own, just as the Cardassians had done with the other eight Tears of the Prophets. But no, her contacts at the monastery were clear: Kai Opaka had, beyond all reason, bade Sisko to take the Orb with him.

And not long after that . . . everything changed.

Sisko had discovered the wormhole—a stable subspace conduit into the unexplored Gamma Quadrant—located inside the Bajoran system itself. Kira had seen the implications of the discovery immediately—Bajor was suddenly at a flashpoint of change for this part of the galaxy. This was an opportunity for her world to rise up from the ashes of the Occupation in a way no one had ever imagined.

Then, as news of the discovery began to spread, word came from the monastery—Opaka's seclusion was at an end. She was ready to speak to the people. And she wished to do so with Sisko at her side.

Sisko . . .

A silence fell over the crowd. Kira shifted nervously, her fingers brushing the newly cropped stubble on the back of her neck as the monastery doors swung open. Kai Opaka emerged from the building. She descended its steps, with an old vedek leaning on her arm, two prylars following behind. She looked older than when Kira had seen her last, but her eyes were full of hope. Kira wondered who was supporting whom, or if they were supporting each other.

The assemblage called to her as one. Cries of *"Opaka! Opaka!"* echoed through Ashalla and, Kira suspected, throughout the valley. Opaka smiled at the sea of faces. Just seeing her gave them comfort—she was a fire, Kira knew, that burned away all fear and doubt.

The crowd fell silent as Opaka stopped in front of Sisko. Kira watched as a smile spread across the commander's face.

"It is good to see you again, Emissary," said the kai.

Sisko's face fell.

Kira's eyes widened.

A murmur spread through the crowd. Kira felt her palms beginning to sweat. *Gotta be a mistake. She can't possibly have said—*

She heard the mumbling questions all around her, questions that were now hammering her own mind.

The wormhole—the wormhole is the Celestial Temple? This is the fulfillment of the Prophecy of the Emissary? Sisko encountered the Prophets?

Who is this man?

"Kai Opaka," Sisko stammered, but his words were swallowed up by the noise of the crowd.

Opaka offered Sisko a knowing smile. Kira caught the look and she realized that the kai had deliberately provoked the uproar that was now surging through the crowd. "Thank you for coming," Opaka shouted over the tumult, speaking directly to Sisko.

She—she really believes it. Her face . . .

"I wouldn't have missed it," Sisko yelled back. "But about this emissary business . . ."

"Time enough for that later," said the kai, looking out over the assemblage. Kira noted some people breaking from the crowd and running back into the city. They stopped to speak to a group of pedestrians along the way, pointing back to the dais—which, in turn, set the newcomers running toward the monastery.

"I see that more are arriving and, I suspect, many more are to follow," the kai observed wryly. She turned to the prylars. "Let us delay the address for now."

"Kai?" said the vedek at her side.

"Just a few hours," Opaka elaborated. "Our people are nothing if not patient, and it seems as though more will soon be inclined to gather here." She turned back to Sisko. "In the meantime, I'd like you and your friends to have a tour of the city. You should get to know the people, and our world. My dear friend Vedek Tanin will guide you."

Tanin bowed his acceptance of Opaka's will. Sisko looked uncertain. But what he told her was, "We'd love to."

The prylars began to disperse the crowd while Tanin led the group from the space station away. Kira followed, trying to control her breathing as she rubbed her sweating palms on the sides of her uniform. She turned around once to look at the kai . . . and was shocked to see that Opaka was looking back at her.

Kira turned away and forced herself to keep moving.

Emissary . . . ?

The crowd around her continued to thin as people ran off to spread the news. Soon, she knew, the whole planet would be buzzing. Before Kira's eyes, the doorway to the future had swung wide open, and the doorway to the past had slammed shut forever.

★   ★   ★

The scars of the Occupation were everywhere.

Sisko could see that Ashalla had once been a city of breathtaking beauty, possessing a serenity that not even the Cardassians could expunge completely. Nevertheless, the last fifty years had left their mark on the city. From a distance, it hadn't looked so bad. Up close, the level of devastation was astonishing.

As the group was led down streets strewn with rubble, Benjamin Sisko draped an arm over his son's shoulders.

"The Cardassians did this?" Jake asked.

"They did," his father confirmed.

"Why do we have to be here?" Jake looked up at Sisko, his eyes pleading.

"We've been over this, Jake-O," Sisko said. He knew the suddenness of his new assignment had taken Jake off guard. Having spent the last two years reestablishing ties with family and friends back home after the destruction of the *Saratoga,* Jake had had to leave all that behind so that Sisko could accept a posting beyond the edge of Federation space. So far, the transition hadn't been an easy one. "We're here today to support Kai Opaka in a call for planetary unity," Sisko went on. "Besides, I thought you'd enjoy getting away from the station and into some fresh air. It's a new world, Jake! Don't you find that exciting?"

"I guess," Jake murmured.

Sisko's forehead creased. *This adjustment may take a little longer than I thought.*

The group halted near a nondescript structure as their tour guide, Vedek Tanin, gestured toward a narrow opening in one corner of the building's exposed foundation. "Do you see that archway?" the vedek asked.

"I see it," Jake said, his tone of voice conveying his complete lack of interest. Sisko winced. Jake's first trip to Bajor was not going as well as he'd hoped.

"What is it?" asked Julian Bashir. The doctor was quite a bit more excited than Jake, for which Sisko was grateful. The last thing he wanted to do was offend the Bajorans this early in their relationhip.

"The building that used to stand here was a warehouse," Tanin explained, "until the Cardassians destroyed it, along with many others, when they withdrew. But the foundation is much, much older. That archway leads to a network of catacombs that runs underneath the city."

"Like where they bury dead people?" Jake asked. His interest was suddenly piqued.

Tanin nodded. "Some of the earliest kais," he said, "along with some vedeks and others revered for their faith."

"Can we see them?" Jake asked hopefully.

Sisko saw Kira smile sadly at the boy's curiosity. "Perhaps later," the vedek said. "But we wouldn't be able to venture in too far; we might never find our way out."

"Why?" Bashir asked. "Haven't the tunnels been mapped?"

"The catacombs are a labyrinth. Knowledge of them was lost to us for centuries and they fell into legend. During the Occupation they were rediscovered by members of the resistance, and only now is the significance of the find becoming public."

At mention of the resistance, Sisko and Bashir both looked at Kira. Shifting uncomfortably, obviously not expecting to share Tanin's task as guide, she said, "Uh, a resistance cell found the opening about five years ago and started using the tunnels as a bolt-hole. No one ever went in too far—the tunnels seemed to extend for *tessijens,* and there hasn't been time to chart them safely."

Bashir's brow furrowed. "But sensors—"

"There are refractory minerals below ground in this region that inhibit sensor scans," Kira explained. "That's what made the tunnels ideal for hiding from the Cardassians."

"We hope to chart them by more conventional means at some point," Tanin said, and then gestured at the battered city around him. "But, as you can see, we have other priorities right now."

"Who built them?" asked Sisko.

"My forebears," Tanin answered. "They were constructed many millennia ago. One of the legends surrounding them—and which may explain why knowledge of the catacombs was eventually lost—is that ancient Bajorans used them to seek the wisdom of the Prophets."

"How did they do that?" Jake asked.

"If a believer had lost her faith," the vedek said, "she would descend into the catacombs to look for it. Supposedly, the lost soul would wander in the darkness until the Prophets touched her, and only then would she return to the light above. For that reason, the catacombs are known as The Paths of the Lost." When his listeners didn't say anything, the old vedek smiled. "It's quite a lovely metaphor, actually."

The tour moved on and, while they walked, Vedek Tanin paused in his recitation of the local points of interest to address Sisko directly. "I just want to say," he offered in a quiet voice, "that I am honored to meet you, Emissary."

Sisko fought the urge to roll his eyes. Instead, he gave the vedek an uncomfortable smile.

Tanin hesitated as if he had something more he wanted to say. It took him several moments, during which the tour group neared the end of the street. As they came upon an intersection, the vedek turned to Sisko once more.

"Emissary," Tanin said, bowing his head. "If it would not be too presumptuous . . . would you offer me your blessing?"

"Blessing?" Sisko asked. He caught Bashir's confused expression, then shot a look at Major Kira, his eyes practically begging his first officer to bail him out somehow.

Kira stared back at him, her expression unreadable.

Sisko shifted uncomfortably. He tapped Vedek Tanin lightly on the shoulder, hoping that was enough.

Tanin lifted his head, a look of complete contentment on his face. "Thank you, Emissary."

Sisko licked his lips, unsure of what to say. He really was going to have to speak to Opaka about this emissary matter; whatever messianic figure the Bajorans were waiting for, he was fairly certain Starfleet wasn't going to appreciate it when they found out he'd been tapped for the job. Besides, it made him uncomfortable as hell.

Bashir finally spoke, breaking the uneasy silence that had settled on their little group. "What's that building?" he asked. He was pointing to a blackened structure that stood out among every other building in that part of the city.

"That is the Taluno Library," Tanin said. "It was constructed over eighteen hundred years ago, and was once the center of learning in Dakhur Province. The Cardassians set it on fire during an uprising of Bajoran laborers."

"No regard for history," Bashir said under his breath.

Off to the side, Sisko heard Kira grunt, as if to say, "No regard for anything."

Tanin reached into a satchel that hung inside his robes and drew out a small handlight. "I would be pleased to show it to you. There are aspects of the interior that are still quite extraordinary, despite the damage."

Sisko smiled politely. "By all means. Lead the way, Vedek."

As the group approached the library, they heard a series of excited shouts coming from the next street over. A group of children were playing in the street.

Jake's eyes widened, the sight of other kids seizing his attention. Kira drew near to him, a wistful smile on her face. "Springball," she explained. "It's a popular sport on Bajor."

Jake Sisko stood there, mesmerized. Aside from the idea of bodies buried beneath them, this was first sign of genuine interest in anything Bajoran he'd shown on the whole trip. Jake hadn't made any friends since they'd left Mars. There was only one kid his age on Deep Space 9 so far, and he was a Ferengi—one with delinquent tendencies, at that. Not exactly the kind of influence Sisko wanted for his son.

Jake turned back to the tour group. *He looks,* Sisko thought, *like the loneliest boy in the Alpha Quadrant.*

Sisko approached his son, pulled him into a tight embrace, and kissed him on the top of the head.

"Jake-O," the commander said, "how're you doing?"

"Fine," Jake said. His eyes wandered back to the kids playing in the street.

"Why don't you stay and watch the game," his father suggested.

Jake's face lit up as he spun out of his father's bear hug. "Can I?" the boy asked.

"Sure," Sisko said. "Have a good time."

Clearly warmed by his father's smile, Jake quickly darted off toward the other children across the way.

Sisko was about to rejoin the tour when he noticed Dr. Bashir lingering in the doorway of the library.

"Do you want to watch, too?" Sisko asked.

"Oh," stammered Bashir. "No, sir, I . . . um . . ."

"Go on," encouraged Sisko. "You can keep an eye on my son."

Bashir grinned. "Of course, sir. I'd be happy to." Moving away from the library, Bashir called out, "Hey, Jake! Wait for me!"

With a final look at his son's receding back, Sisko turned and entered the Taluno Library.

The air was stale inside the ancient building. It smelled of old books and fires that had burned out long ago. Sisko stopped and stood in the foyer of the ruined building, his senses overwhelmed with the loss of so much knowledge. Despite the rays of sunlight lancing through cracks in the damaged roof, the place was quite dark. Making out details was difficult.

"There used to be a painting on the ceiling," Tanin indicated, "a starscape."

"I saw it once when I was in the resistance," Kira added in a quiet voice. "It was beautiful."

No one spoke as the vedek shone his handlight across the broken beams and boiled plaster. Sisko thought he saw some wisps of blue. It reminded him of the wormhole.

★   ★   ★

At the sound of Dr. Bashir calling his name, Jake turned around just in time to see his father step through the doorway into the old library. As Bashir came to a stop beside him, offering a friendly grin as he did, Jake turned his attention back to the game and tried to get a sense of springball. Brightly colored but crudely drawn scoring and foul zones decorated three walls of a wide alley, while four children equipped with paddles stood in the center, chasing after and dodging the wild ricochets of a small blue ball darting from wall to wall.

Eventually deciding the game had a lot in common with racquetball, Jake narrowly missed catching the ball as it went flying wildly into the air. It sailed over his head and into the library through an open basement-level window.

"I'll get it," one boy said.

"I'll go with you," said a young girl who skipped after him.

Without the ball, the game ground to a sudden halt. It was about that time that the Bajoran children noticed the aliens watching them. While their game was in time-out, they turned to Jake and Bashir as the next best source of entertainment.

"Where are you from?" one child asked.

"What's your name?" wondered another. "I'm Ferin."

"Jake Sisko. And this is Dr. Bashir."

"We're from Earth," Bashir added.

"Sisko?" Ferin asked. "Like the Emissary?"

Jake stared at the boy, confused. He had heard Kai Opaka say something about an emissary back at the monastery, but hadn't really been paying attention.

"I'm sorry," Jake said. "I don't know what you're talking about."

"You haven't heard about the Emissary?" The boy was shocked. "He found the Celestial Temple and is here to protect Bajor."

"My dad found a wormhole," Jake offered, wondering if they were confusing his father with someone else.

Eyebrows furrowing as if Jake had just sprouted an extra head, Ferin evidently decided to move on to more important matters. "Do you guys want to play, too?"

"Sure," Jake said. He grinned.

Bashir said, "I'll just continue to watch, if that's all right."

"Okay," said Ferin. "I wonder what's taking them so long to get the ball."

Jake turned to face the building.

"The library was constructed using the most advanced techniques of the time," Vedek Tanin continued. "Note the complexity of the walls and columns."

"Amazing," Sisko whispered, placing his palm against one of the great, blackened blocks that formed the outer walls of the library and finding it cold to the touch. Instead of conventional right angles, the stones had been meticulously hewn—by hand, it seemed—into a harmonious variety of curvilinear shapes and somehow fitted together flawlessly. His mind reeled at the thought of the advanced mathematics, craftsmanship, and aesthetics that the library's ancient builders had combined to create such a structure. *Order from chaos,* he thought. *But not really chaos at all. . . .*

His Starfleet mission briefing had included a great deal of information about Bajor, of course. Not just its current political situation and turbulent recent history, but also its rich and ancient cultural heritage—how the Bajorans had developed art, science, and philosophy long before humans had even walked upright. Reading about it was one thing, though. Experiencing the sheer power and age of that past as a tangible reality was something else entirely.

And, of course, nothing in the briefing had prepared him for the discovery of the wormhole, or his life-altering encounter with the beings within it only a few days ago. That led his thoughts, inevitably, to Wolf 359, where his heart had lingered for the last two years.

When he had first gone to see the kai, Opaka had exposed him to the Orb of Prophecy and Change—an energy construct of some kind that not even Dax understood. The Orb showed him a glimpse of the past—of Jennifer, his dead wife. His heart sank even now as he thought of her—so beautiful; so fragile. Her death at Wolf 359 had plunged him into a chasm of bitterness too deep and dark to climb out of on his own. His encounter with the wormhole aliens had changed him—healed him. He had gone to them lost and angry, and had returned as a man ready to make peace with the ghosts of his past.

He loved Jennifer so much. He would always love her, but he saw now that he had to start living his life again. He owed her that much. He owed it to Jake, and he owed it to himself.

But now . . . What did he owe Bajor? Opaka had been the one to propel him toward the wormhole aliens with an apparent certainty that he would encounter them. She had known, somehow, that by going to them, Sisko would take back his life. She'd even suggested that his future and that of her people were tied together.

"Ironic. One who does not wish to be among us is to be the Emissary."

Emissary. She had used the word again on the monastery steps, and the reaction of the crowd had been disquieting, to say the least—as had the look in Vedek Tanin's eyes when he asked for Sisko's blessing. Even Major Kira kept staring at him now. It was just too much. What did these people expect from him?

Sisko's thoughts returned to the library when he heard the voices of children. He turned, and saw two young Bajorans enter the building.

Kira had strayed to the far side of the room, her thoughts in turmoil. She knew the prophecies that formed the bedrock of her faith as well as any devout Bajoran. She'd known the coming of the Emissary was an event long anticipated, and that he would be known by his opening of the Temple gates. Sisko had explained some of what happened to him inside the wormhole, but for some reason, until Opaka's startling words at the monastery, she hadn't connected the wormhole to the Celestial Temple. But if they were really one and the same . . .

Could Opaka be right? And if it was true, what did that mean for Bajor? That an alien representing a people Kira considered no better than the Cardassians should turn out to be the Emissary of the Prophets—

How did it all happen so fast?

Kira could remember, as a child, looking up into the sky after a day of backbreaking labor in the Singha refugee camp. She could remember seeing the light of Terok Nor hanging over Bajor like a dying star, and wondering bleakly if there was any hope left in the world. That she herself had, only days ago, given the order propelling the station to the mouth of the wormhole *(the Temple?)* was an irony not lost on Kira, nor the station's abrupt transformation in her mind from beacon of despair to one of hope.

Hope. Faith. Sometimes those concepts seemed so hard to take hold in Kira's mind. Fighting was easy. Blowing up buildings and making the Cardassians pay dearly for every inch they stole, every life they took, all that came naturally to her. But to live through the age of *Ha'mara,* the time of the Emissary—it scared her to the very core of her *pagh.*

A commotion startled Kira from her thoughts; she saw two children enter the building. They seemed to be searching for something.

They took no notice of the group standing in the foyer. "Over there," said the boy, moving toward a stairway leading down. The girl followed him. Vedek Tanin looked as if he was about to say something, to call out to them.

The children had just taken their first step onto the stairs when the building exploded.

Jake was being taught how to swing a springball paddle when he heard the blast. He turned to face the library—everyone did. They watched in sick fascination as the building began to collapse, engulfed in black smoke and flames.

"Dad!" Jake screamed. Memories of Wolf 359 played out in his mind. He dropped the paddle and lunged toward the building. He would have rushed headlong to his death, but Doctor Bashir caught him and dragged him away.

"Jake, no!" the doctor shouted. A cloud of dust rushed toward them as Bashir herded as many children as he could around the corner of the alley, out of the path of the billowing gray wave. Fortunately, those out of his reach had the sense to flee on their own.

"Let me go," Jake pleaded. He pummeled Bashir's chest. "Please, my dad's in there."

There was a deafening rumble and the street shook beneath them. The dust cloud spread into the alley, throwing Jake's vision into darkness. Jake clung to Bashir, crying, *"My dad! My dad!"* But he couldn't even hear himself over the screaming around him.

There followed an eerie silence as the ground settled, broken only by the sounds of coughing and a rain of grit descending on the alley. Time seemed to slow to a crawl until, finally, Jake sensed light against his eyelids. He felt himself being pulled again, led away somewhere. He heard voices, felt himself moving into sunlight. Eventually someone splashed water into his face. Slowly, as the grit in his eyes washed away, Jake opened them.

Dr. Bashir, covered from head to foot in a thin layer of gray dust, looked at him in concern. "Are you all right, Jake?"

Jake said nothing.

"Jake, if you think you're injured, I need to know *now*. There may be people here who need my help."

Jake's throat constricted as he tried to form words. "I'm—I'm okay. But my da—"

Bashir gripped his shoulder. "Jake, I need you to stay put for now. Can you do that?"

Jake nodded as sobs began to wrack his chest. Bashir squeezed his shoulder once more and left him, looking for people who may have been injured.

In the distance, Jake saw a pile of rubble, and could only watch as a trail of dark smoke rose from it into the clear sky.

★   ★   ★

Across the city, in the monastery, Kai Opaka felt the ground tremble. She heard the explosion—heard the building collapse. For a moment it was like she had gone back in time. The Occupation had never ended—the resistance had lashed out once more at their oppressors.

Opaka stood at her window, her heart sinking as she saw the plume of smoke rising over the city. She immediately moved to her desk and sought out a newsfeed over the comnet. It wasn't long before she found one and saw that it had been the Taluno Library. The Militia was already on the scene, speculating that an explosive device, left by the Cardassians and overlooked after the withdrawal, had somehow detonated. Soot-covered people, some bleeding, could be seen in the background around the ruins. Even worse, witnesses were reporting that several people had entered the library before the bomb had gone off. Opaka hung her head in sorrow.

A monk entered her chambers. "Your Eminence," he said, his voice cracking. Opaka turned to look at him, her face streaked with tears. "We've just been informed," the monk began. "The people that were inside the library—witnesses are saying it was Vedek Tanin's group."

Opaka felt her knees quiver. She leaned heavily against her desk. *Dearest Prem . . . Commander Sisko and his son . . . Major Kira and the doctor. . . . How can this have happened?*

She watched the scene still unfolding over the comnet, saw the massive stones that had formed the walls of the building strewn in a low pile of rubble. It was horrific, more so for being the likely tomb of innocent people, but Opaka forced herself to look, studying the scene for some ray of hope.

She blinked, replaying her own thoughts. *A low pile of rubble. Why is it so low?* She looked carefully. Though they had clearly been blown apart from one another, most of the stones of the library appeared to have survived the blast intact. *Then why does there seem to be so few of them? Unless . . .*

"The Paths of the Lost," she said suddenly.

"The catacombs?" asked the monk.

"The library rests above the labyrinth," Opaka said. "It's only a slight chance, but if the force of the collapse broke through the earth, Vedek Tanin's group may have fallen through as well."

"That seems impossible," the monk said. "Those stones weigh—"

"With the Prophets," Opaka said, "all things are possible." Driven by renewed hope, the kai pushed away from her desk. She strode across the room, her legs carrying her like a woman half her age.

"Where are you going?" the monk asked.

"Taluno Library," answered Opaka.

"To pray over the fallen?"

"To organize rescue efforts."

The monk stared after her in disbelief as Kai Opaka headed out of the monastery.

A light shone in the darkness.

Sisko felt the floor shift beneath him as he propped himself up on his elbows. His eyes narrowed, trying to make out the source of the light.

The floor must have collapsed, he realized. The weight of the entire building had fallen on top of them.

"Kira!" Sisko called. "Major, are you there?"

He heard someone moan. Sisko had no idea if it was his first officer or the vedek.

"Tanin!"

No answer.

The floor shifted again as Sisko sat up. He bumped his head on the ceiling that was now just centimeters above him.

"Damn," he said.

Sisko rubbed his head as he carefully turned himself around. He realized that death was almost inevitable at this point, but something drove him forward. He crawled. The stones were sharp and uneven, but he managed to gain a few meters.

Focus on your objective; that was what they taught him at

Starfleet Academy. Kira might be dead. Tanin might be dead. The children he had seen just before the explosion were almost certainly dead, but there wasn't anything he could do about that.

Don't think. Don't feel. Just act.

There was a light burning in the darkness, and Sisko was going to make it to that light. He kept crawling.

Had he lost consciousness? He was unsure how long he'd been buried; it felt like he had been down here for hours—maybe even days. For all he knew it was only a few minutes. The jagged stones tore into his knees and the palms of his hands as he moved. He pushed himself even harder.

After an agonizing length of time had passed, Sisko finally reached the source of the light. He collapsed when he realized where the glow was coming from—the vedek's handlight.

Tanin Prem was dead.

The first thing Major Kira saw when she awoke was *his* face. He hovered over her, his features framed in white. The effect unnerved her.

"Major," Sisko said. "Are you all right?"

Kira felt the world spinning as she leaned forward. She closed her eyes and saw Sisko's silhouette outlined on her eyelids. She slumped backwards.

"Easy, Major," the commander said.

A moment later, Kira felt his strong hands lifting her, easing her into a sitting position. Her forehead stung and she could feel blood streaming down her face. *Must be a gash.*

"What happened?" she asked.

"I'm not sure," Sisko said. "There was an explosion, the building collapsed. . . ."

The last thing Kira remembered was seeing two of the kids from the springball game, and then everything was thunder and fire and falling stone. She rubbed her hands through her hair, feeling a sticky residue in her short tresses. Her fingers came away slick and red.

"Tanin is dead," Sisko told her. He leaned back and gave his combadge an anxious tap.

"Sisko to Bashir," he said.

There was no answer.

"Sisko to *Rio Grande.*"

The runabout they had used to travel from Deep Space 9 failed to respond. Kira tried her own combadge and had the same results.

"Maybe they were damaged when the building collapsed," Sisko speculated.

"No," said Kira, realizing the truth as she stared at the oppressively low ceiling. "It's the earth around us. We're in the Paths of the Lost."

Sisko took that in. "Those refractory minerals in the ground you mentioned earlier. They're keeping our signals from getting through."

Kira nodded absently. "It also applies to sensor waves and transporter beams. We're on our own down here."

Then she heard someone crying in the darkness.

Sisko turned toward the sound. "Not entirely on our own, it would seem."

One of the kids, Kira realized dimly. She rubbed her temples, trying to focus. She looked around, saw that Sisko was shining the handlight across the room, searching for the source of the sobs.

Finally, his light settled on two frightened children.

"Hello there," Sisko said.

Kira heard his voice echo softly through the shattered room.

About twenty meters away, a young girl was sitting with her legs crossed, her back leaning against the wall. She held a boy in her arms. The boy was weeping.

"Why don't you and your friend come over here?" Sisko asked the girl. She stared at him blankly.

"They're terrified," Kira said, gritting her teeth to stay focused.

When it became evident that the children were not going to answer, Sisko said, "Then why don't we come to you." He turned to Kira and whispered, "Major, do you think you can move?"

Kira steeled herself. She had lost a lot of blood, she was dizzy, but she wasn't about to admit any weakness to a Starfleet officer, even—especially—not this one.

"I'll be fine," she said.

Kira leaned forward and crept along the rough floor, her mind working to figure out what caused the explosion. What if the Cardassians had returned? What if they had attacked Bajor and were even now marching through the streets above?

Kira pushed the ugly thoughts aside, trying to stay focused on the here and now. Their first priority was to get out of this building before what was left of it finished falling on top of them.

As they neared the children, Kira saw that though they were clearly dirty and frightened, they seemed otherwise unscathed. The commander tried talking to them again.

"My name is Ben Sisko," he said. He offered as warm and reassuring a smile as Kira suspected he could manage in such dismal surroundings.

"Sisko?" the boy asked. He rubbed his eyes with his fists.

"Sisko," repeated the girl. "You . . . you're the Emissary."

Kira looked at the commander. The recognition in the child's voice was startling. Opaka had named him Emissary only a short time ago, a matter of hours at most, yet word had already spread throughout the city.

"Emissary," the girl said, "can you take us out of here?"

Before Sisko could answer, the boy cut in. "Can you blast a tunnel through the stones with your phaser vision?"

Sisko laughed.

"No, I'm afraid . . ."

"Commander," Kira said suddenly, not at all liking where the conversation was going. "We don't have time for this. We aren't safe here. Our only chance is to find a way into the catacombs as quickly as possible."

Sisko nodded. "Agreed, Major." He turned back to the children and asked, "What are your names?"

"Oden Jek," the boy said.

"And I'm Eleth Loral," said the girl. "But you can call me Loral. Jek and I are cousins."

"This is Major Kira," Sisko said, and Kira nodded, but the dizziness swirled back all of a sudden. She managed to steady herself. "I want you both to be very careful," the commander went on, "because we're going to have to help each other to get out of here."

"We'll help," Jek said.

"We'll do anything for you, Emissary," Loral added.

Kira wanted to correct her, but she stopped herself. This was neither the time nor the place.

"We're looking for a tunnel," Sisko said. "Do you think you could help us look?"

The children agreed.

The group spread out. Kira groped blindly through the dark, trying not to think about the kilotons of stone hanging over their heads.

Eleth Loral knew she was going to live.

When the explosion occurred and the building came down, she was sure that she would die. When she awoke in the darkness to the sound of Jek crying, she was sure that they would never be found, that they would starve or be crushed to death.

But when the Emissary came to her, when he told her there was a way out, she knew that she would live to see her father once again.

Loral could almost stand up straight. She squinted into the darkness as she took a cautious step forward. She screamed as she felt the floor give way beneath her.

The girl jumped back, her heart fluttering. Below, she could hear stone crashing against stone.

Jek rushed over from where he was standing. She heard Sisko and Kira crawling toward her as fast as they could.

A gaping hole had opened in the floor at her feet. She peered into the inky blackness but could see nothing. The others arrived moments later, and when Sisko shone his light into the hole, the darkness parted.

Opaka stood in the middle of the street, a cool breeze fluttering through her robes. It reminded her that winter was coming—that the seasons rolled on in their endless cycles in spite of festival or tragedy.

Colonel Day of the Bajoran Militia approached her, his expression stern. "Kai Opaka," he began, "you shouldn't be here. It isn't safe. Come, let me escort you . . ."

Opaka ignored the colonel's condescending tone and brushed aside his outstretched hand. Like many in the Militia, Day had been a resistance fighter—a member of one of the more radical splinter groups, if the rumors were true. Now he numbered among those who seemed to think that their efforts alone had ended the Occupation, and thus had earned them the right to decide now what was best for all Bajorans. It was a dangerous mindset, Opaka knew, one that was certain to propagate strife in the days or months to come if allowed to continue. But it was also a problem for another day. "What news of the rescue efforts?" Opaka asked.

Day frowned, his delicately chiseled features unable to conceal his displeasure at having his will ignored. "The Federation doctor has set up a triage center in the old public shelter," he reported. "Medical personnel from the local hospital should be arriving soon."

"Very good," Opaka said. "What of those trapped inside the library?"

Day blinked as if her question was the last thing he expected from her. "Surely you don't imagine that anyone could have survived in there? There were a lot of people injured in the surrounding buildings, Eminence," Day added. "Nearly a dozen fatalities have been reported so far."

"But has anyone checked the ruins yet?"

"There are no discernible lifesigns under the rubble. And we can't rule out the presence of another explosive device."

Opaka looked to the street where the library once stood. The entire block was in ruins. "With a weapon that powerful," she said, "would you bother to use two in the same location?"

Day's jaw shifted back and forth. *Why is he so angry?* "There's no way of knowing, *Eminence,*" he said tightly. "But enough Bajoran blood has been spilled today for the sake of your alien friend."

Ah. There it is.

Day had raised his voice just enough to draw the attention of several nearby Militia officers, who now frowned in his direction.

"Every death diminishes me," Opaka said quietly, wondering if Day even knew enough of the prophecies to recognize the quotation.

"If that is so," Day said, uncomfortably aware that their conversation now had listeners, "then you should be as reluctant as I am to risk more lives here."

"He is the Emissary," Opaka said, her eyes narrowing. "But even if he were not, his life, and the lives of those who were with him, would still be worth the risk."

"There is no chance that—"

"The Taluno Library was known to have rested atop one of the tunnels of the Paths of the Lost. You know that the catacombs are resistant to scanning. If they survived, their *chance* was to have made it into the Paths. . . ."

Opaka fell silent. Something had caught her attention. There was a small park not far from where they stood, a lonely patch of green that had been untouched by the destruction of the library. Someone was sitting over there in the grass, and he was watching her.

"We must not give up on them," Opaka finished. She turned back to Day, to the other Militia officers who had now gathered around them. "I implore you."

Day stood his ground for a moment, staring down at her, no doubt feeling the eyes of the others on him as they awaited his answer. After an interminable moment, he nodded, saying, "Very well, Kai. But any more blood spilled will be your responsibility.

Not mine." He turned sharply and began issuing orders as he led his people back toward the ruins.

Opaka watched him go, and for the first time since the news came to her, her thoughts for the growing number of victims of the explosion narrowed to one.

"Hold on, Emissary," the kai whispered into the wind.

Her thoughts turned quickly back to the park, to the solitary observer sitting there on the grass. Opaka was past the age of swinging a pickax effectively, but her *pagh* was strong. She'd be of little use in the effort to lift tons of stone, she knew, but there was something else she could do.

Jake watched Opaka walk toward him. The worst of his uncontrollable sobbing was over—for now, anyway. Part of him felt as if it might overwhelm him again at any moment. But right here and right now, as Kai Opaka approached him, he had himself under control.

Opaka approached him slowly. "You're Jake Sisko," she began.

Jake turned away. He nodded.

"May I speak with you?" she asked.

"I guess," Jake said. His eyes stared vacantly toward the rubble.

"I know you're very upset right now," Opaka said as she settled down in the grass next to him. "I just want you to know that it's all right to hope."

Hope? Was she kidding? How could she expect him to have hope? Nothing could save his mother when the Borg attacked the *Saratoga,* and nothing was going to bring his father back to him now. Hope was a lie.

"I'm not sure what you believe in," Opaka said.

"I don't know either," said Jake. His eyes were glassy from exposure to the dust and smoke.

"My faith is all that I have," Opaka said. "It is the same with many here on Bajor. Faith binds us; we are the children of the Prophets."

"What does that have to do with my dad?" Jake asked.

"Your father discovered something a few days ago," said the kai, "something that has great significance to my people."

"The wormhole?"

"Yes. But it is more than that," she said. "What you see as a wormhole, I see as the home of the Prophets, their Celestial Temple."

Opaka stroked Jake's ear, but he didn't pull away. Like her face, her touch was soft and comforting.

"Like Heaven," Jake said. "You think my dad is in this Temple with these Prophets?"

"No," Opaka said, her voice soothing. "But in my faith, it is believed that the one who finds the Celestial Temple is meant to be the Emissary."

"Oh," Jake said, "so that's what this emissary stuff is all about."

"The Emissary will do many things," said the kai. "He will face many challenges, some dangerous, but he will persevere."

"Are you saying that you want me to believe in the Prophets?" Jake asked.

"No," answered Opaka. "That is not for me to decide." She took his hands in hers and grasped them firmly. "But I want you to believe in your father."

Jake looked out at the still-smoking ruin of the library, feeling the control he was working so hard to maintain threatening to slip. Eyes tearing, he turned back to Opaka as if she were a lifeline. "Do you . . . do you think he's alive?"

Opaka smiled and drew him into her embrace. "Have hope, Jake."

"Are you sure we're going the right way?" Kira asked.

"Reasonably sure, given the circumstances," Sisko answered.

"How can you tell?"

"There's a very slight breeze coming from this direction," he said. He gestured the way they were headed. "That may mean there's an opening to the surface up ahead."

The darkness was all around them, broken only by the handlight Sisko held—its glow casting pointed shadows on the hand-carved walls. The stone, what they could see of it anyway, was cold and lifeless.

Beyond the beam of light, the darkness was nearly impenetrable. The tunnel twisted and turned, but Sisko kept them heading in the direction of the breeze. As they walked carefully down the narrow corridor, he feared that they might walk right past an exit and not even know it. His fears were confirmed when he heard one of the Bajoran children speak up behind him.

"Emissary," said Jek, "I think I saw something back there."

Sisko stopped. He turned to face the child.

"Something? Like what?"

"A door," answered the boy.

The group backtracked, and after a moment's search, found the door once they knew what they were looking for. Major Kira gripped the handle, giving it a slight turn. The door creaked open on its hinges.

Sisko leveled the handlight, directing its beam inside. The room was small, carved from the stone by tireless labor. There were hammer and chisel marks crisscrossed all over the walls.

"A shelter?" Sisko speculated.

"Storage room," Kira said, indicating a couple of crates stacked in the far corner of the chamber. "Probably belonged to the local resistance cell."

As the group entered the room, Kira went over to the crates and began to investigate. Sisko sat down in the corner and leaned against the wall, angling the light for maximum illumination and hoping, once again, that the power source would hold out. The children were on him in an instant, Jek sitting in his lap and Loral nuzzling up under Sisko's arm.

"Did the Prophets tell you the way out of here?" asked the girl. "I heard that they told you the future of everyone on Bajor. Do you know who I'm going to marry when I grow up?"

"That's stupid," Jek said. "They didn't tell him the future; they gave him magical powers. Can you see in the dark?"

Sisko fought back laughter as he shook his head.

"Actually," he said, "the Prophets did something even more amazing than that."

The children's eyes widened. They seemed to hang on his every word.

"What did they do?" Loral asked.

"When I went to the worm . . . the Celestial Temple," Sisko said, "I had given up all hope."

"Because of the Occupation?" Loral asked.

"No," Sisko said, seeing Jennifer lying dead in their quarters on the *Saratoga*.

"Emissary?" Jek said, startling Sisko back to reality.

"The Prophets showed me that I should never give up," he said. "That there's always a chance to make a better life for ourselves. That it's better to light a candle than curse the darkness."

Out of the corner of his eye, Sisko could see that Kira's gaze was fixed on him again.

"Anything useful in those boxes, Major?"

Kira turned her attention to the crates. "We're in luck. This one has food rations—looks like dried meat and fruit." She picked up a ration pack, tore it open, and took a whiff. "Smells all right." She took out a dark stick of what may have been the Bajoran analog of jerky, nibbled a piece off the end, and shrugged as she passed the pack over to Sisko. "Still edible. There are water packets, too."

"That's something," Sisko said with a smile. He sniffed the contents of the ration pack—strong, but not bad—and then held it out to the children, who each took some. Sisko turned back to Kira and nodded at the second crate. "Try the other one."

Major Kira moved the first crate aside and opened the one beneath it. Her eyes came up, flicked to the children for a moment, then settled to Sisko. She shook her head slightly.

Sisko frowned, guessing Kira had discovered a cache of explosives, probably stockpiled for attacks against the Cardassians. *Too bad we can't use them to blast our way to the surface without risking a cave-in.*

"What's in that one?" Jek asked.

"Nothing," Kira said as she resealed the crate. "Nothing we can use, anyway." After finding an old blanket and using it to bundle together as much food and water as it would hold, the major tossed Jek one of the water packets, keeping one for herself and Sisko.

The boy stood up and ripped open the seal.

"You share that with Loral," Kira ordered him. With that, she sat down next to the others. She tore open the packet and drank deeply. When she was done, she handed it to Sisko.

"Thanks," he said. He turned up the packet and sucked down the rest of the water.

"Can I ask you something?" Kira said.

Sisko looked at her and nodded. "Go ahead."

"How do you know how to navigate through tunnels?"

"Survival training," he answered, "at Starfleet Academy. We took desert and arctic survival during our first and second years, and spelunking when we were juniors."

The children giggled, even Kira smiled. *"Spelunking?"* she repeated. "What's that?"

"Caving," Sisko explained.

Kira nodded. From the look on her face, Sisko could tell that there was something else on his first officer's mind. "What is it, Major?" he asked.

Kira hesitated, then said. "What you told the children . . . about what the Prophets showed you . . . it's almost word for word in the text of Chinjen's last prophecy."

Sisko shrugged dismissively. "There are many people on many worlds who have said things like that, Major. Including my own."

Her eyes bore into him. "Are you really the Emissary?" she whispered.

Sisko sighed and fell silent, unsure how he should answer. "I really don't know what that's all about," he said at last. "When I met Kai Opaka for the first time, she spoke so strangely. You'll recall that I only went to her on your advice, to ask her to do what was right for Bajor."

"The will of the Prophets," Kira said, "is what's right for Bajor."

Sisko tensed at that, but he tried not to let it show. "Opaka grabbed my ear," he told Kira, "and then she called me the Emissary."

The major's eyes widened. She turned away and stood up, starting to pace the little room. "This is unbelievable," Kira said.

"Then you must feel about it the same way I do," Sisko said. "This is exactly why Starfleet established the Prime Directive. When they find out that I've become a religious icon on Bajor, they'll almost certainly want to reassign me."

"The Prophets wouldn't have chosen you," Kira said, growing more agitated by the second, "if They didn't—"

"Major," Sisko snapped, cutting her off, "I never asked to be the Emissary. I don't share your beliefs."

Kira stopped and stared at him. An uncomfortable silence fell on the room. Sisko felt the children's eyes darting back and forth between him and Kira.

"I'm just trying to do my job here," he said, easing the children off him and rising to his feet. "To bring Bajor into the Federation—"

"Fifty years of fighting for the right to be free," Kira interrupted, shaking her head angrily, "and then you show up to make things better—*after* the fact. Where were you during the Occupation? Or when I was three and my mother was dying? *Where the hell were you then?*"

Sisko stared back silently, uncertain how he should respond.

"What's the matter?" she demanded. "Isn't there some protocol in your Federation rule book about how to deal with people like me? Don't you have an answer? You're the Emissary!"

"I never said—"

"You didn't have to!"

Kira drew close to Sisko, close enough that he could feel the warmth of her breath.

"Are you embarrassed?" she asked. "You've traveled across the stars and brought truth to a race of primitive savages. And we're so stupid, that we think you're a god. Isn't that what your enlightened Federation perspective has led you to believe?"

"You're out of line, Major," Sisko said, his eyes never wavering. He was about to say more when he heard Loral whimpering behind him.

"Please stop fighting," she pleaded. "I'm scared."

Jek paced to the far side of the room. His back was turned to them, but Sisko thought he saw the boy's shoulders trembling.

"All right," Sisko said softly, and looked at Kira again. "No more arguing. We should be moving along anyway." He helped Loral up. Kira was still glaring at him when she went to lay a reassuring hand on Jek's shoulder, coaxing him toward the door. Soon the group was back in the tunnels, the dark earth and stone pressing in all around them as they set off once more in search of freedom. They walked in silence.

Night had fallen over the city. Inside the triage center, Dr. Bashir and the Bajoran medics had done everything they could for the victims of the blast. Only when the worst of the injured had been stabilized and transferred to the nearest hospital did Bashir finally leave the makeshift surgery in order to check on the rescue efforts.

As Bashir approached the blast site, he heard a mournful harmony rising over the rubble. Lanterns had been set up all around to hold back the darkness; clearly, the rescue workers were planning on working through the night.

The singing grew louder as Bashir approached, and after a moment, four Bajoran Militia officers stepped slowly from the ruins. The men and women shared a weight on their shoulders—a narrow box shrouded in white.

The doctor bowed his head as the funeral procession moved past. He heard the arrival of someone behind him, but did not look up until the death chant had faded up the street.

When Bashir did turn around he saw a Bajoran soldier standing at his side—a lieutenant, judging by the rank symbol on her collar.

"That was Vedek Tanin," the lieutenant said. "They found his body about an hour ago."

Bashir shifted nervously. If Tanin Prem was dead, what hope was there for Commander Sisko and Major Kira? "Have any other bodies been found?" he asked.

"Not yet," the lieutenant replied. "There was another cave-in when we recovered the vedek. Unless they made it into the catacombs, their chances are slim."

"That catacombs?" Bashir said excitedly. "Tanin showed us an entryway several blocks from here—"

"Yes, we know about it. We sent in searchers with ropes to thread the way, but they hit a dead end—the collapse of the library has blocked off the tunnel that led toward that exit. Unless we can safely get through the rubble, either from up here or below, we're cut off from the rest of the catacombs."

"Surely your people must know of another way in," Bashir said, suspecting the answer before the lieutenant gave it.

"Not yet, we don't," she told him. "We have people searching the area, but the truth is, there's still too much we don't know about the catacombs. If there were ever any maps of the tunnels, none have survived to the present day."

"And no way to scan for them," Bashir muttered, his growing frustration causing him to fidget even more. He'd been in contact with the station earlier. Lieutenant Dax and Chief O'Brien were working on the problem from their end, but the unusual attributes of the terrain were proving to be a difficult challenge. It appeared the commander and the major's best hope was with these Bajorans.

The lieutenant offered Bashir an encouraging smile. "We haven't given up yet," she said, and moved off to rejoin the diggers and lines of people who were passing buckets of dust and broken stone from the ruins.

Of all the places to become lost, Bashir thought grimly, *it had to be the one place on Bajor where all our technology is useless.* For a fleeting moment, he considered the occurrence within the context of the

Bajoran religion—what little he knew of it, at any rate—but then quickly shrugged off that particularly unscientific train of thought. Lives were on the line—perhaps more than the commander's and the major's—and mysticism wasn't going to help here.

Kira was freezing. The walls were like ice, chilling the air for the wanderers. She had again fallen behind the little group, needing to put some distance between herself and Sisko, even if it was only a few steps.

Up ahead, Sisko and the children had stopped walking. She could see by Sisko's light that the tunnel beyond branched off in several directions. As Kira approached, she heard Loral cry out excitedly.

"Major, we've found stairs! They lead up!"

Kira rushed to catch up, the only thought on her mind now the promise of escape.

Sisko angled his light at the crude stairs cut into the stone and smiled at her. "After you, Major."

Kira began to climb, but realized as she ascended that something was wrong. She reached out with her hand to find the way blocked thirty steps up.

"The stairs are blocked," Kira announced, pounding her fist on the stone. "We can't get through this way."

Sisko's light punctuated her statement. Great boulders were wedged together overhead, the vestiges of a long-ago cave-in.

"I'm scared," Loral whimpered. She began to cry.

"I'm cold," Jek said. He wrapped his arms tightly around himself. His teeth were chattering.

"There are supposed to be several exits to the catacombs," Kira said, trying to offer some comfort. "We just need to keep looking."

"Yeah, right," Jek snapped. "They're probably all like this one. We're going to die down here."

"I don't want to die," Loral cried. "I want to go home."

"You're never going to go home," said Jek. "You're—"

"That's enough of that," Sisko said. His voice boomed against the stone. "We're going to find a way out of here. It's just going to take us a little while longer."

"I'm sorry, Emissary," the boy said. He choked up with tears.

Sisko perched himself on the steps between the two children. He wrapped each of them in a big hug, drawing them close.

"I want to get out of here just as much as you do," he told them. "My son Jake is up there, and I want to see him again just as much as the two of you want to see your families."

Kira sat on the steps above them, watching as Sisko comforted the children.

"Tell me about your families," Sisko said. He nodded at Loral. "You first."

"My father's a doctor. He helps people when they're sick." She paused, and then she added, "My mother died during the Occupation."

The acceptance in her voice wasn't surprising, but it hit Kira harder than she expected. Having lost her own mother as a very young girl, and her father not long after that, she wondered how many of Bajor's children had simply grown numb to what they'd endured during the Occupation.

"How about you?" Sisko asked Jek.

"The Cardassians killed my parents," he said. "I was only a baby, so I don't remember them. I live with my uncle in Singha and we're in town to hear the kai's speech."

"I'm here for the kai's speech as well," Sisko said, "and I really want to hear what she has to say. So why don't we stop sitting around here moping and find a way out of these tunnels?"

The children's faces seemed to brighten somewhat. Loral took Sisko's hand as she and Jek led him back down the steps.

Kira stared after them. She really wasn't all that surprised to learn that Sisko was good with children—he had a son of his own, after all. What she hadn't been prepared for was how easily he seemed to turn their despair into hope. *And not just theirs.*

When he reached the bottom, Sisko stopped and turned, aiming his light up at her. "Still with us, Major?"

Kira let out a long breath, then stood and brushed off her uniform before she started down the stairs. "Still with you," she said.

"Jake. How are you doing?"

Jake Sisko looked up, startled. He saw Dr. Bashir's face without recognition. He didn't know the man, really. Only his uniform. *I'm on a planet of strangers.*

Rather than answer Bashir's question, Jake asked, "Any news?"

Bashir sighed and sat down next to him on the grassy slope facing the library ruins. "They found Vedek Tanin. He's dead."

"Yeah, I know," Jake said, his voice sounding hollow in his own ears. "Nothing since then?"

Bashir shook his head. "You okay?"

"No," Jake said honestly. "I hate this place. I hate these people." The ease with which the words came shocked him, but didn't stop him. "I hate you, too."

Bashir nodded. "Because I'm Starfleet?"

The question surprised Jake. He hadn't expected Bashir to understand. Maybe he knew about Mom. Jake nodded, and in answer to Bashir's question, he said, "That, and because you stopped me from going to him."

"You might have died, Jake."

"At least then we would have died together."

"You think your father would want that?"

Jake shrugged. They sat in silence for a while, watching the rescue workers. Finally, Jake said, "I wish we'd never come here. Everything was fine at Utopia. Why did my dad have to take this stupid assignment? What's the point of exploring if so many people have to die?"

Bashir held his breath for a long moment, and then let it out. "I don't know," he admitted. And then, as if understanding that he had nothing to offer Jake, the doctor got up to go. Jake told himself he didn't care; he wanted to be left alone.

"I don't really hate you, you know," Jake said suddenly.

Bashir stopped and turned, offering him a small smile. "Yes, I know." Then, as if an idea had occurred to him, the doctor opened his medical kit and took out a padd. He held it out to Jake. "I brought this along with me on this trip because I thought I might have some time to work on a medical paper. Why don't you take it?"

"What for?" Jake asked.

"For you to write your feelings down," answered Bashir. "Maybe it will help you to sort things out." At Jake's skeptical expression, Bashir added, "You don't have to use it. Just keep it in case you change your mind."

Jake accepted the padd, murmuring an insincere "thanks." The doctor nodded and walked away.

Alone again, Jake resumed his vigil. His thoughts wandered aimlessly, taking him through a tangle of conflicting emotions. After a few minutes, he looked down at the padd in his hand and slowly, hesitantly at first, he began to write.

The ground was uneven.

Kira had felt the floor descending for some time now. She'd noticed the unfinished workmanship in this part of the catacombs and wondered if this section was newer than the rest.

As her attention lapsed, she took an awkward step and felt her ankle twist under her. "Ow."

"Major?"

Sisko's voice calling to her was followed by the beam of his handlight shining in her face. She winced and shielded her eyes with her hand. "Would you please stop doing that? You're going to blind me."

The glare turned aside. "Are you all right?"

"Twisted my ankle," she said dismissively. "Nothing serious." She took a single step on the treacherous ground and a jolt of pain shot up her leg. "Dammit."

Suddenly Sisko was at her side, one of his arms around her waist, one of hers across his shoulders. He guided her toward one wall of the tunnel and eased her into a sitting position.

"We should try to get some rest, anyway," he said. "This is as good a place as any."

Loral and Jek stood on the edge of the light. They were shivering.

"Come on, sit down," Sisko said to them. "It's dinner time."

He untied the bundle they'd carried from the resistance storeroom and took out four food packs, handing one to Kira and one to each of the children. Jek tore his open eagerly and had his food wolfed down in about ten seconds. Loral savored her meal, chewing slowly and trying to enjoy every bite. Kira saw Sisko cringe as he ate. "Not used to eating rough?" she asked pointedly.

Sisko looked at her. "Major," he said, "I grew up in New Orleans."

"Is that your planet?" Loral asked.

"No, it's a city on Earth."

"So?" Kira said. She had never heard of New Orleans, either, but figured that Sisko was trying to tell them how tough he had it as a child.

"They'll eat anything in New Orleans," Sisko informed her. "Slugs, raw oysters—just about anything you can imagine, especially if it's fried or covered in hot sauce."

Kira laughed in spite of herself. She hadn't expected humor from him. But then, she'd known Benjamin Sisko for only a matter of days, and that really wasn't enough time to make a fair judgment.

She began to realize that she *wanted* not to like him.

As silence settled on them once again, Kira's thoughts turned to their earlier conversation. "You never answered my question," she said.

"What question was that?" Sisko wondered.

"Are you embarrassed to tell me that you're the Emissary?"

Sisko sighed and set down the food pack. "I'm not embarrassed," he said. "I'm just not convinced that I *am* the Emissary."

"So what *do* you believe?" Kira challenged.

Sisko hesitated, then shrugged. "I don't know."

Kira grunted. "I think we've finally found something we agree on."

"Well, we also both want to get out of these tunnels," Sisko said with a smile. "If we're not careful, we may just start to realize how much we have in common."

Kira shook her head. It was so much easier when she knew who the enemy was. Now, she wasn't sure anymore. "I've been fighting for so long," she said. "Everyone on Bajor—resistance is all we know."

"That's what you keep saying, Major," Sisko said. "But we both know that isn't true."

"Excuse me?"

"Granted, I haven't been here all that long," he began, "but I think I'm starting to see the true face of Bajor. I see it in people like you, and Opaka, and Tanin, and in these children. I saw it in Ashalla, and in the Taluno Library. I see it even here in these catacombs. And when I look at all of that, I *don't* see a people spoiling for the next fight. What I see is a unique and remarkable civilization with an astonishing history and a living, ancient culture that even the Cardassians couldn't crush. I see a people that rightly cherishes its past, and yet is preparing to embrace the future."

"A future with the Federation, you mean," Kira said angrily, throwing down her food pack. "The Cardassians promised us a future when they came, too."

"You can't honestly believe that the Federation is anything like the Cardassians." Sisko said.

Kira laughed bitterly. "Can't I? All my life the people in power said that they were looking out for our best interests. They just wanted to do what was best for Bajor. Well, I think it's high time that *Bajor* decided what's best for Bajor," Kira said, feeling her fists clenching at her sides.

"Some would say that Bajor *did* make that decision," Sisko said. "It was the provisional government that invited us here."

"Because they don't have the vision to see that Bajor doesn't need anyone," Kira shouted. "Not the Cardasians, and not *you.*"

Sisko's eyes narrowed. "Major. Ever since I arrived on Deep

Space 9 I have tried to be reasonable with you. Now I see that it was a waste of time. All you seem to understand are the extremes—love and hate and nothing in between. You're so used to fighting that you can't stand peace."

Kira was stunned. She had never seen Sisko so angry. His eyes were like two glowing embers; he stared into Kira's eyes and wouldn't break his gaze.

"You've fought for freedom your whole life. But now that you have it, you don't know what to do with it."

Kira snapped back to herself. *Freedom? This from a man who grew up in a house with both parents—a man who has never known what it was like to starve.*

"How dare you?" Kira said, pulling herself to her feet. "You don't know me . . ."

"You won't *let* me know you," Sisko fired back.

"You think that you put Bajor on the map," she shouted. *"You* found the Celestial Temple. *You* convinced the kai and half the planet that you're the Emissary. Well, you haven't convinced *me."* Her eyes had narrowed into slits.

"I don't believe in you," Kira screamed.

Her voice reverberated off the walls, echoed down the corridors of the Paths of the Lost.

Loral and Jek shrank back from her, terrified. Kira turned away, limping down the tunnel into the darkness.

Sisko lurched forward and stopped in front of her, blocking her path. "Get the hell out of my way," she snapped.

"No, you're hurt," Sisko said quietly. "Take my hand."

Kira stopped, her blood hammering in her ears, her heart feeling as if it would pound its way through her chest. She looked at Sisko's outstretched hand, up into his face, and suddenly felt as if she would sag under the weight of her own uncertainty.

And slowly, she reached out and took his hand.

Sisko gently helped her back toward the children. For their part, Jek and Loral clung to them both as they settled once again on the ground.

"Why are you two always fighting?" Jek asked, shivering as he leaned back against the commander.

"It isn't nice," commented Loral, who had put her head in Kira's lap.

"We just don't know how to talk to each other," Sisko said, wrapping his arms around the boy. "Yet," he added with a smile. "It's all right. Try to get some sleep."

Kira stroked Loral's hair until the girl's breathing evened out. Jek's eyes began to droop, and in minutes, both children were asleep.

Kira studied Sisko's face. "If you were just a Starfleet officer," she said, "it would be easy for me to hate you. But you found the Temple. And Opaka . . ."

Sisko looked down at the ground. "Major," he said softly, "you say that you want what's best for your people, and you told me earlier that the will of the Prophets is what's right for Bajor."

"That's right," Kira said quietly.

"And I don't claim to speak for them," Sisko went on. "But is it really your belief that isolating Bajor is what they want? That shutting out the universe is the only way for your people to find peace?"

Kira had no answer.

Sisko turned to her, his soft brown eyes questioning. "What exactly do *you* believe in, Nerys?"

The question still hung between them as sleep finally overtook Kira.

Dawn came to Ashalla.

Colonel Day sat in a dark corner of a café near the blast site and watched as another injured rescue worker was lifted out of the ruins, the third one since the operation started. Day had hardly slept all night, and was due back on-site in less than an hour. He had just taken a sip of *moba* juice when he heard some of his men talking at a nearby table.

"This is insane. No one could have survived all that. We're putting ourselves at risk for nothing."

"That's what I told the colonel."

"What did he say?"

"He said that the Federation doesn't care how many of us get hurt, as long as they get their man back."

"The Federation!"

"So we risk our lives for one of theirs? I didn't see them lining up to fight during the Occupation."

"I hear you. But the orders come from the top. What can we do?"

"I don't like this. I don't like this one bit."

Day allowed himself a small smile. He didn't like it either, but he had already decided that if he could use one old woman's sick interest in an alien to help wake up Bajor to the Federation threat, it was worth a few broken bones.

The Paths of the Lost wound up and down through the endless stone. Sisko's pulse was up, but he didn't mind. He had always enjoyed a good walk first thing in the morning. Not that this was the ideal environment, but after sleeping on the bare rock last night he was happy to be doing anything besides lying down. Even Kira's ankle was better, and the major was once again bringing up the rear. The children walked together between the adults, their chatter bringing a smile to Sisko's face.

"I'm cold," Jek complained.

"Me too," said Loral. "Do you smell something?"

"I don't know," said the boy. "I think so."

As the group rounded a bend in the tunnel, the smell the children had noticed became suddenly apparent to Sisko. Soon it overwhelmed them, triggering their gag reflexes.

Covering his mouth and nose with his hand, Sisko took a look around at their surroundings. The tunnel had opened into a wide chamber with large, rectangular crevices carved directly into the walls on either side.

Sisko approached one of the openings and quickly realized where the smell was coming from.

"This is a tomb," he said, his voice muffled by his hand.

Kira stepped up and, heedless of the smell, laid a hand reverently on the threshold. She bowed her head and Sisko heard her whisper, but he couldn't make out the words. He turned away to give her some privacy. As Sisko moved further down the passageway, he noticed Jek staring at a picture painted crudely on one of the walls.

"Hey, look at this," said the boy.

Sisko drew near, trying to get a better look.

Something that looked like an old-fashioned sailing ship was floating among the stars. There was a streak of purple, which Sisko assumed represented the Denorios Belt, and beside it, a mouth of blue flame. The Celestial Temple.

Next to the first drawing was another, the figure of a man standing in a white circle.

"Is that you, Emissary?" asked Loral.

"I don't think so," Sisko answered, but found it difficult to tear his eyes from the image.

The catacombs were different beyond the tomb. No more hand carved tunnels—they'd come upon natural caves, untouched by Bajoran artisans. Stalactites dripped overhead, some forming columns with the stalagmites below.

"It's beautiful," Loral said. The child stared in wonder as she passed a patch of purple crystal formations on the wall of the cavern. Something was glistening farther down the wall.

Sisko stopped suddenly.

"Major," he said, pointing at the wall, "do you see that?"

Kira looked. After a moment, she turned back sharply toward Sisko, understanding. "Water."

Sisko nodded. "There's water seeping through the wall."

"So what?" Jek asked.

"These caverns were carved by flowing water," Sisko explained, "and most rivers have underground sources."

"There's a river just outside the city," noted Loral.

"And if this is any indication," Sisko said, feeling himself grinning from ear to ear, "then the way out of here may be very close by. All we have to do is follow the water."

Colonel Day threw down his pickax. He looked at the Militia personnel and civilian volunteers gathered around him. "No more," he said. "This is no longer a rescue operation. As of this moment, it's strictly recovery. I'm calling in the heavy equipment."

The workers gave a hearty cheer.

There had been three cave-ins since the body of Vedek Tanin had been discovered the previous night. The number of injured workers had risen to five.

"Let's get out of here," Day said. He took a lumbering step over some debris and then stopped. Kai Opaka stood in his way.

"Where are you going?" she asked.

"It's over, Eminence," Day said. "The work is too dangerous, and it's been long enough. There's no hope that anyone could be alive down there."

"No hope?" Opaka echoed. "And what of the Prophets?"

"What of our *lives?*" Day asked. He knew he stood little chance of winning a spiritual debate with the kai, and he wasn't fool enough to try. But if he could keep the emphasis on more immediate concerns—

Opaka faced the crowd. She drew them in close, gesturing for them to gather around her. "I know that the work you do here is dangerous," she said. "I know that you've seen your friends and coworkers injured. Perhaps you've even been injured yourselves.

"I want you to know *why* you risk your lives," said Opaka. "Somewhere under these stones, there is a man named Benjamin Sisko. He is the Starfleet commander of Deep Space 9 . . . and he is the Emissary of the Prophets."

A murmur ran through the crowd. Day shook his head in disbelief that Opaka was still peddling that delusion of hers. He'd heard the rumors, of course; they'd been spreading since yesterday. If she thought their people would accept an offworlder as the Emissary so soon after the Cardassians had been forced out, Day's task here would be easier than he thought. Opaka's "good news" would be rejected, Sisko would be left to die, and the Federation would likely abandon Bajor as a lost cause. Then Day's purposes, and those of the group to whom he belonged, the Circle, would be achieved.

In the park across the street, reporters from the comnet had set up imagers to record the proceedings. *Even better,* Day thought. *Now the whole planet will know what a demented old relic she really is.* Day saw that the other two aliens, Sisko's son and the Starfleet medic, were also present.

"We have faced many challenges together," said the kai. "We defeated the Cardassians and survived their brutality. But we must not become like them. We must become like ourselves. We must remember who we truly are, and not what our oppressors tried to make us into.

"A greater challenge is upon us now. To face the future. Our people are weary, angry, divided. We must set aside our differences and recognize that we have not merely survived, but thrived. Because even during the darkest hours of the Occupation, we were united. The only way we can move forward is to do so as one, as the people we know ourselves to be.

"On this day, I call upon the people of Bajor to join together. To gather the strength of the *pagh* within each of us and to embrace the future toward which the Prophets, through the Emissary, are guiding us."

Day looked at the faces in the crowd. Tears filled the eyes of many. Too many. Some wept openly. Others nodded with renewed purpose. Day cursed beneath his breath. Opaka was turning the tide.

"My friend Vedek Tanin Prem died yesterday beneath these stones," she continued. "Before he died, he told me that he believed the path of the Prophets was not always clear, and that he feared for our people's ability to face a new test of our faith—one that would require us to let go of our preconceptions and recognize the Emissary for who he truly is.

"Now, Children of the Prophets, that test is upon us. We have come through the night of the Occupation and now stand at the dawn of *Ha'mara*. The Temple gates have opened."

The kai reached down and picked up Day's abandoned pickax. Then she straightened, meeting his eyes for a long and disconcerting moment before turning back to the crowd. "Vedek Tanin spoke true when he said that the path of the Prophets is seldom clear, and it is seldom easy. But I am willing to walk that path, as Tanin did. I will not turn aside now, after living through so much. And I will not turn my back on the Emissary."

Opaka swung the pickax against a massive stone. The blow was not heavy, but it rang out across the rubble.

Soon the sound of metal on stone intensified as the others picked up their tools and went back to work. Within minutes, the ringing of pick and hammer had drowned out all other sound.

Deep under the city, Sisko had lost all sense of time. The tunnel had been climbing steadily for what seemed like hours. From all indications, Sisko felt they were headed in the right direction, but there was no way to be sure. He kept putting one weary foot in front of another, hoping that the next time he rounded a bend in the tunnel he would see daylight.

Sisko thought he felt a burst of warm air. He stopped moving, and Kira and the others closed in on him, his joy quickly spreading through the rest of the group.

"Is it an exit?" Loral asked.

"I think so," Sisko said. He took a step forward and felt the floor give under his weight.

Strange, he thought. He gently began to retract his foot when an excited Jek raced past him.

"Stop!" Sisko cried, but it was too late.

The floor gave out beneath the group with a crack that rang out like thunder. Sisko tried to jump back but he wasn't quick enough. He felt the handlight slip from his grasp as he fell into shadow.

★　★　★

A few meters back, Kira felt the tunnel rumble as the floor collapsed beneath her. She heard the others cry out as they fell, and suddenly Kira was suspended in complete darkness. She groped for a handhold, her fingernails digging into the unforgiving stone of the floor's jagged edge.

She couldn't hold on. That truth exploded in her mind as she felt herself beginning to slip into the chasm below. She tried to pull herself up, but that only sent more fragments of stone falling into the void.

What did it matter, she thought. Even if she could pull herself back up, where would she go? The light was gone, the floor untrustworthy. If she did somehow climb out of the opening, she would have to walk the Paths of the Lost alone. There was a good chance that she would never find her way out, that she would wander the catacombs until she died of starvation, or slipped into madness.

It seemed she had run out of options. She felt her fingers giving out. She would fall, probably to her death, and she would never see the light of day again. If she did live, her only chance for survival would be to follow Benjamin Sisko—to walk with him wherever he led.

Sisko thought he was dead the moment he hit the underground lake. It sent blades of ice through his veins, freezing him into complacency as he sank through the black water.

Don't think. Don't feel. Just act.

His survival mantra was all that kept him alive. He kicked his legs and began to pull himself through the water. In the darkness he couldn't tell which way was up, so he could only hope that he was headed in the right direction.

As Sisko breached the surface of the lake, he saw the handlight lying on a stone fragment that jutted out of the water. It was focused on the lake, reflecting off the water and filling the chamber with a pale blue light.

Sisko's eyes widened in amazement as he took in the size of the cavern. The remains of the chamber's ceiling stretched like fingers into the darkness. There was a muddy shore about twenty meters away, where Jek and Loral were sitting calmly, smiling at him.

"Isn't this incredible?" asked the boy. "Have you seen the fish?"

Sisko wasn't sure that he wanted to see any kind of animal that lived in this environment. He kicked through the water in the direction of the beach, wishing more than anything for a warm bed and a bowl of hot gumbo.

As Sisko neared the beach he heard Major Kira splash into the water behind him.

"Kira!" he shouted. "Are you all right?"

He was about to turn back for her when her head bobbed up about five meters away from him. She shook her head in disbelief.

Satisfied that she was all right, Sisko trudged onto the muddy shore. He was freezing, but that didn't bother him right now. He looked at himself—the knees ripped out of his pants and his uniform covered in mud.

Sisko laughed, and the sound boomed through the gigantic chamber.

"What the hell are you laughing at?" Kira asked as she too arrived on the bank. She looked as ridiculous as Sisko felt, and seeing her made him laugh even harder. Kira's brow furrowed—her jaw was clenched in anger.

"What's so damn funny?" she snapped.

"We are," Sisko said. "Just look at us."

Jek scooped a handful of mud into his hands and fashioned it into a ball. He took careful aim at Kira and threw.

Kira's jaw dropped as the mud splattered across the front of her uniform.

"You little ingrate!" she yelled, though Sisko could detect no real anger in her voice. The major knelt down and dug her hands into the mud beneath the water. She produced a projectile of her own and threw it toward the beach. It landed squarely in Sisko's face.

He stopped laughing. Sisko reached up with both index fingers and wiped the mud off his eyelids. "Major," he said, "this means war."

The battle that raged in the cavern under Ashalla might never have made it into a Starfleet combat training simulation, but as it became clear that he was facing three-to-one odds, Sisko began to think he was fighting for his life—or, at minimum, his dignity.

Sisko laughed as he hurled another mudball at his first officer. Kira retaliated by scooping her hand through the water and splashing the commander.

"You're going to regret that," Sisko said. He lunged into the water after Kira.

As he lumbered toward her, the lake floor dropped away suddenly. Sisko tried to pull himself back to where there was even footing, but it was impossible—the sudden current under the surface of the lake was sucking him down. He tried to call out for help, but water filled his throat. The cold sent needles of pain through his body. Sisko reached toward the surface—but saw only darkness as the water closed in over his head.

Then, a small, strong hand closed over Sisko's wrist.

Kira pulled with all her strength. She felt her feet slipping, but refused to let go.

"Come on, dammit!"

She cursed into the shadows as she felt one of her boots slip in the muck. She heard Loral and Jek splashing up behind her, felt their hands wrapped around her waist. Together, they pulled with everything they had.

Finally, Sisko emerged from the black water. Coughing and sputtering, the group collapsed on the dark shore of the lake.

"We're never going to get out of here," Kira said.

"We have to try," Sisko insited. "No matter how difficult the road is, we have to keep going. Even if I knew I would fail, at least I'd die knowing that I never gave up."

"I thought everything would be different after we beat the Cardassians," Kira said. "I thought I could finally stop fighting."

"You can stop fighting *me*," said Sisko.

"I'm trying," Kira panted. "I'm trying." Dimly, she was aware that Loral and Jek had gotten up and started wandering down the shore.

"I have a confession to make, Major," Sisko said. "I didn't tell the complete truth about my experience in the wormhole."

Water dripping into her eyes, Kira squinted in his direction, waiting.

"I said that the Prophets showed me I should never give up, but I never explained how." He paused, still breathing heavily. "They showed me my wife. They showed me her death over and over again. I asked them why. I begged them to take me away from there."

"What happened?"

"They said that *I* brought them to Wolf 359. *I* had never left the *Saratoga*. Two years later, and I hadn't lived a day."

"That's understandable . . ."

"No, it's not." Sisko sat up, turned toward her. His face glistened with beads of water. "I owe it to Jennifer to keep living," he said. "It's the debt that all survivors owe the dead. You owe it to your family, and to every Bajoran who died during the Occupation—to live. And to move forward boldly, to make the most out of life."

"And you think I can do that by aligning myself with the Federation?"

"This doesn't have anything to do with the Federation," Sisko said. "It has to do with *you,* with Kira Nerys. You can choose to live in the present or to live in the past. The same choice I had."

Sisko sighed, and went on, "There's been enough death because of the Occupation. Now is the time to bring hope back into the world."

Kira stared at him, and finally dared to speak the thought that had come to her mind. "It seems to me that that's what you're here for," she said, "if you truly are the Emissary."

"I don't know about that," Sisko answered. "For now, though, I'll settle for just being a friend to Bajor, and to you."

In the distance they could hear Loral and Jek shouting in excitement. "A stairway! Emissary, we found the way out!"

Kira and Sisko stared at each other for a long moment, as understanding finally passed between them. Kira stood up, walked over to where Sisko sat, and reached out. "Well?" she said. "Take my hand."

Sisko smiled and let Kira pull him to his feet. They limped together across the muddy shore.

When they neared the stair, which seemed to wend its way up a considerable distance, Kira could see a glimmer of daylight at the top. Sisko turned as if to take one last look at the Paths of the Lost. They had survived, Kira knew, only because they had relied on each other. She wondered if Sisko believed, as she now did, that the Prophets had a hand in all this. But for some reason, she didn't ask. Maybe she no longer needed to know.

They walked up the long stairs in silence. At the top they pushed together through a thin layer of earth on a wooded slope at the edge of Ashalla. It was dusk beyond the Paths of the Lost, about thirty hours after the collapse of the Taluno Library. The light hurt the wanderers' eyes after being so long underground, but they didn't care.

Ashalla glittered with light. In every window Jake could see, a candle was burning. Lanterns lit the sight of the Taluno Library, where rows of candlebearers had gathered near the workers who were still digging carefully through the ruins.

And then, they started singing.

To Jake, it was much like the the song of the people who had gathered at the monastery the previous morning, and it reminded him a lot of the African choral singing his father had introduced him to a few years ago.

Clutching the padd that Bashir had given him—which now contained pages and pages of thoughts and feelings he'd spent half the day wrestling with, Jake found himself repenting his earlier anger toward the people of Bajor. No matter what happened to his father, these people didn't deserve his hate.

Then, as he stood looking on with Dr. Bashir, Jake thought he heard his father's voice.

He turned away from the workers and looked down the street. His jaw dropped.

"Dad!" Jake screamed. He ran toward his father.

Everyone who was watching the progress on Taluno Library turned around at Jake's shout. They saw four muddy people walking arm in arm down toward the crowd.

Jake flung himself into his father's arms.

"You're alive!" he said. He hugged his father as tight as his arms would allow. Sisko hugged him back so hard that Jake's feet were lifted off the ground.

"Jake-O," Sisko said. "I am so glad to see you."

Sisko set his son down and gave him a joyful kiss on the top of the head.

As the weary group walked down the city street, people lined up on either side. The meek and the strong, peacemakers and freedom fighters, farmers and politicians—from every village, from every province they had come. A cheer erupted from the gathered people as the Emissary and his companions passed by. It was a time of joy in Ashalla. It was *Ha'mara*.

It was a time to sing.

The next day, Kira Nerys stood in the main shrine of the monastery, facing a great tapestry purported to depict the grand design of the universe, as imagined by ancient Bajorans. Although in truth, all Kira saw was a complex and seemingly random—albeit aesthetically pleasing—jumble of abstract elements. *Which,* she reflected, *is probably as good a description of the universe as any.* After a moment, Kira closed her eyes, held her hands open and apart, and prayed.

She heard someone enter the room. Kira didn't look, but she

sensed the newcomer standing near and joining her in communion with the Prophets.

When Kira opened her eyes, she was shocked to see that it was Kai Opaka.

"Eminence," Kira stammered.

"Please," the kai said. "I've never liked being called that. Opaka will do. Are you well?"

"I'm mending," Kira said. Dr. Bashir had tended to their wounds as soon as the welcoming crowds began to dissipate.

"May I?" Opaka asked as she extended her hand toward Kira's ear. "Of course."

Opaka breathed deeply as she felt Kira's *pagh*. Her face filled with understanding.

"You are troubled," Opaka said as she released the major's ear. "Would you care to talk about it?"

Kira hesitated. The opportunity she was being given was all that she hoped for and everything she feared at once. "Commander Sisko," she said finally. "I don't understand why the Prophets would choose a nonbeliever as the Emissary."

Opaka smiled, and regarded the tapestry before them. "The will of the Prophets is sometimes confusing," Opaka said. "Often the path they choose for us to walk is not one we would choose for ourselves."

"This is a strange path, Opaka," Kira said.

Still smiling, Opaka turned to Kira and took both her hands in her own. "But you need not walk it alone."

Sisko was in his office on Deep Space 9, seated opposite Major Kira. Three days had passed since their return from Bajor, and in all that time, they had not spoken a word that was not work-related.

Sisko was holding a report detailing the progress on the station's repairs and upgrades. With all the Federation and Klingon traffic expected to come through Deep Space 9 in the weeks and months ahead, work to make the station ready for it was going on around the clock.

"This is fine," he said, handing the padd back to Kira.

"Thank you, sir."

Sisko had expected Kira to return to ops then, but something held her in place.

"Is there something else, Major?"

"Yes," she said, "there is." Then she fell silent.

"Well?"

"I just wanted to say that I'm sorry for the way I spoke to you in the catacombs," Kira said.

"No need to apologize, Major. We were both under a lot of stress."

"With all due respect, Commander," she said, "I need to get this off my chest."

Sisko leaned back in his chair. "Then by all means," he said, "speak freely."

Kira took a deep breath. "I'm still not sure that the Federation presence here is the best thing for Bajor," she said. "But after everything we went through in the Paths of the Lost, I want you to know . . . I consider myself very fortunate to be working with you."

Sisko smiled. "The feeling is more than mutual, Major. Is that all?"

"Yes, sir."

"Then I'd like to ask you a question, if I may."

"Please."

"Do you believe that I'm the Emissary?"

Kira smiled at him. "I believe in the Prophets, Commander," she said at last, "And if they believe in you, then that's good enough for me."

Sisko blinked. "I see."

"Will that be all, sir?"

"Yes. Thank you, Major. Carry on."

Kira nodded and left, leaving Sisko alone in his office. He wasn't sure what he had expected her to say, but her answer left him with a vague feeling of unease about the future.

He had heard from Starfleet the day before, and it appeared they weren't going to reassign him after all. Given the circumstances, taking Sisko away from Bajor now would likely do more harm than good. Or so they seemed to think.

Which suited Sisko just fine. His misgivings about his status among the Bajorans notwithstanding, he felt certain, in a way he hadn't known since before Jennifer had died, that he was where he belonged.

Benjamin Sisko stood up and turned to gaze out the window behind his desk. Suddenly the wormhole flared to life as a starship began its journey into the Gamma Quadrant.

No doubt there were turbulent times ahead. But at least he had made some headway with Major Kira. They still had a long way to go, he knew that, but he took comfort in the knowledge that, whatever lay ahead, they would travel that road together.

The Orb of Opportunity

Michael A. Martin and Andy Mangels

Historian's note: This story is set between the third-season episodes "Life Support" and "Heart of Stone."

Michael A. Martin

Michael A. Martin's solo short fiction has appeared in *The Magazine of Fantasy & Science Fiction*. He has also coauthored (with Andy Mangels) several *Star Trek* novels, a pair of e-books in the *Starfleet Corps of Engineers* series, and three novels based on the *Roswell* television series. Martin was the regular cowriter (also with Andy) of Marvel Comics' *Star Trek: Deep Space Nine* comics series, and has written for Atlas Editions' *Star Trek Universe* subscription card series, *Star Trek Monthly*, *Dreamwatch*, Grolier Books, Wildstorm, and Platinum Studios. He lives with his family in Portland, Oregon.

Andy Mangels

Andy Mangels has coauthored several *Star Trek* novels, two *Starfleet Corps of Engineers* e-books, and three novels based on TV's *Roswell* (all written with Michael A. Martin). Flying solo, Andy has penned *Animation on DVD: The Ultimate Guide; Star Wars: The Essential Guide To Characters; Beyond Mulder & Scully: The Mysterious Characters of The X-Files;* and *From Scream To Dawson's Creek: The Phenomenal Career of Kevin Williamson*. Mangels has written for numerous licensed properties as well as a plethora of entertainment and lifestyle periodicals. He lives in Portland, Oregon, with his longtime partner, Don Hood, and their dog, Bela. Visit his website at <www.andymangels.com>.

Kira Nerys met Winn Adami at the door to the kai's VIP quarters aboard Deep Space 9. "Legate Turrel's transport ship is making its approach, Eminence," the major said.

Winn found Kira's tone stilted and formal, far beyond businesslike. The major's eyes, apparently focused on some point on the gray bulkhead past Winn's shoulder, practically smoldered with barely restrained hostility.

Winn nodded, her clerical robes rustling as she swept through the doorway and past the major. She didn't care much for Kira's angry manner, though she certainly understood the reason for it. Vedek Bareil's death remained an open wound for both of them.

May the Prophets guide her to the knowledge that Bareil Antos gave his life willingly, and for a noble cause—peace with Cardassia. And that his passing has also paved the way for the return of the Tears of the Prophets to their rightful home.

After they'd traveled together in silence to Deep Space 9's docking ring, Kira said, "Did Turrel give you any reason for his having delayed his arrival?"

Winn shook her head. "No, child. But he *did* promise to clarify his reasons once he came aboard." Despite the historic peace treaty Bareil had just helped her negotiate with Turrel, Winn had sensed from the legate the typical Cardassian reticence about explaining himself before Bajorans—a reluctance that also included, evidently, Bajor's spiritual leader.

"I managed to take a good look at his ship from ops," Kira said as they stopped at an airlock. "From the scoring on the hull, it looks like it's been in battle fairly recently."

That didn't sound right. Transport ships, even those of Cardassian design, weren't built for warfare. Winn felt a flutter in the pit of her stomach as she speculated anew about the possible reasons for Turrel's tardiness. Considering the incalculable value of the cargo the legate's transport carried, she didn't like the direction her conjectures were taking her.

A telltale light flashed green. "Turrel's ship has docked," Kira said.

Winn watched quietly as the major keyed an access code into the airlock keypad. A moment later, the heavy door hissed and rolled aside, and Kira led the way into the interior chamber.

Legate Turrel, flanked by a pair of uniformed military aides, entered the airlock from the hatchway on its opposite side. Turrel and his party stopped, the legate standing erect. As Winn remembered from her recent meetings with him across the negotiating table, Turrel's eyes were cold. But there was something else in his gaze that Winn had never seen before in a Cardassian.

She thought it resembled sorrow, or perhaps desperation. Winn's guts went into freefall. Clearly, something had gone terribly wrong.

"Legate Turrel," Winn said after Kira briefly and formally welcomed the Cardassians aboard the station. "What's happened?"

Turrel hesitated for a moment, as though gathering his thoughts. Then he met Winn's gaze squarely once again.

"The Maquis attacked us while we were en route from Cardassia Prime," he said. "And they seized our . . . cargo."

Alone with the kai in his office atop the station's bustling operations center, Commander Benjamin Sisko could hardly believe what he was hearing. "You're saying the Maquis *stole* the Orb of Contemplation right out from under Legate Turrel's nose?" he said.

"Legate Turrel not only offered to return the Orb to Bajor,"

Winn said, taking a seat in front of Sisko's desk. "But he also promised to oversee its transportation personally in order to ensure that nothing went wrong." Sisko heard a fair amount of anger percolating beneath her voice.

"Sounds like that wasn't enough," Sisko said. "Does Turrel have any idea where the Maquis might have taken the Orb?"

"He believes that they took it into one of their secret bases in the Demilitarized Zone. Along with the blindvault they were using to transport it. Turrel thinks the Maquis believed the vault to contain a biogenic weapon."

"A blindvault," Sisko repeated, considering the complications that revelation posed. Blindvaults were scan-proof, sound-proof, transporter-proof, and all but impregnable. The odds were pretty good that the Maquis wouldn't be able to get the vault open, at least not right away.

And since the Maquis had made no ransom demands of which he was aware, the odds were equally good that they didn't yet know what they'd stolen.

"Emissary, I can't begin to tell you what a catastrophe this is," Winn said.

A catastrophe for Bajor, or for your newest political coup? Sisko thought, turning to face the star-dappled spacescape visible from his window as he suppressed a rush of anger. He had witnessed her wringing out every last iota of Vedek Bareil's negotiating expertise in order to obtain a peace treaty with Cardassia. Watching her take credit for that agreement—an effort that had cost the gravely injured vedek his life—had rankled him. It wasn't hard for him to believe that the secret repatriation of one of the Orbs taken from Bajor during the Cardassian Occupation was to become merely another feather in Winn's political cap.

Aloud, he said, "It would have been nice to have received some advance warning that the Cardassians had authorized the release of the Orb. Starfleet could have supplied some protection."

"So might have the entire Bajoran Militia, Emissary," came Winn's tart reply. "Or the Cardassian Central Command, for that matter. Legate Turrel and I agreed that using a large contingent to transport the Orb would have only attracted undue attention to its transit from Cardassia to Bajor."

Sisko took a seat behind the massive black desk that was the centerpiece of his office. He picked up his baseball from the desktop and tossed it from hand to hand. *And a large contingent of escort vessels might also have forced you to share the credit for bringing back the Orb. Even though a lot of that credit ought to have gone to Bareil.* Just three days earlier, Winn had commented on how cordial the late vedek's relationship with the hard-dealing Cardassian legate had been.

"Bringing back an Orb would be quite an accomplishment," Sisko said, trying to keep his tone neutral. It was already obvious that Winn wanted his help. But he wanted to hear her say so.

Winn nodded, obviously not inclined to beg. "Indeed it would. Especially when one considers what a poor job the Cardassians have done in keeping track of them."

"I'd always thought that Cardassian stubbornness was the main obstacle to the return of the Orbs," Sisko said, surprised.

Winn chuckled humorlessly. "Cardassian stubbornness can never be underestimated, Emissary. But their bureaucratic foul-ups and intramural rivalries are at least as big a hindrance."

"I'm not sure I understand."

"Of course not, Emissary. Starfleet doubtless has few such inefficiencies," Winn said, her pleasant expression never wavering. "However, Legate Turrel has just made me aware that the Cardassian Central Command has lost track of nearly all eight of the Orbs they took from Bajor during the Occupation. Which may explain why he wasn't eager to set a timetable for the Orbs' return during the last negotiations."

And it probably gave you quite an effective lever to use on him, Sisko thought, quietly impressed by the kai's ability to pressure a tough negotiator like Turrel into making such an embarrassing admission of Cardassian incompetence, malfeasance, or perhaps both. *If the legate hadn't agreed to revisit the Orb issue quickly, then you could have damaged him pretty badly by going public about Cardassia's allowing the Orbs to disappear.*

"So has Turrel explained what's become of the missing Orbs?" Sisko said aloud.

"Only generally. The Orb of Wisdom seems to have been stolen from the Cardassians at some point after *they* stole it from *us*. The Orb of Memory apparently never even made it Cardassia. Turrel assures me that Central Command is close to discovering the whereabouts of the Orb of Time. But the remaining four Orbs have somehow vanished from the science labs where they've allegedly been kept since the Occupation."

"If I were Turrel," Sisko said, "I'd suspect the involvement of the Obsidian Order." He had no doubt that Cardassia's much-feared intelligence service had always had its own secret agenda regarding the Orbs—and whatever weapons potential they might possess.

"I have already broached that possibility with the legate, Emissary. He claims to have looked into this already, and says that the Order flatly denies any knowledge. In any event, the Orb of Contemplation was the only one of the eight Turrel has thus far been able to locate. Now, he says the Cardassian military is scouring the DMZ for the thieves. He promises that they will be tracked down and punished, and that the Orb will be recovered and returned to us. But there can be no guarantee of success. The Maquis can be very wily adversaries, as I'm sure you're aware."

Sisko noted that her last utterance was accompanied by an ever-so-slight smile. He wondered if she might not harbor some sympathy for those former Federation citizens; after all, they were no doubt as familiar with Cardassian oppression, and with the struggle against it, as she was.

He set the baseball back on his desk and leaned forward, meeting Winn's eyes directly. "I suppose we have little choice at this point other than to take Turrel at face value. So what happens now?"

"Now I need your help, Emissary."

Ah. There it is. "My help as the Emissary? Or as a Starfleet officer?" He sincerely hoped it was the latter. Having to play the role
of one of the most revered icons in the Bajoran religion had always
made him distinctly ill at ease.

"Perhaps both, Emissary. For whatever reason, your destiny lies
along the path of the Prophets, and of Bajor. And should all the
other Orbs remain lost, recovering even a single one would be
enormously valuable to my people."

And to you, personally. Sisko rose, satisfied that he understood what
was at stake. "I'll see what I can do to help you recover the Orb."

"Thank you, Emissary. As a further gesture of goodwill, Legate
Turrel has suggested mounting a large-scale joint mission, pooling
the resources of the Cardassian Military and the Bajoran Militia.
However, at the risk of insulting the legates's generosity, I must
admit to feeling far more comfortable working with you and
Starfleet."

Through the office doors that overlooked ops, Sisko caught a
glimpse of Kira, who was engaged in discussion with Lieutenant
Dax. Dax glanced up at the office occasionally. Kira, however,
seemed to be expending a great deal of effort not to do so. He
knew she must still be grieving Bareil intensely—the vedek had
died only three days earlier—and no doubt didn't relish the
prospect of Winn attempting to turn another of Bareil's hard-won
diplomatic victories to her own personal political advantage.

Sisko moved toward the office doors and opened them. Looking down into ops, he caught the eye of the Deep Space 9's chief
of operations, Miles O'Brien, who had looked up from an instrument panel he was in the midst of repairing. Sisko beckoned
silently to the chief, who quickly made his way up the stairs and
entered the office.

"Yes, Commander?" O'Brien said, nodding respectfully at the
kai. Sisko couldn't help but notice how uncomfortable the engineer seemed around Winn, evidently unfamiliar with the Bajoran
religion and the protocols of dealing with its senior clergy.

Sisko moved to the replicator to get some refreshments—*raktajino* for himself and O'Brien, and cold water for Winn—and then brought O'Brien up to speed about the theft of the Orb.

O'Brien sipped his *raktajino* in the seat beside Winn's. "If you don't mind my saying so, ah, Eminence, your instinct to avoid taking a large contingent of ships into the DMZ was a good one. If Turrel really has a lot of Cardassian vessels combing the region right now, then finding the trail of a single Maquis ship will be hard enough as it is without adding any additional warp signature noise."

"That was my thought as well," Winn said, staring contemplatively at her water glass.

Sisko couldn't help but wonder whether the real reason she had declined Turrel's offer—possibly placing the peace treaty she and Bareil had just negotiated at risk—was that she wasn't comfortable with the notion of delivering the Maquis to the legate's tender mercies. *Or maybe she simply doesn't get along with Turrel as well as Bareil did.*

"And that is why," the kai continued, "I have decided to go into the DMZ alone. I wish to find the Maquis cell responsible for the theft of the Orb and make a personal appeal for its safe return."

Sisko set down his mug. "With all due respect, Eminence, I strongly advise against that. The Maquis are far too suspicious of trickery and infiltration to trust you. And they're desperate enough to see you as a valuable hostage."

Winn set her glass down on the desk as though banging a gavel. By some miracle, the water didn't spill. "I cannot sit idle while the Orb remains in the hands of thieves. Its return is too important to the people of Bajor. I *am* going into the Demilitarized Zone, before the trail goes cold. Turrel has even provided a copy of his ship's sensor log to facilitate matters."

Sisko's gaze locked with Winn's for a protracted interval. He doubted she possessed the expertise to follow a fading Maquis warp trail on her own, no matter what information Turrel might have shared with her. He could also see that he wasn't going to dissuade her.

"All right," Sisko said with a sigh. "But you should at least go with the protection of the Bajoran Militia." He looked toward the chief engineer. "Mr. O'Brien, I want you to assemble a small recovery team and prepare a runabout for launch. Your team will coordinate the search effort with Kai Winn's Bajoran personnel."

O'Brien nodded. "Aye, sir. We can use Turrel's sensor data to track the Maquis from the runabout. I doubt the Cardassian search parties have any equipment quite as sensitive as ours, so I expect we'll locate the Maquis ship's trail and follow it to their hideout before anyone else manages it."

Something else suddenly occurred to Sisko. He cast an eye toward Winn. "Let's just hope that Turrel doesn't resent Starfleet's involvement in the search enough to endanger the new Bajor-Cardassia treaty."

"The legate shouldn't mind your assistance," Winn responded. "So long as it doesn't further embarrass him by becoming common knowledge."

O'Brien shrugged, clearly more interested in planning the details of the recovery operation than he was in the intricacies of Cardassian politics. "Once my team on the runabout locates the Maquis' hideout, the Militia crew can keep them busy while my team slips inside, locates the vault, and snatches the Orb right out from under their noses."

Winn nodded, her expression thoughtful, like a dom-jot player carefully considering every possible bounce the billiards might take. To O'Brien, she said, "The Emissary seems to think it unlikely the Maquis will be able to open the vault immediately. How do *you* propose to do it?"

"My first instinct would be to ask Legate Turrel for the combination," O'Brien said.

Winn shook her head. "The price of that information would have been consenting to a joint Cardassian-Bajoran military operation. I'm afraid that we must find another way."

Sisko frowned. "Chief, the Cardassians don't manufacture blind-vaults, do they?"

"No, sir. They're designed and built by the one people in the quadrant most interested in keeping their valuables safe—the Ferengi."

Sisko felt a grin slowly spreading across his face. "Then it sounds like you'll need the services of an exceptional safecracker."

"I think I have the perfect person in mind for the job," O'Brien said, returning Sisko's smile.

Winn walked several paces behind the engineer as he stepped off of the busy Promenade and into Quark's bar. She was content to let him lead, since he was clearly far better acquainted with this milieu than Winn was.

Or had ever wanted to be.

While O'Brien chatted with one of the Ferengi waiters, Winn stood between the tables at the periphery of the bar's gambling area, taking great care not to touch anything. The evening rush had yet to materialize, though the dabo wheel spun in a desultory fashion while a handful of revelers looked on. An awkward-looking Lurian ogled the young, scantily attired Bajoran woman who presided over the game. Winn looked away, disgusted, and approached O'Brien.

"So how about it, Rom?" the chief was saying, leaning toward the Ferengi waiter. "It's just to the DMZ and back, and the whole thing'll take maybe four days, tops. We could really use your help on this. Those lobes of yours could make all the difference."

"The people of Bajor would be in your debt," Winn offered, prompting a response from the Ferengi that resembled a wince.

The thin, almost emaciated-looking Ferengi was snaggle-toothed and repellent. But Winn had never much liked the company of Ferengi. She found everything about them—from their obsession with material possessions to their very appearance—to be the antithesis of all things spiritual.

It was bad enough having to ask for assistance from the alien whom the Prophets had inexplicably selected to be the Emissary. It was bad enough to be denied the opportunity to speak directly with the Prophets, as Sisko had done. It was bad enough to have to rely on the kindness and competence of Legate Turrell. But to be forced to consort with these large-eared *creatures* as well . . .

But the Prophets may have a plan even for such as these, Winn thought, chiding herself. *After all, Chief O'Brien really seems to think this Ferengi's contribution to the mission could be valuable.*

"Uhhm, why me?" said the Ferengi, who seemed to be cowering even though no one was threatening him. Winn wondered if cringing might not be an ingrained, reflexive defense mechanism for this wretch. In spite of herself, she felt a surge of pity.

"Rom, you are easily the most technologically savvy Ferengi aboard DS9," O'Brien continued, draping a friendly arm around the Ferengi's slight shoulders. "And that makes you the perfect choice to serve as Starfleet's 'safecracker' on this mission."

"My brother is not going to serve as Starfleet's *anything,*" came a harsh, braying voice from behind Winn.

She turned to see the approach of another Ferengi, whose deep scowl and expensive-yet-vulgar-looking suit made it clear that he was far less apt to cower than the Ferengi with whom O'Brien was speaking. She recognized the newcomer at once as Quark, the owner of this establishment—and the one who had recently bestowed upon her the dubious honor of namesake for one of the items on his dessert menu.

Ignoring both O'Brien and Winn, Quark marched right up to the other Ferengi, the one he had referred to as his brother. Winn pondered whether any two brothers anywhere had ever resembled each other less.

"Get back to work, Rom, or I'll dock you *another* hour's pay," Quark said.

"I'm on my break, Brother," Rom replied, sounding lame.

"Your break's over."

"Now hold on a minute, Quark," O'Brien said. "I'm not sure how much of our conversation you heard, but—"

Quark pointed at one of his outsize ears as he interrupted. "Hello? Would you like me to read you the transcript? You want to drag my brother off on a four-day jaunt across terrorist-infested space when I'm already shorthanded as it is."

"But—" Rom began.

"No buts," Quark said, squashing his sibling's words flat. "You're not going, and that's that."

Then Winn noticed another large-eared figure, a youth. He stood on the restaurant's uppermost level, leaning against a railing. His tiny, sharp eyes seemed to be absorbing every detail of the exchange between Quark and Rom. Though the lad was a good eight meters away, Winn had no doubt that his oversize ears were taking in every word, just as Quark's had.

Rom grimaced at Quark, apparently about to put up a fight. Then, to the obvious chagrin and disappointment of the boy on the railing. Rom's temporarily rigid posture bowed into a subservience that he wore like a well-broken-in garment.

"Yes, Brother," Rom said, shifting his scant weight awkwardly from one foot to the other. He was a picture of defeat and dejection.

"Now get back to work before your next paycheck gets all the way down into negative integers," Quark said. With a shamefaced nod, Rom quickly walked away, headed for the kitchen.

"You'll have to forgive my brother for wasting your time," Quark said, speaking to both O'Brien and Winn simultaneously. "I love him, but he's an idiot. It's a full-time job just steering him clear of trouble and keeping his teeth to the grindstone."

"No problem, Quark," O'Brien growled. "Especially if *you* have some skill in breaking into Ferengi-designed blindvaults."

Quark's eyes widened in a stage-play portrayal of surprise and indignation. "Chief! That sounds like criminal behavior to me. Whatever Constable Odo may have told you, I'm far too busy running my entirely *legitimate* food, beverage, and entertainment emporium to have time for such things. Now, if you'll please excuse me . . ." And with that, the large-lobed restaurateur was gone.

O'Brien sighed, his brow furrowed. "Damn. I mean, 'That's certainly disappointing.' Sorry, Eminence."

But Winn wasn't concerned about the chief's language. "What do we do now? Can your recovery team get at the Orb without bringing a Ferengi along?"

"Looks like we're going to have to. I suppose we can always open the vault after we get it back to DS9. After all, what's the difference if it takes an extra day or two to do a job a Ferengi could have done in a few minutes?"

Winn considered O'Brien's question in silence. He'd made a good point. But what if the Maquis thieves had somehow managed to remove the Orb from the vault? If Chief O'Brien wasn't able to settle that question until *after* returning the vault from the DMZ, then the Maquis might succeed in taking the Orb just about anywhere. Its trail would be as cold as a Pagu winter by then. In that event, recovering the Orb would be all but impossible.

She glanced upward again. The Ferengi youth was still standing on the restaurant's upper level. He was gripping the railing so hard with his long, graceful fingers that his knuckles were as white as a sinoraptor's fangs. The boy's gaze seemed to be lingering on the entryway to the kitchen, through which Rom and Quark had just disappeared. His dartlike eyes contained a fire that she would have recognized in any species: frustrated ambition.

Winn decided to find out as much about the boy as she could. Turning her gaze back to O'Brien, she said, "Please continue assembling your team, Chief."

O'Brien nodded. "We can be ready to leave within a few hours."

"Good. I have some business to tend to in the meantime."

Then she strode purposefully back out onto the Promenade. She still needed to contact Militia Command in order to obtain an escort vessel for the Orb-recovery mission, a call she intended to place from her quarters.

But on her way there, she made a brief stop at the station's security office.

★   ★   ★

Nog felt his lobes fairly vibrating with apprehension, though he couldn't exactly say he was afraid. The sensation wasn't as bad as the times Odo had picked him up and tossed him into a holding cell—his most recent experience of that occurred only a few days earlier, when his friend Jake Sisko had acted to settle their recent quarrel over a double date that had gone badly—but it was close. Sure, Kai Winn wasn't the constable; no armed deputies flanked her, nor did she have the authority to summarily lock him up, so far as Nog could tell. And she didn't have Odo's creepy, unfinished facial features. But Nog was well aware of her significance to Bajor's religious community, and felt himself responding to her air of quiet authority in spite of himself.

What would Marauder Mo do? Nog asked himself. He decided that the beloved action-figure/holovid personality would meet Winn's authority with bluster.

"All right, Kai Winn," he said, folding his arms across his chest with practiced insouciance. "Now will you please explain exactly why you've brought me here?"

Winn gestured broadly about her, as though inviting him to study the Bajoran shrine's simple, unadorned walls. "I asked you to come here partly to familiarize you with something I'm seeking. And partly so we can speak in private about its extreme importance to the people of Bajor."

Nog looked about the shrine, which was empty except for the two of them. A pair of prylars had been tending to the tapestries in the outer vestibule when they arrived, but had obediently vanished when the kai had asked them to step outside for a few minutes.

"Well, we seem to have a great windfall of privacy," Nog said. "Let's get on with this before my uncle sends out a search party."

Winn smiled blandly, not rising to Nog's insolent tone. Moving quietly, she led the way into a smaller interior chamber, which was lit only by candles set into sconces. In the center of the room, atop a raised dais, sat a large, dark, roughly cubical box.

"I know all about your many . . . skills," she said, her eyes seeming to bore into him.

"Really?" Nog said, wondering how that could be. After all, he wasn't exactly a public figure.

Her expression turned grave. "Yes. Your Constable Odo has told me a great deal about you. It seems you've misspent a great deal of your childhood learning to crack safes, pick locks, and so forth."

Now his lobes picked up the sound of opportunity. *She needs me,* he thought. *Looks like it's a seller's market for the services of a good lockpick.* And Nog knew that he was good.

But being scrutinized by an authority figure—even one whose authority largely didn't affect him—also made him nervous. He maintained his neutral negotiator's grin as best he could anyway. "I suppose I'm not the sort of person you'd normally turn to for help."

"Be that as it may, your abilities will be invaluable in recovering one of Bajor's missing Orbs from the vault that holds it."

"Let me guess. It's in a Ferengi-constructed blindvault."

Her eyebrows rose. "You're familiar with them?"

"Of course," Nog said, swelling with pride. "The lock mechanism is a kind of tonal puzzle. Sort of a subsonic word-association game where you key in specific notes in response to random prompts from the vault's computer."

She stroked her chin thoughtfully. "That doesn't sound too difficult."

Nog felt an incipient surge of panic; perhaps he had told her too much. Recovering quickly, he pointed to his right ear. "Without the correct combination—or lobes like these—you won't have a prayer of getting a blindvault open anytime soon."

"It is a mistake to underestimate the power of prayer, my young friend."

"I trust latinum more."

Ignoring his comment, Winn said, "The mission will last about four days. You would accompany me aboard a Bajoran Militia vessel, which will be working in tandem with a Starfleet vessel in recovering a missing Orb."

Nog didn't like the sound of that. "Why do you need to bring me along? Why not just bring the vault back to the station and have me open it here?"

"Because if others have succeeded in opening the vault first, recovering the Orb may well prove impossible. I can't risk that. Don't worry, child. You'll be well protected."

Nog's fear persisted. "If you need to bring a lot of protection along, then this must be a pretty dangerous mission."

Her bland smile abruptly turned as hard as duranium. The lines on her face, perhaps etched there during the brutal years of the Cardassian Occupation, deepened. "We live in a dangerous universe, child," she said.

"Maybe. But some parts of it are definitely more dangerous than others. And therefore more expensive."

She blinked in evident incomprehension. Pleased that he was holding his own with her, he pressed on. "I need latinum. Ten bars. Up front. I'll do the mission, but only if you show me the goods first."

She regarded him in silence for a long moment. He expected her to become angry with him. Therefore the sad expression that crossed her broad face took him by surprise.

"I'll show you something better," she said finally. "The Orb of Prophecy and Change." Then she turned toward the box at the room's center and opened it.

He looked inside, skeptical.

Suddenly, a light more brilliant than anything Nog had ever seen before streamed forth, washing over him, enveloping and embracing him. Ageless voices whispered into his lobes, their enticing words just beyond his comprehension. He heard a ringing, not-unpleasant musical overtone underlying it all, which brought to mind the stories he'd been told as a child about the highly paid celestial choirs that worked the Great Lounge of the Divine Treasury. It spoke to him of the infinite, and of answers to questions he lacked the understanding even to ask. And for an instant, he glimpsed something heretical, something he'd dared to consider only occasionally, such as during the times when he watched, disappointed, as his father knuckled under to Uncle Quark's arbitrary will.

It was the notion that there might be something out there even more precious than latinum.

Then, as suddenly as the nimbus of light and thought had surrounded him, it was gone. The box was closed, inert.

Kai Winn was studying him, a look of expectation on her face.

Nog wasn't at all certain how much time had passed. It might have been minutes, or merely seconds, the way time often passed in his latinum-lined dreams.

All he knew was that now he felt more willing than before to listen to what Winn had to say. And that there was a lot he needed to learn about the universe around him, dangerous or not.

He wondered if this was the same feeling his uncle had spent years systematically stamping out of his father.

"Will you do it?" Winn asked. "We can discuss the issue of remuneration later. At the moment, time is of the essence."

"Okay," he heard himself saying, realizing only belatedly that he had somehow dropped his insistence on up-front payment. He hoped he hadn't just disgraced every sacred, heroic, profit-driven principle that Marauder Mo stood for.

Almost in a daze, Nog walked across the Promenade back to the bar. Maybe Marauder Mo wouldn't have struck the deal he had just made with the kai. Ferenginar's favorite superhero certainly wouldn't have been afraid of the mission; it was an adventure, after all, and many were the protagonists of Ferengi holofiction who valued adventure nearly as highly as Acquisition Itself. But being asked to wait for payment until after the fact might have given even the most stalwart action hero pause.

Nog noted with some surprise that he wasn't afraid. A little apprehensive, maybe. But not afraid. Instead, he found himself eagerly anticipating the mission, which would commence with his meeting Kai Winn on the docking ring in a little less than four hours.

The trick, of course, would be getting through those few hours without letting anyone know what he was up to; the kai had made him promise to keep his involvement in the mission absolutely secret. Nog had agreed, aware of how bad she would look if word were to get around that she might be taking someone as young as he was into harm's way. Were that to happen, the kai would no doubt become very testy. And a testy kai could certainly contrive ways to make life very difficult not only for him, but also for his father and Uncle Quark so long as they remained aboard the station.

He wondered: Would the kai have retaliated had he flatly declined to go on the mission? He wasn't sure, but he decided it didn't matter. He *wanted* to go, if only to prove to himself that Uncle Quark couldn't do to him what he'd already done to his father.

Now, as he wended his way toward his uncle's business office, was the time Nog felt most in need of the unfailing courage of Marauder Mo. After all, he was about to disappear for four days, and he couldn't tell anyone why, not even his father. *But I've got to tell my uncle something.*

He entered the office without knocking and saw Quark sitting behind the desk, hunched over an untidy pile of financial padds. Nog saw that his uncle was auditing the secret books for accuracy, while vetting the public ones for plausibility. It was a good, solid practice for any Ferengi businessman.

"I need a few days off, Uncle," Nog said without preamble.

"No," said Quark without looking up. "Now get back to work—"

"—before I dock you," Nog finished, in unison with his uncle.

Nog remained standing beside the crowded desk, watching his uncle work. Quark looked up at him at last, obviously irritated.

"You're still here."

"Just for as long as this takes, Uncle. I *really* need some time off. Four days."

Quark set down the padd he was working on, his eyes narrowing with suspicion. "Why?"

Nog feared he'd already said too much. Quark would surely figure out what he was up to. After all, hadn't he also heard O'Brien's pitch to his father? He had to know that the foray into the DMZ exactly coincided with his vacation request.

But if Quark had done the math, he gave no outward indication of it. He simply returned his attention to the teetering stacks of padds on his desk. "I'm afraid I can't spare you, Nog. You know how shorthanded I am around here."

The reason for Quark's obtuseness suddenly struck Nog like a body blow. *He doesn't take me seriously enough to think Winn would want to take me along to the DMZ.* He only barely overcame a powerful temptation to tell his uncle the truth.

Instead, he said, "I'm *taking* the time off, Uncle. With or without your approval." He turned his back on Quark and made for the door.

Quark pushed the padds to one side with a loud clatter and stood. "Nog, if you leave before your shift is over, you can forget about ever drawing a paycheck from me again."

Nog hesitated in the doorway. The impulse to stay, to remain in the bar doing his uncle's bidding, had evidently become an entrenched habit. How many times had his father caved in to Quark following confrontations like this one? He pictured himself twenty years older, still working in the bar alongside his father and a spiritually broken—and financially insignificant—cadre of Ferengi waiters and Bajoran dabo girls. The horror of the image rivaled his father's tales of the Vault of Eternal Destitution, the impoverished netherworld that awaited the souls of insufficiently profitable Ferengi in the next life.

"Good-bye, Uncle," he said, then continued out the door, steeling himself so as not to react to the shouted invectives that followed him halfway back out onto the Promenade.

Nog found the Bajoran Militia ship *Akorem Laan* surprisingly comfortable and roomy. But then, never having been aboard a Bajoran Militia ship, he'd had no idea what to expect.

Napping in the luxurious cabin where Winn had left him, Nog reflected on just how smoothly things had gone during the first two days since the departure from DS9. *Almost too smoothly.*

An unfamiliar and incredibly loud sound shrilled through the room, startling him so thoroughly that he nearly fell off the bed. He jumped up and ran awkwardly to the companel mounted on the bulkhead.

"Um, bridge?" Nog said, shouting above the alarm. "What's going on up there?"

"Who's this?" responded a stern male voice.

Nog tried to swallow, but found that his mouth was too dry. His ears were beginning to throb with pain because of the blare of the Klaxon. "I'm Kai Winn's, um, mission specialist."

"We're in a state of red alert. Please remain in your quarters, young man. And stay off the comm unit."

Nog nodded, then realized that the person on the other end of the comm couldn't see him. "What's going on?"

"Just stay put and be quiet," said the comm voice. Then the channel was abruptly cut off.

Nog scowled at the silent companel. Hupyrian beetle-wings of fear brushed his spine. *What would Marauder Mo do?* he thought, trying to calm himself.

He went to the door and exited into the corridor, then carefully followed the signs on the bulkheads until he found a turbolift.

The male Bajoran officer who greeted Nog on the bridge of the *Akorem Laan* might or might not have been the same individual who had told him to remain in his quarters. In Nog's experience, Bajorans were usually as hard to tell apart as hew-mons.

"This is a restricted area," said the officer. Another pair of brown-uniformed Bajorans, a male and a female, approached him, their intentions as clear as if they were Nausicaan bouncers.

"I just wanted to find out what was going on," Nog said, splaying his hands imploringly.

"That won't be necessary," said another voice as the pair put their hands on his shoulders and began steering him back into the turbolift.

They stopped. "Yes Eminence," they said in unison, then released their grip on Nog's quaking shoulders.

Kai Winn emerged from behind a bank of arcane-looking equipment and approached Nog and the officers who still flanked him. "It's all right. Why have you come to the bridge, child?"

"I heard the alarms," Nog said. In fact, his lobes were still ringing, even though the Klaxon had been turned off minutes earlier. "I just wanted to know what was going on."

Winn nodded, then turned toward the stern-looking, blunt-faced Bajoran male who stood in the center of the room. The large viewer beyond him at the front of the room displayed an image of a Federation runabout whose port side looked pitted and scorched. "With your permission, Colonel Lenaris?"

"By all means, Eminence," he said deferentially. Nog gathered that this colonel was nominally in command of the ship. But Winn was clearly the one who wielded the real authority here.

Winn returned her gaze to Nog. "We seem to have reached a portion of the DMZ frequented by the Maquis. The Starfleet runabout aiding in our search has been damaged by one of their mines."

Mines, Nog thought, his fear rising, running, and getting out ahead of him. *If the runabout can smack into a mine, then so can this ship.*

"How . . . How bad is the damage?" Nog asked, his heart racing.

The colonel spoke up. "The crew of the *Orinoco* was fortunate. Their navigational deflector apparently set off the mine, but the runabout managed to avoid the brunt of the blast. Chief O'Brien and his team are busy repairing the damage now, with some assistance from our people. We're at full stop for the moment."

Nog considered with mounting horror just how close O'Brien and the other Starfleet people had come to being incinerated by a terrorist booby trap.

"After we get under way again," he asked the colonel, "how do we know we won't run into more of these mines?"

Lenaris smiled beneficently. "We've got a pretty good idea of the mines' sensor profiles now, thanks to the incident with the *Orinoco.*"

"Don't fear, child," said the kai.

Fear is one of the things we Ferengi do best, Nog thought as he nodded a mute acknowledgment. He wondered how O'Brien and the others on the runabout dealt with that fear.

Then, perhaps as a way of managing his own trepidation, he became truly curious about that. How could *anyone* keep his head when faced with such a crippling emotion?

"Could I listen in on their comm traffic?" Nog asked Winn, who batted the request to the colonel with an interrogative glance.

"I don't see why not," said Lenaris. "So long as you don't tie up the channel with any chatter of your own."

The colonel ushered him toward a console in an out-of-the-way corner, where a female Bajoran officer who couldn't have been much older than he was adjusted an earpiece to "passive" mode, then handed the unit to him. It hadn't been built with the Ferengi body plan in mind, so Nog had to hold the earpiece in place with one hand as he took an unoccupied seat nearby. Then he did something else that many Ferengi did extraordinarily well.

He *listened*.

Monitoring the Starfleet crew's secure-channel conversations with each other and with the Bajoran crew, Nog was impressed at how efficiently—and apparently fearlessly—O'Brien, Muniz, Adabwe, and Wright worked to transform a near-catastrophe into a minor inconvenience. His Uncle Quark's management style notwithstanding, Nog concluded that constant yelling might *not* be necessary to get satisfactory results out of one's subordinates after all. The *Orinoco* and its Bajoran escort were both under way again within the hour.

From the confidence Nog heard in the Starfleet team members' voices, he might have concluded that the mine incident had never even happened. He was beginning to think that O'Brien and his staff were either the bravest people in the galaxy, or the most foolish. Or maybe they possessed acting abilities capable of fooling even the most sensitive, empathetic of Ferengi lobes.

Whatever the reason, these people seemed to fear nothing, while Nog and his father couldn't even stand up to Quark. *What am I doing hanging around with people who have this kind of courage?*

Somehow, the Starfleet team had made an acquisition that Nog had never seriously considered making. And he found that it both shamed and inspired him.

"The runabout's sensor link verifies that we're approaching the end of the warp trail," said the young female Bajoran. Nog could see that her words were intended for Colonel Lenaris and Kai Winn, both of whom were still on the bridge. "The coordinates correspond with this system's one marginally habitable planet."

"That has to be where the Maquis took the Orb," Winn said, apparently speaking to no one in particular. A mottled blue crescent was steadily growing on the forward viewer.

Lenaris nodded as he scrutinized one of the many nearby tactical displays. "It would seem so, judging from the sensor data Legate Turrel supplied us. This has to be the location of the base from which the thieves are currently operating."

The colonel gestured to another junior officer. "Open a channel to the *Orinoco.*"

"O'Brien here, Colonel," came the chief's voice a moment later.

"We're ready to make our approach. Is your recovery team prepared?"

"Just say the word."

No fear, Nog thought, lying to himself. He felt as though he was about to hyperventilate. *No fear.*

"All right," Lenaris said. "Let's—"

O'Brien's raised voice cut the colonel off. *"There's a ship approaching us from the planet. From the profile, I'd say it's a small Maquis raider."*

"Confirmed," said an intent young Bajoran man who was seated at a console to the colonel's right.

"We see him," Lenaris told O'Brien. He began barking orders to his crew. "Red alert. Raise shields. Charge weapons."

The klaxons shrilled again. Nog winced as his head rang like a bell.

The battle was fast, savage, and memorable only for its brevity. But the bridge had shaken so much that Nog worried he might develop kidney trouble.

Then something happened that seemed to surprise everyone on board: After exchanging multiple barrages with both the runabout and the *Akorem Laan,* the Maquis raider simply broke off its attack and flew off. *Away* from the planet where the Maquis base was supposedly located.

"Pursue them," Winn said to Lenaris. "We have to find out what they know."

Lenaris gently shook his head. "I'd advise against that, Eminence. This could be a ploy intended to leave the *Orinoco* vulnerable to a sneak attack."

Winn looked angry at being questioned on the bridge. But she also seemed to know the limits of her expertise. *Thank the Blessed Exchequer that somebody does,* Nog thought, wondering not for the first time just how he allowed himself to be dragged into the middle of a combat zone.

Apparently satisfied that he was acting with the kai's blessing, Lenaris resumed giving the bridge crew their orders. "Approach the planet. Cover the runabout's landing from a standard orbit."

Nog knew that O'Brien and his recovery team had no choice other than actually landing; being impervious to transporter beams, the blindvault itself couldn't simply be beamed up from the Maquis base. Once again, Nog marveled at the courage of O'Brien and the others. After all, these were engineers, not marines.

Even Marauder Mo might think twice about doing something like this,

Nog thought as he exchanged a glance with Winn. *Unless he'd been paid up front, that is.*

Nog was glad he hadn't been forced to accompany Chief O'Brien's team down to the surface. But not for the reasons he'd expected.

"*They're dead,*" O'Brien reported gravely, immediately after his team had crossed the curiously quiet Maquis perimeter. "*All of them.*"

Winn looked stricken. "You're saying the Maquis fighters we've been tracking are all dead?"

"*Yes, ma'am. Almost all of them are—were—humans. But we're finding some Bajorans among the bodies as well.*"

Nog watched the entire Bajoran crew as they bowed their heads mournfully. He felt unutterably sad. No amount of latinum could make up for the lives that had been lost.

"How did they die, Chief?" Lenaris asked, his voice somber.

"*A firefight, apparently. A pretty vicious one, from the look of things. We're continuing our tricorder sweeps. O'Brien out.*"

The Bajoran bridge was silent as a tomb for the remainder of the recovery team's search of the Maquis compound. Finally, uncounted minutes later, O'Brien's voice returned, sounding more upbeat this time. "*We've isolated the footprint of the blindvault. It's showing up as a one-cubic-meter blank spot on our scans.*"

"That's wonderful news, Chief," said Winn, brightening.

"How long do you expect the recovery op to take?" Lenaris asked.

"*It shouldn't take us half an hour to get it aboard the* Orinoco, *Colonel. Is your mission specialist ready to assist us in getting the thing open?*"

Lenaris looked in Nog's direction. Nog merely swallowed the lump in his throat and nodded.

It's showtime.

The chief was wrong, Nog realized as he and Winn materialized aboard the *Orinoco.* It had taken the recovery team only twenty-seven minutes to carry the blindvault that held the Orb of Contemplation back to the small ship and then reach orbit.

Nog stepped down from the small, two-person transporter stage located behind the runabout's cockpit, followed a moment later by Winn.

The first thing Nog noticed was the slick-looking black cube, just aft of the transporter, still sitting on the antigrav sled the recovery team had used to bring it aboard the runabout. Each of the cube's sides measured just over a square meter. The next thing Nog noticed was the trio of Starfleet-garbed people who stood about the sled, touching the object's seamless surface in search of a way in.

That's why I'm here, Nog reminded himself. *Because nobody here except me has a chance of getting a blindvault open quickly enough to satisfy Kai Winn.*

The sound of Colonel Lenaris's voice drew Nog's eyes toward the extreme forward part of the cabin, where the gray-blue planet below was visible through a large, front-facing window.

"We're ready to break orbit and withdraw from the DMZ, Orinoco."

Chief O'Brien, seated in the cockpit with his back to Nog, answered crisply. "We're ready as well."

Moments later, the planet dropped away. The runabout was heading back toward Deep Space 9, shadowed by its better-armed Bajoran escort. The worst part of the mission was over, Nog noted with no small amount of relief. Within two days, he'd be back home, trying to explain his mysterious absence to his uncle and his father.

But that was a reality best dealt with after he'd finished the task he'd come here to perform.

Nog approached the blindvault, and O'Brien's team members made room for him. He ran his long fingers across its smooth, light-devouring surface.

O'Brien chose that moment to enter the aft section and address the members of his team. "All right, now let's have a good close look at this blind—"

The chief stopped in mid-word, his mouth forming a silent ellipse of incredulity as his eyes fell upon Nog.

"Um, mission specialist Nog, Chief. Sir. Reporting for duty." Nog assayed a sloppy, left-handed salute.

O'Brien ignored him, glaring instead at the kai, who was now standing beside Nog. The runabout was beginning to feel distinctly crowded.

"What the hell is going on here?" the chief demanded. "What exactly is a teenage kid doing tagging along with you on a dangerous mission in the DMZ?"

Winn seemed as imperturbable as one of the stone gargoyles that guarded the Tower of Commerce back on Ferenginar. "You said you thought a Ferengi would be useful on this mission, Chief, did you not?"

"Of *course* I did. I tried to persuade Rom to come with us, remember? You were there."

"Indeed I was, Chief. Rom declined, so I found another Ferengi who possesses similar aptitudes. I would think, under the circumstances, that you'd be grateful for the help."

"It's your Orb," O'Brien snapped. "And your conscience. *Eminence.*"

Winn's rejoinder was interrupted by the wailing and flashing of a cockpit alarm. O'Brien and a dark-haired hew-mon engineer named Muniz—Nog recognized him from back on the station—immediately returned to their stations. The other two crew members—a hew-mon male and female who, respectively, had to be Wright and Adabwe—began running scans from other consoles adjacent to the main cockpit. The blindvault and the Orb inside it were now all but forgotten.

"Sensor contact with a ship," Muniz said. "No, make that *two* ships."

O'Brien nodded. "I see them, Enrique. O'Brien to Lenaris. Are you picking up what we're picking up?"

"They've appeared on our sensors, too, Chief. One is the same Maquis

ship that attacked us earlier. It's been stopped and boarded by a Galor-class *Cardassian warship."*

"I want to approach and hail them, Colonel. I think we ought to find out what they're up to," O'Brien said.

"Agreed."

A few minutes later, Nog watched O'Brien drop the runabout out of warp and hail the Cardassian ship, which was already visible through the front window as a distant point of light. A glance at Adabwe's tactical readout told Nog that he was actually looking at two vessels—one Cardassian and one Maquis—flying in extremely close proximity to each other.

O'Brien repeated his hail. "Cardassian vessel, this is Chief Miles Edward O'Brien of the Starfleet runabout *Orinoco.* Please respond."

"Strange," Wright muttered, shaking his head at something on his console that Nog couldn't see. "You'd think the Maquis ship would show human life-signs. But all I'm detecting on either ship is Cardassians."

Adabwe's head moved up and down. "I get the same readings. The *Akorem Laan's* science officer confirms our scans as well."

The chief raised an eyebrow at that, but said nothing. Instead, he repeated his hail yet again. He did so twice again before a brusque male voice responded on an audio channel. "Orinoco, *this is the Cardassian warship* Tavracet. *Please state your business here."*

"We've just concluded a . . . salvage operation," O'Brien said in the ingratiatingly familiar voice Nog sometimes heard him use at the bar when in the company of Dr. Bashir, a tankard of beer, and a handful of metal-tipped projectiles. "I was wondering if you required our assistance before we returned to Federation space."

A long beat elapsed before the Cardassian responded. *"Thank you for your kind offer, Chief. However, I believe we already have the matter well in hand. The terrorists have been apprehended.* Tavracet *out."*

"My. That wasn't very neighborly," Adabwe said, still studying her sensor console.

Wright shrugged. "Cardassians aren't the cuddliest people in the quadrant. Even when they're *not* shooting at you."

Nog looked toward Winn, who stood behind the cockpit. Her eyes were focused on the forward window.

"The people on that Maquis ship might have been the ones who stole the Orb from Turrel in the first place," she said.

"Maybe," O'Brien said, turning his seat toward her. "Or the dead Maquis we found on the planet might be the guilty parties. We may never know."

Winn nodded. "I suppose the important thing is that we've recovered the Orb."

"I'm forced to agree," said O'Brien, who then opened a channel to Colonel Lenaris back on the Bajoran ship. After a quick and parsimonious exchange, the chief fed a series of commands into his flight console.

The distantly visible *Tavracet* and its Maquis companion fell away as the runabout went back to warp and resumed its heading for DS9.

Nog was startled by a hand on his shoulder, but calmed when he realized it was Winn. Smiling, she gestured toward the black cube behind the transporter. "Mr. Nog, if you'd be so kind?"

Nog moved deliberately toward the antigrav sled. His fingers felt slippery with sweat as he slowly felt along the blindvault's edges. He closed his eyes to shut out the expectant gazes of Winn and Chief O'Brien's team. He had to marshal all of his concentration to tune out the myriad tiny sounds they made even as they tried to be still. Angrily shushing the fidgety Muniz had done absolutely no good at all.

There. A gentle ringing overtone, perceptible only to Ferengi auditory nerves, sounded as his fingers came into feather-light contact with the first hasp. The second, third, and fourth, each one making its signature chime, followed in sequence. He opened his eyes to see a half-meter-wide flatscreen interface extrude itself onto the blindvault's nearest face, as though conjured by magic.

An icon appeared, rendered in the angular, reassuringly familiar script of written Ferengi. He touched it, and a tone sounded. He calculated a tone an octave higher, then bisected it to generate a pitch a tritone above the original sound.

The process repeated and gradually accelerated, as he heard the pitches and anticipated the response each time. Sweat ran down his bulbous forehead and into his eyes. He ignored it and soldiered on. Though he nearly lost the sequence when someone's badly timed decision to sit caused a cacophonous squeak, he continued listening to the ever-changing tones and keying in the responses that would have made no sense to anyone with smaller, less sensitive lobes.

Throughout the procedure, which seemed to go on for an hour but probably actually occupied a span of perhaps four or maybe five minutes, a single thought recurred continuously within Nog's head, like a persistent *leitmotif* that got stuck in the brain during a concert of Sinnravian *drad* music: *This is way, way too easy.*

Then, just when Nog began to worry that he might have made a critical misstep capable of making the blindvault's computer shut down permanently, the interface panel shimmered and began to vanish, along with the front and top faces of the black cube.

He turned toward Winn, flashing her a triumphant grin.

Then he saw that her expression was anything but happy.

A moment later, he saw a similar, surprised look on the faces of O'Brien, Adabwe, Wright, and Muniz. Only then did he look back into the open blindvault.

It was empty.

What the hell would Marauder Mo do now?

"No," Winn whispered. "By the Prophets, it can't be." Having lived through the horrors of the Occupation, she had known despair on many occasions. But never quite like this. Victory had never been snatched from her grasp quite so ignominiously before.

Nog stood before the empty vault, his mouth silently opening and closing. "Do not blame yourself, child," she told him. "You did everything I asked of you."

Winn became conscious of O'Brien standing beside her. "Obviously somebody got to the vault before we did. And it's the same somebody who killed all those Maquis, unless I miss my guess."

Winn nodded, numb. It didn't matter. The Orb was gone. Just like all the other Orbs that the damned Cardassians had expropriated and then lost.

Nog found his voice at last. "This has got to have something to do with that Cardassian ship."

"Why do you say that?" O'Brien asked.

"Because nobody mentioned finding any sign of Ferengi either down on the planet or aboard the Cardassian ship. And without a Ferengi, whoever beat us to the vault probably couldn't have gotten it open as quickly as they did."

O'Brien nodded, apparently understanding. "Unless they already had the entry code. And nobody had *that* except for Legate Turrel and maybe a very small handful of other Cardassian officers."

Nog's eyes widened as he carried this logic another step further. "That's why I think the Orb might be aboard the Cardassian vessel. Chief, were there any strange energy signatures on that ship?"

"I don't think so. At least, none that any of us recognized."

Winn watched as Adabwe and Muniz called up the records of the scans the *Orinoco* had made of the *Tavracet* and the Maquis ship it had impounded. O'Brien, Wright, and Nog were also watching intently as arcane charts, graphs, and columns of numeric data scrolled across the readouts.

Winn realized she couldn't make heads or tails of any of it.

"There's an unusual-looking energy spike here," Adabwe said, pointing to a sharply rising curve on a graph she'd frozen in place on one of the monitors. "But it could mean anything from a leaky coolant manifold to an inefficient warp core."

"Doesn't exactly scream, 'I'm the missing Orb, come look for me here,' does it?" Muniz said.

Nog spoke up. "No. But it could."

"Excuse me?" Muniz said.

Nog pointed at the cryptic squiggles on the console before them. "Can you run this through the computer or something and convert it into sound?"

Adabwe scowled thoughtfully. "That's a lot of cycles per second. It wouldn't be in the audible range."

Grinning, Nog tapped his lobe. "Let's give it a try anyway."

A moment later, Adabwe keyed in the last of a short sequence of commands. "There it is."

"I don't hear anything," O'Brien said.

"Me, neither," said Muniz.

"Shhhh," Nog said, closing his eyes. A moment later he opened them and a look of recognition passed across his pinched face. "I've heard that sound before."

"Where?" Winn asked.

"In the Bajoran shrine back on the station. Two days ago."

Winn recalled that Nog had been standing with her before the Orb of Prophecy and Change that day.

Hope reignited within Winn's soul. She turned to O'Brien. "Chief, we must double back and find the *Tavracet* immediately."

Another sensor alarm sounded, prompting O'Brien to return to the cockpit to check it. Winn followed him forward. "Looks like we won't have to.

"The *Tavracet* seems to be following *us.*"

Winn immediately beamed back to the *Akorem Laan,* and headed straight for her private cabin there. Activating her personal sub-space transceiver, she instructed the device's control computer to contact Legate Turrel on his secure diplomatic channel.

Whatever deception you're attempting, Turrel, I'm going to put a stop to it, here and now.

Turrel's face appeared on her desktop viewer moments later, and Winn thought she saw a look of surprise flash across the legate's hard, almost reptilian face. The picture on the screen was so sharp he might have been standing right beside her.

"Kai Winn. To what do I owe the unexpected pleasure of this call?"

Winn wished to waste no time on diplomatic pleasantries. Instead, she sought to rattle him with a direct assault. "How long have you been aboard the *Tavracet,* following us?"

He blinked several times, signaling to Winn that she had scored a direct hit. Then he recovered his composure and smiled his negotiator's smile. *"Very good, Eminence. What gave me away?"*

"For one thing, the *Tavracet* appears to be carrying the Orb of Contemplation. I didn't think you'd want to stray very far from it, after all the trouble you evidently took to persuade the Central Command to release it to your custody. And especially after the Maquis allegedly stole it."

Turrel frowned. *"You doubt that the Maquis were responsible for the theft of the Orb?"*

"Let's just say that I now find it hard to believe that they acted alone."

"Why do you say that?"

"The blindvault you used to carry the Orb is transporter-proof. That means the thieves would have had to *board* the vessel you took to Deep Space 9 in order to seize the vault. So if Maquis fighters had been the only attackers, they would have done far more than simply steal from you—they would have slaughtered you and every other Cardassian on board. But there *were* no Maquis on the Maquis ship you've just impounded."

"Interesting speculation."

"Not speculation. We've already opened the blindvault you left behind in the Maquis hideout. The Orb was missing."

The look of discomfiture on Turrel's face spoke volumes. He hadn't been expecting this. Winn thought he had the look of a man whose entire world was now in danger of spiraling out of control.

She pressed on. "Turrel, it's very unlikely that the Maquis could have removed the Orb from the blindvault. But *you* could have done it. Or perhaps the deed was carried out by some of your subordinates. Perhaps by officers who weren't happy with your efforts to repatriate the Orb."

"Ordering the Orb returned was an unprecedented act of Cardassian largesse," Turrel said, somehow managing to sound both cautious and self-aggrandizing at the same time. *"Bold strokes such as these can sometimes inspire fear."*

"Change is often frightening," Winn said, nodding. Having lived under the brutal heel of Cardassian oppressors for decades, she felt she knew what she was talking about. "But perhaps now is the time to challenge that fear. After all, we've both worked very hard on our recent diplomatic agreement. I'm certain that neither of us wishes to place in jeopardy what we've accomplished together thus far."

Turrel's stolid visage changed subtly, moving by degrees from calculating to contemplative. At length, he said, *"All right. Perhaps the whole truth will best serve that end."*

"I am listening, Legate."

"I'm sure you are aware that Maquis raids have been a persistent problem for the Cardassian Union over the past year, ever since a treaty redrew our boundaries with the Federation."

"Leaving a number of former Federation worlds and their populations technically in Cardassian territory."

"Not technically, *Eminence. Those worlds are* ours *now, and their Federation populations have been relocated. Save, of course, for the Maquis—those who opted to use terror tactics in an effort to retain the territory the Federation legally ceded to us."*

Of course, Winn was bitterly aware that one person's terrorist might be another's freedom fighter. But this was a subject she didn't wish to debate at the moment. "I am familiar with the origins of the Maquis," she said. "Please go on."

"Very well. I needed some help in drawing a particularly troublesome Maquis cell out into the open. I also discovered, as you suggested, evidence that certain individuals in my officer corps were not only actively working against our efforts to repatriate the Orb of Contemplation, but had also covertly thrown in with the Maquis to that end."

Winn nodded, beginning to see clearly the picture that Turrel was painting for her. "You needed to draw your own traitors into the open as well."

"Exactly so. And the Orb served as an irresistible enticement for both. The turncoats, you see, wanted to keep the Orb for themselves, and they contrived to use the Maquis to acquire the vault that carried it. Blaming the Maquis seemed an elegant method for covering up their conspiracy. By discreetly monitoring the progress of your search of the Demilitarized Zone, I was able to apprehend the traitors immediately after they had wiped out the Maquis cell and relieved them of their prize. A prize that will soon be back on Cardassia Prime."

"So your offer to repatriate the Orb was merely a ploy. You planned to keep it all along, while making it appear that the Maquis made off with it." Winn suddenly feared that the treaty on which she and Vedek Bareil had labored for so long—the agreement that Bareil had died pursuing—was unraveling right before her eyes.

Then another infuriating realization came to Winn: Had Turrel's plan worked only a little better, she never would have known that he had manipulated her, the Bajoran Militia, and Starfleet into unwittingly abetting the wanton slaughter of people whose only real crime was standing up against Cardassian tyranny.

And some of those people were Bajorans, she thought, her gorge rising.

"So we seem to have a truly thorny problem now, Kai Winn," the legate said. *"It would be terribly costly to me, and to my government, if the accusations you've just made were to become generally known. Obviously, I can't permit that to happen."*

By the Prophets, Winn thought, horrified. *He means to destroy this ship and the runabout, merely to cover up his scheme. No doubt he'll blame the Maquis for that as well. I was a fool to think I could ever negotiate in good faith with this man.*

Her mind raced. There had to be an alternative to a pitched battle, and the abandonment of the treaty that Bareil had given his life to negotiate. If she were to call the bridge now, what were the odds that even Lenaris could act in time to save the ship? Absurdly, she found herself thinking of the games of chance that had seemed so popular in the drinking establishment run by Nog's unpleasant uncle.

She smiled very slightly when an answer came to her.

"The Federation will be extremely interested to learn that the Cardassian government has conspired to entrap and murder its citizens," she said. "Even if they are Maquis outlaws."

"I can jam your transmissions," Turrel pointed out.

Winn shrugged. "That will only ensure that the Federation learns the truth about what you've done to the Maquis. If anything should happen to me on this mission, Legate Turrel, I assure you that the Vedek Assembly will give the Federation all of my files on that very subject."

Of course, Winn was well aware that she had made no such prior arrangements with anyone, either in the Vedek Assembly or anywhere else.

But *Turrel* couldn't possibly have known that.

After a moment's hesitation, Turrel said, *"You're bluffing."*

Winn leaned fractionally toward the visual pickup, her eyes widening. "If you agree to return the Orb now, you won't have to discover the hard way whether or not that's so. And we can both go on pretending, for the sake of both our worlds, that the treaty we just signed still *means* something."

Lapsing into silence again, Turrel seemed to mull her proposal over very seriously. After all, he had spent at least as much time negotiating the recent treaty as both she and Bareil had. Perhaps he, too, didn't want to see those efforts wasted.

"All right," he said at length. *"Perhaps the best solution to this problem is indeed to return the Orb to you as promised—and to rely on your discretion."* Then he smiled unctuously, as though returning the Orb had been his true intention all along.

"If nothing else, you may consider the Orb a token of my sincere thanks. After all, if your Bajoran Militia ship hadn't engaged the Maquis vessel the Cardassian traitors were using, they might have eluded me—and

escaped with the Orb. I applaud your wisdom for involving Starfleet and your own world's military in this situation. You have helped immensely in ridding me of two vexing problems."

Cardassia's political undesirables, she thought. *And the Maquis cell.*

A great bitterness rose within her as she considered just how thoroughly Turrel had manipulated her. Just as she had manipulated Bareil and so many others throughout her life.

Winn laughed then, but without humor. "Of course." She had few illusions. She knew all about the pragmatic, often bruising compromises necessitated by real-world politics, or *realpolitik,* as the Emissary sometimes termed it.

Just as she knew that neither she nor Turrel could ever afford to reveal the truth of what happened today to anyone besides each other; to do so would be far too politically embarrassing for either of them.

She had already forgotten how close Turrel had come to attacking the *Akorem Laan.* Swallowing her anger, Winn reminded herself that she was about to return to Bajor in triumph, carrying before her the long-lost Orb of Contemplation and enjoying the laurels of a grateful Bajor. *A victory has only to look like a victory to serve as such,* she thought. *And sometimes that can be enough.*

Winn smiled. "Please prepare to transfer the Orb to my ship, Legate Turrel. I will instruct Colonel Lenaris to expect the *Tavracet* to rendezvous with us."

Turrel scowled slightly just before his face vanished. Winn consoled herself with the idea that the Prophets had no doubt foreordained Turrel's messy involvement in the Orb's recovery, just as they had predetermined the unfortunate death of Bareil during the recent treaty negotiations—and those of the Bajorans whom Turrel had slaughtered in the Maquis base. She was grateful never to have known their faces.

Seeing Bareil's in her dreams every night was burden enough.

Although it had been slightly less than four days since he'd left the station, Nog thought everything sounded, felt, smelled, and looked different. The Promenade seemed a little livelier, more colorful. The crowd appeared more varied and interesting, even the hew-mons. Maybe *especially* the hew-mons.

As a crowd gathered on the lower level of the Promenade, growing hushed as everyone present awaited Kai Winn's announcement, Nog spied the tall, gangly form of his friend, Jake Sisko. He caught Jake's eye, and the pair moved to a spot from which they both could see the proceedings clearly.

"Where have you been for the past few days, Nog?"

Nog shrugged. "Out."

He barely paid any attention to the faith-and-homily-laden speech Winn made before she'd unveiled the Orb of Contemplation to the awestruck gathering. Cheers rang through the Promenade.

"That's really something," Jake said afterward, leaning across the railing on his elbows. "I wonder how she got her hands on it?"

Nog shrugged again as he watched a pair of prylars carefully guide the antigrav sled holding the Orb box toward the Bajoran shrine. "Who knows?"

"Aren't you even a little curious, Nog?" said Jake, a good-natured scowl on his face. "However it happened, I'll bet it'd make for a heck of a story."

"Maybe." Nog desperately wanted to tell his friend how he'd been an integral part of that story. But he'd promised the kai his silence, and despite what the Seventeenth Rule of Acquisition said, a contract was a contract—even with a non-Ferengi. Especially when the particular non-Ferengi in question, arguably the most powerful person on Bajor, had yet to pay him for his services.

Shame and fascination struggled within him as he realized that he didn't care about the money. At least, he didn't think he cared very much. For the first time in his brief life, he had things other than money to consider. *What would Marauder Mo think about that?*

Nog and Jake walked together along the Promenade, sharing a companionable silence. Just days earlier, the two of them had

agreed to try to be more sensitive to the vast cultural gulf that separated them. *Maybe Ferengi and hew-mons aren't so different after all.*

"*There* you are!" called a familiar voice, coming from directly
behind Nog. He turned quickly in the rapidly thinning crowd and
found himself facing both his uncle and his father. The latter's face
bore a look of worry mixed with relief. The former merely looked
annoyed, though not nearly as angry as Nog would have expected.
Has he figured out where I've been?

As his father embraced him, Nog realized belatedly that he and
Jake had walked right up to the front of Quark's bar.

"I'll catch up to you later, Nog," Jake said, then disappeared
around the curve of the Promenade.

After Rom released him, Nog noticed that Quark was standing
beside him, quickly tapping numbers into a padd. "About our last
conversation, Nog," Quark said, his beady eyes riveted to whatever
was displayed on the device.

"I think you said I should forget about ever drawing a paycheck
from you again, Uncle."

Quark finally lifted his eyes from the padd. "Maybe I was a little
hasty. Since I'm still shorthanded, I'll tell you what I'll do: You can
have your old job back. With a thirty percent pay reduction, of
course. To keep the rest of the staff in line. You understand."

Out of the corner of his eye, Nog saw Chief O'Brien approaching. He turned and caught the chief engineer's eye.

O'Brien paused beside him and spoke into his ear in a low
tone. "You've got some real talent, kid. It would be a damned
shame if you were to waste it."

With a parting wink, O'Brien resumed his course and disappeared into the milling crowd. Nog wondered just how much of
Uncle Quark's generous "offer" the chief had heard.

"Well? What's it going to be?" Quark demanded.

Indecision abruptly seized Nog. It had been easy to walk out on
Quark when he'd been at the start of a grand adventure. But that
lay behind him now. And it hadn't earned him so much as a slip of
latinum.

But then he considered what the chief had just said . . .

Nog looked to his father, whose gaze was imploring. It was obvious to Nog how Rom would have handled this situation. He'd simply go along, as he always had. No matter how badly his brother took advantage of him, per the Sixth Rule of Acquisition.

What would Marauder Mo do?

A confident smile spread slowly across Nog's face. "I think I liked your offer from four days ago better, Uncle," he said.

Then he turned and walked away. And started planning the future.

Broken Oaths

Keith R.A. DeCandido

Historian's note: This story is set shortly after the fourth-season episode "Our Man Bashir."

Keith R.A. DeCandido

"Broken Oaths" is the latest of Keith R.A. DeCandido's many forays into the world of *Star Trek* fiction, which has also included the *Star Trek: Deep Space Nine* novel *Demons of Air and Darkness* and its award-winning follow-up novella "Horn and Ivory" in *What Lay Beyond;* the duology *The Brave and the Bold,* which was the first single story to encompass all five *Star Trek* TV series; the novels *Diplomatic Implausibility* and *The Art of the Impossible;* the comic book miniseries *Perchance to Dream;* the forthcoming *I.K.S. Gorkon* series, the first set of books to focus exclusively on a Klingon ship and crew; several *Star Trek: S.C.E.* eBooks, monthly adventures of the Starfleet Corps of Engineers; and more. He has also written novels, short stories, and nonfiction books in the worlds of *Buffy the Vampire Slayer, Gene Roddenberry's Andromeda, Farscape, Doctor Who, Xena,* and Marvel Comics. The editor of the groundbreaking original science fiction anthology *Imaginings,* Keith's forthcoming work includes the original novel *Dragon Precinct,* editing the anthology *Star Trek: Tales of the Dominion War,* and at least one more foray into the worlds of *Deep Space Nine.* Learn too much about Keith at his official website at <DeCandido.net>.

O'Brien and Bashir's dart board remained unused.

Quark wasn't too bothered by this. The tables and bar stools were occupied by customers consuming their libation of choice. Many were absent-mindedly munching on sand peas, which made them finish their drinks faster, thus prompting them to ask for refills. The dabo tables were all filled to capacity. Off in the corner, young Jake Sisko was hustling a couple of Bolians at the dom-jot table. Upstairs, all the holosuites were booked until closing.

But the dart board just sat on the wall. Quark could afford that, of course. He didn't profit directly from the board's use, nor did its lack of use have a significant effect on his bottom line. He had installed the thing in the first place only because it was small and unobtrusive, and because two of his best customers requested it. As a bartender, Quark was especially mindful of the Fifty-Seventh Rule of Acquisition: "Good customers are as rare as latinum. Treasure them." If the two of them wanted to spend their time in Quark's throwing tiny spears at a series of concentric circles, who was Quark to deny them?

Ironically, those two customers were both present, sitting separately. Dr. Julian Bashir sat at the bar with the ever-delectable Lieutenant Commander Jadzia Dax, while Chief Miles O'Brien was at one of the tables with the less than delectable Lieutenant Commander Worf. In fact, Quark hadn't seen Bashir and O'Brien together at all since they returned from a mission to the Gamma Quadrant weeks earlier. *But hey,* he thought, *as long as they're coming in and drinking, I don't care who they sit with—or whether or not they throw pointy things at a wall.*

As he refilled Morn's ale, he heard Dax and the doctor's conversation.

"I notice you and the chief haven't gotten together much lately. No darts games, no racquetball, no holosuites."

"We just haven't," Bashir said.

As he put Morn's ale glass back on the bar in front of the Lurian, Quark frowned. Bashir didn't normally sound that crestfallen, especially since he got that "secret agent" program of his.

"Well, Quark did go to all the trouble of putting the board in. You should at least play a few games just to give him something to have for side bets."

As if those side bets brought in enough to be worth it. Quark had to admit, though, that those side bets *did* bring a profit, albeit a small one.

With a level of defensiveness Quark had never heard Bashir use with Dax, the doctor said, "I'm really *not* interested in lining Quark's pockets, Jadzia."

"Of course not, but still—"

"Look, I have to go."

Quark glanced over to see Bashir gulping down his tea and getting up from the bar. Dax, for her part, looked as crestfallen as Bashir had sounded moments earlier.

"All right. Don't forget, we need to go over those new radiation protocols tomorrow morning."

Bashir flashed that idiotic smile of his. *Finally, the old doctor.* "I'll be there. And—I'm sorry I snapped at you. I've just been a little tired lately. Good night, Jadzia."

"Good night."

Quark shook his head. Dax stared down at her *allira* punch, looking disappointed in herself. He walked over. "C'mon, Jadzia, what did you expect? Some people don't like having their personal lives interfered with."

Dax arched an eyebrow. "Eavesdropping, Quark?"

Holding up his hands defensively, Quark said, "Just trying to see to the needs of my customers."

"That would be 'yes,' then."

"Look, for whatever reason, Bashir and O'Brien aren't best friends anymore. It happens. It wasn't that long ago that they couldn't stand each other. If I've learned one thing as a bartender—"

"Quark," Dax said with a mild glower, "I've learned plenty of things about friendships over the *centuries* I've been alive, so I really don't need a lesson from you."

"Oh, I think you do. I see people come in and out of here all the time. One minute they're inseparable, betting together at dabo, experimenting with the same exotic Klingon beverages, sharing holosuite programs. The next they can't stand the sight of each other, come in separately, and sit with different people. It happens—especially with these humans."

Dax finished off her drink and gestured for another. "I guess what bothers me is that I don't know *what* happened. I mean, I know they were captured by some Jem'Hadar in the Gamma Quadrant, and then escaped. Julian even found a Jem'Hadar that wasn't dependent on ketracel-white. But *something* happened there. They don't play darts, they don't play racquetball—the chief's been working overtime, and Julian's been spending all his spare time in the holosuite with that secret agent program with *Garak* of all people."

Quark shrugged as he placed a fresh glass of punch in front of the science officer. O'Brien had also been booking extra holosuite time, mostly that kayaking program he'd brought over from his previous posting. So as far as he was concerned, the sundered friendship meant double the holosuite usage. Somehow, though, he doubted that Dax would appreciate a reminder of that.

He looked over at O'Brien, and noticed that both his synthale and the Klingon's prune juice were running low. "Excuse me," he said to Dax, who nodded absently, having gone back to staring at her drink. *No doubt plotting some way to trick Bashir into revealing why he doesn't like O'Brien anymore. Personally, I never understood those two in the first place.*

As he approached the table where the two men sat, he heard a surprising exchange:

"I have observed that you and Dr. Bashir have not engaged in your—'target practice' of late." To Quark's abject shock, the tiniest hint of the most infinitesimal glimmer of a smile approached the beginnings of existing on Worf's face. He knew that the Klingon and O'Brien had served on the same ship in the past—the *Endeavour* or the *Odyssey* or the *Voyager* or some other such ship, Quark could never keep track of them. Indeed, Worf usually only came to Quark's in O'Brien's company—which suited Quark fine. Worf was the most recent addition to the crew of Deep Space 9, and the Ferengi would have been just as happy for him to be the next subtraction. The amusement value of a Klingon who drank prune juice had worn off pretty quickly. If he didn't use the holosuites as often as he did, he'd be of no use to Quark whatsoever—as it was, the floors and walls always needed repairs after he was done with them.

In response to Worf's observation, O'Brien muttered, "We just haven't."

"It is a surprising development. I was under the impression that you enjoyed the contests."

"We did, I suppose," O'Brien said pensively. "But things change. Look, I really don't want to talk about this."

"I understand."

Okay, this is weird, Quark thought. Dax being a busybody, the Ferengi could understand; it was her nature. But Worf?

"Can I refill your drinks, gentlemen?"

Before either of them could reply, a voice sounded from the combadge affixed to the chief's uniform. *"Chief O'Brien—please report to the* Defiant.*"*

O'Brien gave Quark a half-smile. "I guess none for me, Quark." To Worf he said, "Excuse me, Commander."

"Of course."

O'Brien departed, leaving Quark standing staring at Worf's impassive face. "More prune juice?"

Worf's glower was far nastier than Dax's. "No." Then he, too, rose and moved toward the exit.

Dax, however, intercepted him on the way out. "Did you ask him?"

Aha—now it makes sense, Quark thought.

"Yes."

When no more information was forthcoming, Dax, who looked like she was ready to jump out of her spots, asked, "What did he say?"

Impatiently, Worf said, "He said he did not wish to speak of it."

"So then what did you say?"

Worf frowned. "I told him I would respect his wishes and not speak of it."

Dax smacked him gently on the arm. Quark suspected that she was one of the few people in the quadrant under the rank of captain who could get away with such an action. "What'd you say *that* for?"

"Because I saw no reason to pry into Chief O'Brien's personal life. And I *still* see no reason to."

"Well, I do. That friendship is good for both of them. Julian needs someone in his life like the chief—a stabilizing influence. And with Keiko and Molly spending most of their time on Bajor, the chief needs to have more friends around, not fewer."

"It is not our place to interfere."

"Like hell. Julian's my friend. O'Brien's your friend. You delivered his baby!"

Quark blinked in something like shock. The bartender had an active imagination, but even he could not wrap his mind around the idea of Worf's delivering a baby.

Dax continued. "We owe it to them to do whatever we can to bring them back together."

Deciding that this was the point where he needed to reiterate his view, Quark said, "You're wasting your time."

Worf turned angrily on the Ferengi. "This is *not* your concern."

"Hey, they're my customers. And so are you," he said to Dax, "and even you," he added with a quick nod to Worf. Turning back to the Trill, he said, "Look, *I* think this is a waste of time. The commander here thinks this is a waste of time. Now, if the two of *us* agree on something, don't you think it might have a bit of merit?"

Dax pursed her lips. "No. Excuse me."

Quark and Worf watched her go. Silence hung between them for a moment.

"So," Quark finally said, "you delivered Molly?" The Ferengi's sensitive ears heard the growl build in Worf's throat, probably before the Klingon was aware he'd done so. "Never mind—sure you don't want more prune juice?"

Worf then also left the bar.

"Or not."

Quark went back behind the bar, staring at the unused dart board. *Maybe I'll just take the thing down.*

"I'm not sure what you expect *me* to do, Old Man. I can't order them to be friends again."

Dax sat in Benjamin Sisko's office, watching the captain toss his baseball from hand to hand. She had been observing that particular set of gestures for years—it had gone from a method of burning off nervous energy to a habit that Sisko couldn't, and didn't care to, break.

"Well, why not?" At Sisko's glower, Dax smiled. "I know, I know, I'm just frustrated. Worf and I have been trying to get them to open up about what happened in the Gamma Quadrant, but—"

Sisko almost dropped the ball. "Worf? How'd you get *him* to help out?"

Her smile widened. "He owes me one."

"I don't want to know," Sisko said quickly. Dax was grateful. She had been able to play on Worf's gratitude for saving the Klingon's life during the search for the Sword of Kahless. However, the details of that search had of necessity been kept secret, even from Sisko.

"Anyhow, it's not doing any good. They won't talk about it." Dax got up and started pacing across Sisko's office. "And I can't get any clue from their log reports to give me an idea."

"You read the log reports?"

"Actually, I'd already read them—Julian's theories on why Goran'agar wasn't addicted to the white were fascinating reading—but this time I was looking at them to see what actually *happened* there. But the reports were—sparse."

"You think they held back facts in their report?"

Sisko's tone had hardened, the baseball now being clenched in his hand. He had temporarily stopped being her old friend Benjamin and gone back to being her commanding officer. Dax realized that she was now accusing two of her crewmates of falsifying a report. "No, nothing like that, just—" She sighed. "I don't know—the *context* is missing. Some people file reports that are dry recitations of facts." Chuckling, she said, "Remember the way you used to file every report to Curzon so spit-and-polish that he started asking you to provide a stimulant with the reports to keep from falling asleep?"

"I remember." Sisko's lips twitched in that almost-smile of his, and he started tossing the baseball again. "You told me that people would be reading these reports centuries from now, and you didn't want them to think that all Starfleet officers were automatons." In a passing impression of Curzon's imperious tones, Sisko added, " 'Pretend it's one of your father's recipes, young Sisko, and put some *spice* into it!' "

Laughing, Dax said, "Exactly. Well, Curzon would've loved Julian's reports. He's always inserting philosophical asides and odd theories."

"True."

"But not this one. They crash-landed on Bopak III, Goran'agar asked Julian to try to find out why the planet cured him of the white dependence, Julian theorized that it wasn't the planet, but that Goran'agar was born without the addiction, and then O'Brien engineered an escape."

Sisko let out a long breath. "I've read the reports, too, Old Man, and—style notwithstanding—I didn't see anything that's a cause for concern."

Dax shot him a look. "You didn't?"

"I've worked with both of them for over three years now, and I know that they would never leave something out of an official report without a damn good reason, and that they wouldn't do anything to harm Starfleet or this station."

"So you're saying you have no cause for *professional* concern."

Getting up and walking around to the other side of the desk to face Dax, Sisko said, "That's right. As for *personal* concerns—" he tossed the ball in the air toward Dax, who caught it unerringly "—that's outside my purview as their commanding officer."

Again, Dax sighed. Sisko's implication—that it was outside the science officer's purview as well—was, strictly speaking, true. And his comment about leaving something out of an official report hit closer to home than he even knew. *Or maybe he does know. Benjamin's gotten pretty good at keeping his cards close to the vest. Curzon taught him well.*

Holding up the ball for him to take back, she said, "Point taken, Captain. Thanks for letting me vent."

"My door is always open." Sisko grinned, took the baseball back, and walked back around to his desk chair. "And Dax? I'm not telling you *not* to pursue this, either."

Worf reveled in the feeling of the serpent worms wriggling down his gullet.

The transition to living and working on Deep Space 9 after almost eight years on the *Enterprise* was proving more difficult than Worf would have imagined. But those problems were mitigated by the presence of the Klingon restaurant. As much as the replicators on the *Enterprise* had been fine-tuned to provide decent enough Klingon fare, there was simply no substitute for live *gagh*.

When he was done with the meal, he flagged down Chef Kaga and ordered a *rokeg* blood pie for dessert, then took out a padd to read over the latest fuel consumption report from the *Defiant* while he waited.

"Commander, do you have a minute?"

Looking up, he saw Chief O'Brien. This surprised Worf, as O'Brien had—justifiably—been avoiding him for the past few days, probably by way of dissuading further questions about Bashir. If Worf were not so indebted to Dax for saving his and Kor's lives on the Hur'q planet in the Gamma Quadrant, he would not have engaged in such tasteless behavior in the first place. The status of the chief's friendship with the doctor was no more his concern than it was the Ferengi bartender's.

"Of course, Chief. Please, sit down."

O'Brien gingerly took the seat across from Worf. The chief's nose was wrinkled in the manner that many humans' did around Klingon food. Worf had never understood how a species with such inferior olfactory senses could be so averse to food that actually *had* a smell to it.

"I was wondering if I could ask a favor." At Worf's affirmative nod, O'Brien continued. "I've been thinking a lot about—about what happened. With Julian. In the Gamma Quadrant."

Worf blinked. He had not expected this. "How is it that I may be of service regarding that?"

"When we crash-landed on Bopak III, we were immediately surrounded by a platoon of Jem'Hadar. They kept us alive, and were referring to us as 'targets'—right up until Julian said he was a doctor. After that, they put us in a holding cell. We both figured they needed medical assistance. I told Julian not to help them. If we had any kind of power over them, we needed to use it."

"Naturally."

"The Jem'Hadar First was named Goran'agar. He had kicked the addiction to that white drug of theirs, and he thought it was because of something on the planet. Julian and I pretended to help him while I worked out a way to escape, but another Jem'Hadar caught me at it." He shuddered. "I thought they were gonna kill me there, but this Goran'agar was determined to get *all* his men to kick the white habit, and he knew Julian wouldn't keep working if I was dead. Goran'agar was playing Julian, telling him what he wanted to hear. You know what he's like—as soon as he gets a medical problem to sink his teeth into, he won't let go until he's solved it. It never occurred to him to think of what the consequences might be. I mean, he's always been a little naïve, but this *is* the Jem'Hadar we're talking about."

"I assume you reminded him."

O'Brien nodded. "But he insisted. He even ordered me to keep working at one point."

When O'Brien's pause went on for several seconds, Worf prompted, "What happened?"

"I had to get a component from the runabout, but I managed to escape using the transporter. While the Jem'Hadar were searching, I went to get Julian." O'Brien bit his lip. "He wouldn't come. He told me to go ahead and leave if I had to, but he was going to stay behind to try to see if Goran'agar's condition could be duplicated. I knew that nothing I said was going to change his mind—he was gonna stay there. Never mind that the Jem'Hadar are the enemy, never mind that more Jem'Hadar might show up and try to kill them all, never mind that Goran'agar's own men were as likely as not to turn on him.

"So I blew up his research."

"You disobeyed a direct order."

"I didn't have a choice!" O'Brien said defensively, even though Worf was not accusing him of anything, merely stating a fact. "If he stayed behind—" He hesitated. "Of course, he also might've found a cure. And who knows, it might've been the best thing in the end—but we didn't know! At the time I was so sure of myself, but now—" He regarded Worf with an almost pleading look in his eyes. "What would you have done in my place, Commander?"

Worf leaned back in his chair and folded his arms. "I would not have been in your place. I outrank Dr. Bashir."

"That's *not* what I meant."

"My point is, Chief, this is *your* story. I cannot act in it, only interpret it." He paused. "In Klingon tradition, obedience is paramount. As a rule, one does not even question the order of a superior."

"As a rule?"

Nodding, Worf said, "But—if a superior is acting in an irrational manner, Klingon Defense Force regulations require a challenge to remove that superior rather than obey an order from such a warrior. Do you feel that the doctor was acting irrationally? He was, after all, consorting with the enemy. Aiding them."

"Well, I don't know that I'd go *that* far."

"But you did what you felt was right."

"Yes."

Kaga came by then with the blood pie. After he set it down, he asked O'Brien if he wanted anything. "The *taknar* gizzards are fresh today!"

Again, the chief's nose wrinkled. "No, thanks, I'm not staying."

"As you wish." Kaga bowed and took his leave.

Worf took a bite, which was the best he'd had since the last time he'd had his human foster mother's pie. "If the doctor was consorting with the enemy, then your actions were proper, and you were true to yourself. In the end that is all we can aspire to."

"Well, he was and he wasn't." At Worf's questioning glance, O'Brien added, "I mean, he's a *doctor*. To him, they weren't Jem'Hadar, they were patients. He was trying to cure them. That's what he does."

"Then *he* was true to *him*self. In which case, neither of you has anything to be ashamed of."

"Maybe." O'Brien got up. "I'll leave you to your dessert, sir. Thanks for your help."

"You are welcome," Worf said, though based on the fact that O'Brien looked as perturbed when he exited as he had when he came in, the Klingon doubted that he truly provided a service.

On the other hand, perhaps now Dax would leave him alone on the subject . . .

* * *

"Mind if I join you?"

Dax turned around to see Bashir catching up to her on the Promenade. "I was just heading to the replimat to get a *raktajino*. And of course you can join me. I even promise not to say a word about Chief O'Brien."

At that, Bashir chuckled, which Dax took as a good sign. She'd asked the occasional probing question over the past few days, with even less luck than she had the first time in Quark's, to the point where the doctor seemed to be avoiding her company.

"Actually, the chief is what I wanted to talk about."

They each ordered from the replicators—Dax her Klingon coffee, Bashir a mug of chamomile tea, claiming that his stomach was a bit upset—and found a two-person table.

After an awkward pause, Bashir finally started to speak. "You've read the reports we wrote about what happened on Bopak III?"

Dax nodded.

"What we didn't include in the report was what happened between Miles and myself." Bashir hesitated, drank some of his tea, then proceeded to tell Dax about the *Rubicon* crash landing, their capture by First Goran'agar, and Bashir's ever-more-futile attempts to find out what in the planet's atmosphere led to that one Jem'Hadar's ability to produce the health-stabilizing enzyme that others of his kind could obtain only from ketracel-white. "Miles didn't want to have anything to do with it. He said we shouldn't help them under any circumstances." Bashir blew out a breath. "Actually, his exact words were, 'We do not help them, and that's the end of it.' "

At that, Dax had to put down her *raktajino* or risk spluttering it. "He said that?"

Bashir gazed at Dax with his wide eyes. "I actually had to give him an order to cooperate. It was an odd feeling, I can assure you."

"You were the ranking officer, Julian. What I can't believe is that you had to do it in the first place. Chief O'Brien had no authority to make a statement like that." *Even if he had a point,* she thought, but didn't say aloud. O'Brien's concerns were legitimate, though Bashir's enthusiasm also wasn't without cause.

"I sent him to the *Rubicon* to retrieve a part, but he used the transporter to escape. The Jem'Hadar went off to chase him down, and he doubled back to get me. He wanted to leave—but I couldn't. I told him to go ahead and take the runabout, but I was staying behind. I couldn't just abandon the Jem'Hadar. Leaving aside any other considerations, they only had a limited supply of white left. If I didn't find a cure soon, they were all going to die."

Dax knew where this was going. She knew both men well enough to know that neither was likely to back down in these circumstances. "He destroyed your research?"

"Yes," Bashir said, surprised. "He said I could bring him up on charges later, but now we had to leave. There was nothing keeping me there now." Bashir finished off his tea. "It was—odd. I mean, he's the chief. He's been in Starfleet for ages. And he's my friend. I thought he had more respect for me than that. But to so utterly dismiss my orders, my opinion—*me*—like that . . . By just saying I could bring him up on charges obviously meant that whether I did or not was irrelevant. That *I* was irrelevant. And that he was unrepentant." He shook his head. "That's ultimately why I didn't— bring charges, I mean. What would be the point?"

"I can't believe he did that," Dax said, though truthfully, she had no trouble believing it. "He had no business even questioning your orders like that—and to out-and-out ignore your authority, it's just—" She slammed her mug down. "It's not like he doesn't know you. I mean, there are some noncoms who think that officers are all useless, but I thought O'Brien had more sense than *that*— especially regarding *you*. Honestly, Julian, I think you *should* bring him up on charges. I know it's been a few weeks, but I think Benjamin will understand. You—"

Bashir put a hand on Dax's wrist. "Jadzia—"

About time, Dax thought. "What?"

"I don't think Miles would have done what he did without

good reason. If he didn't think it through. If he didn't—didn't *believe* in what he was doing."

"Did you think through what *you* were doing?"

Bashir straightened, and only then did Dax realize that, uncharacteristically, the doctor had been slouching throughout the conversation. "Of course! I had a chance to *cure* them! I could hardly turn my back!"

"Have you told the chief that?"

Whatever puppeteer returned Bashir's posture then clipped the strings, and he slouched again.

They sat in silence for several seconds before Bashir got up, went to the replicator, and ordered another tea.

But instead of returning to the table, he wandered off toward the infirmary.

Letting out a growl worthy of Worf, Dax finished off her *raktajino. This is worse than I thought.*

When Miles O'Brien entered Garak's tailor shop, he realized with a start that it was the first time he had set foot in the place since it blew up a year ago. O'Brien had never trusted Cardassians—he'd seen too much during his time on the *Rutledge*—and Garak was especially untrustworthy. However, the shop's door wouldn't close, which was something of a security concern, so O'Brien—at the request of both Garak and Odo—went to fix the problem.

Garak spoke amiably when O'Brien arrived with his toolkit.

"Thank you for coming, Chief. While I am normally loath to take you away from what must be more pressing duties, I fear that my shop would be far too tempting a target for vandals if the door were left wide open at any time other than normal business hours."

"No problem." He knelt down and pried the cover off the door control panel. There were no customers in the shop at the moment, which disheartened O'Brien. It meant he was in serious danger of being the only object of Garak's seemingly endless capacity for conversation. There were people O'Brien could talk to while working—Dax, Worf, most of the *Defiant* engineering staff, the captain—but Garak was most assuredly not one of them.

Sure enough, the tailor kept talking. "It's good to see such dedication. I freely admit that there is much about your Federation that I disapprove of, but the work ethic among you of Starfleet is quite unparalleled. I'd say it's worthy of a Cardassian—which I suppose doesn't mean as much to you as it does to me, but still, it comes from the heart."

"I'm sure it does," O'Brien said for lack of any better rejoinder.

"And, of course, you could have passed this on to one of your staff—especially given your antipathy toward me."

O'Brien gritted his teeth as he searched for a programming cause for the door to be broken, but the computer functions were all fine.

Garak obviously noted O'Brien's displeasure, as he added, "Now then, Chief, don't try to hide it. I would be a poor shop owner if I did not have a certain capacity for observation, and even the meanest intelligence can see that you don't like me. I'm sure you have your reasons, especially given your past history with my people, and I respect that. I respect even more your willingness to put that aside to help me out of my little difficulty."

Does he ever shut up? O'Brien wondered as he checked the physical mechanism to see if it was jammed in some way. *And who is he fooling, anyhow? It's not like his past as an Obsidian Order agent is much of a secret anymore—if it ever was . . .*

"Then again, you seem to have a great deal more free time of late, what with your lovely wife and child spending most of their time on Bajor and you and Dr. Bashir having ended your friendship."

That tears it. O'Brien switched off his magnospanner, stood up, and faced the Cardassian. "Look, I'll fix your door for you, Garak—and I'll also thank you to stay out of my private life."

Looking shocked at O'Brien's reaction, Garak held up his hands, and his mouth formed an O. "My apologies, Chief. Believe me, offending you was the last thing I intended."

"Good." He knelt back down and switched the magnospanner back on. *Worf is one thing—he's a friend.* But he saw no reason to let this Cardassian pseudo-spy stick his neck in, as it were.

"Besides, it was a foregone conclusion in any case."

A fervent desire for Garak to shut up warred with curiosity as to what he meant by that last statement within O'Brien's mind. Against his better judgment, the latter prevailed. "What was?"

"You and the good doctor. The amazing thing is that you've been able to stand being in each other's company at all. After all, you're an enlisted man, an engineer, a family man. Dr. Bashir is an officer and a gentleman, as you humans put it, with no family to speak of. You don't have the same interests, except for a few silly games. Indeed, your sojourn to the Gamma Quadrant quite admirably displayed just how little you two have in common. It was wise of you to go your separate ways. I doubt that any other outcome was even possible."

Before O'Brien could even consider formulating a response to this, two things happened: A Lissepian walked in, and O'Brien noted that two isolinear rods were in the wrong place. While Garak asked how he could help the Lissepian, O'Brien put the rods in their proper slots, and then closed the door.

"Ah!" Garak said. "Excuse me a moment," he added to the Lissepian, who bowed by way of affirmation. "Thank you, Chief. I am most grateful."

Opening the door once again, O'Brien said, "I'd watch out for those vandals you mentioned. Someone switched a couple of the the isolinear rods—it caused the commands to reroute. Any time the computer received an instruction to close the door, it was read as a request to open it."

"I will maintain vigilance, as you suggest. Again, Chief, my thanks."

"Don't mention it." *Please don't mention it.* Without another word, he turned his back on the meddlesome tailor and headed to his quarters to change. He had a date with a holosuite.

★　★　★

An hour later, he was dressed in the one-piece black outfit with the blue-and-yellow highlights that he wore when he went kayaking. The suit kept him warm and dry, leaving only his head exposed. As he headed up the stairs to the second level of Quark's where the holosuites were housed, the bartender flagged him down. "Chief, there's been a slight change in plan—you're in Holosuite Three. Rom has to do some kind of maintenance thing or other on number two."

"Whatever," O'Brien said. He didn't care which holosuite they put him in, so long as it had a kayak and a facsimile of the Colorado River in it. Working his way down the Colorado, with nothing to focus on but his arms' movements with the oar, was just what he needed right now. He'd spent most of the last week cleaning up the mess Rom made of the *Defiant* when the aftermath of the True Way's assassination attempt on the station senior staff necessitated hooking the warship's transporter to the holosuites. Between that and his usual duties, he'd been going full tilt.

Now, though, he could lose himself in the rhythm of kayaking. Left stroke, right stroke, left stroke, right stroke. No need to figure out why the door is broken, or which Cardassian subsystem still, after over three years, wouldn't interface properly with a Federation processor, or what Rom was thinking when he wired the *Defiant* transporter, or why everyone and her bloody sister seemed concerned with whether or not he and Julian were talking to each other.

If I can just get through this without hurting my shoulder again . . .

Just as he had that thought, he came upon a sharp bend. O'Brien sliced his oar through the water on his left twice to get the kayak to turn, but he didn't move fast enough. The kayak started to capsize.

Bloody hell. Water filled his mouth, nose, and ears as he found himself unceremoniously dunked into the river. Pinwheeling his arms and legs in an attempt to right himself, he tried to swim for shore, but the current took control of him. *If I can just get my head above water,* he thought frantically, *I can get the computer to shut this damn thing off.*

Pain shot through his left shoulder as it collided with something heavy, just as his eyes cleared. Realizing that he was at the shore, he clambered forward, hoping that it would take him away from the river and not back into it.

Coughing water, he managed to crabwalk his way out of the river, his kayak and oars lost to the current. *But they're not real, anyhow.*

The pain in his shoulder lessened a bit. *If I'm lucky, it's just wrenched a bit, and I won't have to see—*

Feet.

O'Brien coughed some more, and blinked the water out of his eyes, but, as he lay there on the shore of the Colorado River, he definitely saw two feet. Human feet, shod in what looked to be leather shoes—too well polished for someone standing on the shores of a river, truth be known. Above them were immaculately tailored ankle cuffs.

He looked up.

Clad in an old-fashioned tuxedo and holding some kind of projectile weapon was Julian Bashir, who asked, "What are *you* doing here?"

O'Brien's attempt to answer resulted in more coughing, as some of the water was still lodged in his throat. Bashir kindly helped him up and slapped him on the back in an attempt to get him to cough up the remaining water.

"How did you wind up kayaking on the French Riviera, Chief? I thought you preferred the Colorado."

"French—this *is* the Colorado!" Then O'Brien looked up and saw the resort just a few meters away. He shook his head. "Rom."

"Probably melded the programs by mistake. Or Quark misassigned the holosuites."

"Or both."

O'Brien stared at Bashir for a moment.

"Look, Julian—"

"Chief, I—"

An awkward pause followed.

"You first, Chief."

"No, Julian, it's all right, you go first."

"Please, I insist." Then Bashir let loose with that idiotic grin of his—the one that made O'Brien want to punch him the first time he saw it. "Age before beauty."

The chief decided to just give in and go first. But seeing that damn grin made the apology he was going to utter catch in his throat, as he found himself remembering all of the doctor's most annoying qualities all at once. "You know, it's funny, when we first met—I really really hated you."

Bashir blinked. "I knew you didn't care much for me—"

Snorting, O'Brien said, "If you *did* know, you did a lousy job of showin' it. You were pretentious, annoying, irritating, self-centered." He bared his teeth—it wasn't really a smile. "You, Julian Bashir, are a ponce." The not-a-smile waned. "And yet, I remember you tellin' me one time that you admired me and respected me, and for the life of me, I couldn't understand why. I mean, what in God's name would you look up at *me* for? I'm just a regular engineer going to work every day. You, you're a doctor, top of your class, you're good-looking, athletic. You beat Vulcans at racquetball. You put together alien comm systems with just a dying engineer to give you half-baked instructions. You *save lives*. I just put machinery together. What the hell do you see in *me* to respect?"

Shaking his head, Bashir said, "Don't you see, Miles—that's it."

"What's it?"

"You're a regular engineer going to work every day. Yes, I've done all that you say. All my life, I've always known the things I wanted, and whatever they were, I got them—easily. *Things* have always come easily to me. Yet there you were, happy with your family, your life, your career—much happier than I've ever been able to be. I found true love in medical school, and I gave it up for my career. You found true love on the *Enterprise* and made it work *with* your career. Not only that, but look at what you've done: fighting the Cardassians, the Borg, the Romulans, yet all the while you're still—you. Still happy, still content, still—" Again, he let that damn grin loose. "Still the chief. You don't know how much I envy you, Miles. Because with all I've accomplished, it can't even begin to compare to what you have."

Remembering Garak's words, O'Brien said, "I guess what we have in common is that we don't have anything in common."

"Perhaps." Bashir started to pace around the rocky shore. "And that's what made Bopak III hurt so much."

Here it comes.

"Yes, I admire you, respect you, as much or more than anyone else on the station. That's why what you did hurt so much. And it also made me second-guess myself."

O'Brien put a hand on Bashir's shoulder. "You've got nothing to second-guess, Julian."

"Don't I? You were right, about everything. Leaving aside every other possibility, I was never going to figure out a way to work around centuries of genetic engineering with one makeshift laboratory in the twenty-six hours I had left before the platoon's white ran out. If we stayed behind, we would have died, whether or not I found any kind of cure."

"Maybe—but you swore an oath to save lives. To do no harm. And I took an oath as well, to obey my superiors. Even though I disagreed with you, I never should have acted the way I did. I should've raised my objections, not lectured you like you were some kind of Academy cadet. And if you still insisted on helping Goran'agar, then it was my duty to do as you said, not undermine you like that."

Bashir turned to face O'Brien. "Remember what you said after Goran'agar refused to come with us?"

"I'm not sure," O'Brien said. In fact, he was fairly sure he knew what the doctor was referring to, but if he was wrong, he did not think it would be politic to remind Bashir of it.

"You said, 'He's their commander—they trusted him.' I was your commander, and you didn't trust me."

O'Brien found he couldn't look Bashir in the eyes. "No, I

didn't. I guess—" He hesitated, then chuckled. "I guess I was still thinking of you as a ponce."

Bashir smirked. "Well, I do make a good one." He looked down. "Especially in this outfit."

"I'm sorry, Julian." The words that wouldn't come before came tumbling out of O'Brien's mouth now. "I shouldn't have thought so little of you to disobey you so easily." Now he did look the doctor in the eyes. "It won't happen again—sir."

Bashir returned the gaze for several seconds, then that grin came out again. Somehow, though, O'Brien didn't find it irritating this time. "Don't call me 'sir'—I work for a living."

The chief snorted. "Nice try, *Lieutenant.*"

"Come on," Bashir said, "why don't we let Quark know that the holosuite's not working—and then see if the dart board's free."

The dart board rang out with the sound of a bull's-eye.

Quark thought, *Someday, someone's going to have to explain to me what a "bull" is, and what its eye has to do with this game.*

The sound was certainly not unwelcome. It mixed in nicely with the cries of "Dabo!" from the wheels, the hum of conversation from the tables, and the wails of anguish from the two Tellarites Jake Sisko was hustling at the dom-jot table.

Of course, the visuals were a little bizarre, even by Quark's high standards. Usually when Bashir and O'Brien played their dart game, they were in uniform. Now, however, O'Brien was wearing that unfortunate one-piece thing that he always wore when he kayaked, and Bashir was dressed in that outfit Garak referred to as a *tuck-see-doh.* Quark was considering taking bets on which one of them looked more foolish, especially since it was impossible to choose between them.

They were also laughing like old friends.

At the end of the bar, Dax sat next to Morn, nursing an *allira* punch and grinning ear to ear. "Well," Quark said, approaching her, "I haven't seen you looking this happy since the last time you fleeced me at the *tongo* wheel."

"Oh, I'm happier than that. Look at them."

"Do I have to? Look at them, I mean."

"Fine, don't." Dax laughed. "Just take their money."

Grinning, Quark said, "*That* I'm glad to do."

Dax then regarded him with those beautiful eyes. "Thanks, Quark. I owe you one."

"Oh, you owe me more than one. You know how long it took Rom to rewire the holosuites so those two would each think they were in the right program?"

"Knowing Rom, about fifteen minutes. Nice try, Quark. I owe you *one*."

Quark shrugged. "Can't blame a Ferengi for trying. I'll settle for a rematch of that *tongo* game. Tonight, after closing."

"You're on."

"Good. Now, if you'll excuse me, both of our dart players have empty glasses. I need to rectify this appalling situation." He then grabbed a tray and approached the pair just as Bashir's dart hit very close to the middle. "Gentlemen," Quark said. "Who's winning?"

Bashir looked at O'Brien. O'Brien looked at Bashir. Each then pointed to the other and said, "He is." Then they started laughing.

On the other hand, maybe those two have had enough. After a moment: *Nah.* "Can I refill your drinks?"

"Definitely," Bashir said.

"And keep 'em comin'," O'Brien added.

Quark smiled. "Your wish is my command."

And for the rest of the evening, O'Brien and Bashir's dart board remained used.

... Loved I Not Honor More

Christopher L. Bennett

Historian's note: This story is set during the fifth-season episode "Soldiers of the Empire."

Christopher L. Bennett

At the age of five and a half, Christopher L. Bennett saw his first episode of *Star Trek*, believing it to be a show about a strange airplane that only flew at night. As he continued watching, he discovered what those points of light in the sky *really* were. This awakened a lifelong fascination with space, science and speculative fiction. He often made up *Trek*-universe stories set a century after Kirk's adventures (an idea years ahead of its time), but soon shifted to creating his own original universe. He eventually realized he did this well enough to make a career out of it. Years of rejections failed to disabuse him of this arrogant notion, and the magazine *Analog Science Fiction and Fact* fed the delusion by publishing his controversial novelette "Aggravated Vehicular Genocide" in November 1998 and "Among the Wild Cybers of Cybele" in December 2000.

" . . . Loved I Not Honor More" is Christopher's second work of professional *Trek* fiction, following the eBook *Star Trek: S.C.E. #29: Aftermath*, published in July 2003. At this rate, he may never recover from his delusions.

The universe was finally starting to make sense again.

Quark was back in business—licensed Ferengi business, to be precise. His yearlong exile from entrepreneurial civilization was over, thanks to his dogged perseverance, his unwavering faith in the Rules of Acquisition, and his shrewd negotiating acumen. Well, that and the fact that his mother was sleeping with the Grand Nagus, but he wasn't about to mention that to anyone; not only was it a scandalous state secret, but it wasn't an image he wanted to think about if he could avoid it. To sweeten the deal, that officious FCA greeworm Brunt had been put in his place (namely the unemployment line), Quark now had the ear of the nagus himself (well, Moogie did, but there was another image to be avoided), and to top it all off, his beloved Marauder Mo action figures, kept in storage by Moogie all these years, now stood proudly displayed in his quarters here on DS9. *Yes*, Quark thought as he strode through the Promenade this fine morning, *life is good*.

And the stern, suspicious look on Odo's face was a special bonus. As he walked past the security office, Quark could see it in the constable's simulated eyes—he was worried. Odo had held an edge in their ongoing game for a time, but now Quark was no longer handicapped. Already he was on the prowl like never before, making new deals, seizing opportunities, weaving his old Ferengi connections together with the new ones he'd made during his exile—and capitalizing on the insider information he'd gained during his fleeting career as the Nagus's financial secretary. In the few days since getting his license back, Quark had already erupted onto the business scene as a force to be reckoned with, determined to make up for lost time, with interest. And Odo could tell the momentum had shifted in Quark's favor.

Not that the changeling would ever admit it, of course. Indeed, mere moments after Quark passed the security office, Odo was at his side, affecting his usual superior sneer. "I'm glad you're looking so cheerful lately, Quark."

"Oh, really?" Quark asked evenly, refusing to take the bait.

"Yes. It means you're overconfident. You're so eager to get back in the game that you're bound to make a mistake. And when you do, I'll be there. Enjoy your *freedom* to do business while you can."

"Believe me, I will." Quark smiled as he worked the elaborate lock that secured his bar—after shooing Morn out of the way, a ritual so routine he barely noticed it. "I'm enjoying everything today, Odo. It could be *thloppering* right here on the Promenade," he said, using the Ferengi word for a particularly cold, hard, and miserable variety of rain, "and I'd be giggling like an apprentice and jumping in the puddles. So I'm not going to be bothered by that dark cloud that always hangs over you."

"*Nothing* bothers you?" Odo challenged as the doors slid open barely fast enough to let Morn plunge through. "Not even the fact that your brother Rom has given away his entire fortune, petty though it was, to please Leeta?"

Oh, yes—without Quark's levelheaded presence to keep him on track, that idiot had fallen under the sway of the hew-mons and that uppity Bajoran fiancée of his and thrown his life savings to the orphans. So what if it proved she didn't want him for his money, like Rom's first wife, Prinadora—he'd ended up just as penniless. But no—Quark shook it off. "Not even that, Odo. At least Rom is consistent in his idiocy, and that's a comfort in its own way. Better a broke idiot for a brother than a cunning competitor." *Hmm, that's good,* Quark thought to himself. *Could be a new Rule of Acquisition. I'll have Moogie run it by the Nagus. . . .*

"Just as well," Odo scoffed. "It's not as if your meager business skills could stand up to any real competition."

"Scoff away, Odo," Quark said fondly as Morn, now settled in his stool, reached out to a glass that stood on the bar. "Nothing's going to break my good mood today."

"How about a health inspection?" Odo countered, snatching the glass from Morn's hand. "Don't you bother to clean up before you close anymore?" Morn glared silently—the big Lurian rarely had much to say before his first drink, claiming the station's air dried his throat.

Quark fully registered the glass for the first time. "That wasn't there last night, Odo." He took the glass, felt the temperature, sniffed it. "This is a fresh drink." He frowned. "Maparian ale . . . with a hint of . . . *Pazafer?*" he finished, the frown quickly fading.

"Barkeep!" came a harsh cry from the shadows. "What kind of *petaQ* keeps a lady waiting for her drink?"

Quark whirled, beaming. "Grilka!"

The fearsome Klingon stepped forward, a broad grin belying her harsh tones. "That's *Lady* Grilka to you, Ferengi. Of the House of Grilka."

Quark stepped forward and offered her the ale with a courtly bow. "My lady. All honor to your House." He smirked. "Though I still think 'House of Quark' has a nobler sound to it."

Grilka laughed and pulled him against her. "It's a good thing I like you, Quark, or you'd be long since dead."

"The way you show affection, I'm lucky to be alive," Quark half-chuckled and half-gasped, before she pulled him into a savage kiss that proved his point. Odo and Morn exchanged a disgusted look that spoke volumes.

When Grilka finally let him up for breath, Quark noticed Odo leaving the bar, shaking his head in disbelief. *Could this day get any better?* Quark wondered as he tried to regain his sense of balance and guide his Klingon lover to a table.

"How did you get in here?" Quark asked. Just because he was

deliriously happy didn't mean he wasn't concerned about a security breach. If Rom had broken his locking codes again . . .

"I wanted to surprise you, so I arranged it covertly with Commander Dax. She said she was 'always happy to engineer a romantic gesture,' and allowed me to beam in here from my transport vessel." Quark was relieved that his codes were safe and that no one less skilled than Dax had pierced his beaming shields. Jadzia was one Starfleet officer who was always welcome to invade his privacy—well, so long as neither Grilka nor Worf were around to see it.

"Well, it was a lovely surprise," he told her, keeping those thoughts securely to himself. Certainly it was a nicer surprise than Grilka's first visit to his bar, which had led to a shotgun wedding, a battle to the death, and other unpleasantness. Ironic that they hadn't become lovers until well after their divorce. "Did you come all this way just to see me?"

A Klingon noblewoman would not deign to shrug, but she tilted her head in a suitably classy and dignified equivalent. "The affairs of a mighty House weigh heavily at times. I felt I could use a . . . pleasant distraction."

"Pleasant distractions are my stock in trade." Quark leered. "I still have dozens of . . . holoprograms for couples . . . which we haven't sampled together yet."

"Call me a traditionalist, but I prefer to stick with *Kahless and Lukara*. If you still wield a *bat'leth* as well as you did against Thopok when you wooed me," she smiled seductively, "then we may share a passion as great as theirs."

Quark's good mood faltered just a touch. "Well . . . I may have let myself get a little out of practice." Especially without Worf puppeteering his muscles through a telepresence relay like before. "Business keeps me busy, you know."

"Well, you were feeble at first, but caught on swiftly," she reassured him, patting his hand. "With our love to fire you again, you will rally to the fight in no time."

"I–if you say so," Quark chuckled nervously, and hastened to change the subject. "So . . . these House affairs. Everything going well financially? Beneath your notice, of course, but . . ."

"Yes, my Ferengi, I know how such things amuse you." Her smile faded. "In truth, things are not so well on that front. But such are the wages of battle," she finished dismissively.

"Oh, I'm sure. But if there's any small way I could help keep the war machine running smoothly . . ."

"Here is a catalog of our recent losses," Grilka interrupted, all business, whipping a padd from her belt. "Our enemy has struck hard, doing much damage to my estate. He is one you know, Quark: D'Ghor."

"D'Ghor?" Quark gasped. "But I thought he was in disgrace! The High Council did that . . . shunning, back-turning thing when he tried to kill me."

"Fortunes changed during the recent war. Alliances shifted, factions rose and fell. Cousins of D'Ghor won honor on the Cardassian front, and he has borrowed some of their prestige for his own. And, I must confess, he fights honorably now, with open force rather than devious accounting tricks. No offense."

"None taken," Quark said patiently.

"He has allowed my men glorious deaths, as I have done for his, and I can honor him for that, at least. But his forces favor disruptors over blades."

"Is that honorable?"

"It is . . . somewhat more vulgar than good honest metal, but we have disruptors too, so it is fair. The main problem is that their aim could be better. My estate is full of holes, and many priceless antiques have been sent to join their former masters in *Sto-Vo-Kor*," she smirked.

Quark shook his head. "Barbaric—such a waste of good merchandise. Maybe you should keep your valuables in storage until this blows over. Substitute replicas in their place, or holograms."

"That would be deceitful."

"No, you don't have to lie, not if anyone asks. It's just being cautious. Announcing your resources without exposing them, say."

Grilka nodded. "It is an interesting idea." She smiled and stroked his lobe just the way he liked. "I look forward to hearing more . . . later."

"Odo, you really have to get out more," Quark said airily. "If the routine business dealings of a simple bartender are of such consuming interest to you, then you desperately need to take a good, long look at your life and what it's missing." He smiled. "And then we can discuss where I can get it for you and how much you'll pay for it."

Odo almost accused him of offering a bribe, but he realized it was nothing of the sort—just a Ferengi's reflexive response to every situation as a business opportunity. Had it been a bribe, Odo knew, it would've been delivered in a far oilier tone. Besides, even Quark knew better than to try a bribe on him—even in the middle of the lovestruck haze he'd been drifting around in for the past few days. Odo couldn't begin to understand what a Klingon noblewoman could see in a degenerate like Quark—honestly, it stretched Odo's faith that there was justice in the cosmos when this ratlike reprobate could attract so many respectable females while an upstanding lawman . . . well, never mind. It wouldn't have bothered him so much if Quark's recreations with Grilka had managed to distract the Ferengi from his extralegal schemes. But if anything, she'd energized him, heightened his focus and his confidence—and his caution. The mistake Odo had expected him to make hadn't materialized yet. But maybe, if he kept the pressure up, Odo could throw Quark off his balance. Or at least wear him down.

So he peered at Quark with his most intimidating peer. Odo had few equals when it came to peers. "All I'm missing, Quark, is proof. If I find out you're selling espionage technology to a hostile power . . ."

"Really, Constable! Such paranoia is unbecoming. The Reletek are a peaceful, neutral people. They invented the transphasic sensor array as a scientific tool, nothing more." He segued smoothly into sales-pitch mode. "It's for scanning phenomena that exist out of phase with normal space and time—things undetectable by normal means. Nothing more than ghosts to us. What could be the harm in that?"

Odo knew he was basically telling the truth; the Reletek were a small, herbivorous, molelike people who had never done much harm to anyone and barely attracted any notice. Their one noteworthy feature was the genius for sensory technology that they'd developed to compensate for their own limited senses. But Odo was more concerned with how others might abuse the fruits of that genius. "Dax tells me that transphasic scans could be used to bypass sensor-jamming fields, or to listen in on encrypted subspace transmissions."

"They can also be used to penetrate certain kinds of cloak, or to detect interphasic beings like those sneaky Devidians. In fact, they could be a positive boon to station security. You shouldn't be browbeating me, Odo, you should be making me an offer."

"And this no doubt explains all the fine, security-minded scientists on your client list. The warlords of Alrakis . . . the Nachri insurgents . . . the Tzenkethi. . . ."

"None of whom are currently at war with Bajor, the Federation, or their allies," Quark hastened to point out.

"And I'm sure the Lady Grilka wouldn't be upset to learn that a certain House of D'Ghor is also in business with the Reletek?"

To Odo's satisfaction, that finally got a reaction out of Quark. "You haven't told her, have you?" he asked furtively.

"Any reason why I shouldn't?"

Quark recovered his nonchalant air, though it wasn't as pristine as before. "I just . . . don't want to bother her with irrelevancies. I mean, it's not as if I'm the one who brokered that deal. It was made weeks ago, before I even went into business with the Reletek. And from what I gather, it was for a general sensor upgrade package. D'Ghor isn't really into anything as subtle as espionage, from what I hear."

Odo had to concede privately that Quark was right—other

than Grilka, there was nothing to connect the Klingon to Quark. He'd vaguely wondered if Quark might have arranged the attack on Grilka's estate in order to create a financial crisis that would bring her here to consult with him. But it had only been a month since Quark's failed flirtation with arms dealing, which had demonstrated that he had *some* trace of conscience within that misshapen head of his. He wouldn't directly engineer dozens of deaths merely to satisfy his carnal pleasures. Odo had been secretly relieved when Quark had chosen not to follow his cousin Gaila across that line—though only, he rationalized to himself, because it verified his assessment of Quark as more a nuisance than a genuine menace. He was tempted to pursue this further just to make Quark squirm, but it would be pointless and prurient.

Still, the smug look on Quark's face irked him. "Face it, Odo," the Ferengi said, "you've got nothing. You're wasting your time harassing me when you should be out tracking down some real lawbreakers."

"Quark, whenever I'm around you I can practically hear the laws breaking. You've never seen a law you haven't tried to break."

"You think so, do you?" Quark leaned forward intently. "Between the two of us, who follows the rules more, hmm? Me, that's who." Odo scoffed reflexively, but Quark didn't let him go further. The changeling realized their banter had given way to something more serious. "Why do you think Grilka likes me? Because she sees that I'm a man of honor. I live by a clear ethical code, the Rules of Acquisition. Maybe it's not your code, or the Federation's, but it's the code of my people, and I work hard to live by its dictates.

"You, on the other hand—you break the rules all the time. You broke the Cardassians' rules, to protect people they would've killed. You break Starfleet's rules whenever it suits you, if they get in the way of your precious 'justice.' And what about that shapeshifting? It gives you an unfair advantage. It's *cheating*. But that never bothers you, does it?" Quark shook his head. "You don't even obey the normal laws of physics! An eighty-kilo man one moment, a hundred-gram goblet the next. How do you even *do* that?" Odo sometimes wondered that himself. Dax's theories about folding his mass into subspace sounded reasonable, but proof had been elusive.

"And on top of all that," Quark went on, "you're in love with a terrorist! The ultimate criminal!"

"Be quiet!" Odo hissed, trying to make it sound contemptuous rather than furtive, and failing miserably.

"Ha!" Quark exclaimed, pointing a finger. "And you call me dishonest. How much longer are you going to lie to Kira about your feelings?"

"I've never lied to her! I've merely . . . been circumspect."

" 'Evasive' is more like it."

"*It wouldn't be appropriate,*" Odo said, emphasizing every word. "Kira's happy with First Minister Shakaar. I've . . . learned to move on." He was trying to persuade himself as much as Quark, he knew. Kira had been going on so much lately about her plans to visit Shakaar on Bajor next week, to take him to the Glyrhond Falls, the Kenda Shrine, and other romantic locales. It was the most cheerful she'd been since the recent death of her friend Tekeny Ghemor. Her bond with Shakaar was good for her, something stable and secure, and the last thing Odo wanted was to disrupt her happiness with his regrets.

"If you say so." The frank sarcasm in Quark's tone galled him—especially because it was warranted. "But would she have ended up with him if you'd been honest with her when you had the chance?"

"You're one to talk about honesty in relationships," Odo shot back, unwilling to confront the question. "If you're so honest, why don't you tell Grilka how you really won her over? What does Klingon honor say about letting someone else do your fighting for you?"

"Hey—Worf may have been doing the moves, but *I* was the one whose skin was on the line!"

"Do you think she'd appreciate the distinction? Why don't we ask her?"

Quark seemed genuinely panicked now—yet somehow that didn't satisfy Odo as much as he would've expected. Perhaps the sense of potential loss in his eyes looked too familiar. "Odo, you're kidding, right? There's no need to do anything crazy here. . . ."

"I don't need to, Quark. You can't keep making excuses forever—sooner or later you'll have to spar with Grilka. And with Worf and Dax off on the *Rotarran,* you'll have to rely on your own, *hunh,* 'skills.' I'd recommend wearing a combadge so you can be beamed directly to sickbay."

Somehow his taunt seemed to backfire—Quark was growing more smug. "Don't buy me a condolence card yet, Odo. When the time comes, I intend to be ready." He sidled closer, conspiratorially. "I've been practicing every day in the holosuite. You know, the *bat'leth*'s not that hard to handle, once you get the hang of it."

Odo scoffed again. "You? The man who objects to exercise because it makes you sweat?"

"Can you believe it?" Quark chuckled. "The things we do for love, as the hew-mons say. But I tell you, Odo," he sighed, "that is one female who's worth it all. Ninety-Eighth Rule, my friend: 'Every man has his price.' I guess she's mine. She makes me feel . . . *honorable.*" He shook his head. "Who knew that could be a good thing?"

Odo realized he'd run out of comebacks. This wasn't some fleeting exercise in lust—Quark really *cared* for Grilka, and that threw Odo for a loop. Quark may have used deceit to win Grilka's affections, but at least he'd been forthright about his feelings. And that was more than the chastened changeling could say.

"This is odd," Quark murmured as he lay next to Grilka in his quarters, studying the account of her estate's losses.

"Hmm, what's that?" she said distractedly, while making a casual yet somewhat effective effort to distract him in turn.

"It's uncanny how many of the things D'Ghor's forces have destroyed were valuable. I mean, this is just collateral damage, right? Random destruction?"

"Correct."

"Then either you have the luck of Slug the Loser, or . . ." He shook his head. "It just doesn't make sense. Why would D'Ghor go out of his way to *destroy* your valuables? I thought your property was what he most wanted for himself."

"And he failed to win it. Perhaps all he cares for now is vengeance," she growled.

"*Ow.* Hey, relax those fingers, sweetheart. I'm pretty attached to that lobe."

"Sorry." But then she sighed in frustration. "Oh, Quark, I detest the timing of this virus of yours. All this lying around and talking, when your presence makes me burn for *action!*"

"Oh, I couldn't agree more, my dear—it's an awful shame," he said with a weariness that wasn't entirely feigned.

She poked him teasingly. "The symptoms don't seem so horrible. Sweat, sore muscles, fatigue . . . I endure worse in my daily exercise."

"Oh, so do I, of course." Rule 270: *A near-truth is an economical lie.* "But those are just the side effects of battling a viral foe that would do far worse if my body let it. I need to focus my energies on the, uh, the battle within!"

"But for how much longer?" she groaned in a way that sent a shudder through him.

He stroked her muscular arm. "Just a few more days, and then we'll battle side-by-side once more, my Lukara." That satisfied her, and what she did in response more than satisfied him. "Oh-h-h-h, yes. Uh, but keep in mind I'll be a bit slow getting back into the, ah, swing of things."

"I'll try to be gentle. But no promises."

"I can live with that. I hope."

They spent a few minutes on other things, but his mind refused to let go of one niggling thing. "It just doesn't make any sense! *Destroying* precious artifacts . . . gemstones . . . all that latinum destroyed forever. . . ." His shudder had nothing to do with Grilka's attentions this time.

Grilka sighed and stopped what she was doing, recognizing that he couldn't let this go. "D'Ghor must simply wish to ruin me, as we ruined him."

"But he was doing that before, in a sensible way. Not just . . . *wasting* all that wealth, but acquiring it for himself. It's the nature of the Great Material Continuum—wealth isn't created or destroyed, just transferred from one owner or source to another. One man's loss is another man's gain. D'Ghor is violating the Law of Conservation of Property! It's just not natural!"

Grilka tried to settle him down, but Quark was just too distraught at the tragic loss. "To understand D'Ghor's actions, Quark, you must forget all this Ferengi superstition and think like a Klingon!"

"But—"

"Quark." She silenced him with a kiss. "You are the only Ferengi I have ever known who could do this. Who could transcend his beginnings and find the warrior's heart within, make himself worthy of a Klingon lady's love. It is what makes you the noblest, most exciting male I have ever known. Do not doubt yourself, my *par'machkai*. You mastered our ways of fighting, and of loving . . . you can master our way of thinking, too."

Quark's spirit soared. The caress of her hands, her eyes, her voice made him feel ten times his size, filling him with confidence and pride even beyond what the return of his business license had done. He felt he could lift DS9 with one arm and battle Fek'lhr's hordes with the other, while his feet amassed a fortune that would make Bilgat the Monopolistic look like a beggar. "Yes, Grilka, yes! And you're the only Klingon I've ever known who could see the worth of a Ferengi spirit. I don't normally do this with females, but I'd love to discuss *The Exploits of the Nagi* with you, teach you to play *tongo* . . . maybe even show you some of the advantages to living like a Ferengi female," he leered. "You'd save a fortune on armor polish. . . ."

Grilka laughed. "You say the funniest things, Quark. But seriously—why don't we try a *mok'bara* session? That shouldn't be too hard on your poor ravaged body. And the meditative focus will help your body battle its invader. And then I'll have Tumek bake you a *rokeg* blood pie; there's nothing better for fortifying the immune defenses. . . ."

Quark was surprised, but he let the matter drop, happy to accept her eager ministrations. Getting her interested in Ferengi culture could wait . . . they had plenty of time.

Rom was helping out at the bar when he heard his brother calling him, in the irate tone that usually accompanied that action. He looked up to see Quark limping down the stairs from the holosuites, still dressed in Klingon-styled workout gear—a sight which caused Chief O'Brien's throw to miss the dartboard altogether. Dr. Bashir was torn between teasing the chief and coming to Quark's aid, but Quark waved him off irritably. "Are you all right, brother?" Rom asked as the chief began arguing with Bashir about whether the throw should count.

"I'll live, no thanks to you. I think I twisted my ankle," Quark went on, glaring at Rom. "But I know I had the safeties on. Are you *sure* you installed those upgrades right?" When Quark had let Cousin Gaila lure him into arms dealing, using the holosuites to simulate demo models of powerful weapons, he'd insisted that Rom enhance the safeties first.

Looking over his brother apologetically, Rom said, "Uhh, the safeties can keep a holographic weapon from hurting you, or . . . catch you if you fall off a holographic cliff—but they can't stop you from hurting yourself if you're not . . . uh, not careful."

"You mean all that stuff we tell the customers about not being liable for this kind of thing applies to me, too?" Rom nodded sheepishly. "Now, that's just not fair."

"I'm sure the doctor would be happy to fix your ankle."

"That's not the point. I can handle a little pain," he asserted, straightening with dignity (and with difficulty). "Pain is just another obstacle to overcome—it flees before a true warrior spirit." He planted his fists on his hips . . . then winced and rubbed his shoulder. "Well, maybe not *flees* exactly . . . but I've still got the upper hand! Ohh, I need to sit down," Quark groaned, plopping himself wearily on a barstool.

Rom was proud of his brother's determination, and had complete faith in his ability to triumph . . . but still he didn't look too good. And his approach didn't seem to match up with the things Leeta had been teaching Rom about physical fitness. "Maybe you're pushing yourself too hard," he suggested. "You've been spending every free moment in that holosuite—you really ought to pace yourself more."

"Believe me, Rom, I'd love to. But Grilka's patience isn't eternal. She's a very *passionate* female," he laughed—then broke off in pain. "Ahh—even my *lungs* ache."

"Uhh, speaking of patience, brother—or rather, people who don't have it—I've had to take several calls from the Alraki warlords. They say they're getting tired of waiting for your answer."

"Ohh, that's just typical warlord bluster. They'll keep. Besides, I wanted to see if I could get that arcybite mining contract first."

"I-I don't understand," Rom said.

"I explained that to you already," his brother sighed. "Before deciding on their offer of industrial disruptors, I need to know if I have any use for them."

"Oh, I remember that, brother. But the bidding on that contract already closed."

"What? But I thought that wasn't until Stardate 50780."

"That was yesterday," Rom said apologetically. He realized that the forward progression of time in response to the increase of cosmic entropy wasn't something he could personally be blamed for, but he figured he should be apologetic anyway, just in case. If Quark got angry enough, he'd undoubtedly find some way to hold him responsible for it.

But Quark just frowned a bit and shrugged it off. "Oh, well. Never mind. Plenty of other suckerfish in the River."

"Like who?" Rom prodded.

"What do you mean?"

"I-if you let this deal fall through, then you must have an even better one lined up . . . right?"

Quark had picked up the Klingon dictionary he'd been carrying around lately and begun muttering gutturally to himself. He interrupted this briefly to say, "Not particularly."

"Oh." Rom processed that for a moment, and came to the conclusion that he was confused. "Now I'm confused."

"Quick—call the news services. Rom is confused. *Rom mIS-moHlu'taH.*"

"I'm serious, brother. Just a few days ago you were so excited about all the new deals you had lined up. Now you're hardly even bothering with them. You're letting deals fall through . . . passing up investments . . . you've barely even looked at the stock reports lately."

"Don't worry, Rom, I'm not losing money."

"Maybe not, brother . . . but you aren't making it either. How can you reestablish yourself in the Ferengi business community if you aren't aggressively pursuing profit?" Rom knew he didn't understand business all that well, but he felt pretty clear on this point. He'd never accumulated much profit, even before he'd given it all away for love, and other Ferengi generally didn't think much of him. On reflection, he was glad Leeta was Bajoran and not Ferengi, or she wouldn't have appreciated him giving up his profits to prove he was happy with her not being Ferengi. Or . . . wait a minute . . .

"Rom, there is more to the universe than the Ferengi business community," Quark said, mercifully distracting him. "And there are other things worth aggressively pursuing. Like the love of a lady from a noble Klingon house," he finished with a proud tilt to his head.

"A noble *broke* Klingon house," said Chief O'Brien as he bellied up to the bar. "Two pints, Rom—on Bashir's tab," he added smugly. Rom could understand why—since the doctor had admitted his genetic enhancements and stopped holding back, O'Brien's victories had been few and far between, even with a handicap. Of course, Rom had even more reason to be smug—he hadn't just won a dart game from the genetic superman, he'd won Leeta. But he wasn't the smug type, so he decided to let the chief be smug for both of them.

"She's not broke yet, Chief," Quark countered. "And she won't be if I have anything to say about it."

"Well, she can't be too well off," Bashir observed between glares at O'Brien. "She only ever comes to see you when she has money trouble."

"How little you understand our relationship, Doctor," Quark said, unfazed.

"Well, she *does* have money trouble, doesn't she?" the doctor pressed. "Didn't I hear you just the other day, lamenting how all those precious heirlooms were 'gone, gone forever'? "

"Don't remind me." Quark was lost in thought for a moment, reflecting on the tragedy, but then he shook himself. "But that's beside the point. She doesn't care about the losses. It's the wages of battle."

"So it's just coincidence that she came to see you now. And happened to bring along a copy of her financial records."

But Rom's mind had caught on an earlier statement. "Gone where?" he asked.

"What?" Bashir asked.

"The heirlooms. Where did they go?"

"They were disintegrated, you idiot," said Quark.

"I knew that."

"So be quiet." He turned back to Bashir. "Of course she brought her financial records—she knows I enjoy helping her with them."

"She's using you, Quark," O'Brien sighed.

"Well, of course she is."

The chief did a take. "You mean you realize it?"

"What you hew-mons don't realize is, every relationship is about using. Sometimes we use each other for profit or lust, sometimes to give us children, sometimes for companionship, or to make us happy. It's all using."

Rom was still frowning. "But where did they go then?"

Nobody listened. "What about love?" O'Brien demanded. "Real, selfless love, I mean?"

"Even 'selflessness' is fundamentally selfish. Think about it—why do you do nice things for your wife?"

"Because it makes her happy!"

"And that makes you happy, right?"

"Of course."

"So ultimately, you're acting out of self-interest. If it didn't make *you* feel good, you wouldn't do it."

"So what you're telling us," Bashir said, "is that everything you're doing for Grilka is ultimately for your own gratification."

"Of course."

"And exactly *how* much pain are you in right now?"

In the lull that followed, Rom tried again. "Where did they go then?"

"Where did who go?" O'Brien asked.

"The heirlooms."

"You mean . . . *after* they were disintegrated?" Rom nodded.

Now he had everyone's attention. "Rom, have you been sampling the drinks again?" Quark asked. "When something's disintegrated, it's just . . . *gone. Foosh."*

"Maybe—but what about the particles that made it up? Matter can't be destroyed, brother. You can change its form, but all the mass still exists."

"So I guess it gets vaporized."

"But that can't be! That means the particles would gain massive amounts of thermal energy and expand to fill a much larger volume. That would cause an explosion!"

"He's right," O'Brien said. "That's how chemical explosives work—sudden vaporization and expansion."

Rom nodded. "But when something's disintegrated by a disruptor, it just . . . glows and disappears. No *boom,* just *foosh*. So it can't be vaporized."

"Then obviously it's turned into energy," Quark said impatiently.

"Oh, no, brother!" Rom said, taken aback. "With the amount of raw energy contained in matter . . . if it were all released at once, it would be like a photon torpedo exploding! That's why transporters don't really turn matter to energy like people think, just into a particle stream."

"Okay, so it isn't turned into energy." Quark clearly didn't care one way or the other.

"So what *does* happen to the particles?"

"Don't they transition out of the continuum?" Bashir asked, much more politely than Quark. He was a good loser. That was why it was hard for Rom to be smug.

"That's right," the chief said. "With a disruptor or an old-style phaser on disintegrate, at least half the matter undergoes a quantum phase shift. It's effectively gone from our universe."

"But *where does it go then?*"

O'Brien shrugged. "Another dimension . . . some kind of interphase space . . . never really thought about it."

Rom turned it over in his head. "So . . . all those valuables Grilka lost . . . they haven't ceased to exist, just gone to another place."

"No, Rom, they're completely disintegrated. Only, maybe, fifty to ninety percent of their mass would've phase-shifted—the rest would just be ordinary vapor here in our dimension. And even if there were some way to, say, lock a transporter onto that other phase space, the pattern information is completely lost. It's just random atoms. And I assume they'd disperse throughout the phase space as a fine mist—wait more than a few hours, and you'd never be able to widen the beam enough to lock onto more than a few milligrams' worth."

"Bu-ut there is a way to lock onto them. The Reletek sensors, brother! They scan other phase spaces. Maybe we could use them to find . . . what's left of Grilka's property. Some of it, anyway."

"A bunch of atoms?" Quark scoffed.

"Atoms of latinum. Or gold. Or indurite." The acquisitive light began shining in Quark's eyes again, cheering Rom up. "Wouldn't D'Ghor be surprised, brother?" he chuckled. "He thinks he's destroying Grilka's valuables, but we might be able to recoup some of her losses!" But Quark's growing smile had frozen and was now turning into a look of dread. "What is it, brother?"

"D'Ghor . . . he's one of the Reletek's buyers! He already has the transphasic sensors!"

"Wow. Isn't that ironic."

"No, you idiot! Don't you get it? This explains everything! Why D'Ghor is attacking with disruptors, going out of his way to disintegrate Grilka's valuables. He's not just destroying them out of revenge—he's *stealing* them!"

O'Brien leaned forward. "You mean . . . he disintegrates an object, then locks on with the transphasic sensors and beams its atoms back from interphase before they dissipate too much?"

"Right! He . . . what you said." He shook his head. "It's brilliant. He gets to acquire her property, like before, but now he can make it look like he's waging honorable combat. On top of which, all the precious metals are automatically 'melted down,' so to speak, so they're totally untraceable."

"Awful lot of trouble to go to, though," O'Brien said. "Mining transphasic space for lost atoms? It's a clever idea, sure, but incredibly inefficient. It'd never be practical."

"Since when are Klingons practical? They'll do anything to look honorable, even when they're robbing you blind. And it's the only explanation for what D'Ghor's been doing, the way he's singling out Grilka's most valuable objects for disintegration." He grabbed a padd, brought up some figures. "Look here—valuables like paintings and stonework aren't getting hit as much as the precious-metal items. And look at D'Ghor's recent economic activity—an increased trade in *refined metals.* I'm telling you, Chief, it all fits."

Rom was impressed as always with his brother's keen insights.

"So . . . D'Ghor's able to do all this because he's in business with the Reletek."

"Right."

"But you're in business with the Reletek too."

"Well . . . yeah."

O'Brien and Bashir exchanged a look. "Uh-oh," the chief said. "I wouldn't want to be you when Grilka finds out, Quark."

"I don't see the problem," Quark said defensively. "I can't be blamed for how some other client of theirs misuses their technology. Even by Federation law, I'm not doing anything wrong. Grilka will certainly understand that."

"Who are these Reletek?" Grilka shrieked. "Where can I find them? I'll rip their lungs out!"

"All right, that's one option," Quark said in a reasonable tone. So far she hadn't been taking the news as well as he'd hoped. She hadn't even apologized after vilifying D'Ghor for plotting and scheming "like a Ferengi," but Quark had chalked it up to her understandable distress. "Although I'm not sure how feasible it is to do it to an entire species. Besides, we really can't blame the Reletek. All they did was build a perfectly innocuous sensor system that has many legitimate, peaceful applications. And . . . provide D'Ghor with technicians to install and operate the system," he added in a small voice, striving for nonchalance. "But they're just giving the customer what *he* pays them for, so there's really no reason to hold it against them . . . or . . . against anyone else who might have their own, *entirely unrelated* marketing arrangements with the Reletek."

Grilka softened marginally. "Do not worry, Quark. I cannot blame you for doing business with them before you knew of their perfidy. And that is in the past now."

"Right! Absolutely right. Our partnership *began* in the past. Before the circumstances changed. So . . ." Quark sensed the minefield ahead, but had to make sure anyway. "So any contractual relationships carried forward from that period were made in good faith and can be continued without prejudice. Right?"

Grilka frowned. "Quark . . . you *have* severed your ties with them, correct?"

He stared. "Grilka, I don't think you understand. I won the *exclusive* marketing rights to this technology throughout the greater Ferengi trading community. Not only does that bring me a hefty profit, but it's pivotal to my efforts to restore my good standing in the business world."

"How can you prattle on about business and profits when there is honor at stake?" Grilka loomed over him angrily. Quark's instinct was to recoil, but he stood his ground, locking his gaze with hers.

"This *is* about honor. It's about restoring my reputation. Erasing a stain from my good name."

She backed down, respect in her eyes, but then spoke in a calmer tone. "How can you restore your good name by associating with those lowly enough to work with D'Ghor?"

"The one has nothing to do with the other! Grilka, can you honestly tell me that D'Ghor doesn't buy any of his food or armor or weapons from the same manufacturers you do? Come on, everyone in your whole empire wears the same suit of armor! Somebody's got one hell of a monopoly."

"That is a traditional design going back centuries. It is a national symbol, not a private possession. And it does not give D'Ghor an advantage over my House! These Reletek do!"

"I'm not responsible for that."

"But you can make a statement, Quark. Defend my honor by rejecting their tainted money. Surely that will do much for your good name."

"Not by Ferengi standards. There's no valid business logic for doing that. And boycotts are rarely effective, especially if you're doing them by yourself."

"Ferengi standards," Grilka sneered. "Why care about them? What has the 'Ferengi trading community' done for you, except dismiss and ridicule that good name of yours?"

"Exactly," Quark hissed, leaning forward. "That's why I have to prove them wrong."

"By fighting on their battlefield?" she countered, mirroring his motion and coming seductively close. "Why do that when you can claim a high ground of your own choosing? Then you control the battle." She took his head in her hands. "Stand by my side, Quark. Strike a blow for the honor of my House and cleanse your hands of those who stand against it. Your name already rings with honor in my ears, Quark, son of Keldar. Stand with me and we will make that name immortal in the songs of history." Now she was stroking his ears, and he could taste her hot breath. "You are mighty on your own—you need no Reletek or Ferengi to validate your name. Cast them aside. Cast aside everything that stands between us!"

She began to do just that, in a literal and immediate sense. "When you put it that way," Quark gasped, helping her unfasten her national symbols, "how can I refuse?"

However ingenious D'Ghor's latest attack on Grilka's finances might have been, in some respects he apparently preferred to stick with the tried and true. As Quark swaggered down the corridor a couple of nights later, on his way to meet with Grilka and feeling pretty good about himself, a large hand reached out, grabbed him by the collar and slammed him into the bulkhead. When D'Ghor's less-than-aesthetic face thrust itself into his, Quark experienced a strong sense of déjà vu. "Quark!" the burly Klingon growled. "We have . . . *business* to discuss."

"D'Ghor! What a . . . pleasant surprise!" Quark gasped, struggling for air. "What brings you to DS9?"

"You have heard of my partnership with the Reletek. It is why you severed your contract with them, no doubt at Grilka's urging."

"That's the Lady Grilka to you," Quark snapped, surprised at his boldness. It seemed his intensive studies of Klingon custom were taking hold. The thought heartened him—surely Klingon custom contained plenty of insights on how to live through a confrontation like this.

But D'Ghor merely barked a curt laugh at his presumption and moved on. "What you may not have known, Ferengi, is what my end of the deal is. My House is providing . . . *security* for the Reletek. They are a small, timid people . . . they need the help of powerful warriors to . . . *protect* their business interests."

"In other words," Quark shot back, "you've hired yourself out as a thug." D'Ghor's hand around his throat tightened, and some Ferengi instinct reasserted itself. "Which is certainly a valid career choice. I've known many fine thugs myself." *If only a few of them were here now,* he thought.

"Be silent and listen! You have violated your agreement with the Reletek. They are not willing to tolerate that. It sets a bad precedent if others feel they can do the same. So I am here to tell you, Quark: either resume your business with the Reletek . . . or attempt to bargain your way off the Barge of the Dead before it reaches Gre'thor."

"Ahh, don't you think that might be a little excessive?" Quark wheedled. "I mean, it would raise questions, right? Some might even see it as an admission of guilt." Grilka had petitioned the High Council to investigate D'Ghor and punish his House once again; but with only an elaborate hypothesis and no hard evidence that he was engaged in anything other than honorable combat, the Council was unwilling to act. Quark would've been glad to see D'Ghor do something that would reveal his guilt, but not if it involved killing Quark in any way.

But D'Ghor sneered at the threat. "You are aiding a sworn enemy of my House. No one would ask questions if I say I killed you in open combat. I don't actually need to let you fight back— just *say* that I did. As you should know well, 'slayer' of Kozak!" he finished with a laugh.

"*D'Ghor!*" Quark had never been happier to hear that name— since it was uttered in Grilka's voice. D'Ghor let him drop, and he turned to see his Klingon lady standing in the corridor, her disruptor leveled at her enemy's head. "You are careless and stupid, as always. Did you not think my servants would monitor your Reletek freighter when it docked?"

"Do you think I need to hide from the likes of you?" D'Ghor snarled back.

"I would shoot you where you stand, but I will not sully my hands with the blood of such a coward. Though if you would care to come at me honorably now, I will kill you gladly."

"You call *me* a coward," D'Ghor scoffed as Quark ran to Grilka's side (well, her rear side), "when your own consort needs a female to rescue him." He began moving slowly back, his bluster belied by the presence of the two large, armed Klingon bodyguards who now emerged from the corridor behind him. "If you would prove the valor of your House," he went on, "have your Ferengi stand and fight me when I come for him again. No females or politicians to hide behind—just him, me and two *bat'leth*s. We'll see if he can last two seconds."

"You'd be surprised," Grilka said with a proud toss of her head. "We accept your challenge."

"Now, let's not be hasty," Quark advised. "Not that I'm not up to a little friendly combat, of course, but why spill blood needlessly over a simple business dispute?"

"There is far more at stake here than business, Quark," Grilka told him fondly but impatiently. "You wish to defend your good name? Well, D'Ghor has spat on it. You must not stand for that."

"Make your choice, Ferengi," D'Ghor said. "I will come for you tomorrow, and one of us will die. Unless you care to resume your business with our mutual Reletek friends."

"Quark." Grilka cradled his head in one hand, without lowering her disruptor in the other. "You are ready for this. You deserve better than to associate with him and his minions. He is a coward, a bully, and a cheater." She smirked. "You may have been a cheater yourself, but you are an honorable warrior now, with as much valor as cunning. And that means he has no advantage over you. You cannot fail. Quark," she finished in her sultriest tones, "I know you will not fail me."

Quark was getting that ten-times-his-size feeling again. He turned to face D'Ghor, feeling like he was on autopilot, seized by a power greater than himself, a power that could not be defeated. "You tell your Reletek friends that the deal is off for good. And if you have the lobes to face me without those walking mountains to hide behind," he said, gesturing at the bodyguards, "then I'll be waiting in my bar after the close of business tomorrow. BYOB— bring your own *bat'leth.*" As he heard himself speak, he felt terrified yet delighted, like a passenger on a thrill ride. But then, he felt the same way every time Grilka took him. For her, he would do this. And for her, he would not fail.

Odo couldn't believe what he saw when he entered the holosuite: Quark, in full Klingon regalia, locked in combat with a holographic Klingon twice his size and actually appearing to hold his own. When Rom had told him, Odo had assumed the idiot-savant engineer had gotten confused on the details, as he so often did on matters not related to electroplasma systems and anodyne relays. But here was the evidence, plain as day. There was only one explanation. "You've gone mad," the changeling scoffed. Startled, Quark stumbled, and his programmed opponent waited patiently for him to regain his footing. Odo harrumphed at the absurdity of it. "That's the only explanation. After all these years of my relentless scrutiny, you've finally snapped under the pressure."

Quark glared at him for a moment before resuming his sparring. "Don't try to talk me out of this, Odo. This is a matter of honor."

"Oh, please. You may have deluded yourself into thinking you've mastered Klingon ways, but you can't fool me. Even when you're preparing to fight for your life, you still cheat! You think D'Ghor is going to wait politely if you stumble?"

"I wouldn't have stumbled if you hadn't distracted me!"

"If you really had sufficient training for combat, you wouldn't have *been* distracted." As though taking him at his word, Quark chose to ignore him. "Quark . . . just file an assault charge against D'Ghor. I'll arrest him. That will give me time to investigate him further and . . ."

"And how would that make me look to Grilka?" Quark hissed between panting breaths. "Like a coward! Like a . . . a . . ."

"Like a *Ferengi?* Quark, that's what you are! Or have you forgotten? Just last week you were telling me how hard you strove to live up to the Rules of Acquisition. Well, how about Rule Fifteen, 'Dead men close no deals'? Or while we're at it, Number 125, 'You can't make a deal when you're dead'? Apparently it's an important enough principle to mention twice."

"And you just assume that I'm going to lose this fight, is that it?" Quark demanded. "What makes you think D'Ghor is such a tough fighter, huh? A Klingon who'd rather use deceit and dirty tricks to get ahead, who needs bodyguards to protect him? You'll see—he's all bluster. Besides—he's not inspired by love like I am. He doesn't have a prayer."

Odo crossed his arms. "I see. So you intend to kill him? Are you actually willing to commit homicide to impress Grilka?"

"He made the challenge, Odo, so it's self-defense. Anyway," he allowed, "I'll spare him if I can. That will disgrace him worse than death."

Something about this seemed familiar to Odo. He grasped at the possibility. "Wait—is this some kind of scheme, Quark? That's it, isn't it—this is all just an act to impress Grilka, or draw in business for the bar. You've got some last-minute cheat or escape up that armored sleeve."

"You're wrong, Odo," Quark said so simply that Odo knew it to be true. "There's been enough deception already. If I'm to move forward with Grilka, I have to prove myself—for real this time." He paused, along with his obliging opponent, to meet Odo's eyes intently. "She *believes* in me, Odo. I *have* to be worthy of that belief."

Odo shook his head in dismay. "I was right the first time—you *are* mad. Or maybe you're just a fool. Can't you see how she's exploiting your infatuation, seducing you into serving her purposes? How can you believe she truly loves you when she's willing to talk you into killing yourself in her name?"

"You don't know a thing!" Quark cried, channeling his vehemence into a renewed attack on the holo-Klingon. "You're just jealous because the woman *I* love actually knows I exist!"

That did it. Odo strode forward and got right up into Quark's face, ignoring the *bat'leth*s flailing about. "Kira knows I exist!" he shouted. "And she values me for what I am. She respects my opinions, my values, my desire to explore my culture, even when she doesn't share in them."

"Try not to get so close, Odo," Quark advised with sincere concern, stepping around him to continue sparring. "These things can be dangerous." But Odo interposed himself again, determined to be heard.

"Grilka only values you for your pliability—your willingness to let her mold you into something you're not. To abandon everything you believe in if it makes her happy. Think about it, Quark—has she made any effort at all to learn Ferengi culture? Has she treated your values with anything other than contempt?"

"Look who's talking." Quark kept trying to get around him, with little success. "I'm warning you, Odo, step aside before you get sliced in half!" he said, his solicitousness becoming tinged with frustration.

But Odo stayed in his face, singularly unconcerned, and continued to goad the Ferengi. "Some 'man of principle' you turned out to be. True to your own ethical code? Hah! You've tossed it all aside in record time. What happened to the deal, Quark? What happened to the give and take, the pursuit of profit?" His voice grew harder, more contemptuous, eagerly feeding Quark's slow burn. "Tell me, Quark, what is Grilka giving you in exchange for your devotion? What has *she* risked or lost or given up for you? Not her profits. Not her culture. Not her safety. From where I'm standing, it looks like you're giving away your soul for free! At least Rom can make more money. You're an even bigger sucker than he is!"

"All right, you asked for it!" Quark cried. Dropping the *bat'leth,* he lunged at Odo and tried to toss him out of the way with a *mok'bara* throw.

Odo didn't budge.

Quark glared, and tried another throw.

And another. Odo crossed his arms and waited.

Quark tried kicking his legs out from under him, and only knocked himself on his butt. He leapt bodily onto Odo, trying to knock him down, but ended up clinging to his torso and pulling ineffectually at his shoulders and elbows. Even the holographic Klingon seemed to have a touch of pity in his eyes.

Odo morphed his face out the back of his head and said, "Are you finished?" The sight startled Quark into losing his grip. To his credit, he tried to turn the fall into a backward roll, but came down badly on his right ear and banged his knee, and ended up lying on his side, gasping in pain.

Restoring his features to their normal place, Odo moved to stand over Quark, gazing pityingly down on him. "You know what the sad part is? I wasn't even trying that hard to stay in place."

"You're just—saying that to rub it in," Quark gasped.

"Can you be sure of that?" Odo reached down to help him to his feet. "Are you really willing to gamble your life on that?"

"No," Quark admitted, wincing in pain.

"Are you all right?"

"I think you'd better get me to the infirmary." Odo could tell it was a hard admission for Quark. There was much more than physical pain in his eyes. "I've been fooling myself," Quark said as Odo helped him limp toward the exit. "D'Ghor's gonna kill me."

"If you fight him."

"If I don't, Grilka will kill me. Or at least she'll never talk to me again."

"Would that be such a bad thing?"

Quark paused in the doorway, resting his weight against it. "Oh, don't blame her, Odo. She's just being a Klingon. I'm the one who was stupid enough to think I could be one too."

"So do you want to file that assault charge against D'Ghor now?"

Quark pondered. "Hmm, maybe I could blame him for these injuries, demand compensation, huh?"

"Back to your old Ferengi self already, I see," Odo snarled, privately pleased. "But it wouldn't work, since I'd be the investigating officer and I know what really happened."

"And you're annoyingly immune to bribery. Well, it would only delay the inevitable anyhow." Quark sighed. "It wouldn't solve the fundamental problem." Steeling himself, he strode forward again. "No, Odo . . . there's only one way to resolve this now."

Quark was waiting behind the bar, cleaning glasses, when D'Ghor stormed through the entrance. Although the place was closed, empty and dark, Quark greeted him with routine good cheer as the doors slid shut behind him. "Welcome to Quark's! Finest tavern and gaming establishment this side of the wormhole. And what can I get you this fine evening?"

D'Ghor glared suspiciously. "What is this, Ferengi? Do you intend to fight me, or just stand there while I chop your head off? Take a look around—there's no one to save you this time." He narrowed his eyes suspiciously. "Or is there?"

"The bar is closed." Quark shrugged. "No one here but the two of us." Luckily, Morn was off on a cargo run, or that would've been harder to arrange. Quark met D'Ghor's eyes unflinchingly and said, "I swear it on my honor."

"Then you are an honorable fool!"

Still his gaze didn't waver. "There are all kinds of honor, D'Ghor. I simply realized that I make a much better bartender than a warrior. So if I'm going to go, I might as well go out doing what I do best. Better to be remembered as a good Ferengi than a bad Klingon."

"Either way is fine with me!" D'Ghor cried, hefting his *bat'leth*.

"Are you sure?" Quark asked. "Seems to me you're in the same boat."

That gave D'Ghor pause. "What do you mean?"

"You're trying to be a Klingon and a Ferengi at the same time, just like I was. And you're making just as much of a hash out of it."

"You will suffer for that!" But D'Ghor was listening now, curious to know the precise parameters of the insult before he avenged it.

"A true Klingon wouldn't care about profiting from his enemy's defeat. He wouldn't use the pretense of honorable combat to hide the fact that he was stealing. So obviously you're not much of a Klingon."

That was enough for D'Ghor. He lunged, but Quark's defensive reflexes were faster. He ducked under the bar, and by the time D'Ghor leapt over to search for him, he'd scurried out from behind, disappearing into the darkness. "But as a Ferengi," he went on, positioning himself so the room's acoustics would mask his position, "you're a joke. Retrieving disintegrated elements from interphase? You call that cost-effective?" D'Ghor stormed over in his general direction, swinging his *bat'leth* and knocking over tables, the noise handily masking Quark's movement elsewhere. "I mean, the expense of it all . . . the sensors, the operators, the retooling of the transporters . . . and all for a few sprinklings of precious metal. You can barely break even with a scheme like that! You could make much more profit marketing the Reletek sensors for other uses. Really, D'Ghor," Quark laughed from under the dabo table, "as money-making schemes go, this is one of the most idiotic ones I've ever heard of."

"PetaQ!" D'Ghor snarled, smashing some more furniture. "You think this is just about profit?"

"Isn't that what it's always been about?" Quark was already scuttling toward his next hiding spot. "Acquiring Grilka's wealth any way you could?"

But he felt D'Ghor's grip on his collar, and then he was flying through the air to slam against the bar. He scrambled to his knees, cornered, as D'Ghor loomed over him. "Maybe before it was. But she—*and you*—forced me into disgrace! You ruined my good name! This way, I humiliate Grilka by stealing her wealth from before her eyes, with her left none the wiser! The metals I retrieve from out-phase may only just balance the expense, but it is worth it to wreak vengeance upon her, while regaining my reputation as a warrior!"

Yes! Got it! Quark kept talking to distract him for a few seconds more. "So your reputation is a sham by Klingon rules, and your profit-making scheme is a sham by Ferengi rules. You're pathetic, D'Ghor—you don't make the grade by anyone's standards of honor!" *Where is he?* "At least I'm true to my Ferengi principles. So I die a more honorable man than you."

"So long as you *die!*" The *bat'leth* swung, and Quark squeezed his eyes shut, convinced he'd miscalculated at the final moment and hoping the Divine Exchequer would place the blame where it belonged, on Odo. But then he heard a welcome squishing, oozing sound. He opened his eyes to see D'Ghor's sword centimeters from his head, held in place by a golden pseudopod stretching down from the ceiling. A second later, a large mass of goo landed on the Klingon, knocking him to the ground, and swiftly re-formed into Odo.

"What took you so long?" Quark demanded. "You had his confession! Didn't you?"

"Yes, Quark. It's recorded. You can always count on Klingon bluster." He turned one of his contemptuous excuses for a smile on Quark. "I just wanted to see if *you* had any last confessions you might want to make."

"Never." Quark smirked. "Secrets are valuable—I wouldn't help my chances of getting into the Divine Treasury if I gave them away at the last moment."

As Odo pulled the dazed, disarmed D'Ghor to his feet, the Klingon glared daggers at Quark. "You *swore* on your honor that we were alone!"

"What can I say? I told you I was true to my principles." He lifted his head proudly. "I lied."

" . . . So that's the bottom line," Quark said. Facing Grilka was, in its way, even harder than facing D'Ghor had been. This time he didn't have Odo to protect him from the consequences. "The person you've been trying to change me into . . . it's not the person I'm supposed to be. I let myself forget that . . . because I love you." To his surprise and relief, she was listening patiently, absorbing his words, rather than throwing the usual Klingon fit of melodrama. But Quark's fear was that she was just building up slowly to one hell of an eruption. He couldn't tell one way or another from her stony countenance.

"So . . . because I love you . . . I used trickery to win you over. Made it look like I was a fighter, went through all the motions of Klingon romance. And that got me what I wanted . . . at first. But I've had to keep lying to hold onto you, to make the lie bigger, and it got to the point where I was lying to myself." He shook his head slowly. "I'm not a warrior, Grilka. I'm a businessman. I live by a Ferengi code, not a Klingon one.

"And a Ferengi doesn't give something away for nothing. But that's just what I've been doing. This is a one-sided relationship, Grilka—I put my business, my health, my self-respect, my *life* on the line to please you, and all you do is ignore and ridicule everything I believe in. Any way you add it up, I'm taking a huge loss here.

"So if you can't make an effort to respect my culture . . . to accept me for who I am . . . to let me be true to my own kind of honor . . . then it's over." He winced at the sound of it, but refused to falter. "I don't want it to be over, Grilka. I love you. But this is the way it has to be."

She studied him silently for several long moments more. Then she rose and moved slowly toward him. "I admire your conviction, Quark. And what you say is . . . very wise."

He brightened. "Then . . . you can change? Learn to love me as a Ferengi?"

Grilka met his gaze, held it intently, and said . . . "No." Quark sagged. "I am sorry. But only a Klingon heart can beat as one with mine." She looked away. "Perhaps that is my failing, not yours. You deserve someone who can accept and love a Ferengi as an equal. I am not that one."

Quark tried to sort out the feelings that churned through him . . . and settled on the safest one. "Fine," he snapped, striding toward the exit. "It's your loss, sweetheart." He stopped to throw her a smug look. "Well, at least you still have your financial solvency. Oh, wait . . . thanks to me and my filthy Ferengi ways. Isn't that ironic."

He resumed his dramatic exit, but Grilka's voice stopped him in mid-huff. "In fact . . . my finances could stand some improvement after recent events. But a good advisor is hard to find."

A few moments passed. "I know someone who might be persuaded . . . for a reasonable fee."

"Certainly. Such compensation would be only fair."

Quark shared a bittersweet smile with himself. "Give me some time. I'll let you know."

The last thing Quark wanted to see right now was more Klingons. So naturally this was the day the *Rotarran* had returned, and its crew had commandeered Quark's bar to carouse and head-butt and *Qapla'* the hell out of each other in celebration of some glorious victory. It would've given Quark a headache even if it hadn't been a reminder of what he'd just been through. But at least the *Rotarran*'s return meant that Jadzia was back, and she'd taken time out of the Klingonalia to commiserate with him. No matter what, he could always count on the beautiful Trill to lend a sympathetic . . . dainty . . . incredibly sensual ear. But he shook off that line of thought. That way lay madness.

"My mistake was in not paying attention to the Rules," he insisted. "The warnings are all over. 'Females and finances don't mix.' 'Latinum lasts longer than lust.' 'She can touch your lobes but never your latinum.' "

"But," offered Jadzia in return, " 'Beware the man who doesn't make time for *oo-mox*.' Two-twenty-three, right?"

"But that," Quark countered, pointing a finger, "is because that man has his head together. He isn't distracted by lust or . . . or other emotions. He's focused on his business like a laser. And that's what

I need to be. I have to rebuild my reputation as a businessman. I need to get back the momentum I had going there. I was really on a roll, Jadzia! I could feel it all coming together. Because I was focused on *profit*. No distractions, no females to warp my priorities . . . just the bright, beaconlike glow of latinum pointing the way."

"Hmm . . . bright but cold," Jadzia said with one of those sexy— one of those thoughtful pouts of hers. "And lonely. What's the point of accumulating all that wealth if you can't share it with a special lady? Or at least use it to impress the ladies." She smirked, a Curzonian leer peeking through.

"That's Federation thinking."

Jadzia took his hand, her touch sending chills through him like a shot of ice-cold Aldebaran whiskey. "It's your way of thinking, whether you realize it or not. Face it, Quark—you're an incurable romantic. You crave love just as much as latinum."

"Well . . . if it pleases you to think so, go right ahead." He sighed. "But even if that's true . . . why do I keep falling for all these alien females? Cardassians, Klingons . . . strong, independent, assertive," he sneered. "No wonder it always goes badly for *me*. No—from now on, I should stick to nice, pliant Ferengi females, who do what they're told and don't cause trouble."

"Like Rom's ex-wife?" Jadzia challenged. "Or your *mother?*" she added even more pointedly.

"Aa-ah," Quark cautioned. "Rule Thirty-one!"

"I'm not making fun of her. I'm just saying, Ishka was your main female role model growing up. So maybe it's no wonder you like strong, independent, assertive women."

"I do *not* like that kind of female. If Moogie's had any influence at all, it's been to set a bad example that I need to get away from. No. From now on, it's quiet, unassuming, passive females for me."

Jadzia glared at him like a *tongo* player calling his bluff. "You'd be bored out of your mind within a month! Where's the *challenge* in a relationship like that?"

"Challenge?"

"That's right, Quark. That's why you keep going after that type of woman. Because it *isn't* easy. Because what you want isn't just handed to you—you have to work for it, *bargain* for it." She leaned her face close to his, those vivid blue eyes sparkling like the purest sapphires. "It's the thrill of the deal, Quark. That's what you love. Taking a chance. Going up against the odds. Negotiating with a tough, canny competitor for romantic gain. 'The riskier the road, the greater the profit.' " She clasped his shoulder. "You are far too much of a Ferengi to be satisfied with anything less."

Quark had no idea how long he spent gazing into those eyes. But eventually some of the Klingons called out to Jadzia, insisting that she join in their carousing. "Think about it." She smiled at Quark and went over to them.

What a woman, he moaned to himself as he watched her glide gracefully away. *A challenge, hmm? Like, maybe, winning you away from Worf . . . ? Ohh, yes, Jadzia dear. I'll think about it.*

Three Sides to Every Story

Terri Osborne

Historian's note: This story spans the sixth-season episodes "Behind the Lines," "Favor the Bold," and "Sacrifice of Angels."

Terri Osborne

Terri Osborne escaped the wilds of Indiana shortly after college, spending ten years in Boston, Massachusetts, before finding her way to the urban jungle of New York City. Her first story was written at the tender age of six.

While sitting in a convention hall at the age of twenty-three, Terri heard Ronald D. Moore talk about how he'd sold the script for "The Bonding" at that age. In the arrogance of youth, she immediately thought that she could do that. That was 1993.

In 2001, Keith R.A. DeCandido finally managed to convince her that her work didn't actively suck and might be publishable after all.

"Three Sides to Every Story" marks her first professional sale. She can be found on the Web at <http://www.terriosborne.com>.

She owes innumerable words of gratitude to Marco Palmieri for being willing to take the risk on new writers, suggesting things that *always* made the story better, and generally making the experience a good one.

This story is dedicated to the memory of John Haznedl, another talented artist taken too soon.

"Again?"

Jake slumped back onto the sofa with a sigh, filing away his twenty-second rejected article in as many days. No matter how much he tried to bury his writing style or how much he fought his instincts and tried to portray the Dominion objectively, nothing worked. Weyoun never failed to find something in an article that wasn't "balanced" enough for his liking. Jake was beginning to think that, despite the Vorta's insistence to the contrary, nothing short of Dominion propaganda would get his articles for the Federation News Service past Weyoun's watchful eye.

Leaning his head back, he stared at the relentless gray ceiling of his quarters. In the months since the Dominion had taken Deep Space 9—he refused to think of it by its Cardassian name of Terok Nor—he'd felt like a hamster on a wheel, going through the motions and getting nowhere.

Home had never felt so much like a prison.

He'd heard stories from the local Bajorans about what life had been like during the Occupation—the forced labor, the stench of poverty, the wails of starving children lining the Promenade—and wondered if that would happen again. With Dukat in charge, even though he now answered to Weyoun, a return to those conditions was a possibility that couldn't be ruled out. Dukat was still Dukat, and some things were as inevitable as the sun rising over the Dahkur Hills. The Bajorans fighting Cardassian rule was high on that list.

Kira and Odo had both denied it when he'd approached them, but Jake was sure they were putting together a resistance cell. He'd caught wind of it from one of Quark's dabo girls. Besides, Jake had known Kira for five years. She would never willingly work with the Cardassians without trying to get rid of them. Kira Nerys was no collaborator.

There has to be a way to help, something she can't do that I can.

A smile crept across Jake's features as an idea hit. "Nothing like killing two birds with one stone," he said, pulling his eyes away from the depressing blandness of the ceiling. It would work. It *had* to work.

He needed some way to get his stories out there, in the faint hope that they might somehow make it to the FNS. He'd overheard Kira say something to Odo about trying to find a way to communicate with their contacts on Bajor, but without going through the usual subspace channels. Combining the two objectives was simple.

He didn't have any idea how it was going to work, but that was a bridge they could burn when they got to it.

Everything would depend on Kira going for the idea. *Where would she be at this hour? Probably Quark's. She's been spending more time there lately. Can't say as I blame her, with all of the Cardassians in ops these days.*

Grabbing a padd, he headed for the door.

"Solve Kira's problem, and she might let you in," Jake muttered as he walked through the hustle and bustle of the Promenade. While the place was still as busy as it had ever been under his father's command, Jake couldn't remember feeling so alone. He was surrounded by a sea of Cardassian gray, broken only by one of the preternaturally pale Vorta or the scaly features of a Jem'Hadar. The few Bajorans he could see looked as though they wanted nothing more than to fade into the proverbial woodwork.

The difference in the sights he could handle. Life as a Starfleet brat had long since accustomed him to that. What bothered him the most was that even the smells were different. The Klingon restaurant had closed shortly after the first Dominion troops began heading toward Cardassia, and Jake found he missed the harsh smells of fresh *gagh* and *rokeg* blood pie that had been a part of the place for as long as he could remember. Sometimes, walking by Chef Kaga's establishment reminded him of the days the crawfish were delivered to his grandfather's restaurant.

Where the Klingon cuisine was distinctive in smell, Jake found Cardassian food to be something purely nauseating to anyone with a respect for food. He wasn't sure of the source, but the aroma of Cardassian *tojal* wafting his way smelled more like something from the garbage heap behind Sisko's Creole Kitchen than from the menu of a legitimate eatery.

The vendors who'd been there for as long as Jake could remember were having a difficult time with the transition. His old friend who ran the *jumja* kiosk smiled as Jake passed, but turned a hollow expression to an inquisitive Vorta inspecting his wares.

Quark, however, had done nothing but adjust the settings on his replicators. It was still the same business, just with a different clientele. Jake took a small amount of comfort in the idea that some things never changed.

He noticed one other thing missing as he walked toward Quark's bar—the noise. He'd spent the last few years growing accustomed to the endless chatter and intermittent screams of "Dabo!" Cardassians, however, weren't as demonstrative as Bajorans or humans when they won. More often than not, they simply pumped a fist in the air and placed their next bet. Between that and the ever-present, distressingly silent Jem'Hadar—who Jake figured visited the bar only because Weyoun had ordered them to mingle—the volume in Quark's had decreased by several dozen decibels since the Dominion's arrival.

Jake searched the bar for Kira, but found it filled with off-duty Cardassians and Jem'Hadar soldiers. He was about to head back to his quarters to begin putting his idea into writing when he caught sight of someone sitting at a table on the second level. *Is that who I think it is?*

It looked like a Cardassian female, but there was something very different about her. Her features had a soft innocence to them, attractive, but still childlike. There was a pinkish cast to her skin that Jake had never seen on a woman with neck ridges. Her black hair—he couldn't tell how long it was from that angle—sat pulled up into an attractive arrangement on the back of her head. Her dress seemed typical of the few Cardassian women he'd known, tastefully fitted, but with a touch of Bajoran simplicity to the design. No, it was the color that set her apart. Jake couldn't remember seeing a Cardassian woman wearing burgundy before.

Curious, he walked into Quark's and up to the second level, ignoring the understaffed barkeep's latest attempt to get him to wait tables. Scanning the level, he found a vacant table from which he could observe this woman. If this really was Dukat's daughter, it made things more interesting. Every source he had said that Kira had sent Tora Ziyal to Bajor to keep her safe during the Dominion occupation. What was she doing back?

One of the overworked Ferengi waiters brought him a root beer, which Jake gratefully accepted. Quark had tried to get rid of all the Earth foods after Starfleet relinquished control. But, never one to miss an opportunity, Jake's continued presence on the station made him keep a small supply on hand. His waiters evidently had standing orders to bring Jake root beer whenever he entered the bar.

As Jake had no intention of developing a taste for *kanar,* it was a small favor that he appreciated.

He pulled up his most recent article on the padd's display in an attempt to cover the fact that he wasn't working. A clattering brought his attention to the floor, where a charcoal stylus had fallen and rolled toward his chair. Jake quickly reached for it.

"You dropped this," he said, backing it with the most winning smile he could manage as he handed the stylus to its owner.

"Thank you," the woman replied with a polite smile of her own.

At this distance, Jake could see the faint ridges at the bridge of her nose. "Excuse me, but aren't you—?"

"Tora Ziyal," she said, smiling. "You're the Emissary's son."

"Jake Sisko," he replied. "I thought you'd gone to Bajor?"

Ziyal gestured for him to sit down. When he had relocated to her table, she quietly explained. "I did, but it didn't work out. This is the only place that I feel at home."

Jake almost laughed. "I know the feeling."

"Really?" With a slight cant of her head, she asked, "Don't you have family on Earth?"

For a moment, Jake thought better of revealing any personal information, even if it was otherwise easy to obtain. There was something a little too disarming about her, something that made him feel comfortable almost immediately. That, in itself, was dangerous. If Ziyal reported any of it back to her father, he might never see his family again. Did he dare give Dukat that kind of leverage? His gaze wandered to three Jem'Hadar soldiers on the lower level, their overbuilt sidearms holstered, surveying the bar in a manner that suggested they were ready to draw their weapons at the slightest provocation.

They could kill me whenever they wanted and Dad would never know.

Why worry about giving Dukat more leverage when he had all he needed sitting comfortably in the barrel of a Jem'Hadar pistol?

I've got to trust somebody. The others will barely even give me an interview, let alone talk.

"My grandfather and my aunt," he finally replied.

Ziyal stared down at the sketchpad on the table, a wistful look in her eyes. "You're very fortunate. All I have is my father."

Setting aside the urge to ask her about Major Kira, Jake followed Ziyal's gaze to the piece. It was a deceptively simple rendering of what looked like a pool of water in a forest, a bird dipping its beak for a drink. It reminded him of some ancient Japanese art that Mrs. O'Brien had shown them in school, full of subtle detail. He could almost feel the energy flowing through the strokes, few as they were. The design had the effect of a tidal current, moving him through the work like a leaf on a gentle breeze. "That's beautiful."

"Thank you." Jake swore he could almost see a blush in her cheeks. "I'm thinking of calling it 'The Seat of Power.' I tried to imagine what the station might be like if it were a place on Bajor, with all of the ebb and flow of the universe coming through it. It's a place of great importance, and great energy. My father has already said he wants to display it in his office when it's done." Her lips pursed as she stared down at the unfinished piece. "It's not quite what I envisioned, but it'll do."

It'll do? I've never seen anything like this! This needs to be someplace where everyone can see it, not just Dukat. Is that bird supposed to be her father? I heard she had a blind spot for him, but if she thinks he's half as innocent as she's drawing him, she needs to take another look.

Six months ago, someone so blatantly naïve living in a war zone might have worried him. However, after being accused of such naïveté for something as simple as expecting freedom of the press from the Dominion, Jake was no longer sure that was such a bad thing.

"It's—it's beautiful," he repeated.

Ziyal took a deep breath. "I want to see if I can do more pieces like the ones the Cardassian Institute of Art wants to exhibit."

Jake's eyes widened. He may not have been a painter, but he knew what recognition like that meant to an artist. "That's wonderful! Congratulations."

"Thank you," she replied politely. If he hadn't been watching, he would have missed the brief flash of discomfort that crossed her features. "I heard that you're a writer?"

Jake shrugged, trying to cover his curiosity. "Sort of. I mean, it's hard to be a writer when nobody but Weyoun is reading your stories."

"But, you still write, don't you? How can you continue to put the words together and not consider yourself a writer?"

She's got a point. I was writing long before the FNS job came through.

Now I'm just a writer with no readers. When Dad gets back, that'll change. Dad won't stop until he takes the station back, I know he won't.

"My father is having a dinner party tonight," Ziyal said. "He invited a few of the Bajoran shop owners to help everyone get used to working together. Will you come?"

Jake felt his cheeks warm. The idea certainly was appealing. There was something genuine about Ziyal, something he would never have expected from Dukat's daughter. Something beyond his journalistic curiosity was piqued.

The idea of being there for part of the peace process interested him, and might even be an article that would get past Weyoun, if he spun it just right.

However, Jake couldn't shake the feeling that showing up at one of Dukat's parties, even if he *had* been invited, might be overstepping his bounds. They'd think that he was only there as a reporter, which wouldn't be wrong, but his stomach churned at the thought of how any display of friendliness toward Ziyal might be taken.

"I'd like to, but I'm not sure your father would like that," Jake replied. "I'm not exactly one of his favorite people around here."

"You will be welcome if you should change your mind," she said.

He leaned back in his chair. Every instinct he had said that there was a major news story waiting to happen in Tora Ziyal. His grandfather once said that you could tell people who were going to make a difference in the world. He hadn't appreciated that until now.

What Jake couldn't tell was whether the difference was going to be with her art, or with her personality. He couldn't see how it would be possible to dislike Ziyal. If they did, she'd probably manage to change that with just a few words.

Fodder for an article, artist for his books, whatever else she might have been, Tora Ziyal was someone that Jake knew he could just sit and talk with.

They chatted about anything and everything that crossed their minds for the next two hours, from the way her mother would sing her to sleep when she was a toddler to his grandfather's method for peeling eggplant. Once he explained to Ziyal what an eggplant was, he was even able to get Quark's replicators to manage some passable aubergine stew. The fact that Jake couldn't remember every measurement of the recipe made the sampling of the end product more of an adventure.

She liked the taste of the Terran dish, and they made a pact that every time they met in Quark's, they would try to sample a delicacy from the other's culture. The Bajoran food he could live with, but after some of the smells around the Cardassian eateries, Jake was sure that Ziyal had gotten the better part of that deal.

No subject seemed to be off limits for either of them. Before he realized it, they were talking about things he'd never even told his father. The story of her mother's death in the *Ravinok*'s crash hit Jake particularly hard, forcing him to share the story of his own mother's death on the *U.S.S. Saratoga* at Wolf 359.

"I heard a little about the Borg when my father took me back to Cardassia," she said. "That your ship took them on and there weren't any survivors at all. . . ."

That was when the alarm on Jake's padd went off.

"What's that?" Ziyal asked.

Jake sighed. "It's when I was thinking of going to bed." A yawn pulled at his lips, but he managed to fight it off. It was so comforting talking to Ziyal, almost like the long conversations he and Nog used to have. He hadn't realized how much he missed having Nog around.

"Maybe you should listen to it," she said, a gentle chiding in her voice. "We both have a lot of work ahead of us."

Looking down at his padd, he realized that she was right. Somewhere along the line, he'd begun making notes about little things Ziyal was doing, the way she would stare intently whenever she was listening to someone, how she would glow with pride whenever the subject of her father came up, details that he hadn't even realized he was noticing.

"I'll talk to you again sometime?" he asked.

Ziyal smiled. "Of course."

As Jake headed back toward his quarters, he found himself looking forward to 'sometime' more than he had since the Dominion's arrival.

Tora Ziyal watched Jake leave the bar with a mixture of trepidation and happy anticipation.

The misgivings were becoming an unfortunate part of everyday existence. Life as the daughter of Gul Dukat hadn't proven to be the grand experience that she'd imagined when they'd left Dozaria. Ziyal had witnessed her father's fall from grace firsthand, and it hadn't been pretty. Her own people—at least, that was what she'd wanted to consider them—had wanted her dead for the simple crime of being half-Bajoran. She'd never told her father about the night that an anonymous figure in a Central Command uniform cornered her as she was coming home from the market, threatening both herself and her father if they didn't leave the planet. Dukat had been troubled enough just trying to keep his wife from carrying off Ziyal's half-siblings.

Tora Naprem, Ziyal's Bajoran mother, had always said that the Cardassians valued family above all else. Memories of the love that had rained upon Ziyal's head before they first left Terok Nor never failed to remind her of the promise of that statement, but the level of hatred she'd experienced from her own stepmother on Cardassia made that love pale in comparison.

Ultimately, it had all fallen down around them, their home, her father's power base, any stature they had possessed, all of it gone in a heartbeat thanks to the racism of a people she wasn't sure she wanted to belong to anymore.

She knew her father wanted nothing but the best for all Cardassians, no matter what they may have thought of him. Dukat was doing the best he could, and his deal to bring the tattered remains of the Cardassian Union into the Dominion was just another step in that direction.

She'd grown accustomed to feeling trepidation. But the happy anticipation? That was something new.

She'd met the Emissary only on a couple of occasions before Starfleet had been forced to abandon the station, but she got the impression that the father was not that much different from the son. Her own father seemed to believe that Sisko would eventually bow to Dukat's inherent superiority, but Ziyal didn't share that belief.

Unlike her father, Ziyal also knew Benjamin Sisko as the Emissary of the Prophets, a man of holy writ. She felt a sort of kinship with him, a comfort in the thought that, like her, Sisko was someone caught between two cultures. They were both living bridges between worlds. She aspired to the kind of success that Sisko had found in his role as Emissary. If her art could bring that about, then so be it. It was a mantle that she would gratefully accept.

She hadn't expected to like Jake Sisko, but she found him just as intriguing as his father. The young man must have been groomed for Starfleet, so for him not to follow in his father's footsteps had to have been a difficult decision. He had a creative spirit, but he needed encouragement. Why was Weyoun the only person reading his stories? Maybe if she gave him the audience he so desperately needed, it might be enough to keep him going. She knew the path that Jake strode far better than she'd ever care to admit. She'd thought herself comfortable with the idea of her art only being for her own benefit for the longest time, until Vedek Nane had encouraged her to follow her talents.

Perhaps she could offer Jake the same encouragement.

As she watched him leave the bar, she saw a Cardassian soldier standing in the entryway, also watching Jake. She wasn't sure who he was, until he turned back toward the bar.

Her stomach sank at the sight of a familiar sneer on Damar's face.

Kira turned the chair in Rom's quarters around, sitting with her arms folded atop the back. "A newsfeed?" She appeared to consider the idea for far longer than Jake had anticipated. "Jake, are you sure about this?"

"Yeah," he said, pausing in his pacing of the room. "We could get stories out to the station's general population about what's going on. We might even be able to get the information to Bajor. If we can get it to Bajor, I just might be able to get someone to send it to the Federation News Service. Didn't the resistance use something like that during the Occupation?"

Kira nodded. "Dukat used to have an entire team of soldiers scouring every Bajoran publication for secret messages to the resistance. I think it became an obsession of his after a while."

"The only thing bothering me is, how do we get it out there without Dukat finding out it's me?"

One red eyebrow raised. "Good question. If it's going to come from within the station, he may think it's you anyway."

Jake didn't like the sound of that. "Rom, can we play around with it in the comm system? Scramble its origin?"

The Ferengi seemed momentarily perplexed by the question. "Um, if I had the current access codes, put in something that will bounce it through the system a bunch of places, we can have every transmission come from a different origin. Maybe if we run it through a triphasic subspace oscillation router, or couple it to a code scrambler."

"So, you think this will work?" Jake asked.

Rom nodded. "The only problem is putting the router into the system. Ooh! There may be something my brother has that can help."

"Do I want to know about this?" Kira asked. Seeming to think better of the idea, she said, "No. No, I don't. Not yet. Rom, do whatever you need to do to get this going. And if you can find a way to mask the signal and get it through the subspace transmitters to Bajor, do it."

The Ferengi nodded.

A thin smile spread across Kira's features. "I'll bet Dukat will bury his nose in it just like he did during the Occupation. So let's lead him on. Don't put anything substantial in it, Jake. No matter how we end up getting it out there or how much we try to hide its existence, Dukat will find out about it. He always does. If there's nothing to the stories, he'll drive himself to a frenzy just trying to find messages that aren't there."

Jake rolled the idea around in his mind for a bit. It wasn't what he'd hoped for, but it was a way to help the cause. He didn't care much for the idea of tying his hands in such a manner, but he could use it as an exercise in creative writing. Trying to keep any kind of meaningful information out of the articles would take more creativity than he'd attempted since his admissions tests for Pennington.

Dukat on a wild-goose chase might be exactly what we need. He'll probably know it's me, but anything that makes his job more difficult is good for the resistance.

Jake took a deep breath, not sure if he wanted to broach the next subject. Finally deciding that he didn't have much to lose, he asked, "Maybe if I worked on an article about Ziyal for the FNS, Dukat wouldn't think I had time for the newsfeed?"

Kira flinched, but recovered quickly.

"I thought maybe if somebody told Ziyal's story, how she wants to be a bridge between the Bajorans and the Cardassians, it might help heal a few old wounds. She definitely is news. The fact that the Cardassian Institute of Art wants to exhibit her work needs to be mentioned. She's got to be the first person of Bajoran ancestry to have their work shown like this."

Kira leaned forward in the chair. "They did steal a lot of Bajoran art during the Occupation, but I think you may be right."

Before he could devote another word to the subject, Dukat's voice came over the comm. *"Major Kira, please meet me in my office."*

Jake gave her an inquisitive look. She just shrugged. "What is it, Dukat?" Kira said, an edge of accusation in her voice.

"The Cardassian freighters carrying those industrial replicators for

Bajor will arrive in the morning. I would like to discuss the transition arrangements with you in person, Major."

Sighing, Kira pulled herself out of the chair. "On my way."

As she strode through the door, Jake realized what was wrong. Something had come between Ziyal and Kira, something that was making the major uneasy. It took about a half-second for Jake to deduce that the something in question was Gul Dukat.

Ziyal instructed the lift to go to her level of the habitat ring, heading for home. Perhaps if she had a good night's sleep, she'd be able to figure out how to handle the problem with Damar.

He had to have been keeping an eye on Jake. The predatory look he'd shown the other night when Jake left Quark's was just like the one that glinn had given her that night. The fact that Damar tended to fawn like a sycophant over her father wasn't far from her mind. The idea that he might do something to Jake to gain Dukat's favor was unsettling.

As the lift doors opened, she thought she heard a very familiar voice.

"What is it, Damar?" her father asked in a hushed tone.

"It's Sisko's son, sir."

"Keep your voice down." Her father's voice grew softer, but the design of the corridors was acoustically generous. "Why worry about him? There's nothing Jake Sisko can do that we won't know about."

The mention of Jake's name from her father's lips in such a conspiratorial tone perked Ziyal's ears. The recessed entry to the lift allowed her to step off just far enough for the doors to close, but not so far as to be visible to anyone down the corridor. She just hoped the lift didn't decide to drop off another passenger anytime soon.

"I think he represents a danger. The Bajorans trust him. He has some sway with them. I've been watching his actions, sir, and I'm concerned. He's close to many known former resistance members. And . . . your daughter has been fraternizing with him."

Her father softly laughed.

"Sir," Damar said, "respectfully, Ziyal could be exposed to even more Bajoran propaganda if she associates with Jake Sisko. It could turn her sympathies toward the Bajorans."

"She spent months on Bajor. If she were going to be affected by any Bajoran propaganda, the damage would certainly already be done, wouldn't it?"

The sarcastic tone with which her father had said "Bajoran propaganda" gave Ziyal a sick feeling. Her history instructor at the university had been in the Ornathia resistance cell, and had told her some stories about things her father was supposed to have done, things Ziyal had never heard of before that time. She'd heard that her mother wasn't the only Bajoran woman in whose arms he'd found solace. She'd also heard of the many things he'd done to both the Bajorans and his own people, even so far as to taking the son of fellow Cardassian Kotran Pa'Dar and putting him into an orphanage. Ziyal wasn't sure what to believe, but the tone in her father's voice made her worry that at least some of it might have been true. Would it matter if it was?

"Yes," Damar replied. "It would."

Her father's voice turned cold. "I don't care for your tone, Damar. Nor do I understand this sudden fixation with Jake Sisko."

She heard someone, presumably Damar, pacing. "I don't trust him, sir. If there is an organized resistance on the station, he'll be involved with it."

Ziyal's heart jumped into her throat at that. A resistance? On the station? They couldn't be that desperate, could they? She could remember some of the horrors that the resistance had brought upon themselves during the Occupation. The tragedy at Gallitep was still something she didn't fully understand.

The idea of Jake Sisko involved with another Bajoran resistance movement gave her a bad feeling in the pit of her stomach. Her childhood hadn't been full of friends, but of the few who had been able to see past her ridges, she'd lost too many over the years. The last thing she wanted was to add Jake to that list.

"Don't let Jake Sisko worry you, Damar," her father said in an icy voice. "I have him right where I want him, firmly under my control. If he does anything to offend my hospitality, I have no problem reminding him of his status."

Ziyal had to fight to control her breathing. She had never heard such a ruthless tone in her father's voice before. Was there really something to what Kira had been telling her? What right did she have to believe Kira over her own father? Why would Dukat lie to her?

He was her father, and she knew he would tell her the truth. That was what good fathers did. And one thing she believed with all her heart was that Skrain Dukat was a good father.

"Come with me."

Jake looked up from his padd to find Glinn Damar staring bullets at him. "Why?"

Damar smiled thinly, a gesture that Jake realized only made the Cardassian look more reptilian. "Gul Dukat wants to speak to you."

Certain that he was making a mistake, Jake rose from his seat and followed Damar out of the Replimat. "What does he want to talk to me about?"

"I was ordered to find you, not answer questions."

Jake's pulse began to race. There were only four people on the station he could think of who could get away with ordering Damar around: Odo, the "female" Founder, Weyoun, and Dukat. He couldn't think of anything he'd done in the past twenty-six hours that would have irritated any of them.

He tried to come up with a good way out of the situation. Striking out, he opted to follow Damar down the Promenade to the turbolift.

They rode in more awkward silence for several seconds before rising into the familiar surroundings of ops. The only thing unfamiliar about it was the sea of gray Cardassian uniforms where there should have been Starfleet and Bajoran Militia manned stations.

"Move, human," Damar ordered.

Human? Until that point, he hadn't seriously considered that Damar might injure him. Threaten, intimidate, and make his life miserable weren't out of the question, but would Dukat actually allow Damar to hurt him?

Jake took a few steps forward, down into the central pit of ops. It was a quick walk, navigating between the various members of the duty shift, then up the steps that led to the door of what was once his father's office. Fear hit Jake square in the chest as the doors slid aside and Damar pushed him over the threshold—

Into an empty office.

"Where is he?" Jake asked.

"Not here," Damar replied. As the doors closed behind him, the Cardassian walked over to the edge of Dukat's desk.

"Then why—?"

"You will not speak to Tora Ziyal anymore."

Jake stared at Damar, mystified.

He didn't get a chance to reply, as the doors slid aside again, this time for Weyoun.

"Mr. Sisko," the Vorta said cheerfully. "So good to see you again."

Jake wasn't sure which to fear more, the thinly veiled disgust in Damar's expression, or the obsequious look on Weyoun's face. His eyes darted between the two men for a long moment before he said, "What am I doing here?"

The Vorta arched an eyebrow. "An interesting question. Perhaps you'd enlighten us, Damar?"

The Cardassian's upper lip curled into a sneer. "Sisko's son has been talking with Gul Dukat's daughter. It will stop. He remains on this station at Gul Dukat's sufferance. If he wants to continue living here, he'll do as he's told."

Before Jake could even formulate a response, Weyoun's voice turned cold. "Mr. Sisko is living here at *my* sufferance, not Dukat's. And he will continue to live here, unharmed, for as long as he likes."

"This human is a threat to the Dominion's control over Terok

Nor," Damar shot back, rising to his full height in an obvious attempt to intimidate the Vorta.

Weyoun, however, was not cowed. "Whose threat assessment is that, Damar? Yours?"

"Yes," Damar replied, not backing down. "If he's allowed to continue fraternizing with Tora Ziyal, it will be detrimental to the Dominion's relationship with the Bajorans."

The look of complete disbelief on Weyoun's face, under any other circumstances, would have gotten a laugh out of Jake. "This young man poses no threat to anyone. He is merely a reporter trying to write an article that I will allow him to send to his superiors. He has my permission to interview anyone willing to speak to him. You will not harm a hair on Jake Sisko's head. Doing so would put relations between the Dominion and Bajor at risk. Do I make myself clear?"

Mystified by Weyoun's sudden support, Jake could do nothing but stare as the Vorta turned toward him, his arms wide. "Mr. Sisko. Please accept the sincerest apologies of the Dominion for this unfortunate incident."

"I-I was planning to do an article on Ziyal, something to commemorate her exhibit," Jake said, trying to find his voice.

Weyoun smiled his most placating smile. "Of course, what a wonderful idea. I look forward to reading it when you're through."

The Vorta took a step to his left, just far enough to trigger the automatic doors. "Now, if you will excuse us, I have a few things to discuss with Damar."

Jake shot out of the office like an animal fleeing two hunters. Once he was across ops and safely ensconced in the turbolift's cab, he ventured a gaze up to the clear office doors. Weyoun and Damar were in what appeared to be a heated discussion.

As the lift took him away from ops, Jake hoped they weren't arguing about him.

Jake took a long sip from his root beer. He still wasn't sure how to take the grief he'd gotten from Damar, but he knew he had to keep talking to Ziyal. If he was going to do an article about her, he'd have to interview her at some point, whether Damar liked it or not. *Besides, I think I'm beginning to like her.*

"Jake!"

A flash of panic was quickly replaced by relief as he recognized the voice. He stopped drawing stick figures in his catsup with a French fry just long enough to catch sight of her walking up to where he sat on the bar's second level.

"Ziyal. Hi."

She gave his plate a puzzled look. "What's that?"

"Cheeseburger and fries. Wish I could say it was a good cheese-burger." Gesturing with the fry that was still in his hand, he asked, "Wanna try a fry?"

Shaking her head, she pointed toward his drink. "Although, that certainly smells interesting.".

Smelled interesting? Root beer? He'd never thought of it that way before. "It's called root beer." Grabbing the unused straw that the waiter had brought him, Jake stuck it into the mug. "Have a sip."

She gave the mug an odd stare before taking a quick sip from the straw. He hadn't noticed her being tense before, but her shoulders visibly relaxed as she considered the taste. "It tastes interesting, too."

Jake gestured toward the waiter, requesting another mug.

"Jake." Ziyal's voice turned conspiratorial as she leaned toward him. "I heard what happened with Damar."

"You did?" he asked, not sure whether he should be happy or worried by the revelation. "How? All of it?"

Ziyal nodded.

"Damar doesn't approve of us talking."

"I'm well past the age of being able to make my own decisions," she replied. "Who I choose for my friends is my decision to make, not my father's, and certainly not Damar's."

If any of the women he'd met on the station since moving there had been more like Ziyal, Jake briefly wondered if his life wouldn't be very different right now.

"I think I've got Weyoun's blessing, so Damar can't do anything. I hope."

"You've got Weyoun's blessing for what?"

Jake took a long sip of his drink before he pitched the idea. "I'd like to do an article for the Federation News Service about your work. It's a great step forward for interspecies relations, and it'll help you get your message across to more than the people on Bajor and Cardassia." Raising his eyes to hers, he added, "I really want to do this article, but I promise I won't do it without your permission."

For a very long moment, she seemed to consider the idea. Finally, she replied, "What about my drawings? You'll need to put a couple of them with the article."

All right! "Yes. Whatever you want to put in."

"I don't know," Ziyal said, her lips curling. "The Institute asked me do a holovid for them, introduce myself, talk about my work." She wrung her fingers. "It's easy to tell you about what I do, I guess. It just seems so inconsequential in the face of everything going on out there. Bajorans hate me because I'm half-Cardassian. Cardassians hate me because I'm half-Bajoran. There are times when I think one person can't do anything to change that."

Jake reached out and put a hand over hers. "Look, you're exactly what people need to see right now. Someone who's going on with her life, even here. Everyone needs to have something to live for. When there's a war that could take that life away any second, having something like that matters even more. We're going to get through this, Ziyal. We have to think about what we're going to do when it's all over. I want to go back to being a writer, and you want to be an artist. Right?"

A wistful smile worked its way onto her features. "Yes."

"Then we need to think long-term. You're the daughter of a public figure, and you're starting to get famous for your drawings.

If people see you doing what they should be doing, you might be able to get more than your message across."

Jake wasn't quite sure where the speech had come from, but he watched her expression for any signs that it might be working. Her smile turned into a beleaguered stare, then a slow nod.

"You're right."

Jake's face split into a grin. "Really?"

Ziyal nodded. "I'd be honored to have you do an article about me."

The sound of her father's fist coming down on his companel woke Ziyal out of a deep sleep. Even with the solid thickness of her bedroom door between them, Dukat had let out enough energy in that one movement to wake the dead.

"Damar, come to my quarters now!" he yelled. "Why can't I delete this thing? Who did this?"

Crawling out of bed, she padded to the door that separated her quarters from her father's. As it slid open, she noted with disconcertion the disheveled state of her father's usually slicked-back hair. "Father?"

He pushed back a strand of hair that had fallen in front of his right eye as he turned toward her. "Ziyal," he said, his voice turning silky smooth and calm with a speed that frightened her. "I didn't wake you, did I?"

"What's wrong now?"

Dukat's eyes flicked toward the viewscreen. "Nothing, my dear. Nothing at all."

Her curiosity piqued, she cautiously stepped toward his desk. "If it's nothing, then why are you angry? Did something go wrong at your meeting?"

Dukat didn't reply at once, absently picking up a bit of silver metal from his desk. Her heart ached as she realized it was her mother's earring.

She knew he had recovered the earring along with a pledge bracelet from Tora Naprem's gravesite on Dozaria two years ago.

Nerys said that he'd gone looking for confirmation of her and Ziyal's fate, only to find that Naprem had died in the crash of the Cardassian freighter *Ravinok,* while young Ziyal had been consigned to a life of toil under the Breen. Together with Nerys, he had liberated her from that horrible existence, taken her back into his life.

Ever since that day, Dukat had kept both mementos of her mother, and Ziyal sometimes caught him fingering the earring when he seemed troubled, although only in the privacy of their quarters. But he never took out her pledge bracelet, seeming content to let it gather dust among his stored personal effects. This had always puzzled Ziyal, since the pledge bracelet was much more symbolic of the bond he and her mother had shared.

Dukat continued fingering the earring as he looked up at his daughter, smiling thinly. "I'm not angry," he said.

Ziyal's shoulders slumped. Dealing with her father could be so frustrating at times. "I am not some small child that you have to coddle and protect from the world. It's obvious that something has made you angry. What?"

Dukat stared at the viewscreen beside him. "Someone has found a way around the station's communication system. They're sending out files that haven't been approved for distribution. It's nothing for you to be concerned about, my dear. Now go back to bed and let me take care of this."

Before she could pursue the subject any further, the doorchime rang. "Enter," Dukat said, his fist closing around her mother's earring.

"Reporting as ordered, sir," Damar said as the door slid aside.

Her father gestured at the viewscreen. "Do you have any idea what this is?"

"No," Damar replied, "but I already have people working on it. Someone got the signal through the subspace transmitters."

"They got this to Bajor?"

Damar opened his mouth to reply, but stopped when Weyoun strode through the doorway, padd in hand. A confusion that she'd never seen in the Vorta was etched across his features. "Well, this is interesting."

"I already have a list of suspects, Weyoun," Dukat replied. "I will make an example of whoever perpetrated this."

"Suspects, Dukat? Is this a criminal act? The Bajorans are merely setting up a method of communicating information. These articles are harmless. Springball championships. Who could possibly care about that?"

With an exasperated sigh, Dukat replied, "I am on top of the situation, Weyoun, and I assure you, these articles are not as harmless as they appear."

Weyoun glanced down at the padd. "Really? Well, I suppose the followers of the Dahkur Hills players might find the article harmful, as they were not the victors."

Ziyal recognized the look her father gave the Vorta. It was one he usually reserved for the astoundingly inept officers. "It's not what the articles are about, Weyoun, it's what's hidden in them." Dukat punched a few buttons on his desk, engaging what appeared to be a data analyzer. "When Cardassia first annexed Bajor, the resistance used to conceal coded messages in the text of Bajoran publications to spread messages to other cells. Why start up another news service if they didn't intend to use it for the same purpose? We have a resistance cell on board."

"Do you have anything to base that suspicion on other than this harmless document?" Weyoun asked, his voice arch.

"Not yet."

Ziyal didn't like her father's tone at all. "What do you mean, Father?"

"It means," he said, his voice hard as a rock, "that it's nothing for you to worry about. You should get back to sleep."

Dukat stood and put one hand on her shoulder, his grip tight. She felt him urging her back toward her quarters. Something was wrong, of that much she was sure, but Ziyal did as she was told, walking back into her room and crawling under the covers.

Going back to bed was easy. Sleep, however, was another story.

No sooner had the lock clicked into place than she threw off the covers and made her way back to the door. Kneeling, she managed to hear her father cursing at something.

"Dukat, it's a harmless publication. You're seeing things that aren't there."

Ziyal raised an eyebrow at Weyoun's tone. It was the same mollifying tone Dukat often used on her.

"That's the *idea,* Weyoun. I tell you, it's not harmless. Maybe I'll have a little talk with Major Kira. If there's a resistance cell on this station, she'll know. Damar, find her."

"Yes, sir." The distant sound of a door opening and closing followed him.

Ziyal reluctantly agreed with her father. It felt like ages since she'd last spoken with Kira, but if Ziyal were looking for some sort of underground on the station, Nerys's connection to the old resistance movement would be a good place to start.

What she could disagree with, however, was the salacious edge to his voice when Dukat mentioned speaking to Kira.

"No, Dukat. The Dominion intends to maintain good relations with the Bajorans. Interrogating Major Kira would put that at risk. If you intend to prove the existence of an organized resistance here, it will be without the unprovoked interrogation of Bajorans. Do I make myself clear?"

Ziyal didn't like the kind of things her father was saying, or that he felt comfortable with the idea of interrogating Nerys like that. As far as Ziyal knew, the worst thing Kira had done to Dukat was spurn his advances. The anger she felt from her father reminded her a little too much of the hard, oppressive edge her anonymous attacker had shown in that Cardassian alley. Was her father capable of the same brutality?

"Yes," Dukat snarled in reply.

Ziyal's knees were beginning to ache from the kneeling. Shifting her position, she stopped cold when her foot brushed against a small stand. It felt like the stand that she used to hold the beautiful blue clay pot from her sculpture class. She frantically prayed to as many deities as she could think of—both Bajoran and Cardassian—that she hadn't brushed it too hard.

Before she could get very far in her oaths, she heard the pot begin to roll.

She scurried around in the dark room, cursing the fact that she had thought herself too old for something so simple as a nightlight. She could hear the blasted pot moving, but her fingers were fumbling to catch the thing before it fell.

She was too late.

The pot fell to the solid surface of the floor, breaking with a spectacular sound.

"What was that?" Weyoun asked.

"That came from Ziyal's quarters."

Ziyal rushed back to her bed, throwing the covers over her just as the lock beeped open. As the door slid aside, she propped herself up on one elbow, rubbing her eyes as if she'd just been awakened. "What was that, father?" she blearily asked. "I heard something break."

Dukat looked down at the foot of the door.

Following his eyes, she could see the shattered pieces of the pot. "I guess that was too close to the air vent after all," she said, feigning dejection.

Her father's face softened. "Perhaps it was. We'll clean it up later."

Ziyal nodded. "All right, father."

"Sleep well, my dear."

No sooner had the door closed behind him than Ziyal fell back onto the bed, her mind whirling over the possibilities that a resistance cell on the station might hold.

UNKNOWN SENDER.

Two simple words had never given Jake so much glee. The first issue of his newsfeed had tumbled into his inbox, as well as the inboxes of every resident of the station, promptly at 0600 that morning, full of sound and fury, and signifying absolutely nothing.

It was perfect.

He'd used the previous day's springball results as the lead story, something he thought no self-respecting journalist would ever have attempted. He'd been surprised at how easy composing vapid, useless news articles had been. He'd even adjusted his own writing style to something more staunch and formal just for the occasion. Dukat might recognize it, but after Kira told him about Weyoun's lack of aesthetic perception, Jake wasn't sure that the Vorta would be able to figure it out. So far, it looked like it was working just as planned.

He wasn't sure exactly how Rom's gadget worked, and with Rom in a holding cell after a disastrous sabotage attempt Jake couldn't ask him, but he was grateful that it did. The first newsfeed looked as if it had gone through every comm station from the old ore processing facilities to a tiny comm unit in the Assayer's Office as it was distributed. Several inboxes had even received multiple copies of the file, just to make it look more supsicious. Jake chuckled as he noted the name of one such recipent—Corat Damar.

That had *to have been Kira's idea.*

Jake made a mental note to see if Ziyal mentioned anything about her father during dinner. It was their eighth meeting—he hesitated to call them 'dates'—in two weeks.

Slipping on his shoes, he checked his appearance one last time before heading to the Promenade. After spending the entire night working on Ziyal's article, he was anxious to see what she thought of his work.

He didn't think Bajoran noses could wrinkle like Ziyal's did when she finished reading the first draft of his article. "Jake, I don't know. You've made my father sound like some kind of tyrant, like I'm some sort of *legna* fathered by a *Pah-wraith*. He's not that bad."

"What's a *legna?*"

"It's an old Cardassian word. It means something that's divine, but not a god."

Jake's eyes sank to the plate of *hasperat* on the table in front of him. He'd spent the last several days fixing up the article about her in-between work on the newsfeed, and now the subject of the piece hated his work. Jake had tried so hard to portray every side of the story, but somehow he couldn't help but feel as though he'd ended up hurting her. "I'm sorry, Ziyal. I only used the information the Bajorans gave me about the Occupation."

She nodded. "I know. That's the problem. He wants to repent, Jake. He wants the Bajorans to understand that he was doing what he was forced to do. He's not a bad man."

Jake almost laughed. "If he wants to repent, Ziyal, why did he let them get rid of freedom of the press? If he went up against Weyoun and let me tell the Federation News Service what really goes on here, your father might be judged more fairly."

"They're already telling themselves," she said. "Whoever is doing that newsfeed is only trying to get into more trouble. Nobody's patience is infinite, Jake, not even my father's. He'll find whoever is doing it, and I'm worried about what it'll force him to do when that happens."

He took a bit of pride in the notion that if Ziyal didn't know who was behind the newsfeed, then there was a good chance that Dukat didn't, either.

They sat in companionable silence for a bit longer, until Ziyal said, "Is it you?"

"Huh?"

"Doing the newsfeed. Is it you?"

Jake took a deep breath as he worked up an answer. "Why do you say that?"

"I've gotten to know you, Jake Sisko. Besides, it's a newspaper, and you're the only real journalist on the station."

Mustering his courage, he forced a blank expression onto his face and said, "No. I've been too busy working on the article about you."

She didn't look convinced.

"I'm serious, Ziyal."

Ziyal placed her napkin beside the plate as she stood. "I know. Good night, Jake."

His stomach churned at the tone in her voice. She knew he was lying.

He grabbed her arm before she could get too far. "He's going to execute Rom, Ziyal. Is that repenting? How do you think the Bajorans are going to see it?"

She jerked her arm out of his grasp. "Good night," she said, this time with more force.

Jake watched her leave, not sure if it was right for him to follow. She looked as if she wanted to be alone, but something told him that might not have been the case. Should he tell her the whole truth? What would she do if he did? He didn't know. He was so deep in thought that he didn't even notice the approach of one of Quark's dabo girls, a slender, raven-haired Bajoran named Maiki.

"Jake," she whispered. "Jake!"

Shaking himself out of his reverie, he replied, "What?"

She leaned down, her lips a few scant inches from his ear. "Morn just brought back word. The Federation is coming. They'll be here in a few days."

Jake wanted to cheer, but restrained himself. Dad was coming back!

His hopes were quickly doused by one realization. "Ziyal."

He stood, making sure his gaze remained on Maiki's face. From the waist up, her costume was one of the skimpiest that Quark made his dabo girls wear, with bits of flesh-tone mesh holding together the few strategically placed scraps of emerald green fabric covering her chest and pelvis. The costume was handy in getting Cardassian soldiers to cozy up to her for "favors," which made Maiki one of his best informants. Still, he'd long since learned the lesson about looking her in the eye if he wanted to be kept in the loop. "Meeting tomorrow?"

She nodded.

Jake wandered out of Quark's and down the Promenade toward

his quarters. His father was coming back, but if Dukat were forced out, would Ziyal go with him, or stay? He hoped for the latter, but feared the former. If she wanted to stay, she'd stay. But she had just enough blind devotion to her father to make Jake worry.

As he walked, his eyes wandered up to the Promenade's second level. He could still remember sitting along the railing with Nog, their feet hanging over the edge into the open air as they watched the people go by, the innocence of youth personified.

The sight that greeted him from the upper level scarred that mental image. Odo and the female Founder were looking down like a king and queen surveying their domain.

So that's where Odo's been. Explains Kira's bad mood for the last few days.

Jake continued on toward his quarters, receiving the occasional pat on the back from Bajorans as he went. "The Emissary will deliver us from the Dominion, Jake," the owner of the *jumja* kiosk whispered. He overheard one Bajoran saying that the Emissary had found a way to ensure the minefield's safety, that there was no way the Dominion would be able to take it down and get reinforcements from the Gamma Quadrant once the Emissary arrived.

If they were going to get through the next few days, Jake knew that he and the rest of the resistance cell could not show any weakness. If his father really had found a way to keep Dukat from bringing down the minefield, he was going with the boldest plan Jake could ever remember him concocting. "Fortune favors the bold," one of his teachers had once said, "but abandons the timid."

Timid was something Jake Sisko had no intention of being.

He hoped.

No matter what happened, he promised himself that he'd do whatever it took to help free the station.

Ziyal looked around Quark's for Jake, but found no sign of her dinner date. She walked over to the crowded, understaffed bar and managed to catch sight of the proprietor. "Quark? Sir?"

It was the "Sir" that got Quark's attention. The Ferengi raised a hand. "Be right with you, Ziyal."

She scanned the bar once again. There was no sign of Jake, Kira, or even Leeta.

"What can I do for you?" Quark asked.

"Have you seen Jake? We were supposed to meet for dinner."

Ziyal didn't like the apprehensive look that flashed across Quark's face at that. "What happened?" she asked.

He put a hand on her shoulder, ignoring customers as he led her to a quiet area of the bar. That alone was enough to tell her that something serious had happened. "They've been arrested. Damar's accusing them of treason."

"No." She felt like she'd been kicked in the stomach. "Arrested?"

If Damar got them arrested, he had to have Father's permission. Kira was right. My father really has been lying to me.

Quark nodded and whispered, "Resistance."

Ziyal's ears perked at that. "There really is a cell on the station?"

"There was."

Her heart sank. Something told her that Quark had known all along. Mustering her courage, she said, "There still is. Where do I sign up?"

The Ferengi's eyes bulged. "*You?*"

"Yes."

Quark stared at her for a long moment before shaking his head. "No. Dukat won, Ziyal. It's over. Do yourself a favor and find someplace to hide until the smoke clears."

She couldn't decide whether to be angry at the barkeep, or do as he suggested. Her mind instead chose that moment to realize something. "If Rom's going to be executed for treason, that means—"

"Kira will be right after him," Quark said. "And Leeta, and—"

"Jake," she whispered.

The Ferengi nodded. "It might not be so easy for Dukat to get away with killing them, but he'll do it."

A part of her couldn't believe what she was hearing, but in her heart she was beginning to accept that it was true. The fact that Leeta and Kira were Bajorans would only slow her father down, but Jake didn't have that luxury. She had no idea what was going to happen to him.

Working her way out of the crowded bar and back onto the Promenade, she frantically tried to think of some way to get Jake and the others out of jail. *I'm not strong enough to do it myself. I need help, but who?*

It wasn't as if she could go back to her father. She still couldn't stomach his reaction when she'd appealed to him to free Rom. It was so perfectly Cardassian that it sickened her. How could he even consider that she might want to become that kind of person? How could he be so callous? What would he do if she went to him for someone like Jake or Leeta? How could they possibly be enemies of the state?

How can he let them execute Nerys? The way he watches her, it's obvious that he cares for her. What purpose would be served by her death?

As she stepped into the turbolift, she came to the crushing realization that her father probably would let Kira die as an example to others. Kira's death would drive a wedge between the Bajorans and the Cardassians that Ziyal doubted she could ever overcome on her own.

There *had* to be a way to stop the executions.

Maybe if I just went to Weyoun. Maybe he'd listen. He let Jake's newsfeed go, even though Father wanted to get rid of it. Maybe he'll let them go when he finds out about this.

The lift stopped at ops just in time for her to see her father, Damar, and Weyoun gathered around the situation table in the pit.

". . . The *Defiant*'s no match for this station," she heard Dukat say. "If Sisko wants to commit suicide, I say we let him."

Ziyal felt herself beginning to tremble. Before they could realize she was there, the lift took her out of ops.

She was still shaking when the lift stopped at her level of the habitat ring. The Federation was coming. Whatever was about to happen would change the station forever, she was sure of that. If she couldn't find a way to keep everyone safe, there were still things she needed to protect as best she could.

When the door to her father's quarters opened, she immediately went to his desk. Where would he keep it? She searched every object on the desk for it, until a glint of silver caught her eye. She reached around the small chronometer, and lifted it into the light. *Mother's earring.*

She used to think he kept it to remind him of happier times. But as his true nature became clear to her, she began to understand why it was that he took comfort from the earring and not her mother's pledge bracelet. The earring was his trophy. He clung to it precisely because it *wasn't* a reminder of any intimacy he and Naprem had shared, but was instead a symbol of one of his victories. He didn't remember her mother as a woman he loved. To him, she was merely a Bajoran. Something he had conquered.

She needed it more than Dukat did. Ziyal knew that if she could only keep a few things safe in the coming chaos, it had to be what little of her mother remained. *Now, what do I put this in?*

She went into her room and grabbed a small scrap of blue fabric from her dressing area. It was frayed at the edges, faded and worn from years of being wadded up in whatever pocket she had, but it was all that she'd been able to keep after the crash. The Breen had taken everything else or buried it with the bodies of the *Ravinok* dead, but Ziyal had somehow managed to keep the small scrap of her mother's favorite dress.

The half-used canvases and papers that were littered through the room stared at her, almost mocking her that she would put a long-dead woman ahead of the future. Ziyal loved her art, there was no questioning that, but the chain of tarnished silver that she held in her palm was even more irreplaceable than her creations. And despite the fact that her holovid and portfolio had already been shipped to the institute on Cardassia, she knew now that the dream it represented was dead.

Wrapping the earring in the soft scrap of fabric, she shoved it deep into her pocket when an alarm went off somewhere in the distance.

She walked out into the corridor, trying to figure out how close the problem might be. Finally deciding that it was far enough away to not be an immediate threat, she went back into her quarters. That was when the hand came down over her mouth.

"Don't scream. I'm not going to hurt you. I just have one question."

She relaxed for an instant as she recognized the voice. Quark. *Has he been lurking in the corridor?* When he finally took his hand off of her mouth, she asked, "What's that?"

"Do you know how to make *hasperat* soufflé?"

Jake stared at the ceiling, trying to decide if killing Rom before the scheduled execution would make Dukat angrier.

The Ferengi was driving them all crazy with his incessant bemoaning of the gloom and doom he was convinced was about to befall them. Kira had long since abandoned any attempt to talk reason into Rom.

His wife would utter a few words of encouragement every now and again, but even Leeta's patience only went so far.

Don't think about it, Jake. Work on more of the article. Article, more like a biography now. You've got shots of every drawing you can get, now what? The piece for Dukat. That's the cover right there.

It's too big to put in the newsfeed, that's for sure. Does it matter? Once Dad comes back, I'll be able to get my stories to the FNS again. I won't need the thing. The thought crept back into his mind unbidden, and unwanted. *If Dad's coming back, then Dukat'll be gone. If Dukat's gone, where's Ziyal going to go? I've got to talk her into staying. Kira and Garak need her. She's like the kid sister Kira never had.*

The more Jake considered his reaction, the more he realized one other thing, he needed Ziyal to stay, too. His biggest problem was figuring out how to talk her into it.

"All right! No one move!" Quark yelled.

Jake couldn't believe what he saw—Quark, disruptors in each

hand, and Ziyal shadowing him. Within seconds, the Ferengi had taken care of the Jem'Hadar guards and freed them all. Kira took Rom with her, instructing the rest of them to find someplace safe.

He followed behind as Quark led him, Leeta, and Ziyal through the hustle and bustle of the bar to a back room Jake had never seen before. It was no larger than Jake's bedroom, but not a storeroom, even though a *tongo* wheel gathered dust in a corner behind a spotless table and chairs. *One of Quark's meeting rooms.* For the next few hours, he occupied himself with fine-tuning his biography of Ziyal, having snatched his padd from the security office during their escape.

For her part, Ziyal calmed the distraught Leeta with promises of Rom's safety and the Emissary's arrival. There were times when Jake admired Ziyal's capacity for faith and times when he found it disturbing. He wasn't sure which of those times this was. He wished he could find a way to convince her to stay on the station, convince her to stay with him.

A distant alarm broke in on his thoughts.

Evacuation.

Jake fought down his own hope and watched Ziyal closely. "Dukat's evacuating," he whispered. "Dad must be winning."

Ziyal stared at the door. "Father will probably be looking for me."

"Probably."

A look of sadness passed over her. "He's not going to be happy when I don't go with him."

"What?" Jake's eyes threatened to pop out of his head. "You're staying?"

Ziyal nodded. "This is my home. They don't want me on Cardassia."

"What about Bajor?" Leeta asked.

"It's the same. They're only more polite about it."

The door slid aside. "They're leaving," Quark said, stepping into the room. "It should only be a couple more hours before you can get out of here."

"I have to go now, sir," Ziyal stated matter-of-factly.

"Bad idea," Quark replied. "Not unless you want to go with your father."

Ziyal shook her head. "I need to tell him I'm staying here. I should say good-bye."

"He doesn't deserve to know," Leeta said. There was a bitterness in her voice that Jake had never heard before. "I don't see how you can love that man."

Hands falling to her side, Ziyal said, "I can't *hate* him, no matter how much I want to. He's my father."

"Let her go," Jake said. Ever since Benjamin Sisko had beamed out of the Promenade that day, Jake had fought against thoughts of how many times his father could have died and how many cruel ways the Cardassians could have accomplished the task. He felt so stupid for never telling his father that he was staying behind. The least he could do was spare Ziyal the same feelings. *I can't believe I'm about to say this.* "She deserves the chance see him one more time. I know what it'll be like if she doesn't. Until a couple of days ago, I wasn't even sure Dad was still alive. If she's never going to see her father again, she needs to say good-bye."

"I wish I had said good-bye to Rom," Leeta said. "I hope he's okay."

Quark rolled his eyes. "I'll leave you people to work this out. I need to make sure my idiot brother doesn't get himself killed. But if you want my advice, kid, you'll stay put." With that, Quark left the room, closing the door behind him.

Ziyal turned to Jake. "I have to go to him."

"Maybe I should come with you," Jake said. "Quark's right. It's not safe."

Ziyal shook her head. "It's less safe for you. I'm still part Cardassian. I'll be fine."

Jake sighed. "Go," he said quietly, "I'll catch up with you later."

"That's right, you will," Ziyal assured him. "Listen, Jake . . . will you look after something for me until I get back?"

She has to ask? "Sure, what?"

Ziyal reached into her pocket, pulling out a folded piece of peacock-blue fabric. He caught a glimpse of silver as she unfolded it, and marveled at the intricate Bajoran earring that it protected. "This is all I have left of my mother," she said. "Keep it safe for me."

Jake held out his open palm, allowing her to place the package in it. "I'll take care of it," he promised, surprised at how much he meant it.

Ziyal smiled. "Thank you." She stood on her tiptoes just long enough to kiss him on the cheek. "You're a wonderful friend."

Jake watched her go. "So are you," he whispered.

He kept himself and Leeta calm by reading aloud from the article. She seemed to welcome the distraction, wringing her hands no matter how hard she tried to control them. The alarm droned on in the background, until finally he wasn't sure if he had just begun tuning it out, or if it was actually gone. He paused, and discovered that it had grown silent.

"Do you think it's over?" Leeta asked.

Jake stared at the door for a long moment. "Maybe."

He walked toward the door, not sure if he wanted to venture out into the open. Was his father back in control of the place? Was Kira? Had Ziyal found her father before he left? There was only one way to answer those questions.

He opened the door on a corridor filled to capacity with silence.

"Go find Rom," he told Leeta. "He needs you."

The redhead looked unsure of something. "What about you?"

Jake stared down the corridor. "Getting the station back up and running is going to take everybody, Leeta. Everybody but me. I'm going to go find Ziyal."

Leeta pursed her lips, putting a hand on his shoulder before she took off down the corridor.

Jake followed her more slowly, trying to figure out where Ziyal might have gone after bidding farewell to her father. The first place that sprang to mind was her quarters.

It took a few seconds for the turbolift to take him to their level. As he rounded the corner toward the quarters she had once shared with Dukat, he called out, "Ziyal? Ziyal? Where are you?"

A deep—whimpering?—answered. Jake quickened his pace, until he found a Cardassian hunched over against the wall. He appeared to be curled around a body.

Jake caught a glimpse of burgundy. "No."

He scanned the corridor walls until he found a companel. "Jake Sisko to the Infirmary. There's someone injured in the habitat ring. Bring Security. Level two, Section 145."

Jake recognized Nurse Jabara's voice. She'd worked with Dr. Bashir for as long as he could remember. "I'll be right there, Jake. Just one victim?"

"Yes. Hurry!"

He ran over and tried to pull Dukat away from Ziyal. "Dukat, put her down! What did you do? Put her down!"

It took all of his effort just to get one of the Cardassian's hands pried from Ziyal's body. "Dukat, give her to me. Please. We may be able to help."

It took a few more seconds of wrestling before the Cardassian collapsed in a heap against the wall, releasing his grip on the girl.

Jake collected Ziyal's body from the floor, instinct sending his fingers to her neck.

Her skin was colder than he'd ever felt.

He leaned over and held his cheek near her lips. He couldn't sense breathing.

"Ziyal, don't do this to me."

Her chest had been charred by weapons fire, but whether it was a Jem'Hadar pistol, a Cardassian phase-disruptor, or even a Bajoran phaser, he couldn't tell. "How long ago was she shot?" he asked Dukat.

Dukat stared straight ahead, helpless panic in his eyes. Something small was clutched in his hand—his father's baseball.

Jake ran his fingers down Ziyal's midsection, fighting to remember the medic training Bashir had given him. Did she have the same organs as a full-blooded Bajoran? He didn't know, but he had to try. He found what felt like a sternum, and began attempting to resuscitate her as best he could. "Come on, Ziyal," he whispered.

Tilting her head into what he remembered as the proper position, he pinched off her nose. Lowering his lips to hers, he began blowing into her mouth. Placing his fingers back on her sternum, he began performing the chest compressions that he hoped would get her heart going again.

One compression.

Two compressions.

How many was he supposed to do?

The number ten popped into his mind, so he began counting off. He wasn't sure if he was doing it properly, but at least he was doing *something*.

She couldn't die. She had too much ahead of her that she deserved to see. The world needed her vision of life, her caring, her compassion. It needed her belief that the races could all get along, even if the leaders didn't think so. Ziyal was living proof of the power of one mind to change the world. She needed to be an example to everyone else.

The universe needed Ziyal almost as much as he did. Memories came flooding back to him, sharing root beers in Quark's, watching her work on "The Seat of Power" for her father, hearing her talk about her mother, just the sound of her laughter. Her friendship had been just the tonic he'd needed during one of the worst times of his life. There was no way he was going to let go of that without a fight.

He kept up the compressions and breathing, the sound of Dukat's sobbing his only companion, until Jabara arrived.

"What the—? Oh, no."

"Jake," a male voice said, "tell me what happened." It took him several seconds to realize that the voice belonged to Odo.

Jake heard Jabara get something out of her med kit, most likely a tricorder. "I don't know," he tried to answer as he began another round of chest compressions. "I was looking for Ziyal and I found him here." He gestured toward Dukat with a jerk of his head. "She'd already been shot."

He heard Jabara's tricorder begin its work, the tiny electronic pings and whistles not assuaging his fear in the least.

"Jake." He knew that tone in the nurse's voice, knew it better than he ever wanted. "Jake, it's too late. There are no life signs. She's been gone for too long."

He stopped mid-breath, still not ready to admit what he'd known the moment he'd turned the corner. "No," he whispered.

Jabara's hand came to rest on Jake's upper arm. "I'm so sorry, Jake," she said, her voice sincere and compassionate.

Jake's legs began to weaken under him. He managed to lean back against the wall before they collapsed. He closed his eyes tight against the welling tears.

Across the hall from him, Dukat never stopped muttering as Odo tried to get him to stand. Jake was able to make out the occasional utterance of Ziyal's name, but the rest was gibberish.

An image flashed in Jake's mind: Wolf 359, the *Saratoga,* his mother wrapped around him while the world ended. Even though it had happened years ago, Jake could still remember the sight of his normally stoic father deep in grief when they'd gotten off the lifepod.

The sight of Ziyal's lifeless body on the cold floor shredded the thin gauze that had bandaged his emotions since that day. She was so still, so quiet. If it hadn't been for the charred cinder that was her chest, he wouldn't have believed it. *I wonder if Mom looked like that.*

One of the medtechs brought a gurney to take Ziyal's body back to the Infirmary for an autopsy. Jabara helped him to his feet, and Jake leaned on her as they walked back toward the Promenade.

"Are you all right?" she asked. "You don't look that good."

Jake shook his head. "One of my best friends was just murdered. How am I supposed to look?"

★　　★　　★

Jake was working on the last chapter of what had evolved into Ziyal's biography when a cheering emanated from the Promenade. He looked up from his vigil in the Infirmary just long enough to see Kira staring back at him. Neither of them had left Ziyal's bedside for hours. He wasn't sure why they both elected to stay, since there was no way to bring their friend back.

Kira didn't move from the wall she was using for support. "Your father just docked."

Jake's eyes wandered to Ziyal's body. She looked so peaceful, so content. A part of him didn't want to leave her side, but a part of him knew that his father would be wondering how he was doing. "I should go," he told Kira as he pulled himself out of the chair. "He's going to be worried."

Kira reached out and caught his arm as he passed. "If you see Garak, just tell him that she's here."

With an absent nod, Jake walked out of the Infirmary and into the chaotic mass of people packing the Promenade. There were Bajorans everywhere, all jubilant over the Emissary's return. When the airlock door slid aside, Jake's father walked through to the cheers and applause of what looked like a hundred people. For a moment, Jake thought they might actually pick his father up and carry him around on their shoulders, they were so emotional.

After greeting his father and sending Garak toward the Infirmary, Jake headed back to his quarters. It was everything he could do to not go back to Ziyal's side, but he knew that would be a fruitless gesture. With Garak back, there was someone else to keep Kira company.

Jake had a biography to finish.

It took a while for Jake to get through everything, fine-tuning each word until he had a perfect final draft. Sleep was a foreign concept to him after thirty-nine hours of revision and *raktajino*, pushing forward on his quest. Telling Ziyal's story had become a mission, one he couldn't abandon until it was completed.

He saw bits and pieces of messages that had been sent back and forth during that time about a memorial service, something that might encompass everything about her life. Sisko gave Kira and Garak the tasks of arranging things from the standpoint of their respective cultures. It surprised Jake when his father came knocking on *his* door.

"Jake-O?"

Jake didn't even look up from the padd. "Yeah, Dad?"

"Odo found out who killed Ziyal."

That got his attention. Scrolling to the end of the piece, he went to the chapter about her death and looked up. "Who?" he asked, dismayed by the exhaustion he heard in his own voice.

"Damar."

Jake exhaled slowly, putting the padd down. "Damar? He's sure?"

His father nodded. "The security cameras backed up Dukat's statement. Well, what Odo could get out of him, at least. Damar thought she was working against him."

Damar. So Weyoun didn't stop you, after all.

"How is Dukat?"

"Not good. He's barely coherent. Odo has him in a holding cell just to be safe." Sisko walked over and sat in the chair nearest Jake. "Major Kira said you were working on an article about Ziyal?"

"Yeah," he replied. "Only now it's more like a biography."

Sisko raised an eyebrow. "Can I read it?"

Jake handed him the padd, watching his father's reaction as he read.

"This is really good, Jake. I didn't even know you two had met."

An image of Ziyal working on the drawing for her father appeared in his mind. "She was my friend."

"She's going to need a eulogy," Sisko said, gesturing with the padd. "Do you mind if I show this to Kira?"

Jake felt his frazzled brain trying to wrap around the notion, and failing. "A eulogy? She can't use this. It's too long. I'll write—"

"No, Jake," Sisko said, concern in his voice. "Kira can use what you've got here. There are things in here she might not even know about. You need to get some sleep."

Jake tried to figure out a way to convey what he was feeling, but the words wouldn't come. All he could manage was, "I need to be there, Dad."

Sisko put a hand on Jake's shoulder. "If you don't go to bed," he said, "you aren't even going to be awake for Worf and Dax's wedding."

Jake couldn't deny that his father had a point. "I'll try," he replied.

And try he did.

Jake tossed and turned for hours, but sleep eluded him. His mind kept wandering back to the corridor, Dukat whimpering over his daughter's lifeless body.

She was gone before I got off the lift. And I convinced them to let her go.

He stared at the ceiling for hours, trying to think of any way that the outcome might have been different, anything that might have saved her life. Eventually, his sleep-deprived brain couldn't take it anymore, and he looked at the clock.

It was almost time for the memorial.

He downloaded a copy of the entire biography, images of her drawings and all, into each of two padds as he dressed. His hand brushed the cloth-wrapped earring on his desk. He'd kept it safe, but he couldn't help feeling that he'd let her down in the end. Picking up the small package, he set it alongside the two padds.

He slurped down a warm *raktajino* while he finished getting ready. There was one more thing that he needed to do before he left. "Jake Sisko to Captain Sisko."

"Yes, Jake?"

"Dad, I want to give Dukat a copy of Ziyal's biography."

Jake presumed that the silence that answered his statement was his father thinking it over. *"Are you sure, Jake?"* his father replied.

Would I ask if I wasn't sure, Dad?

"Yes."

"All right. But I want Odo with you."

Jake smiled, albeit weakly, for the first time in over a day. "Thanks."

★   ★   ★

Jake had been surprised when he learned Quark had offered to host the memorial. *But then, wasn't this where he had his own funeral?*

The turnout was dismal. Although the tables in Quark's had been cleared away and the chairs set up to face the dabo stage, most were empty. Jake walked in and saw that most of the senior staff had already arrived, but very few others. *Where is everybody?*

He nearly fell into the closest chair, blinking away fatigue. He was fighting a losing battle with consciousness, and had consumed far too much *raktajino*. His hands shook as he held on to the padds.

Jake heard people around him talking, but his mind barely registered what was said. His eyes were focused on the framed charcoal rendering where the dabo wheel usually stood: "The Seat of Power."

His father stepped up to the dais, speaking words he didn't hear to the pitifully meager gathering of mourners. Jake watched as speaker after speaker followed: Kira, Garak, even a representative from the university on Bajor. They all rambled on about Ziyal, talking about what they thought she was, what she wanted, what she believed. Jake felt the padds in his hands. He knew all he needed to know about that.

When it was all over, Jake went off alone and sought out the cargo bay where Ziyal's sarcophagus awaited transport to Bajor. Dad used his influence as Emissary to find a quiet spot in Kendra Province where Ziyal could be laid to rest.

Padds in hand, he stepped up to the sarcophagus. Jake had heard it was considered a dishonor for aliens to view Cardassian remains, but no one would ever know. And truth be told, at the moment, he didn't care. What he needed to do was too important. He took a deep breath, and lifted the lid.

Even in death, she still looked like a flower floating on the breeze. He lifted Ziyal's cold hand just enough to slide the padd underneath. Then, reaching into his vest, he pulled out the blue scrap of cloth and unfolded it, exposing her mother's earring. He had thought to leave it with her, but now found that he couldn't go back on his promise. Wrapping it back up, he gently placed the earring back inside his vest.

I'll keep it safe for you, Ziyal. I promise.

Dukat was curled up in the corner of his cell, muttering on as if the recording that had begun playing in the corridor were on an endless loop.

Jake nodded to Odo, and the force field that kept the Cardassian securely contained came down.

"Ziyal," Dukat whispered. "Is that you?"

Jake stepped into the cell, his heart in his throat. "No." He couldn't help thinking that Dukat had, in a matter of hours, lost everything. He couldn't go back to Cardassia. His wife had taken their children away because of Ziyal, and by staying behind, he lost his position in Cardassia's Dominion-run government. He couldn't live on the station now that it was back under Federation control. He didn't even have his old ship, the *Groumall,* anymore. All he had was Ziyal, and memories of everything she'd been.

Jake could understand that much. He had the same memories, and they weren't tainted by the blind devotion of a father toward a daughter—or vice versa. He could remember all of Ziyal's wonderful idealism, her sincere belief that she could bring Cardassia and Bajor together, her exuberance over her work. It was all part of the natural wonder that was Ziyal.

He tried to imagine what it might have been like if he had lost his father, and there had been too many missions when Jake thought he would never return. What would he do then?

For that matter, if it had been the other way around, and Jake had been the one killed, what would Ziyal have done? Jake's fingers fiddled with the padd. He knew what Ziyal would have done. If she had it in her power, she'd have given Benjamin Sisko back whatever of his son she could manage.

Jake cued up the first image, "The Seat of Power."

"Dukat," he began, "I know it isn't much, but I finished the story about her."

He held the padd out for Dukat to see, placing it in the Cardassian's hand when he didn't reach out for himself.

"Thank you," Dukat whispered, clutching the padd as if it were a lifeline. "I'm so sorry. Things will be fine. We'll go home, Ziyal—"

Jake winced as he saw how the mere mention of Dukat's daughter's name sent him into another fit of convulsive sobs, curling his body even further into the corner of the cell. The hum of the force field that served as the cell's door provided a strange harmonic with the Cardassian's whimpers. Dukat's entire demeanor softened as he looked at the padd's screen.

"My sweet Ziyal."

The Devil You Know

Heather Jarman

Historian's note: This story is set after the events of the sixth-season episode "In the Pale Moonlight," in the days leading up to "Time's Orphan."

Heather Jarman

Heather Jarman grew up fantasizing about being a writer the way many little girls fantasize about being ballerinas and princesses; she had all the lyrics to the Beatles' "Paperback Writer" memorized by age six. But in her wildest suburban childhood dreams, she had no idea how Saturday afternoons spent lazing in her beanbag chair watching *Star Trek* would dramatically affect her lifelong aspiration.

Indeed, the *Star Trek* universe played host to her professional fiction debut, *This Gray Spirit*, the second novel in the critically acclaimed *Mission: Gamma* series of *Deep Space Nine* books set after the TV series. Her follow-up, *Balance of Nature*, is part of the *Star Trek: S.C.E.* series. In 2004, her second anthology contribution (a short story coauthored with Jeffrey Lang) will be published in *Tales of the Dominion War*. She's also currently writing an original young adult novel.

She lives in Portland, Oregon, with her husband and four daughters. She rarely finds time to lounge about in beanbag chairs these days, much to her deep regret.

Jadzia asked to be transported directly to her quarters. Walking through the corridors of Deep Space 9 during the busiest part of the station's day would be a bad idea under the circumstances. Worf would have left for his shift more than an hour ago, sparing her from having to explain why she'd been gone all night, never mind the blood spatters on her uniform.

As the familiar walls materialized, she couldn't help wondering if she'd been dreaming. Everything looked as it always had—the holos from her wedding, the couch whose upholstery she'd always hated but had been too lazy to replace, the gleaming bat'leth mounted on the wall—all of it looked the same, so why did it feel so alien? Her brain and body, addled by fatigue and hours of standing on her feet, offered no answers. Pushing a stray lock away from her face, she felt gummy residue crusted on her hair. She combed it out with her fingers, examined her hand, smudged with coagulated blood and bone-white grit, then wiped it off on her uniform.

Tossing the datachip she'd been clutching onto the coffee table, she removed her pips and her combadge, stripped off her uniform, and threw it into the recycler. How did I come to be in this place? she wondered, not for the first time. She hadn't had an answer yesterday, or the day before, or the week before that, and she saw no reason to expect one today.

The thought would keep—long enough to take a shower, at any rate. Naked, she padded off toward the bathroom.

A nap might be good. Assuming she could sleep. Sleep hadn't been much of a refuge lately. Heading straight to her duty shift might be a better idea. The list of tasks awaiting her attention would help her avoid Benjamin's questions until she'd figured out plausible answers for him. By *staying busy, blending into the ops routine, she could effectively vanish from notice into the sea of bodies and computers and desperately important duties that all good Starfleet soldiers were about these days. She almost laughed aloud at that last thought. A good Starfleet soldier. Looking in the mirror, she traced her reflection.*

"Who are you?" Jadzia muttered as she crouched down beside the stasis chamber. She activated her tricorder and took a reading off the transmitter embedded inside. Comparing the name and the numerical code on her tricorder with the list on her padd yielded a match: 'Shavnah Hakim, human, age 72' lay within the chamber. She dropped to her knees where she could access the next one. *One down, a hundred fifty to go.* "So Quark was okay with converting his wine cellar into a morgue?" she asked her companion, still incredulous at the Ferengi's generosity. When she'd heard how quickly Quark complied with Benjamin's request, she wondered how much arm-twisting and bribery had been required.

Looking up from his own padd, Julian peered at her through the space between two stacked stasis chambers in the adjacent row. "Apparently, wartime brings out latent nobility—even in Quark—"

Jadzia arched an eyebrow.

"—and the captain might have smoothed the way with a sufficient sum of latinum," Julian confessed. "But you have to admit that moving his collection of rare libations and artful erotica holo-programs to accommodate several hundred corpses—"

"—is still impressive," she said, pursing her lips. On every side the rounded chambers silently rippled row upon row, rising and falling dark matte waves, glints of blue light reflecting on their smooth faces. The ventilation fan's soft *chu-chu-chu* stirred the air like a ship churning through deep water. Only the shuffle of their feet against the gratings and the occasional irregular breath hinted that any living creature worked in this chilly, dimly lit place. Ironically, the cargo bay reminded her a little of the underground caverns where the symbiont pools were located on Trill. How life-changing illumination, in the form of symbionts, could emerge from such dark, murky beginnings never ceased to astonish her. Besides herself and the other station personnel who had occasion to work down here, nothing living would emerge from this place.

Jadzia sighed deeply and scanned the next chamber. "I didn't even know we had this many stasis units." Immediately, she regretted her shallow-sounding words. As if a tragedy like this could be measured in supply statistics. She mentally corrected: *this many dead.*

"We don't. The Bajoran Health Ministry made them available after the *Moon Zephyr* was attacked. We hoped we'd need them to stabilize survivors requiring medical treatment. Instead . . ." Julian's voice trailed off. He sighed.

Jadzia checked "Tihana Elkhur, Bajoran, age 36" off her padd. *At least he won't have far to travel to go home.* "Death is the currency of war."

"I'd rather it be dealt less freely," Julian said. "Thanks, by the way—volunteering your off-duty time to help out."

"It's not a big deal. When Kira told me that she'd helped Dr. Girani identify the bodies—" Jadzia shuddered, imagining what a gruesome task that must have been. "Helping you compile the database was a small thing."

"Anyone with friends or family aboard *Zephyr* who hasn't already heard the news probably expects the worst, but allowing them to claim the remains can offer them closure, even comfort. Hardly a small thing."

I've died seven times, Jadzia thought as she moved to the next row of chambers. Preferring instead to focus on the business of living, she seldom contemplated Dax's previous host deaths. Random, rapidly cycling scenes—from Lela's peaceful good-byes to her children to the madness consuming Joran at his end—occasionally broke into her consciousness during combat or other high-intensity experiences. She grew accustomed to the sometimes disquieting images the same way she learned to cope with sensations evoked by a whiff of fragrance worn by one of Emony's lovers or a phrase of music loved by Tobin: She embraced them as part of the rich tapestry that was Dax. But lately, almost without her being conscious of it, her perspective had changed. Her aversion to probing death memories had given way to a grim, albeit pragmatic, curiosity.

She first noticed her thoughts wandering when Worf was away with Martok. The usual Klingon posturing would filter into their good-byes—about it being a good day to die and how they'd meet at *Sto-Vo-Kor*'s gates should this be Worf's last battle. Their parting words were offered in teasing tones and with half-smiles between kisses. Then he would leave, and slowly, the totality of their separation would creep up on her, forcing her to consider the worst possibilities. Truth: She could lose him. He could lose her. She didn't want to imagine a life without Worf, but hundreds of years of experience didn't leave her a lot of room for denial. Recalling the process of death and dying might help her prepare to accept whatever fate handed her.

She would lie alone in the dark, unearthing long-buried memories. . . . The timid, frightened squeezes of a child's hand slowly giving way to numbness . . . agonizing brilliance of light in an exploding shuttle . . . senses drowning in cascading ecstasy . . . the blurry haze as the passageway connecting two minds misted . . .

Inevitably a comm chirp would stir her from her contemplations and, in a shadow of the knot in her chest, she imagined Dax twisting painfully inside her. *This is it. This is the moment.* And she would steel herself in anticipation of the blows inflicted by Benjamin's words telling her that part of her had died far away.

Of course the dreaded message had never come.

But Jadzia learned anew with each false alarm that no memory could possibly prepare her; each host, like every individual in the universe, had to fumble their own way through death. *One aspect of my life I share in common with everyone in this cargo bay,* she thought.

Moving on to the next stasis chamber, she resumed the cataloging routine, beginning with scanning the ID transmitter affixed to the body. She stopped abruptly, pulse thudding in her ears, her thoughts stammering. *What—wait, I—this has to be—read it again. Read. It—*Her eyes bore into the display.

The tricorder slipped out of her hands, clattering onto the floor. Her knees gave way. Spine against the shelving, she slid to the floor, her knees tucked against her body, her hands falling limply to her sides.

"Jadzia!"

Julian sounded worried. She should reassure him. *Never mind me,* she wanted to say, *I'm fine.* She sensed him crouching down next her, touching her shoulder, but she didn't see him, the black waves swimming before her eyes blinding her to all but the dark.

"Are you ill?" He started to wave a medical scanner over her head.

She blinked a few times, breathed deeply and turned her gaze on her friend. "I just—I didn't—" She took another breath. "—I didn't know he was on the *Zephyr.* It hadn't even occurred to me that he might have—" Trying to slow down her racing thoughts, she took a deep breath and swallowed hard.

Julian picked up the fallen tricorder, studying the readout. " 'Setheleyis th'Rasdeth, Andorian, 58.' You knew him."

"I wouldn't have gone back without him," Jadzia whispered. Off Julian's questioning look, she explained, "To the initiate program. When I washed out the first time, Starfleet sent me to a counselor. My commander believed, correctly, that I was pretty depressed about it. She didn't want it interfering with my job performance . . ." Jadzia leaned forward, resting her chin on her knees, smiling as she remembered. "Dr. th'Rasdeth tended to take an unconventional approach. The occasional transport to Rio for a 'pick-me-up' trip. Wonderful seven-course meals. Music. The hours he spent—I've rarely seen a counselor so committed to his work." Smiling at the memory, she looked at Julian and presented him with her best imitation of th'Rasdeth's serious face, his whispering voice: " 'If you don't go back to the initiate program, you'll destine yourself to a lifetime of doubt and wondering "if." ' "

Dropping down on the floor next to her, Julian picked up the padd, ostensibly searching for information on th'Rasdeth. His eyes lit up in recognition. "He taught at the academy, didn't he? I believe I took a course from him on the benefits of positive visualization in psychotherapy."

Jadzia nodded. "He wanted nothing to do with the war, and left the academy last year. He didn't dispute that the Federation's military response was justified, but he considered himself a pacifist and had come to believe that he'd compromised those principles by working for Starfleet. So he resumed his civilian practice in the colonies closest to the Cardassian border, helping the populations cope with the traumas of wartime." She ran her fingers over the chamber's face, imagining the feel of his warm hand resting atop her cool one. "In our last subspace exchange, we'd decided he'd come for a visit next month. I wanted him to meet Worf."

"I'm sorry, Jadzia. Really." Julian squeezed her hand.

She studied his face, saw the sincerity there. *What a dear he is,* she thought, feeling a flush of gratitude for their years of friendship. He meant well, Jadzia knew, but at this place and time, this loss wasn't about her. Gently, she disentangled her hand. "I should have been sorry before I learned Dr. th'Rasdeth died." She picked up the padd, scrolled through the list and clenched her teeth. "All of it, Julian," with her hand she indicated the hundreds of occupied stasis chambers—now coffins—in the cargo bay. "*All* of it is so senseless and I've been processing their bodies like I'm shuffling padds with status reports off to Benjamin's desk."

"Don't personalize it, Jadzia. Professional detachment is one of the first things they teach you in medical school," Julian said sagely. "Feel the loss of your friend and let it represent all the others. Trying to make sense of it all will drive you mad."

"A little madness might be a good thing. For all of us. Because it might push us a little harder to win this damn war—"

Her combadge chirped. *"Sisko to Dax."*

Suddenly, Jadzia felt extraordinarily tired. "Go ahead."

"I need to see you in my office in ten minutes, Commander. Bring the doctor with you."

Jadzia exchanged a look with Bashir. "That doesn't sound good," she observed. "Is anything wrong?"

"It all depends on how you look at it, Old Man," Benjamin said. *"The Romulans have arrived."*

Jadzia stepped over the threshold of her quarters, greeted by an atonal aria from *Kahless and Lukara* blasting over the comm system. Another voice to add to the cacophony in her head. She massaged her sinuses with her thumb and forefinger, feeling the beginnings of a headache coming on. *Worf must have already come off his shift,* she thought, sniffing for the salty richness that would foretell *gagh* for dinner. Maybe they could go to Quark's instead; he'd supposedly added a whole list of rare Rigellian favorites to his replicator files. In her present frame of mind, one of Sirella's steaming, spicy, blood-based puddings might put her off food for a week.

As if he sensed her thinking about him, Worf emerged from their bedroom, a *mek'leth* cradled in one arm. Uncertain whether his first words would be endearments, a to-do list, complaints, or questions about her day (which, at present, she wanted to forget), she raised a hand to hush him. "I need a minute," she muttered, dropping onto the couch.

"Of course," he said, and ordered the computer to mute the music. On their dining table, he placed the *mek'leth* alongside a rag and a bottle of polish and took a seat where he had a clear view of her.

Throwing her feet out in front of her, she rested her neck on the curve of the cushions and slouched down. Her neck and shoulders ached—all those hours hunched over her station, followed by the unpleasantness in the cargo bay. And the meeting with Benjamin had put the already stressful day over the top. A massage would be great. *Maybe I should call Kira and we could make a spa appointment . . .* What began as a sigh became a yawn; she closed her eyes and tried to clear her mind of all the distracting flotsam.

Her thoughts drifted to Dr. th'Rasdeth, as she suspected would happen frequently in coming weeks during moments when the hectic pace of her life lessened. *I'll just have to stay really busy.*

She felt Worf's eyes noting each time she inhaled and exhaled, making it difficult for her to fully relax. Yes, he was diligently polishing the *mek'leth*—she heard cloth shimmying over the blade—but he was watching her, waiting. She needed to project the "don't push me" energy a little more forcefully or he'd wait all night exhibiting the patience of a *lIngta'* hunter sitting stock-still in the brush.

In the nearly three years since they'd first met, he'd developed an uncanny knack for drawing information out of her, particularly information she wasn't in the mood to share. *When it comes to interrogation, he's more Cardassian than Klingon.* Of course, under the right circumstances, interrogation by Worf definitely had possibilities . . . She smiled drowsily, drifting into a daydream.

He cleared his throat. "I understand you had a meeting with Captain Sisko this afternoon."

So much for the patience of a Cardassian. She groaned in exasperation and left the couch, crossed over behind Worf, draped her arms around his neck and nuzzled her face in his hair. "Take me away from all this, lover," she said softly. "We've never had a real honeymoon. After all we've done for the Federation—and what I've done over several lifetimes—I think we're owed."

"While that might be true, we cannot escape our duty. Though, clearly, you wish to avoid talking about yours." He caressed her hand, placed a velvet kiss in her palm.

"This is more fun," she whispered, brushing her lips against his ear.

"Jadzia," Worf said, his tone stern.

She sighed. "Fine. You want a report? You'll get a report." She pulled out a chair and scooted it close beside him. "Benjamin called Julian and me into a briefing. Apparently, the spirit of cooperation has fallen over Starfleet. Someone at headquarters came up with a *brilliant* idea," she said, allowing the sarcasm dripping off the word *brilliant* to hang in the air for a long moment (lest Worf take a too literal interpretation of what she said). The more she considered her conversation with Sisko and Bashir, the more skeptical she became; the urge to contact Benjamin and protest her assignment became more powerful with each passing hour. *Might as well find out what Worf thinks* . . . "Julian and I have been assigned to spend half our duty shifts working on Project Blue Sky, a scientifically oriented war research project—a think tank. While I like swapping stories about exploding test tubes and witty algorithms as much as the next lab *gerk,* it's who we're swapping with that makes me nervous. You want to guess?"

"A warbird of Romulans?" he deadpanned.

"You knew." She shook her head with a grim chuckle.

"Of course. My job requires that I be aware of such information," he said, sliding his arm around her back, tracing her vertebrae with his thumb. "I did not know why they were coming to the station, only that they were coming. Because this is one of the first co-ventures to come out of the Federation's strategic alliance with the Romulans, Admiral Ross is more—anxious—than he would typically be."

"What are they thinking, trying to hatch covert war ops with *them?!*" she said, throwing up her hands. "I'm as thrilled as the next Starfleet officer that the Romulans are on our side against the Dominion, but in any universe, this is a marriage of convenience. When the war's over, who's to stop them from turning against us with intelligence they gained from this alliance? Consummating this marriage could be our undoing." Leaning forward in her chair, Jadzia rested her forehead against his and inhaled deeply, savoring the musky tang of her mate, and closed her eyes. Worf continued to stroke her spine.

I could stay like this forever.

Running away would be nice—any escape would do. She could withdraw into the warm circle of his arms where she didn't need to *think* anymore, to be lost in sensation, drifting to a place where all this death and insanity would dissolve. The whole Alpha Quadrant could go to hell, and she'd be so blissfully content that it wouldn't matter. She placed a soft kiss on his cheek.

Cupping her chin in his hand, he tipped her face up to meet his. "No one wishes more than I that there was an alternative to allying with the Romulans," he told her softly. "But the luxury of such a choice is not ours."

Jadzia stared deeply into Worf's eyes. So much of who he was had been shaped by the Romulan onslaught that had killed his parents when he was child, an attack he himself had barely survived. She hadn't stopped to consider how this alliance was affecting him—and how he was forcing himself to put aside old hatreds for the greater good.

"The war has not gone well for the Federation or the Klingon Empire," Worf went on. "To have any hope of victory against the Dominion, we need this alliance."

"I know—I know!" Jadzia sighed—partly out of exasperation. They'd had this discussion many times: How Starfleet, with its often conflicted identity as both an agency of peaceful scientific exploration and a defensive fighting force, wasn't truly prepared, culturally, psychologically, or militarily, for a war on the scale it was currently faced with. Many argued that its transformation into a force able and willing to battle the Jem'Hadar on their own terms was challenging the Federation's most fundamental ideals, in ways those ideals wouldn't survive. Some believed that even if the Federation won the war, it would be unable to return to being the civilization it once was.

Pragmatically, Worf placed his hopes on General Martok, believing that the Klingons might be able to hold back the Dominion threat long enough for Starfleet to find their footing.

"It's just—and believe me, I feel foolish saying this to you, of all people—" Jadzia began, and stopped. She reconsidered what she was about to say, then shrugged wearily. "I guess I'm just channeling my past-host experiences with Romulans." She placed a feather kiss on his neck, followed by another. *His earlobe looks nice . . .*

Shifting in his chair, Worf drew her into his lap so she straddled him, placing his hands on her hips and pulling her tight against his body.

She grinned playfully. The sooner they could abandon this depressing war talk, the better.

He attempted to look serious but couldn't hide the smile in his eyes. "You are referring to Tobin's encounter with them during their war with Earth—"

"—no small thing—"

"—and their agents breaking into Audrid's lab."

"Also, not a small thing," she said as she unfastened his uniform, pushing the jacket away from his chest. His hands fumbled for the fasteners of her uniform. "And we are left with—?"

"Me following orders, even though I don't want to." She shrugged off her jacket.

Baring his teeth, he growled, low and throaty. "Which is the honorable thing to do."

"And I'm all about honor," she said, pulling him roughly against her. Her teeth found purchase in his lower lip and she flicked at the salty burst of blood with her tongue. He freed her hair from the clasp, fanning her hair over her back with his fingers. Throwing back her head, she bared her throat, her body thrumming in anticipation. He lowered his face and she could feel puffs of hot breath on her neck for what felt like endless moments.

Twining her legs around his waist, she hissed, "Now, *jIH'-Doq* . . ."

Grabbing her by the hair, Worf pulled her back, forcing her to meet his eye. "We are not done."

"Oh, yes, we are."

"Jadzia—your friend, the counselor—"

Ignoring the ache in her chest, she placed a finger on his lips. "Shhhh . . . later."

"But—"

"Shhhhhh. . . ."

* * *

With a start, she awoke, the last vestiges of her dream ghosts fading away as she saw the pale blue illumination from the computer interface near the wall, felt the weight of Worf's arm around her waist. A thin sliver of light from the living room cut through the gloomy half-light of their bedroom. Her heart slammed loudly in her throat, her pulse shushing in her ears; she willed her limbs to stop trembling. For a long moment she lay there, trying to persuade her senses that she'd returned to reality.

When she realized sleep wouldn't be forthcoming, Jadzia disentangled herself from Worf's embrace, knowing from the timbre of his snoring that he was deeply asleep. Shivering, she retrieved a sheet from the floor and wrapped it around herself, hoping that covering up her bare skin might alleviate the chills. She crept into the living room on tiptoe and whispered a command to the computer to raise room temperature. She checked the companel's chrono. 0200. Five more hours and she'd be on the forefront of a new era of interquadrant cooperation, feigning goodwill toward a room of Romulans who were undoubtedly Tal Shiar operatives searching for the easiest way to bypass every security protocol they could figure out.

She went to the replicator. "*Tranya,* on the rocks."

Scooting into a corner of the couch, she stretched out, feeling the first hints of bruises emerging on her ribs and thighs. The pain was strangely comforting tonight, serving as an ever-present reminder of living flesh, another witness of her capacity to feel. She cradled the chilled glass in her palm, listened to the ice clink against the sides with each burning swallow. Placing the empty glass down on the table, she saw the padd containing the *Zephyr*'s casualty list where she'd thrown it when she came home.

She replicated another drink.

Gazing up at the ceiling, she watched the shifting shadows, forming pictures in her mind with the light and shade until the time arrived for her to get ready for her duty shift.

★   ★   ★

A double *raktajino* (with her customary shot of cream) in hand and workbag over her shoulder, Jadzia stepped out of her quarters and discovered Julian waiting, she presumed, to walk with her to the conference room. She opened her mouth, the beginnings of "What the hell are you doing here?" on the tip of her tongue, but "Good morning" managed to slip out instead.

"Thought we could talk before our meetings began," he said, by way of explanation. "Unless you have to swing by ops first or—"

"No. No—I'm headed for Blue Sky." She offered him a smile that she hoped would reassure him. Taking a deep breath, she fixed her focus on the day ahead. Dax's predisposition toward mistrusting the Romulans could easily interfere with her work on this project; she'd have to make an earnest effort to overcome those prejudices—or at least figure out a better way to hide them.

"Excellent," Julian said, rubbing his hands together. "I've had a few ideas about how to approach our research and I'd like your input."

"Whatever you've come up with is brilliant, I'm sure. It always is," Jadzia said with as much politeness as she could muster. Julian sounded too damn chipper for this early hour. He'd be more sympathetic if he feigned being as sleep and stimulant deprived as most humanoids tended to be after their sleep cycles. His unrestrained exuberance at the chance to work on Blue Sky further annoyed her. From the start, he'd embraced Sisko's order with enthusiasm, like a child being granted his chance to sit at the adult table. Julian recognized a bona fide opportunity when he saw one; Romulan methodology was largely unexplored territory for a Federation-trained scientist. At another time and place, she might share Julian's excitement. But this wasn't another time and place. So she listened patiently as he talked nearly nonstop for a few moments, answering him by nodding her head or saying "Uh-huh."

Midway through a dissertation on training regimens that might help the Allies better counter the Jem'Hadar in soldier-to-soldier combat scenarios, Julian stopped in his tracks. Furrowing his brow, he studied Jadzia's face intently. "If you don't mind me saying, you look like you didn't sleep a wink last night."

Jadzia repressed the urge to growl at him. Maybe Worf was wearing off on her. "How long have you known me, Julian? I've always been a night owl. Besides, you should know how it is with newlyweds—we took things easier last night or I might have been rousing you around 0300 to take care of my"—she cleared her throat—"injuries."

"Ah," he said, becoming suddenly tight-lipped. "I just thought you might still be upset about . . ." his voice trailed off.

"I'm fine," she said, knowing fully what Julian intended to say. She didn't want to talk about it this morning any more than she'd wanted to last night. "You and Worf—you're both assuming I've never done this before. That loss is something new. I have seven lives' worth of experience, Julian. Seven. I've survived the losses of lovers, friends, children, siblings—hell, I know what it's like to *die*. This latest loss of mine . . . it's just another pointless death among thousands of pointless deaths." As soon as the last word passed over her lips, Jadzia immediately regretted her sharp tone. Julian had been her longtime friend. He was reaching out to her in kindness and didn't deserve her pique of temper. She sighed, composed herself, and said softly, "Isn't that why we're working on this project? To prevent more of those pointless deaths?"

"Yes. Of course it is," he said simply.

They strode down the hall toward the turbolift in relative silence, nodding to some Bajoran Militia personnel Jadzia recognized from gamma shift. Once the turbolift doors had closed, they stood side by side, Jadzia sipping her *raktajino,* Julian's gaze fixed ahead. Out of the corner of her eye, she saw Julian take a deep breath, open his mouth as if he were about to speak, then quickly close it.

"Say it," she said.

"Excuse me?"

"Just say it. You have something else to say."

"Yesterday. In Sisko's office. You think Blue Sky is a bad idea."

THE DEVIL YOU KNOW 233

"I have reservations. But if the number of ideas you've come up with since yesterday is any indication, Blue Sky should be very successful."

"From the standpoint of advancing pure research, you're right—I am pleased," Julian conceded. "But I, too, have—" he paused "—concerns. Maybe not the same as yours."

She looked at him, inviting him to share his thoughts.

"Doesn't it bother you at all that we're being asked to use our scientific expertise to devise more effective ways of killing—even if we're planning on killing Jem'Hadar?"

Jadzia raised her eyebrows. "Is this about 'first do no harm'?"

"That," he said with a nod, "and devising methods to destroy civilizations isn't why I joined Starfleet in the first place. Our whole mission is to pursue exploration. This project, on the face anyway, runs counter to that mission."

She met his eyes, saw the earnestness in them and chose to swallow the argument into which she was about to launch, offering him, instead, a gentle smile. Not long ago, she would have agreed with him wholeheartedly. Today . . . Today sleep deprivation, frustration, and sadness underscored each crick in her neck and the gritty irritation behind her eyes. Hundreds of years of memories—and yesterday's potently personal visit to a cargo bay—reminded her that rarely could circumstances be as ideal as Julian wanted them to be. "You're right," she said finally. "But right now Starfleet needs me to be a soldier. So I'm going to be a soldier and get it over with."

At least the food is good, Jadzia thought, taking a bite of spicy *hasperat.* The wardroom had already been crowded with scientists when they arrived, many of them craning their necks to get a glance of the assignment list posted on the screen at the front of the room. A small buffet of breakfast and brunch snacks, glided in on a cart and pushed against the back wall, had been less busy. *The brass must be very serious about impressing our guests,* she thought, noting a platter of luscious—and rare—Romulan anemones. Not exactly enthusiastic to begin her Blue Sky assignment, she'd taken her time putting together a breakfast plate before assuming a place in line, waiting for her turn at the assignment list.

Almost as soon as they'd walked in, Julian had recognized a colleague from Daystrom talking with a sour-faced Romulan *(Could Romulans ever be classified as anything but "sour-faced,"* Jadzia wondered) and had excused himself from her company. She was not pleased to be abandoned—an atypical reaction to be certain. Most of the time, she loved social events, even work-related ones, and made friends quickly. Plunging into the group dynamics, figuring out whom she needed to charm in order to get what she wanted was a challenge she usually relished. Today, she figured it would be easier to persuade Quark to donate his day's profits to the kai's charity fund than sort through the conflicting agendas and motives she sensed in this group.

A friendly veneer barely camouflaged the bristling tension. Jadzia overheard a sharp exchange of words between the head of the Romulan delegation, who had made a cutting political remark, and Admiral Ross. A Romulan engineer began seething when Commander Vanderweg accidentally spilled some of her drink on his sleeve. Trying to figure out who she might talk to before the keynote, Jadzia scanned for familiar faces. *Fargo is here from the Centauri Institute; Captain Anjared from the Corps of Engineers . . .* she pivoted to take in the rest of the crowd. A Bolian she didn't know. A couple of Klingons who might be known to Worf or Martok. She felt a tap on her shoulder and turned, finding a slight Romulan female standing behind her. A stir of recognition niggled at her. *I know this woman. Well, well . . .*

"Commander Dax. It appears that once again we will be colleagues." A curt nod.

"Colleagues?" Jadzia grinned. "I have to confess I'm a little surprised to hear you refer to us as colleagues, Subcommander T'Rul. Are you planning on making friends this time? Because last time you were at Deep Space 9, I had the distinct impression that you were working with Starfleet only because your superiors ordered you to—and becoming socially involved was definitely not part of your assignment."

A hint of a tight-lipped smile appeared on T'Rul's face—one that didn't quite reach her eyes. "Our governments have put aside their differences to work together. So we must as well. Wartime doesn't allow us the luxury of allowing our personal objections to supercede the greater goal. In this case, the goal is defeating the Dominion."

That's almost exactly what Worf said. Coincidence, or surveillance on my quarters? Making a mental note to sweep her cabin for spying devices, Jadzia raised her glass. "To defeating the Dominion."

T'Rul nodded her head politely.

"I understand why you've been assigned to this project," Jadzia said. "We're still very appreciative of the work you did to help make the Romulan cloaking device compatible with the *Defiant.* Your expertise in weapons systems would make you a natural for this project. No clue what assignment I've drawn."

"You haven't had a chance to check the list?"

Jadzia shook her head.

"I've been assigned to the munitions task force," she said. "As have you."

Jadzia snorted. "I wonder whose idea that was. I'm the station's science officer—I study pulsars and quantum singularities. Astrophysics is more my expertise."

"Your work on the self-replicating mines was . . . impressive. I know the Vorta were amazed by your ingenuity—particularly Weyoun."

Clenching her teeth behind her smile, Jadzia was reminded that until only a short time ago, the Romulans maintained friendly diplomatic ties with the Dominion. *What's to keep them from renewing those bonds of friendship and sharing all our tactics with the Dominion?* she thought, adding yet another reason to the list of why this Romulan-Federation scientific exchange was a bad idea. "You know our old friend Weyoun, do you? How was he the last time you saw him?"

"Alive, unfortunately."

Startled by her response, Jadzia laughed, nearly snorting her juice up her nose. She dabbed the juice off her face with a napkin grabbed from the buffet cart. Noting the amused expression on T'Rul's face, Jadzia believed she might be seeing the first evidence of a sense of humor she had ever observed in a Romulan. The two women studied each other for a long moment.

"Colleagues, huh?"

T'Rul nodded.

"I've never been much of a team player in these kinds of things, so don't take it personally if I'm not the best partner," she said, making light. "I tend to prefer finding my own way."

T'Rul smiled. "As do I, Commander Dax. As do I. We might be better partners than you think."

Jadzia marched down the darkened hallway, hoping she could remember which of the lookalike lab doors was the right one. Unfortunately, there wasn't anyone around to ask: Security staff had relocated to perimeter areas and her fellow scientists had left for the day. She had followed her group when they left the wardroom, not exactly paying attention to which of the dozen laboratories Blue Sky had been assigned to inhabit. *Teaches me to go along with the crowd,* Jadzia thought, discovering as she scoured the halls that DS9's research facilities were more expansive than she remembered. *How long has it been since I was down here, engaged in genuine scientific inquiry? Too long, obviously. Ever since the war started . . .* She clamped down the thought before it could go any further.

Turning the last corner, she thought the hallway looked familiar, so she chose what she hoped was the right door and waited for the retinal scanner to confirm her ID.

Except for leaving her padd behind in the lab, the first day had gone as well as could be expected.

T'Rul had been correct: Jadzia had been assigned to study both

Allied and Dominion munitions in an effort to better understand
the strengths and weaknesses on each side. The hope was that the
scientists might be able to devise more effective tactics to counter
Jem'Hadar weaponry as well as designing more innovative offen-
sive weapons.

All the team members had been given access to a comprehensive database that contained the specs for all Allied weapons as well
as any available data on Dominion weaponry. Several Federation
torpedoes and phaser bank designs were singled out for group discussion with individual scientists pointing out what they considered to be the flaws or shortcomings in those designs. Each time
another classified Starfleet document appeared on the viewscreen,
Jadzia cringed inwardly. Dax, for many lifetimes, had struggled to
prevent secrets from falling into the hands of the very kinds of
people sitting beside her. Allowing the session to proceed, without
verbalizing her protests, was counterintuitive; replaying her conversation with Worf in her mind helped her keep her mouth shut.
Still, Garak's wisdom made more sense than Worf's: He was fond of
saying "Enemies make dangerous friends," an adage that Jadzia
found fit the situation perfectly.

The session had ended with virtually no new ground being
covered. The bulk of the day had been spent on information gathering and determining what subjects warranted further study. Even
though the subject matter had been relatively neutral, politically
and scientifically speaking, Jadzia was tightly wound when she left
for the evening. The tension had alleviated somewhat by spending
an hour in the holosuite, with Worf, reenacting a chapter from *The
Final Reflection,* one of his favorite novels. He'd even encouraged
her to spend some time playing *tongo.* And who was she to miss an
opportunity to play *tongo* with Worf's blessing.

Dr. Girani had contacted Jadzia on her way back to the habitat
ring, asking if she knew where the *Zephyr*'s fatality database had
ended up. It was then that Jadzia realized that she'd left her padd in
the laboratory—and that she'd forgotten to pass off the *Zephyr*'s
database to Julian when she saw him earlier. Knowing that Girani

planned to work in the morgue overnight, she'd decided to re-trieve the padd and drop it off at the doctor's office on her way to her quarters.

The lab door hissed open; Jadzia stepped over the threshold. Blue-violet light strips running around the room's perimeter of-fered adequate illumination for her to quickly make her way to the corner spot where she'd been sitting. Weaving in and out of several workstations, she bent over to check under desks or chairs as she walked.

Nothing.

She paused, scrutinizing various computer terminals, worktables and cabinets, wondering if someone had moved her padd, perhaps locking it up for the night.

And that's when she noticed a sliver of shadow play.

Her eyes flicked over the back wall, seeking the source of the shadows. The door to the adjoining lab had been left open. A protruding workstation blocked most of the light spilling into the munitions study team's lab, assuring that she—or anyone else visiting—wouldn't notice that the connecting lab, a lab not being used for Blue Sky, was occupied. Anyone working on their project had security clearance allowing access to highly classified materi-als; there wasn't anything *hidden* among them, unless a scientist was working on an unauthorized, even illegal, project. . . . The hair on her neck prickled.

She edged, silently, toward the open door. Flattening herself against the workstation, she listened.

The hum of machinery. The tonal responses of an interface console being tapped. Slow, regular inhalations. *Too bad for Admiral Ross that they certainly didn't waste any time, but oh how I love being right . . .*

Retrieving a Jem'Hadar pistol from among several samples tagged for study, Jadzia pivoted into the doorway, and thrust her weapon out in front of her. "Move away from the terminal."

Hands went up. The slender Romulan stood, took several steps backward.

The short, androgynous hair and military uniform gave few hints as to the trespasser's identity. "Turn around. I'd like to know who I'm turning in to station security." Jadzia's eyes never left the Romulan, who complied without comment. She needed only a profile to ascertain the intruder's identity. If the "spy" hadn't been so obvious, she might have laughed. "Let me give you a piece of advice, Subcommander T'Rul," she said, "if you want to make friends, breaking house rules is a guaranteed way to get off on the wrong foot. You haven't had a chance to catch up with Captain Sisko yet, have you?"

Pacing back and forth in the hallway outside the interrogation room did little to alleviate Jadzia's anger. She'd brought T'Rul to Odo's office *three hours ago*. Three hours. What did it take to determine if security protocols had been violated? Wasn't it obvious?! Of course they'd been violated—she'd been an eyewitness. Why hadn't they put T'Rul in a holding cell or dispatched a team from Starfleet intelligence to question her? She muttered a few potent Klingon curses that Curzon had been particularly fond of.

"Take it easy, Old Man," Benjamin said, raising a warning hand. "I know the Standard translation of that little diatribe and I assure you, this situation doesn't warrant that level of anxiety." He sat in the visitor's chair, his hands palm to palm, flexing his fingers, a calmer version of Jadzia's pacing rhythm.

She turned on her heel, eyes blazing. "Then what does? A full-on takeover of the station? At least you have a hint of what she was up to. Apparently I don't have clearance to be in the loop."

Benjamin shook his head. "That's not true, and you know it. Until the specifics of her story are confirmed, details are on a need-to-know basis."

"Yes, Benjamin, you already told me," Jadzia said, dropping into a chair. "I still have a hard time believing that she didn't even try to excuse herself. She admitted that she was attempting to hack into our database!"

"From everything I've seen, T'Rul has cooperated with security. We ought to find out what prompted this procedural breach before we turn her over to higher authorities."

"Procedural breach? Is that what we're calling it now, because I'll be—"

A door slid open and both Sisko and Jadzia stopped, their attention fixed on Odo.

"Starfleet Intelligence just uploaded a transmission to my database. You'll want to see this, Captain," he said. "You ought to come along too, Commander Dax." And he ushered them into the interrogation room.

Odo took a seat beside T'Rul; Worf was already positioned on her other side. Jadzia noted with some satisfaction that the Romulan had been cuffed to the armrest of her chair. *At least Odo isn't a fool,* she thought. Jadzia and Sisko took seats facing her. *I dare you to lie to my face,* she thought, fixing her stare on T'Rul.

Without the slightest change in her facial expression, T'Rul met Jadzia's eyes.

So that's how it's going to be, feeling grudging admiration for the Romulan's tenacity. *I'll still win.*

Worf tapped some commands into the tabletop interface. A screen on the forward wall lit up.

"Before we watch the recording," Odo said, addressing T'Rul, "I'd like you to tell Captain Sisko and Commander Dax what you told me."

Apparently unwilling to concede defeat in her battle of wills, T'Rul kept her eyes locked with Jadzia's as she began speaking. "The Dominion's assassination of Senator Vreenak surprised my government. Having seen no prior sign of Dominion treachery in our dealings with them, we found ourselves in the unfortunate position of having personnel in hostile territory. A full diplomatic contingent was on Cardassia Prime when Romulus declared war, including my mate, a senior attaché to the Romulan ambassador, and my two children, who worked as interns.

"State Securty claims that they sent advance warning of the Senate's war declaration to all Romulan nationals within enemy territory in the hopes that they would evacuate." Her eyes narrowed and she buried her fingernails into her palms. "I have no proof of those claims, nor do any of the others whose family members were trapped on Cardassia. It was the only excuse State Security offered us when they delivered word of the wholesale slaughter of all Romulans by the Jem'Hadar."

T'Rul lowered her eyes to the tabletop. "When I asked for proof of the massacre, they refused to provide it." Her voice dropped. "They laughed when I suggested that our people might not be dead—that they'd be valuable prisoners, possibly used as currency in a future deal. The knowledge they'd have about the Empire's intelligence networks and military capability could be invaluable to the Dominion. State Security refused to entertain answering my questions, saying only that if I pursued the matter further I would be turned over to the Tal Shiar for a lesson in patriotism." She spat. "When the opportunity came to leave Romulus to work on Blue Sky, I took it, hoping that I might find the proof—proof that the Tal Shiar was lying—in a Federation database." T'Rul's eyes met Sisko's. "My reasons for accessing your data systems were personal, not political, Captain. I acted without the consent or knowledge of my superiors."

An awkward silence permeated the room as the ramifications of T'Rul's story settled on them. Jadzia hardly dared breathe aloud. Secret battle plans, codes to defense networks, ship movements—a Romulan seeking that information would have been predictable. This . . . this had taken her off guard.

"Mr. Worf, I assume you have the next piece of the puzzle," Benjamin said, looking at her husband.

Leave it to Benjamin to smooth the way, Jadzia thought gratefully. She took a small amount of pleasure in knowing that some of Sisko's diplomatic finesse came from the time he'd spent with Curzon.

"There was nothing in the station database related to the event Subcommander T'Rul describes," Worf said. "However, through back channels, Starfleet Intelligence had evidently obtained a recording that they say should clarify the situation." Worf touched the interface again, and the monitor came to life.

A dark, cavernous judgment chamber—clearly of Cardassian design—appeared on the screen. Identifying the participating parties in the sea of gray faces proved challenging for Jadzia, especially since the recording device shifted in and out of focus. What wasn't in question were the Jem'Hadar soldiers lined up behind what appeared to be dozens of kneeling, bound Romulans. A clumsy zoom-in revealed a cluster of Cardassians, Damar among them, standing with a Vorta who may or may not have been Weyoun. Damar appeared to be holding something in his hand, and only when he raised it to his lips and threw back his head did she realize it was a fluted glass of *kanar.*

A Jem'Hadar First stepped toward the pair. The Vorta seemed oblivious to him, gabbing away cheerfully, though the words were inaudible to Jadzia. She saw Damar nodding, looking impatient. The Vorta finally seemed to notice the First and with a careless wave of his hand, gave the signal. The camera jerked and zoomed out.

The Jem'Hadar standing in the back drew their pistols as one and fired on the first row of Romulans, point-blank shots to the backs of their heads. Shattering skulls sprayed bits of bone and brain into the air, spattering both the Jem'Hadar and the other Romulans.

Stunned, Jadzia couldn't stop staring.

When the first line of bodies fell over dead, the Jem'Hadar stepped over them and repeated the act on the next line. Row by row, the Jem'Hadar were making their way forward as each subsequent line of Romulans fell dead.

Jadzia closed her eyes and whispered, "Enough."

"I agree, Commander," Sisko said, his voice tight with emotion. "Turn it off."

The relief in the room—the release of tension—when Worf stopped the recording was palpable. Jadzia looked around at the others, seeing her own horror reflected in each of their faces.

"I take it, Mr. Worf, that this is authentic?"

Worf nodded. "Starfleet Intelligence has independently confirmed the authenticity of the record through an informant on Romulus. They've also been able to determine that Subcommander T'Rul's family was among those in the judgment chamber."

T'Rul was shaking. Her shoulders convulsed; a wail escaped her throat.

Jadzia looked away, her own senses still reeling with the images of slaughter. And what must T'Rul feel, now knowing what fate her loved ones suffered? Her chest tightened.

Benjamin walked around the table, stopping in front of T'Rul. "Under the circumstances, Subcommander, reporting you to Starfleet security or to your delegation would only bring further suspicion and mistrust between our peoples." He signaled to Odo, who unfastened her restraints. Her arms slid bonelessly off the armrests, into her lap.

"But I expect that for the duration of your stay you will comport yourself like an ally," Benjamin continued. "Even a hint of misconduct, and I assure you, I won't hesitate to hand you over. Am I clear?"

"I will not violate your trust, Captain," T'Rul said, the emotionless façade falling once again.

"For what it's worth, T'Rul, I am very, very sorry for your loss," he said.

The Romulan swallowed hard and nodded her head.

Jadzia sat stone-still, gazed fixed downward, as Odo escorted T'Rul out of the room. She stirred only when Worf touched her shoulder, indicating the time had come for her to return home.

"Commander Dax? Here are those shield matrix configuration tables you'd requested."

Jadzia stirred from her reverie and accepted the proffered padd. "Thanks."

As her associate, a Bolian lieutenant, returned to his own workstation, she turned her attention back to watch, for the twentieth time, a simulation of a reworked quantum torpedo against a

Jem'Hadar battle cruiser. No matter how much she tinkered with the torpedo's targeting sensors, trajectories, or detonation mechanism, she came up with the same result—failure. Examining the shield data, she reformulated the simulation's calculations, and requested the computer rerun it. When the torpedo detonated *before* it reached the cruiser, Jadzia knew the time had come for a mid-afternoon *raktajino*. She shoved back her chair and made for the replicator, her steps slowing when she saw T'Rul standing there, studying the menu. For a moment, she considered returning to her workstation, and she slowed down her walk. She hadn't exchanged words with the Romulan since their first day working on the project, fully fifty-two hours ago. Mustering up remotely neutral small talk that didn't sound ridiculous under the circumstances wasn't possible. "How's it going?" hardly addressed T'Rul's very real losses. Recommending exotic pastries from the replicator file would be shallow. But before she could think up a plan, Jadzia found herself standing beside T'Rul at the replicator.

As T'Rul struggled to make the computer understand what she wanted, Jadzia stood by, fidgeting with her hands linked behind her back. When T'Rul threw the replicator's latest mistake into the recycler, Jadzia unthinkingly stepped in, told the computer what she *thought* T'Rul was asking for. A ceramic mug, filled with a steaming red liquid topped off with a mountain of foam, materialized.

"Is this it?" Jadzia said, offering her the soup.

"Your computer didn't understand what I was—"

"My last host—Curzon—spent some time on Vulcan where he had a chance to sample some of their native delicacies. What you described to the computer was similar enough to *shav'rot* that I thought it was worth a try."

T'Rul sipped off the edge. "While not entirely the same as what we brew on Romulus, it is close enough. Satisfactory." She offered Jadzia a curt nod in acknowledgment of her help, and began walking away.

I can't believe I'm saying this. . . . "T'Rul."

The Romulan turned around.

"I know there's no possible way I can understand what you've been through lately. But I do know that this war—this war is costing us all far too much," Jadzia said quietly. "A few days ago, I found out I'd lost someone—an old, dear friend who changed my whole life. He was killed when the Jem'Hadar attacked an unarmed civilian transport outside the Cardassian border. I know it's not the same as losing a husband and children, but I wanted you to know that you're not alone. In your grief, I mean."

T'Rul paused, scrutinizing Jadzia for a long moment before saying, "There is no question in my mind that the Jem'Hadar are a plague. They are a disease that must be wiped out and destroyed." The subcommander started to turn away.

And for Jadzia, everything suddenly fell into place.

Her mind raced, and the more she thought, the more ideas tumbled out of the recesses of her mind, revealing a new world of possibilities in an instant. She reached over and grabbed T'Rul's arm. "Wait."

T'Rul stopped and looked at her quizzically; Jadzia felt her pull away slightly. She probably should let go, but T'Rul was part of this. She needed the Romulan woman to stay put.

"I think I've figured something out," Jadzia whispered, heading for the exit. "Follow me. We can't talk here."

Once out in the hall, Jadzia launched into her explanation before T'Rul could siege her with questions. "If the Jem'Hadar are a plague, why aren't we treating them like a plague? When there's an epidemic, how do we defeat it? We neutralize the organism, develop a vaccination or wipe out the source. *Wipe out the source.*"

Whatever protest had been on T'Rul's lips when they left the room evaporated as comprehension of Jadzia's words dawned on her.

Their eyes met.

And Jadzia knew they understood each other.

The conversation between them started slowly. For her part, T'Rul talked about her mate, how they'd spent most of their married lives apart and how pleased she was that their children had decided to follow their father in such a prestigious career. Jadzia reciprocated with anecdotes about Dr. th'Rasdeth. They had just moved from discussing their impressions of Blue Sky to the war when several doors opened admitting several dozen scientists into the hallway, including Julian.

"Mind if I join you?" Julian called out.

Jadzia and T'Rul separated, allowing him to step in between them.

"Sorry I haven't had a chance to welcome you back, Subcommander," he said, offering her a smile in lieu of the usual human handshake.

"I believe we meet under better circumstances this time than last," she said. "Not in terms of the war, of course, but as allies."

"Speaking of our being allies, how do you think Blue Sky is going?"

Jadzia and T'Rul exchanged looks. Both of them agreed that their munitions team had covered very little new ground so far. Trying to be sensitive to various cultural and political differences meant the team took baby steps to avoid offending one side or the other.

He looked first at Jadzia, then T'Rul. "Ahhh. I see you're as frustrated as I am."

"We didn't say that," Jadzia said.

"You didn't have to. If it makes you feel any better, the efforts to create a more efficient, more effective Allied soldier are equally bogged down," Julian said. "Devising a universal training regimen that can be used by all the various species in our forces is proving to be unworkable. Say, I'm off to the infirmary. Walk with me to the turbolift?"

Jadzia gestured "after you," and they began walking.

"Have you considered using performance-enhancing agents?" T'Rul asked.

Julian shook his head. "Starfleet's reluctant to embrace a strategy that at least on the surface resembles what the Founders have done with the Jem'Hadar and ketracel-white."

T'Rul sighed. "But it works. The Jem'Hadar can fight without eating or sleeping."

"True enough."

"That's one thing I don't understand about the Federation. Your naïve morality."

"I can't think of a place where our ethics have interfered with our fighting ability," Julian said.

"Biogenic weapons. Why not use them against the Jem'Hadar? They wouldn't hesitate to use one against us."

Julian frowned. "Leaving aside that biogenic weapons are outlawed by interstellar treaties signed by the Federation, the Romulans, the Klingons, and even the Cardassians before the war," he said, "such weapons often have catastrophic ecological consequences, not to mention the potential for rampant mutations or other unforeseeable complications. Starfleet isn't willing to accept those consequences."

"Treaties and weapons bans are designed to fit the times," T'Rul said. "And as we have seen, times change. Circumstances change."

"Desperate times call for desperate measures, is that your view, Subcommander?" Julian asked. "Consequences be damned?"

T'Rul's eyes narrowed. "I know something of consequences, Doctor—particularly those that result from the failure to act in time, with every resource at hand."

Jadzia swallowed, hoping Julian would just let it go. He seemed to be considering a response when T'Rul suddenly looked at her and asked, "What do you think, Commander Dax?"

"Yes, Jadzia," Julian said. "I'd be fascinated to hear your perspective."

Jadzia sighed. "Truthfully, I'm surprised that Command hasn't put more options out on the table. Even *theoretical* options such as biogenic weapons—and before you get all worked up, Julian, let me explain. You should know, as a human, that one of the most critical wars in Earth's history was decided by what was, for its time, an unfathomably horrible weapon."

"The Manhattan Project. But this is—"

"How is it different, Julian? Hundreds, if not thousands, are dying every week, civilians and Starfleet. We're losing starships, equipment, and emptying our stockpiles of raw materials faster than we can replace them. Can we really afford to *take* options off the table?"

The trio reached the turbolift.

"Too bad my patients need me, or we could continue this conversation at Quark's."

"I guess we'll just have to continue it without you, Julian. Truce?" Jadzia smiled and gave his arm an affectionate squeeze, before he disappeared into the turbolift.

"So, can I buy you dinner?" Jadzia asked her companion.

T'Rul studied her intently, giving her the distinct feeling she was being tested. "Did you mean what you said just now?"

"What? The part about putting options on the table? Yes. I think so."

T'Rul smiled, a narrow, tight-lipped smile. "Then, yes, I'd very much enjoy sharing a meal with you."

The first few days they'd worked together had been predictably awkward, filled with uncomfortable silences and fumbled attempts to figure out which direction their research should take. They'd worked surreptitiously in the Blue Sky labs, probing the database for any relevant files but found, unsurprisingly, that the Federation's ethical quandary over genetic engineering made research on the subject difficult to find. Other than obtaining comprehensive studies on the Jem'Hadar—provided for use in Blue Sky by Julian—Jadzia and T'Rul had come up with little to nothing. So both women had fallen back on their personal resources—T'Rul's access to Romulan files on the subject and Jadzia's high-level clearance to sensitive Federation materials—for answers. Answers that Jadzia hoped would be forthcoming. Every day that passed without a breakthrough was another day of casualty lists and missing ships and squandered opportunities.

T'Rul was waiting at Jadzia's quarters when she arrived back from her ops shift. Within minutes, both women were hunched over their computer terminals studying. Time passed with little comment, their studies requiring all their focus. The densely written papers had been written for experts in their field. Even with Audrid's memories and biological expertise, Dax had to stretch her abilities to fully understand the complexities of genetic engineering. She marveled at the precision—the elegance—of the techniques and the astonishing potential results they offered. But while she found the articles on curing the Mabgonian plague fascinating, she began to wonder if either she or T'Rul had a chance at accomplishing the task they'd set for themselves. She closed down a particularly tedious analysis of a food-based parasite and moved to the next file, "The Challenges of Interspecies Conception."

Her eyes flickered over the text, and as she studied, the same instinct that told her that Grilka wasn't the woman for Worf told her she might have found what she was searching for. Barely able to contain her excitement, she gestured for T'Rul to come over and check out the article she was reading.

"Listen to this." Jadzia began reading from the article, " 'Ovarian resequencing uses enzymes to rewrite specific sections of DNA.' "

"I'm not sure how this pertains to our project . . ." T'Rul said dubiously.

"If incompatible gametes can be changed so that fertilization can take place, can't genes that produce undesirable Jem'Hadar traits be switched off? If we could resequence Jem'Hadar DNA, switching off traits that give them superior strength or encourage aggression . . . ?"

A triumphant smile—the first Jadzia had ever seen—spread over T'Rul's face. "Fighting them would be a new thing entirely. The complexion of the war would change."

Holding the padd behind her back, Jadzia walked purposefully through Quark's booth, her jaunty step belying her internal trepidation. All their work—the hours of painstaking analysis—all of it came down to the conversation she was about to have. She was within a meter of the table when she realized she would be interrupting an ongoing game. *Julian will make swift work of winning and then I'll approach him,* she thought, slipping into a vacant chair where she could keep an eye on things.

"Don't tell me you think you can pull it off this time," Miles O'Brien said, and took a pull off the mug of ale he'd been nursing. He turned a skeptical eye on the dartboard hanging on the wall. "Besides, I can't decide if that Manchester board makes it easier or harder."

"Between my legs, my back to the dartboard, dart in the right hand in one bull's-eye, dart in the left hand in the other," Julian said confidently. "If that's not a handicap, I don't know what is."

"You say that every time and every time, you still win." Miles fiddled with his few remaining darts. "Just take your shot already. I'll pay your tab and get on my way home."

Not surprisingly, Miles's green hadn't yet scored.

With exaggerated grace, Julian bent at the waist and walked each foot out several paces. A dart in each hand, he counted to three and made his toss.

Jadzia winced—for Miles—who had instantly dropped his head to the tabletop.

"I don't know why I let you do this to me, Julian," he said, rising from his chair. He reached out to the Ferengi waiter who had been waiting patiently nearby and thumbed the padd displaying the tab.

Bashir slapped his friend on the back good-naturedly. "I don't know why you do it either, but I'm certainly grateful to have my bar bill paid, if it makes you feel any better."

Miles shook his head, and mumbled good-bye.

Jadzia saw her opening. "Julian!"

He spun around. "I take it you saw my latest triumph."

"Impressive. But since I know it's just a matter of you calculating trajectories and how much force to apply, I'm less impressed than I would be if it were just raw luck."

"Fair enough," Julian said. "Join me?" He gestured at the table he'd been occupying with Miles.

"Absolutely." She slid into the chair opposite Julian, placing her padd on the table between them. "Can you look at something I've been working on?"

"Blue Sky?"

Jadzia nodded.

While Julian perused the padd, Jadzia waved a waiter over and ordered a Black Hole. Julian still hadn't said a word a few minutes later when the drink arrived. *Whether that's a good sign or a bad one*—she took a deep breath—*who can say?* and she swallowed a mouthful of synthehol.

"Fascinating stuff, really," Julian said, still scrolling through the pages. He paused for a long moment, then put the padd down and crossed his arms. "A theoretical analysis of how to alter the DNA of a fully matured Jem'Hadar."

Hearing the tight, higher modulation in his voice, Jadzia steeled herself for his next words.

"A biogenic device." He shoved the padd across the table.

Jadzia caught it.

"Since when did the project take this approach?"

"What do you mean?"

"Don't play coy with me, Jadzia," he whispered harshly. "You know exactly what I mean. We discussed this. This isn't about teaching officers trained in astrophysics to combat Jem'Hadar soldiering or weaponry. That thing you have in your pocket—" he leaned over until he was nose to nose with her "—is about genocide."

Shaking her head, Jadzia took another swallow of her drink. "It doesn't kill, maim, or infect the Jem'Hadar with disease. This isn't the Quickening. We're not damning them to a slow, painful death."

"That's not the point!" he said through clenched teeth.

"What's wrong with switching off the genes that make the Jem'Hadar practically invulnerable? Even if they'd get tired, we'd stand a better chance!"

"Every sentient creature has the right to self-determination, Jadzia. Altering a species without their consent, is no different than what the Founders do—what they did with the Vorta and the Jem'Hadar."

"So says the man with the miraculous ability to hit a double bull's-eye by throwing darts between his legs."

"For every Julian Bashir there's a Jack, a Patrick, a Sarina, or, yes, a Khan Singh. And when a couple of amateurs—" He shook his head. "Who's to say that the Founders, anticipating just such a strategy as yours, haven't built a failsafe into the chromosome? Tampering could potentially make them more deadly. Setting loose an entire breeding facility of half-crazed Jem'Hadar . . . My, my, that sounds like a sure way to win a battle."

"I think it's a risk worth taking. To not even consider a cleaner alternative to having to send ship after ship into combat is foolish."

"A cleaner alternative," Julian repeated. Scowling, he looked away, clearly seething. Finally he seemed to rein in his emotions and met her eyes again. "You know, Jadzia, there was a time, not all that long ago, when a standard-issue Starfleet hand phaser had a setting capable of *dematerializing* its target. A living being hit by such a weapon would, to all intents and purposes, simply vanish in a burst of light. No blood, no bodies, no mess. It was quite . . . tidy."

"That's very interesting, Julian, but—"

"I'm not finished," Julian said. "Starfleet records show that, historically, when lethal force was required, more phasers were discharged at that setting than at any of the more conventional 'kill' settings of any Starfleet hand weapon before—or since. Do you understand the implications of that? When dealing death became 'clean,' it also became easy. Once those statistics became known, Starfleet ceased producing phasers with a dematerialization setting."

When Jadzia refused to reply, Julian got up from his chair and crouched down close to her. Whispering in her ear, he said, "When war becomes painless, when our consciences are slowly, gently lulled to sleep, we stop having reasons to end the fighting. War becomes a game. People become expendable pieces to be moved around at whim, or gambled casually on a wheel of chance. Think about this carefully, Jadzia."

Picking up one of the darts Miles had left on the table, she rolled the shaft between her fingers. "I'm willing to see how lucky I am," she said, and carelessly tossed it in the general direction of the dartboard. She pushed her way past Julian and toward the exit, never once looking back to see if she'd hit her mark.

"He never said it wouldn't work, correct?" T'Rul said, as they stepped off the turbolift at the bottom of lower pylon two.

"No. But he did raise several valid points about the general safety of testing the enzyme. Such as, what if we let it loose on a large population and we turn them into crazed out-of-control maniacs instead of calm, cold in-control maniacs."

"I believe we can address your concerns."

"You know as well as I do how unreliable simulations can be when it comes to modeling genetic interactions. I'm simply—"

"Here we are," T'Rul said finally. "Go through this airlock and we will be in sovereign territory of the Romulan Star Empire."

Jadzia took a deep breath, threaded her hands behind her back and set her jaw determinedly. "And there's not a squad of disruptor-bearing soldiers behind that door waiting to take me hostage?" she said, trying to make light.

"I cannot guarantee that, but I have been assured by my superiors that you will be safe aboard our ship."

"I'm supposed to take the word of a Romulan?"

T'Rul nodded.

"Fine then. I'll take *your* word. Lead the way."

As earthy and greasy as the interior of a Klingon ship felt, the shadowy interior of a Romulan warbird felt neat to the point of claustrophobia, as if every rivet and air duct had been crafted for a very specific, very controlled purpose. Cautiously, she followed behind T'Rul, alert to ambient noise, wondering how many pairs of hidden eyes analyzed her every millimeter. Squaring her shoulders, she lengthened her strides.

T'Rul approached a cargo hold door armed with, Jadzia recognized, a sophisticated security device mounted on a side panel. T'Rul laid her hand, palm up, on a small platform in front of the device. A needle-thin projectile emerged from the box and pricked the tip of the Romulan's finger. A brief pause was followed by a second needle-device emerging from the box and puncturing another finger. *Barbaric.*

"It checks DNA from a physical sample," T'Rul said. "Retinal scanners and handprint sensors are easily duped. A complete fabrication of cellular tissue is nearly impossible."

"It's rather—"

"Crude? Possibly. But it reminds all who approach the price for deception. You see, the first needle not only samples DNA, but it injects a small dose of poison. Upon confirmation of the applicant's identity, the antidote is administered."

She offered T'Rul a weak smile. The host of reasons why Jadzia mistrusted Romulans suddenly came flooding back to her, but she didn't have time to indulge her paranoia: The cargo bay door had opened.

Her eyes widened; her heart hammered in her throat. *Please don't let this be what I think it is.* She forced her leaden feet to move over the threshold until her limbs stiffened.

On all sides of the room, six stasis chambers hummed along. Dropping to the floor beside a chamber, Jadzia let her hand hover over the chamber's face, hesitating—as if touching the smooth metal skin would connect her with the thing inside. Her thinking ability kicked in long enough to prompt her to pull out her tricorder. *Jem'Hadar.* "You've had these—these chambers the whole time."

"How is it the humans put it? An eye for an eye?"

Tightness in her chest bespoke the horrible realizations now cascading over her. "This is what your people had in mind all along. You were using us—using me—to help you design a weapon you knew the Federation would be squeamish about using themselves."

A grim laugh escaped her throat as she remembered how much she loved being right about Romulan motives. And lo and behold, they hadn't disappointed her, proving that they were every bit the lying, slippery sneaks she'd always known them to be.

"If it hadn't been you," T'Rul continued, "it would have been someone else. Dr. Bashir, perhaps."

Julian. Would Julian have been as stupid as I . . . I can't deal with this right now. I . . . "I need to think this over," Jadzia said, scrambling to her feet. Pressing the heels of her hands against the side of her head, she closed her eyes, trying to squeeze the thoughts from her mind.

T'Rul grabbed her by the arms. "We could do it, Jadzia. We could design the prototype here, aboard the ship, run the test and no one would have to know."

"I have to go." She reached for the door panel, hesitated—"This isn't going to kill me if I try to get out?"

T'Rul shook her head.

Jadzia rushed through the warbird's empty, twisting hallways, certain that her every step was being observed and recorded by some unseen camera. The air in the ship felt thin and each inhalation parched her throat. She hugged her arms close to her body as she exited the airlock, and fought to keep her hands from shaking as she rode the turbolift back up the docking pylon and on to ops.

When she reached Benjamin's doorway, she was still shaking. The moment he saw her face, he dismissed the young officer he was conversing with.

She collapsed in his visitor's chair. And perhaps because she was tired, or because she had wearied of keeping it all bottled up inside her, the story began spilling out, from her first encounter with T'Rul in the wardroom to her last chilling moments in the Romulan warbird.

Benjamin contemplated her last revelation for a long moment. "Do you have reason to believe the Romulans have more than six Jem'Hadar prisoners aboard their ship?"

"I can't even guess," she said. As her adrenaline energy seeped away, she slumped deeper into the chair. "What are you going to do about it?"

A pause, and then, "Nothing."

Jadzia's eyebrows shot up; she shook her head, wondering if she'd misheard him. "Excuse me? The Romulans are conspiring to develop biogenic weapons—and they've nearly succeeded thanks to me, the unwitting dupe sitting here. You're not going to shut down Blue Sky?"

Rising from his chair, Benjamin stood before his window, his back to her. Jadzia found her own gaze following his as she was drawn into the space-night, the white-blue starlight holding the blackness at bay.

"You've done your duty as a Starfleet officer in reporting this to me," he said. "That you did tells me that you have an ingrained sense of right and wrong that takes over when, eventually, you come to your senses." He turned to look at her. "The decision is yours, Jadzia."

"But, Benjamin—"

"I trust you. If anyone can sort through the light and the shadows and the dark, it's you, Old Man."

Time slipped away as she wandered the Promenade, past restaurants and repair shops. She walked by the classrooms, continued through the atrium, and followed obscure service corridors wherever they led. The rhythm of her footsteps gave a steady cadence to her thoughts.

She played and replayed Julian's arguments against testing the biogenic enzyme and couldn't honestly say she disagreed with him—in theory. But theories dealt in ideals, predicting outcomes based on known, measurable variables. The random elements—the unknowns she couldn't foresee—troubled Jadzia. Say she agreed with Julian's arguments and decided to not go ahead with the testing, scuttling any potential use of a biogenic weapon. Most likely, the war would continue as it was currently. For every Jem'Hadar lost, the Founders would breed ten more. If the allies attacked every known hatching facility, the Founders would build more. *The Jem'Hadar are expendable to the Founders, so why are we reluctant to see them as the Founders see them—as just another bioweapon?*

Not doctors. Not engineers. Not parents. Not friends.

She wandered up to the balcony level and stepped over to the railing, watching the flow of people on the main level. Sometimes, as she walked through the habitat ring, she looked at the closed doors and wondered what was happening behind them. Arguments, lovemaking, lazy mid-shift naps, mind-numbing entertainment, the writing of an award-winning play, or working through a formula that would transform the fortunes of worlds. *And the enzyme we've developed. The enzyme could determine who among all those people lives and who dies. We'll never know if I don't test it.*

Can I live with myself if I walk away from the chance to effect change?

She touched her combadge. "Dax to Worf."

"Worf, here."

"I'll be late tonight, so don't wait up. Miss me?"

"My blood sings for you and you alone."

"Hold that thought. Dax out."

She started in the direction of the docking ring.

Jadzia reexamined each tool on the tray, making certain that the hypospray had been correctly calibrated and that the neural sensors were transmitting properly. She'd checked and rechecked the tools more times than she cared to count over the last hour. "So how'd you know I'd be back?"

"Because you are not a fool," T'Rul said as she input the last series of algorithms into the vitals monitor. "I believe that takes care of it. We can proceed."

A beep from the console signaled that the test subject had been successfully revived from stasis and would be arriving momentarily.

Linking her hands behind her back, Jadzia pulled her arms away from her body in a stretch; her shoulders and arms had started to ache. She'd been standing for several hours as she and T'Rul worked through the last few steps in the test process. Replicating the enzyme had been the easy part; devising a mechanism to deliver the enzyme to the test subject required a singular, but physically exhausting, focus.

When and if the weapon was ever deployed, T'Rul had designed a mechanism that delivered the enzyme via inhalation, making it easier to target large groups of Jem'Hadar no matter where they were based. A canister, for instance, could be transported inside a Jem'Hadar cruiser and a ship's ventilation system would quickly distribute the enzyme throughout the ship, exposing all the Jem'Hadar on board. In theory, only micrograms of the enzyme were required to initiate the physiological changes. Still, Jadzia wanted to measure the quantities inhaled by the test subject and be able to chart how quickly the enzyme became absorbed; pouring a vial into the laboratory's air didn't offer her enough control. She solved the problem by figuring out how to dispense the enzyme through a rebreather.

The laboratory door hissed open.

Two Romulans—Jadzia assumed they were techs—wheeled in the gurney with the heavily sedated test subject. Placidly, she watched them prep the subject, twisting the rebreather tubing between her thumb and her forefinger while she waited. A fan's *chu-chu-chu* sounded distant—muffled—in contrast to the percussive tympani of her heart. Feeling her limbs grow thick, unsteady, she swayed forward . . .

"Commander Dax. We are ready to proceed."

She braced herself against the edge of a worktable.

A long pause. "Can I connect the sensors?" T'Rul asked.

Jadzia shook herself back into the moment. "Yes. Of course. If you like." Through rapid eye blinks, the numbers on the readouts blurred together and she felt dizzy; she placed a hand on her stomach. *I should walk away. Let T'Rul finish the job.* She closed her eyes, shutting it all out.

Rapidly firing sensations assaulted her. She recognized them immediately as pieces of seconds lived over hundreds of years . . . prickly summer grass, wailing siren, bitter wine, a musical phrase, a spinning light, warm skin to warm skin, carving knife sinking into her belly, Dax dissolving into descending darkness. And a whirling sea. Her sea. A sea of coffins. The muted dead. The sum total of their lives, the meaning, the memories, torn away and lost in the endless vacuum of space.

Unlike Jadzia. Jadzia would live as long as Dax lived. She had a sort of immortality: the luxury of time to make mistakes, knowing that in another life, she could correct them if she chose. Even with all her present fears and doubts, she still could choose to act now.

And in the end, She made her choice. Because the dead could not.

Turning around, she glanced at T'Rul. The sensors had been attached to the test subject. A brief glance at the monitors indicated that all equipment was functioning. Consoles displayed sinus rhythms, neurological activity, respiration, heart rate.

Her last thought before she placed the mask over his face was how surprised she was that the subject had blue eyes.

. . . A loud crash. The scream of one of the techs. A frantically blinking yellow light. Warning beeps simultaneously erupting from a room of consoles. Jadzia spun around from her monitoring station in time to see the Jem'Hadar jerk his legs free from their bonds and leap from the table. Her hand flew to her phaser. The Jem'Hadar clutched the tech by the throat, choked the life from her, and threw her corpse against the wall, shattering her skull. Jadzia's first shot singed his shoulder. Her second burned a hole through his chest.

Her third blew his head off.

She stepped back quickly enough to avoid being pinned beneath him.

Time to regret and recover wasn't an option. Jadzia and T'Rul immediately began an inquiry into the data they collected. What they learned was, in attempting to rewrite Jem'Hadar DNA, they'd destroyed the creature's ability to process the white. The enzyme's effect hastened, and intensified, the effects of white deprivation, rendering the test subject more dangerous.

After several hours of compiling the data, the Romulan scientists, who had been overseeing T'Rul's and Jadzia's work from a distance, decided to abandon further pursuit of their line of inquiry. All records of the experiment, including the bodies of the Jem'Hadar and the Romulan tech, would presumably vanish. Save one small memento Jadzia would need when she was ready for answers.

Dax asked the Romulan transport chief to send her directly to her quarters. Walking through the corridors during the busiest part of the station's day would be a bad idea under the circumstances. Besides, Worf would have left for his shift—being alone in her quarters would free her from having to apologize for having been gone all night. And the blood spatters on her uniform? She couldn't plausibly explain those.

As the familiar walls materialized, she couldn't help wondering if she'd dreamed the events of last night. Pushing a stray lock away from her face, she felt gummy residue crusted on her hair. She combed out the residue with her fingers, examined her hand, smudged with coagulated blood and bone-white grit, then wiped it clean on her uniform. *So I wasn't dreaming.*

She removed her pips and her combadge, stripped off her uniform, and threw it into the recycler. Whether or not the stains came out, she never would wear it again. She padded off toward the shower.

Considering that she couldn't recall the last time she'd slept, a nap might be good. She could take a personal day. See if Lieutenant Commander Vanderweg could take her shift, which began—she checked the chronometer—in a little over an hour. She could crawl between the covers and sink into the blissful numbness.

If she *could* sleep.

Staying busy might be a better choice; blending into the ops routine, she could effectively vanish from notice into the sea of bodies and computers and desperately important duties that all good Starfleet soldiers were about these days. She almost laughed aloud. A good Starfleet soldier.

Maybe I should contact Worf and let him know I'm on my way. Her eyes teared at the thought of him—they'd hardly had enough time together lately. She looked for her combadge on the nightstand and the vanity table before the thought occurred to her that it might still be on her uniform. But she'd taken her uniform off. *Where did I . . . what was I going to do again? Oh yeah. Shower. Damn, but I'm tired.*

She stood in the sonic waves long after she needed to. Impertinent thoughts kept encroaching on her solitude. Leaving the shower finally silenced the nagging voice in her head; she moved thoughtlessly through her routine until she was nearly ready to go. The sense of having forgotten something pulled at her; she ignored it.

Her swift fingers deftly wove the last strands of hair into a braid and she fished around in her drawer for a hairclip. Pips and combadge? Living room. She passed the replicator. Raktajino. *I haven't had my morning* raktajino.

There. On the coffee table were her pips and her combadge. She wondered, irrationally, if anyone would notice anything different about her. *Like, that last night I witnessed a killing.* She quickly suppressed an escaping giggle, appalled by her inappropriateness. But the memory of the Jem'Hadar's death pulled her thoughts backward into the night; she reviewed them with cold objectivity.

Of course Julian had been right about the consequences of experimenting on the Jem'Hadar. He was, after all, the Federation's expert on the subject. And that aside, Julian tended to be right about everything.

The enzyme, at first, appeared to be working exactly as Jadzia and T'Rul had predicted it would. She vaguely recalled watching the morphing colors on the neural monitors with fascination as, hour by hour, the intensity of brain activity shifted from one hemisphere to another—neural pathways rewritten in front of her eyes.

It should have worked. We did everything right! Brusquely, she attached her pips to her collar. A dull twinge of a headache radiated from her temples. *Did I get that* raktajino *yet?* She paused. Surveyed her quarters, seeing, but not seeing.

Jadzia spied the datachip sitting on the coffee table.

When . . . ? A stretcher bearing one of the shrouded corpses had passed, she'd averted her eyes, and then saw the chip—a download of the visual record of the experiment that one of Romulan scientists had made, forgotten during the flurry of mop-up activity. She'd forgotten that she had it.

Twenty minutes before her shift. *Probably should get going.*

Fixed where she stood, she stared at the datachip.

Who am I fooling? I'm gonna be late. . . .

Pulling a chair up to the monitor, she scanned the datachip contents into the computer memory and sat back to watch. She wanted answers. *Now.* Pretending to review ships' logs and casualty reports at her science station would be an exercise in futility as long as her thoughts lingered elsewhere. She held her breath, waiting, waiting . . . The screen flickered. The footage began.

The recording device had been mounted on the ceiling, giving her a global view of the laboratory. From this vantage, were it not for their uniforms, their dark hair might have made it difficult to distinguish between her and T'Rul. Jadzia found their apparent similarity amusing: the possibility of being mistaken for a Romulan had never occurred to her.

"Get on with it," she muttered, scooting in closer to the monitor so she could fast-forward through the gurney being brought in, the techs connecting the monitors to the test subject's body. *I'm leaning against the worktable, prepping the rebreather, cover his face, administer the dose. . . .* For long moments, she impassively studied the pictures until the juncture where the Jem'Hadar broke free of his bonds. She held her breath.

In rapid succession: The Jem'Hadar assaulted the tech; she reached for the phaser, releasing a blinding blaze of energy—

Firing. Her stomach tightened.

And again. She shivered. "Computer, halt playback." Something didn't feel right, but she couldn't say exactly what or why.

"That's not what happened," she finally said aloud, her voice sounding thin to her ear. What she'd seen wasn't right—it couldn't be; confusion still seethed inside her. Answers meant reason. Reason meant order. Principles of scientific inquiry and order governed her life and voided confusion. She would not accept anything less.

She ordered a replay of the previous minutes.

Again the Jem'Hadar broke free. She pointed her phaser at the back of his skull. She fired.

Involuntarily she gasped, jerking back, refusing to believe her eyes. *That's. Not. What. Happened.*

She blinked. She saw rows of dutiful Jem'Hadar, weapons drawn, aiming at their victims' heads. She blinked. Clinically detached Jadzia Dax, scientist, secured the rebreather to the test subject. *All for the cause.* She blinked. She saw cold fear in the faces of Romulan civilians prepared to die. *All can be justified.* She blinked. She saw Jadzia with a snifter of *kanar,* throwing back her head in a great belly laugh and she cried out to the woman in her vision.

I'm like them.

Staggering out of her chair, she collapsed on her knees, hot silent tears washing down her face. Through her tears, she fumbled for the controls, for the datachip, longing to make it all stop. To make it all disappear. But she knew she didn't have the right to look away. She had demanded answers and now she had them.

In her mind's eye, the room receded, giving way to a cavernous emptiness that surrounded her, pressed down on her, rendering her small and swallowed. Dizziness washed over her and she doubled over with waves of nausea.

She sobbed. She sobbed for all she had lost. Sobs became hiccoughs; hiccoughs became short, irregular breaths until finally, exhausted silence. She lay still on the floor, her head pillowed on her hands.

Emotionally spent, she could finally see a crucial truth that she had avoided acknowledging since Blue Sky had begun: For all her protestations, she *wanted* the Romulans involved, counting on their amoral pragmatism to push the war in a direction she knew the Federation would never take. Had her research with T'Rul proved effective, the Romulans would have used the weapon without a moment's hesitation while Starfleet would have wrung its hands over the moral imperatives. And she wanted it used. She wanted to bring down every Jem'Hadar killing machine in the galaxy. She simply wanted someone else to do the killing. The Romulans hadn't deceived her; she'd chosen to look the other way. *Benjamin's faith in me is misplaced,* she thought. *I have no idea how to find my way through the shadows.*

"*Ops to Commander Dax.*" A long pause. "*Commander Dax?*"

She shook her head, willed her voice to be steady. "Go ahead——" She took a deep breath.

"*There's been an emergency. Molly O'Brien has disappeared. We think there's some kind of anomaly——*"

Wiping her eyes on her sleeves, she said, "I'll be there as fast as I can."

How so much could go so wrong so quickly never ceased to astonish Jadzia. She'd been redirected to the *Defiant* before she even reached ops. During their brief journey to Golana, she'd been in constant communication with Miles, doing her best to assess the problem and brainstorm possible solutions. She'd been so hopeful that she could solve this mystery that she hadn't been prepared for the grim reality of witnessing Miles's and Keiko's shock. The O'Briens' distress had strengthened Jadzia's resolve to find their missing daughter. And she found Molly—after a fashion. The wild, rangy teenager they'd pulled through the time portal might have been genetically Molly, but she bore no resemblance to the playful child who loved storybooks and colored pictures to decorate Miles's workroom.

In all the confusion about how to proceed with Molly, Jadzia had volunteered to baby-sit Yoshi—it was the least she could do. And from a more selfish standpoint, she knew that going back to her quarters feeling helpless and worried would only plunge her into a black mood. She didn't want to be alone with her own thoughts.

She had swung by the O'Briens' quarters to pick up Yoshi's things. Having vivid memories of Audrid's colicky daughter, Jadzia knew that sometimes the difference between a happy baby and a screaming baby was the availability of a favorite toy or blanket. Neema had been fond of a tattered square of violet crochet; she'd rubbed it against her face to soothe her when she needed to sleep.

Jadzia discovered when got back to her quarters, after he'd been changed and fed, that Yoshi had his own unique taste.

"And Mister Froggy goes 'rbbt–rbbt,' " Jadzia croaked.

Yoshi giggled, and grabbed for the stuffed toy. The slobber-covered amphibian went straight into his mouth.

She ruffled his fine silken hair, amused by how intently he gummed the webbed foot. "I'd think you were slurping down *jumja* instead of sucking on artificial fur," she said. *Babies' needs are so much simpler than adults',* she thought. She watched Yoshi bash Mister Froggy's head repeatedly into her coffee table. He soon became bored, casting the toy away. He looked at Jadzia, looked down at the couch, dropped on all fours and peered over the edge.

"All gone," Jadzia said and shrugged. "All gone."

His face screwed up into a tight, wrinkled frown and he catapulted himself into her chest with a frustrated sob.

"There, there." She inhaled deeply, savoring his clean, sweet scent, and was carried back more than a hundred years to the last time she had mothered a baby. Savoring the nostalgic moment, she rubbed his back while simultaneously craning to see over the armrest of the sofa. Scooping him up into her arms, she walked over to where the hapless amphibian had landed. Yoshi's tears promptly dried up. "All better?"

He giggled.

I wish making it all better for me was as easy as it is for you, she thought, feeling a twinge of envy.

As she watched him play, she thought of how lucky he was to be oblivious to his parents' current crisis. *Keiko must be in agony,* Jadzia thought. *I know I would be.* Even Kira was upset. She'd grown so close to their family during the time she'd carried Yoshi that she'd become like a favorite aunt to the children and a sister to Miles and Keiko. *But little Yoshi here. Little Yoshi can just play and play, without a care in the world while his mother—while both of his mothers— worry. Both of his mothers . . .*

Intellectually she'd known what a technological wonder it was that Keiko's baby had been transported into Kira's womb. Sitting here, listening to Yoshi's uninhibited, gleeful laughter reminded her that it had been nothing short of a miracle.

A miracle would be required if she and Worf should decide they wanted to have children.

They'd agreed to put off serious discussions about starting a family until after the war, but the possibility always lived on the fringes of her thoughts. Even during her hell-bent pursuit of a weapon to defeat the Jem'Hadar, Jadzia acknowledged to herself that the infertility technology she'd adapted for the weapon was the same technology she'd need to conceive. Especially now, in retrospect, the irony of using a technology developed to create a life in order to take a life wasn't lost on her; she'd thrown something inside herself out of whack. She had to make it right. She had to. The slow hemorrhage of loss had to stop.

"Buda-buda-buda!" she said, wiggling Mister Froggy back and forth in front of Yoshi's eyes.

Yoshi tried grabbing for the stuffed animal, but Jadzia would make the frog run away and hide whenever he came too close. His eyes widened and he leaned forward, straining to reach the pillow where Jadzia had hidden the toy. In his efforts, he toppled over, landing face-first on her lap. Impulsively, she pulled him up on her chest, holding him tightly against her. She looked deeply into his wide eyes, bent forward and rubbed his nose with her own.

T'Rul's words came back to her unbidden—her invocation of an old human saying: *an eye for an eye.* It could go the other way, *should* go the other way—a life for a life. Replacing one life she'd taken with the creation of another.

I could have a baby. The thought prompted a smile. *It might be a place to start.*

Yoshi wiggled out of her arms, plopping back onto his haunches, looking at her expectantly.

Jadzia pulled Mister Froggy out from behind the pillow.

"And Mister Froggy goes . . ." she tickled him. "Wee!"

The door hissed open. She knew without looking that Worf had returned.

"Hi," he said.

Amazing how even his "hi" sends shivers up and down my arms. "We have a visitor."

Bending over, he placed a kiss on her forehead.

Dax smiled inwardly. *And so I begin again.*

Foundlings

Jeffrey Lang

Historian's note: This story is set during the three-month period between the sixth and seventh seasons of *Star Trek: Deep Space Nine.*

Jeffrey Lang

Jeffrey Lang is the author of the novel *Star Trek: The Next Generation—Immortal Coil* and the short story "Dead Man's Hand" in *Star Trek: Deep Space Nine—The Lives of Dax*. He's also the coauthor (with David Weddle) of *Section 31: Abyss;* and (with J.G. Hertzler) the two-volume tale *The Left Hand of Destiny.* He lives with his family in Wynnewood, Pennsylvania. Thanks to Joshua for contributing the first line of "Foundlings."

Odo asked, "Are you sure arresting Quark is the best first step in this investigation?"

As he strode down the Promenade with his companion, Odo watched the faces of the men and women coming from the opposite direction. Many of them were new Starfleet recruits passing through Deep Space 9 on their way to a new ship or posting. Every one of them did a doubletake as they passed. If animosity was a measurable thing, the readings around his Cardassian guest would have been off the chart.

Only the old station hands, longtime residents and merchants who considered DS9 a second home didn't glare, but stopped and stared as *this* Cardassian threaded his way through the crowd. One or two recognized him and halted in their tracks, then turned to watch as he walked past. Odo heard someone whisper, "Thrax!" but the tide of the crowd swept the caller away before Odo could see a face.

Watching Thrax move, Odo saw that, even after so many years, his predecessor as chief of station security still had a policeman's walk: a loose-hipped, stiff-kneed gait that could carry a man effortlessly though a crowd, or across kilometers in pursuit of his objective. Odo recognized the walk because he had one very like it himself.

In response to Odo's question, Thrax clenched his jaw and pressed his lips together in an expression that, if pressed, Odo would have grudgingly categorized as a smile. "Come now, Constable. You've been at this for—what is it?—ten years now? When a crime has been committed, isn't arresting Quark *always* the best first response?"

Odo snorted appreciatively. There was no denying that this was often his first reaction. Certainly, when he had learned the facts of the case that had brought Thrax to Deep Space 9, his first impulse *had* been to track down Quark, but only to question, not to arrest. "While I agree that an investigation is necessary," he conceded, "I'm not convinced this incident should be considered a crime. But perhaps you know something I don't."

"Just that Quark is Quark. Crime is crime. And punishment . . ."

"Is not quite so quick to follow as it was in your day," Odo said. Thrax was a civilian now, and although he claimed to have returned to DS9 for the first time in a decade as a private citizen with humanitarian concerns, Odo wasn't about to lower his guard or leave any doubt about whose jurisdiction they were in.

Thrax gave Odo a questioning look while skillfully sidestepping a bolting Bajoran child who had escaped his father's grasp. "Some might not consider that a change for the better."

"But those who were unjustly accused and convicted under the old regime might," Odo said sternly as they stopped outside the double doors of the security office. "As much as it pains me to say this, I think in this instance that category may include Quark. He's been involved in many shady deals over the years, but this . . . event, this . . ."

"Tragedy?" Thrax suggested.

Odo pressed his lips into a thin line and shook his head. "People are quick to apply that word to circumstances that are, by definition, not tragic. For tragedy to occur, there must be *hubris* and the one who suffers must bring it upon himself. Whatever else may be true of these events, these individuals did not bring their fate upon themselves. Or—again—do you know something I do not?"

"I'm in possession of certain facts that may elucidate matters," Thrax said. "But before I discuss them I'd like to interview Quark."

" 'Interview'? " Odo asked. "Not 'interrogate'? "

"We'll see," Thrax said as he and Odo stepped together through the doors.

Quark was seated in one of the two chairs habitually set in front of Odo's desk. The Ferengi looked over his shoulder when the doors opened, and Odo saw Quark's eyes widen first in surprise and then, surprisingly, in delight. "Thrax," he said, rising from his chair and bowing in Cardassian fashion. "How the hell are you?"

Bowing in response, Thrax asked in proper Ferengi protocol, "As well as can be expected in current economic circumstances. How is business, Quark?"

"Unpredictable, but I see better days ahead," Quark said, returning to his seat and indicating the chair next to him. Rolling his eyes, Odo walked around his desk and sat in his chair across from his visitors. He had been under the impression that these two had each been the other's worst enemy during the Occupation. The way they were talking he wondered if they expected him to order some tea, excuse himself, and let them get caught up.

"Really?" Thrax said. "And why do you say that?"

"War's got to end sometime soon," Quark said amiably. "One way or another."

"And you'll adapt no matter which side wins?"

The Ferengi shrugged. "A good businessman has to build flexibility into his plans. I like to think of myself as someone who can accommodate the needs of any clientele."

"Indeed," Thrax said. "I suppose this must be true, seeing as you've survived so many years under so many—hmph, what's the word? Administrations?"

Quark grinned and spread his hands modestly. "What can I say? I'm a people person."

"I am not," Odo snapped, attempting to regain control of the meeting. "And yet here I sit with you two. Could it be it's because I have an investigation to conduct?"

"Of course, Constable," Thrax said. "Apologies. We have serious matters to discuss." He turned to Quark and said matter-of-factly, "Why don't you just confess now and save us all a lot of time and energy?"

Still smiling, Quark crossed his arms and settled back into his chair. "Why don't you tell me what I'm being charged with first? Then I'll decide."

"I don't know what the final charges will be, Quark. That's up to Odo, but I have a few suggestions. Smuggling. Criminal negligence. Conspiracy to commit murder. Those are the first three to come to mind, but I'm sure we could think of more."

Shifting his eyes over to Odo, Quark's smile slipped the millimeter that separates pleasure from paralyzed rictus. "Is he serious?"

"Is he?" Odo asked. "I'm not completely certain myself. Perhaps the time has come for the recitation of facts. Then we can decide together." Picking up a padd, Odo read, "Forty hours ago, a Lurian freighter, registry NRX–01772, outbound from Cardassia, experienced a catastrophic core failure less than a light-year from Bajor. The ship was lost with all hands, and two hours after the station detected the explosion, a Bajoran Militia patrol ship found the debris. Does the registration number ring a bell, Quark?"

Quark seemed to consider the question carefully, then, apparently deciding there was no reason not to tell the truth, said, "Sure, I owned a piece of the ship. Silent partnership. One of the owners sold me his share to cover a gambling debt." He sighed. "Guess I'm going to have to write that one off. But, so what? It's not my fault the ship exploded."

Thrax impaled the Ferengi with a stare. "That's not what we're charging you with, Quark . . ."

"*We're* not charging him with *anything* yet, Thrax," Odo snapped. "I suggest you keep that in mind."

Thrax ignored him, and continued addressing Quark. "Since you claim to have been a silent partner, I'll assume you knew nothing about the freighter's cargo."

"Assume away," Quark said, flattening the crease of his trouser leg.

"The freighter was supposed to be carrying bodies."

"Really?" Quark asked. "Whose?"

"Starfleet personnel," Thrax said.. "The civilian authority I represent has been working to recover the remains of our war dead, so they can be properly honored and interred on Cardassia. We have an arrangement with a similar group in the Federation. Nothing official, mind you. We exchange remains through neutral third parties."

"Like the Lurians," Quark said, his mind like a fish on a mating migration unerringly swimming back to commerce. "Not a bad idea. Wish I'd thought of it myself. I could have made a killing."

"Quark!" Odo snapped.

"Sorry. Slip of the tongue," Quark said, sounding genuinely contrite. Then, brow furrowed, he asked, "How's the Dominion letting you get away with this? Doesn't sound like something they would be too thrilled with."

"The Dominion are our allies," Thrax said, his tone conveying precisely how unconvinced he was of this fact. "They respect our conventions and traditions."

"For now," Quark inserted.

Thrax's eyes narrowed at the Ferengi. "For now," he agreed. "I commissioned the Lurians personally for this run. When I learned that they failed to make their scheduled rendezvous yesterday with a Yridian transport hired by the other side, I knew something had gone wrong."

"So here you are," Quark said. "But I'm still not seeing what this has to do with me," he continued, turning to Odo. "The ship was destroyed, the crew was lost. Okay, I feel for their families, but the cargo was—no disrespect intended—a bunch of corpses. If they were vaporized, so what? What difference does it make?"

"No difference," Odo said, before Thrax could react to Quark's attitude. "You're absolutely right. But they weren't vaporized."

"Why not? When a ship's warp core goes up, every living thing . . ."

"The cargo pods appear to have been jettisoned before the engines went critical," Odo explained. "The Bajorans retrieved them and towed them back to the station."

"Then *what* is this all about?" Quark asked, turning back to Thrax. "If the bodies have been recovered . . ."

"They aren't the right bodies," Thrax said flatly.

Mouth hanging open, momentarily struck dumb, Quark stared at the Cardassian. *I'm going to treasure this moment,* Odo thought. *I know I shouldn't, but I will. It almost makes up for the "made a killing" comment.*

"Not the right bodies?" Quark asked. "Then who are they?"

"That," Thrax said, "is what I'm here to find out."

Odo was surprised when Quark insisted on following him and Thrax to the infirmary, and even more surprised when the Ferengi remained silent through the doctor's recitation. "My staff has autopsied the forty-seven Cardassians found in the cargo containers and determined that most of them died of essentially the same thing," Bashir said. "Namely, suffocation and exposure. Their blood supply had been starved of oxygen, and they all showed frostbitten extremities and extensive cellular damage due to radiation and dehydration."

"So they were alive before they were jettisoned," Thrax concluded. "Can you tell me anything about their identities? Were any of them carrying indentification rods, personal articles, anything?"

Bashir shook his head. "No ID rods, no personal articles beyond the clothes they were wearing under their environment suits and the metallic bands most of them wore around their wrists. Some of them were quite ornate and beautiful." He held up his padd for Thrax to see a close-up of one. "Matrimonial bands, aren't they?"

Thrax nodded. "You know something about our customs, Doctor?"

"Yes," Bashir said, "but it wouldn't have taken much to figure it out. We noticed that there were frequently pairs of bands that were similar, one on a man, one on a woman." He hesitated, obviously disconcerted, but then continued. "And many of the those people were found clinging to each other."

Showing no signs of having heard, Thrax handed the padd back to Bashir. "It's an old custom, not much used anymore. I'm surprised to hear you found so many people wearing them."

"Might that not be a clue to their identities?" Bashir asked.

"It might," Thrax said, "but it would be much faster if you just gave me access to the genetic data you took during your autopsies."

Having anticipated this request, Bashir handed Thrax an isolinear rod with a copy of the files.

"Doctor," Odo asked, "can you tell us how long they lived after they were jettisoned?"

"We can estimate. The answer is, not long. The first deaths occurred immediately after the explosion. Trauma. The ejection system the ship used to launch the cargo containers wasn't meant to be used on living beings. The rest died of asphyxiation soon thereafter."

"How soon?" Odo asked.

"*Very* soon. Apparently, they all had about the same amount of air and power . . . which was to say, none."

Odo already knew the answer to the question he'd asked—he and Bashir had conferred briefly earlier that day—and he watched Quark's face carefully as the statement sank in.

Ever a quick study, the Ferengi only required a moment. "What are you saying?" he asked.

"I'm saying . . ." He glanced at Odo for permission, then continued when he got the nod. "When the bodies were found, they were wearing EV suits. But they had neither air supplies nor battery packs."

No one spoke for several seconds, but then the absurdity of the idea sunk under Quark's skin. "That doesn't make any sense," he said. "Why have environment suits, but no batteries or air?"

"The other question that suggests itself," Bashir replied, maintaining his reputation as the cleverest man in any room, "is, if they did have air and batteries, what happened to them?"

"These are precisely the questions Colonel Kira has asked me to investigate," Odo explained. "One possibility is that these men and women did not wish to be identified."

"You're about to suggest a military mission," Thrax said.

Odo looked at him. "Even you can understand that the Bajorans and the Federation would both be concerned about the possibility—some kind of covert operation gone awry."

Before Thrax could protest, Bashir interrupted. "These men and women weren't soldiers, Odo. Most of them were middle-aged if I'm any judge of Cardassian physiology—which I am—and a few were even older than that. None of them was in particularly good shape, certainly not compared to most Cardassian military men and women I've seen."

"Spies, then," Odo said. "They would be able to blend in."

"Spies?" Thrax repeated. "Spy on *whom?* And where? No doubt the movements and activities of any Cardassians within Federation territory are closely monitored."

"Nonaligned planets," Quark offered, obviously sensing an opening. "Like Luria and Fereginar."

"If that was the case," Thrax said, temper flaring, "and I emphasize the word 'if,' then we would just *go* there. In a ship. *Not* inside a cargo pod. There are no laws against it. The Federation doesn't *rule* the spaceways."

"And neither does the Dominion," Quark retorted. "That's the point, isn't it?"

Thrax lifted the hand holding the datarod as if he was about to strike the Ferengi. Quark flinched and Odo willed his arm to a more pliable state in preparation for blocking the blow, but then he saw that there would be no need. Thrax lowered his arm. Turning back to Odo, Thrax said, "I have a hunch about who these people really are, and I brought with me records that may prove it. May I use your office to check this data?"

"Certainly," Odo said and beckoned to one of his men standing watch outside the infirmary. "Sergeant Shul will escort you."

"I know the way," Thrax said.

"I realize that," Odo said. "But there are enough people still on the station who remember your work that I suspect I'd have another investigation on my hands if I let you move about unescorted."

The corner of the Cardassian's mouth lifted ever-so-slightly. "And I would regret having to put you to the trouble, sir." He glanced at the Bajoran deputy who was now standing beside him. "Lead the way, Sergeant."

Odo watched him go, reflecting—not for the first time since Thrax's return—that his predecessor was both everything and nothing like what he'd imagined.

Quark turned and said with practically no trace of sarcasm in his voice, "Thanks, Odo. I know that must have been tough for you—giving up a chance to turn me over to the Cardassians."

Odo grunted. "It was tempting," he admitted. "But for your sake, you'd better hope I continue to believe that this isn't one of your schemes."

"Oh, come on, Odo! You know me, I would never do anything like this."

Odo's eyes moved to the door leading into the morgue and watched as one of Bashir's many assistants came out carrying a small case, full, no doubt, of tissue samples and instruments for taking them. "I suppose this would be a little low, even for you," Odo said. "Locking people in a windowless box, only for them to be set adrift . . ." His mind drifted then and he felt a flash of emotion, a mingled rage and impotence, and saw an image of an endless void dotted with tiny white lights. The strength and suddenness of the feelings shocked him and Odo felt seconds ticking past where neither he nor the Ferengi spoke.

When he finally glanced up, he saw that Quark was staring at him with a confused expression. "What's wrong with you?" he asked, and Odo worried that the Ferengi had somehow read his thoughts, but his next comment showed that, as ever, Quark was more concerned with his own affairs. "If the price was right and the customer told me that it was something they wanted to do, of *course* I would do it. But they were *Cardassians.* Everyone is at war with them; their currency is basically worthless. What would a bunch of Cardassians have that they could use to pay someone to take such a chance?"

Ignoring Quark's cynicism, Odo pondered the question. "That," he said, "is a very insightful question. But you *were* invested in the freighter."

"Like I said, silent partner," Quark reminded him. "No say in what they did. If I had known they were stupid enough to get mixed up in something like this, I never would have accepted the deal. There are better opportunities to take risks on."

"And you would know."

Quark smiled toothily, but otherwise remained silent.

Odo noted with approval how alertly Shul watched each passerby as they sauntered or scurried or meandered along the Promenade. More than one person slowed as they passed the security office, straining to look through the glass and catch sight of the Cardassian. Obviously, word of Thrax's return had spread around the station.

Thrax was just turning off a Cardassian padd as Odo entered. The lines of his face were, if possible, even grimmer than when last they spoke. He began to rise from the chair, but Odo waved him back down. Looking around the room, Thrax commented, "It hasn't changed much since my day."

"No reason why it should," Odo said, seating himself in one of the two chairs facing the desk. Oddly, he had never sat here before, never faced "the constable" from this angle. A disconcerting sensation, he decided. *Good.*

"Even the chair is the same," Thrax mused, bouncing in the seat a little. "It needs new springs. Doesn't this bother you?"

"No," Odo said. "No muscles or bones, unless I want them."

"Ah, right. But didn't I hear somewhere that you were briefly a 'solid,' as your people call us?"

"Briefly," Odo said, wondering how this information had filtered through to Cardassia and wondering, too, whether Thrax had no more connections to the military as he had claimed. "But by the time I realized the chair was bothering me . . ."

"Yes, I see," Thrax said. "Time passes." He ran his hand along the edge of the desk. "It seems like only yesterday I was in this office . . ."

Seeing his opening, Odo asked, "Why did you leave?"

Thrax leaned back in the chair, stroked the armrest and stared at the walls, but did not respond.

When the seconds had stretched uncomfortably into a minute, Odo asked, "Have I offended you?"

"Offended? No. I'm just not used to hearing such direct questions, and I'm sorting through all the possible reasons why you'd wish to know the answer to that one." He locked eyes with Odo. "The peculiar thing is that I'm not able to think of any ulterior motive."

"There is none," Odo said. "I'm simply curious."

"An admirable trait for a security chief, except, alas, when your commanding officer would rather it was not."

"This has never been a problem since the Federation took over the station," Odo said.

"Good for you," Thrax said, then sighed. "All right. The answer is because I grew weary of Dukat. His displays of . . . what? Ego?" He shook his head. "I simply couldn't trust him, and I'd reached a point where I felt I could no longer be a willing instrument of his authority. Despite his claims that he had no animosity for the Bajorans, he had a capacity for brutality that didn't require much provocation. Have you had to spend much time with him?"

"Yes."

"Then perhaps you know what I mean."

"I do."

Thrax frowned. "Then why didn't *you* leave?"

Odo was taken aback. "I beg your pardon?"

"The Bajoran Occupation ended four years after I left. That means you, a non-Cardassian, worked under Dukat for four years. Why?"

Odo grunted. "Maybe I was trying to clean up the mess you left me with."

"Or maybe that's what Dukat wanted you to believe," Thrax

mused. "It's not hard to imagine. My resignation would have made it easy for Dukat to blame the harshness of station life on me, and give him the opportunity to seem more just by bringing in a non-Cardassian security chief with a less . . . forceful hand. But only slightly less, am I right, Constable?"

Odo's eyes narrowed. "Think what you like, Thrax. Your opinion is of no interest to me."

"Oh, come now, Odo. Can you honestly say that once I was gone, Dukat didn't blame me for the conditions Bajorans had been enduring on the station while I was here?"

"That's because you *were* to blame."

"Really? And how much did matters improve after *you* became chief of security?"

Odo felt his hand harden involuntary into a mallet capable of crushing Thrax's skull. The impulse surprised him; he wasn't one to allow himself to become provoked. He had to wonder if it was really because he was angry at Thrax, or at himself. He was still haunted by some terrible choices he'd made during the Occupation, before he'd thrown his support behind the resistance very late in the game. He tended to avoid asking himself why it had taken so long, preferring to believe that while he was doing the job Dukat had forced upon him, he'd might actually have been able to make a difference.

Thrax was right about one thing, though: Dukat had presented Odo to the station population with assurances that the new security chief would be a vast improvement over the departed Thrax. And looking back on his own career under the Cardassians, Odo knew he had always tried to serve justice first. But had he really made a difference for anyone on Terok Nor other than Gul Dukat?

Don't be a fool, he told himself. *Maybe you weren't perfect, maybe you couldn't end the Occupation single-handedly, but you damn well did your best to make life here less brutal, less unfair.*

Less hopeless.

"You don't talk very much, do you?" Thrax asked.

Odo forced his hand to relax. "What do you want me to say?"

"You haven't really answered my question. Why did you stay?"

The image of distant lights in a silent, oppressive emptiness filled Odo's mind again. He blinked it away. "Because someone had to."

Thrax nodded, as if Odo had just confirmed something for him. Odo decided he was growing weary of the man.

Thrax held up the Cardassian padd and said, "I imagine you're curious to know what I've found out."

"I'm waiting," Odo said.

Thrax sighed, set the padd on the desk and slid it across to the edge where Odo could pick it up. Touching the READ button, Odo scrolled through a list of names, each one followed by a string of Cardassian alphanumerics. "Crime codes," he said. He scanned the first several, then looked up at Thrax. "Thieves, extortionists, petty thugs, prostitutes. A little of everything this side of murder and rape."

"Yes," Thrax said. "As I had suspected. Those people were using my body-recovery program as a means of escaping the Union."

"Criminals . . ." Odo mused. "So the Lurians thought they were carrying Federation bodies to be exchanged for dead Cardassians, but instead they were transporting live Cardassian fugitives?"

"That, or these Lurians were in on it. Which may support the idea that Quark was as well."

Odo scanned down the list of names. Icons next to them indicated that the data files contained medical records. "I'll need to show this to Dr. Bashir," he said.

"Of course," Thrax said. "But what about Quark?"

"What about him?"

"Don't you think he's complicit in all this?"

Flicking off the padd, Odo replied, "As you pointed out, whenever a crime has been committed on Deep Space 9, it's always a good first assumption to think Quark had something to do with it. However, the burden of proof is ours."

Thrax shook his head reproachfully. "In my day, things were so much . . . *simpler.*"

"In my time here," Odo said, "both under the Cardassians and the Federation, I have observed that *law* is simple; justice is a more difficult matter."

"You may be correct," Thrax responded, then changed the subject. "I'd like an opportunity to question the team that retrieved the cargo pods."

Odo nodded, though he was surprised. He'd anticipated the request, of course, but had expected Thrax to be more interested in getting background on the Lurians first. "They're still aboard the station. I can arrange to have them meet us in the wardroom."

"Excellent," Thrax said, and began to rise, then paused, both hands pressed against the top of the desk. "I almost hate to ask this," he said. "But you *did* find the safe, didn't you?"

Odo smiled despite himself. He'd wondered when Thrax would bring that up. "Eventually."

"Good. And the contents have been useful?"

"At first. Not much of the information was still relevant after the Cardassians left, but, some of it, yes. Thank you."

Thrax nodded magnanimously. "Happy to be of service."

Following the Cardassian out the door, Odo wondered, *And what will I be expected to do to pay for* that?

As Odo suspected, the two Militia officers—a pilot and a sensor tech—were both wary of Thrax. Neither of them had lived on the station during the Occupation—and therefore neither had known the former chief of security—but Odo suspected part of their unease stemmed just from seeing Thrax juxtaposed with Odo himself. Odo had encountered this sort of thing before, whenever he and Garak were seen together after Dukat had allied Cardassia with the Dominion. It seemed to have become the natural response to seeing a Cardassian and a changeling in the same room.

Unfortunately, the men knew very little about the cargo pods beyond what was in the report. They had discovered the debris field after Kira had deployed them to investigate the explosion.

"Did you come across anything that hinted at the cause of the explosion?" Thrax asked.

The sensor tech shook his head. "There was very little left intact."

"How large were the fragments?"

"Not large," said the pilot. "No larger than the cargo pods, anyway. At least, as far as we could tell. The debris had spread out over quite a distance in two hours."

"Did you chart the dispersal pattern?"

"It's in our report," the sensor tech said.

"Yes, I have that here," Thrax said, glancing down at a padd he held. "It says you found the cargo pods *within* the debris field."

The tech and the pilot glanced at each other. Finally, the tech said, "That's right. What's your point?"

"Only that it seems strange that the pods weren't farther out, somewhere *beyond* the debris field. That would be consistent with their being launched before the explosion took place, then propelled by the blast front. Wouldn't it?"

Odo frowned. *Where is he going with this?*

The pilot said, "What difference does it make? The whole ship went off like a bomb. With all the radiation, the only reason we found the cargo pods at all was because they were all strung together like a chain and the sensor image was huge."

Thrax brightened. "Really? That isn't in the report. They were chained together?"

"Right. All seven of them," the pilot said. "It was the kind of cord they use to tow loads in zero gee, that stuff that can go flexible or stiff as they need it to. They're not supposed to keep containers connected with it after they leave port, you know? But everyone does."

"And you didn't notice anything else about the containers? You just towed them back to the station?"

"Right. Standard procedure," the pilot said. "What are you hoping to find out?"

Exactly what I was wondering, Odo thought.

The pilot's question had a remarkable effect on Thrax: he hesitated. "Only the truth," he said after a moment.

"Is there anything else you want to know, or can we go?"

When the Cardassian didn't answer, Odo asked, "Thrax? Any other questions?"

Again, Thrax didn't answer right away, as if he was trying to decide what he should say next. "No," he said at last. "Nothing." He looked at the two Bajorans. "Thank you for your time. And for recovering my people."

"Not a problem," the pilot said, rising. "Only sorry we couldn't get to them a little sooner. Has anyone figured out why they were in there in the first place?"

"Not yet," Odo replied. "We're pursuing several possible explanations."

After exchanging skeptical glances, the Militia officers rose, then headed out the door.

When they were gone, Odo looked at Thrax, who appeared to be lost in thought. "Is that what you expected to hear?" he asked.

Thrax shrugged. "More or less."

Odo wrapped his arms across his chest. "I have to say I was surprised by some of your questions."

"Oh?"

"You must admit," Odo said, watching Thrax, carefully, "if your objective was to build a case against Quark, that was an odd way to go about it."

"Maybe it was," Thrax admitted, then met Odo's gaze. "But I've been doing this long enough to know that it's easy for little things to slip through the cracks. I don't want that to happen here. You shouldn't, either."

"I don't," Odo assured him. "But it seems to me that an investigation into the crew of the freighter would be more illuminating than the retrieval."

Thrax sighed, keyed a file on his padd, and handed it to Odo. "I've been there. It's a black hole. See for yourself."

Odo examined the file, a compilation of records on the Lurian crew, and saw that Thrax was right. He had encountered countless like them during his career: men and women who, while not precisely upstanding citizens, were also not criminals. Only the captain, Ra'Chet'ka by name, had any kind of serious record, and even the charges against him were most often the minor shipping offenses any neutral merchant would accumulate over a long career. The rest of the crew were more or less the same: petty thugs, drifters, social misfits—but no hardcore criminals.

More telling, their bank records revealed nothing suspicious. One crewman—an engineer—had made an unusually large deposit several months earlier, but closer inspection revealed that he had recently settled on a work-related insurance case. Most of the money had been spent on a vacation to Risa, then the rest frittered away on a variety of frivolous purchases. "You'd think he would have saved *some* of it," Thrax commented when he saw Odo reading that part of the file, and Odo almost laughed out loud. He had thought precisely the same thing.

"You're right, there's nothing here," Odo said. "Or, at least, nothing unusual. There's no doubt that they'd been smugglers at one time or another, but there's nothing to suggest they were aware of anything unusual about their cargo, or that Quark had anything to do with it."

Thrax nodded. "I checked them out thoroughly before I hired them."

"And the Yridians they were supposed to rendezvous with? You said your Federation counterparts hired them."

"I looked into that on my way to Terok—excuse me, Deep Space 9. Another black hole."

"Where was the rendezvous to take place?"

"In neutral space, near the Celeth system."

"Quite a distance from Cardassia."

"Just as well. Even though the Dominion doesn't prevent us from making these rendezvous, Jem'Hadar tend to err on the side of caution and will investigate or even attack any vessels they think are suspicious."

"This has happened?"

"Twice. Both times all hands were lost."

Odo shook his head. "How can you believe that these people have your best interests at heart?"

Thrax stared at Odo, the lines around his mouth etched with repressed anger. "How can *you* work with the Federation when your people are the ones guiding the Dominion?"

"They aren't my people. I believe what the Dominion is doing is wrong."

"And I believe what my people are doing is wrong, too. It was a terrible mistake to ally ourselves with the Dominion." He glanced around the room then as if looking for hidden cameras or microphones, but then shrugged, abandoning all caution. "Even a great people can make foolish mistakes," he concluded. "I can't abandon them. If I did, I'd be worse than a fool. I'd be a traitor."

With that, Thrax stood and excused himself, telling Odo he needed to update his superiors back on Cardassia. His escort met him at the door, leaving Odo alone to contemplate traitors and fools. And which of the two he might be.

Much later, a restless Odo was about to begin a midnight circuit of the Promenade before his next meeting with Thrax when Nerys stepped off the lift directly opposite the security office. Spotting him, she smiled, but Odo could see the lines of weariness around her eyes. Like him, she'd been working many late hours in recent days. She fell in beside him and Odo slowed to match her pace, happy to see her.

Walking close enough that her hand could brush against his, Nerys asked if he had time for a late dinner.

"Not tonight, I'm afraid." She knew he didn't need to eat, so he knew what she really wanted was his company. He was anxious to talk to her, vaguely aware that he was plagued by some noxious thoughts, and he valued her ability to help sort through these kinds of emotions. "I have to follow up with Thrax concerning the dead Cardassians."

"Admiral Ross was asking about that. Any ideas how they got there yet?"

"A couple," Odo said. "None of them good, and none of them provable."

Seeing that their paths were going to diverge, Nerys halted and laid her palm on his wrist. "Then I'll let you go. Call me later if you want to talk."

He smiled. "I will," he said. "There's nothing I would like better."

Smiling in response, she turned and left him to his work. Watching her walk away, he found his thoughts straying to the men and women clutching each other in the dark, cold cargo containers, wondering what it might have been like to feel the heat go out of each other, to listen to the shortening breaths as the oxygen ran out. What would he do in such a situation if Nerys was with him? Wrap himself around her? Envelop as much atmosphere as possible? But, no, of course not. There wouldn't be any atmosphere to capture. What could he do in such a situation? What could *anyone* do?

Right on time, Thrax entered the security office and, handing Odo his padd, announced, "My business here is finished."

"What do you mean?" Odo asked. "There's been an arrest?"

"No," Thrax said. "I mean that, as of this moment, we're closing the investigation."

The news stunned Odo. "You're not even pursuing Quark?"

"Much as it pains me, no. My superiors have instructed me to return to Cardassia as soon as possible with the bodies. Can you help me make arrangements?"

"Of course," Odo said, then worked his way back to the original thread of the conversation. "But why aren't you pursuing the investigation?"

Thrax gave him a grim look. "Because these men and women are better off dead." Without hesitating for a beat, he continued, "I plan to leave with the bodies on my ship tomorrow." With that, Thrax exited the security office without waiting for an escort.

How cold could a man be? Odo wondered as he watched the Cardassian's back recede. *Better off dead . . . ?*

★   ★   ★

" 'Better off dead'?" Nerys asked. "What does *that* mean?" An hour after he had last spoken with Thrax, she sat on the small sofa in her living area, her boots lying carelessly on the floor, her feet tucked under the small blanket she kept on the sofa arm.

"I don't know." Odo could not sit down. As soon as he stopped moving, the wheels of disbelief began to spin faster than he could comfortably accommodate, so he paced. Whereas motion did not necessarily equal progress, inactivity definitely felt like stagnation. "But I think I have to find out."

Stifling a yawn, Nerys stretched and attempted to look alert. "Is there anything I can do?" she asked.

Odo glanced at the chrono on the companel and was surprised to see how late it was. "No," he said. "You're tired. Stay and rest."

Smiling faintly, her eyes drooping, Nerys asked, "You need to rest too. We can both rest." She knew, of course, that he did not sleep, at least in the manner that she did. He enjoyed being with her when she slept, but Odo never closed his eyes while she slumbered. Rather, he listened to her breathe, felt her body move slowly up and down as breaths entered and left, and allowed his mind to both drift and focus in a manner much like he imagined Nerys did when she prayed.

"Not yet," he said. "Soon, maybe. There's something I want to check on."

Sliding down onto the couch and pulling the blanket up around her shoulders, Nerys said, "Nothing illegal, I hope?"

"Illegal?" he asked. "Me?"

Closing her eyes, the faint smile still playing around the corners of her mouth, she murmured, "I'll just wait here in case you need an alibi."

"You do that."

Odo knew he was perfectly within his rights checking the logs of a public comm station *if* he was pursuing a criminal investigation. Even the Federation, notorious in its advocacy of rights to privacy, understood that law officers needed to have such latitude. He also knew, however, that he was mucking about in a gray zone: Was this a criminal investigation anymore? If the people against whom the supposed crime had been committed said that they no longer cared if the misdeeds were brought to light, did he have any reason to investigate? All the rules of conduct neatly filed in his office computer said, "No."

Men like Sisko, who was presently on an indefinite leave of absence on Earth, had always seemed adept at negotiating the narrow channels between law and justice, a trait Odo admired. There was the rule of law and there was justice, and he knew which one he served. Still, he also knew what a conflict of interest was and, to assuage his unease, accessed the logs from his quarters, not the security office.

The logs came up quickly, and Odo skimmed through them with practiced ease. Thrax had logged into station terminal twenty-three at 25:45, and the call had been to Cardassia, which was assigned frequencies between 1000.20.304.234 and . . . *Damn machine,* Odo thought. He must have keyed the wrong number into the interface. He checked again, and then a third time. "This can't be right," Odo said aloud, then felt like a fool for doing it, but couldn't stop himself a moment later from saying, "This doesn't make any sense."

"Why would he send a one-way message to a planet in neutral space?" Nerys asked. She had dozed off with her head cradled on her arm and the texture of her uniform was pressed into her cheek.

"I don't know," Odo said. "That's why I keep saying, 'This doesn't make any sense.'" He saw the brusque response register and tried to apologize, but Nerys waved it away.

"What time is it?" she asked.

"Late. Or early depending on how you look at it. I'm sorry for waking you, but I needed to talk to someone . . ."

Smiling as she twisted her head from side to side to loosen a crick, Nerys said, "It's okay. I understand. I should get out of this uniform and go to bed, anyway." She rose and stopped halfway to her bedroom. "Is there anything else you can do to check on this tonight?"

He considered the question seriously and said, "I could check on the registration number for the message and see what planet Thrax contacted."

Nerys rolled her eyes. "You can do that in the morning."

"He's *leaving* tomorrow."

Nerys made a detour to her interface console to check the docket. "Not until the afternoon," she read. "If we get up early, you'll have plenty of time to talk to him."

"*We* get up early?" Odo asked, but she had already left the room. Considering the options, he followed her. There were worse ways to spend the next few hours.

In the morning, after Kira had left for ops, Odo decided to turn to the one person on the station besides Thrax who could offer the perspective he needed.

"Constable," Garak said, sipping his tea in the Replimat, "you'll have to forgive me. I'm not really quite awake yet. Perhaps you could stop by the shop later this morning and we could go to lunch?"

"No, Garak. *Now.* It has to be now."

The tailor lowered his face over the mouth of his mug and inhaled the pungent, smoky aroma. Odo had to admit that it did not appear as if Garak was faking. The Cardassian's usually alert expression was conspicuously absent.

"I was up late with Colonel Kira and half the general staff discussing Cardassian culture. General Martok would not let me leave until I had told him everything I knew about opera."

"Opera?" Odo asked. That would explain why Nerys had looked so weary. She didn't like Bajoran opera, let alone Cardassian.

"The general believes that a people's soul can be gleaned by how they present themselves in their high arts. If he can understand their soul, he says, he can crush their spirit."

That gave Odo pause. Loath as he was to admit it, he and Garak shared an unusual bond—both of them were aiding the Federation in a war against their own peoples. Odo knew well the kind of exhaustion Garak was feeling, the weariness that came from grappling with guilt and loneliness.

Odo tried to engage him without being too obvious about it. "Interesting theory. What is Cardassian opera like?"

"Discursive," Garak admitted. "Even our arias are *sotto voce*, as the humans say." Amused by his joke—which was fortunate since Odo barely understood it—Garak perked up. "Very well, Constable. Since my generosity of spirit seems to be virtually unbounded, what is it I can do for you?"

Odo sat down and pushed the padd with the details about the criminals across the table. "These men and women were the ones found in the cargo containers. You've heard about this?" Garak's expression made it plain he was pained that Odo needed to ask such a question.

"What about them?" Garak asked.

"The codes next to the names? I recognize most of them, but not all."

"Where did you get this?"

"From Thrax."

"Ah, yes," Garak said, his eyes growing wider. "I heard he was paying us a visit. Still the same sanctimonious prig he always was?"

"I wouldn't know. I never met him when he was here before. We traveled in different circles."

"No one traveled in Thrax's circle except Thrax. He's the most antisocial man who ever graced our little community. Well, until Commander Worf came aboard."

"*Enough*, Garak. These codes." He tapped the padd screen. "What do they mean?"

Pursing his lips, Garak picked up the padd. "I'm flattered that you should expect a simple tailor to know about such things. Couldn't you just look them up in the Cardassian legal database?"

"I did. They aren't in there."

Garak studied the notations more carefully. "You're sure?"

Now it was Odo's turn to give Garak a *"Please consider who you're asking"* look.

Garak studied the padd for another ten seconds, all the while shaking his head. "Then it's come to that."

"Come to what, Garak?"

"They've begun to manipulate the legal system to their convenience. They're unmaking history."

"I don't understand."

"I realize, Constable, that many of the Federation worlds don't think much of the Cardassian legal system, that you don't agree with the way we do things . . ."

"Don't include me when you say 'Federation,' Garak," Odo said. "I'm not the Federation."

Garak flashed one of his most insincere smiles. "Of course, Odo. My apologies. What I meant, of course, was, *they* don't agree. . . . And they don't, do they?"

"No."

"It's all backwards to them. 'Innocent until proven guilty.' " He smirked. "As if any of us is truly innocent."

"I had no idea that Cardassians were so quick to merge morality and law."

"Then you know nothing of my people, Odo, which, frankly, surprises me. I thought you, of all the denizens of our community, might grasp what it means to be Cardassian."

Growing impatient with Garak's meanderings, Odo growled, "The codes?"

"Or, for that matter," Garak continued, seemingly oblivious, "our legal system. My, my, so many escapees." His eyes glittered. "Doesn't that strike you as strange?"

Odo's irritation with Garak evaporated like rain on hot tarmac. "It didn't," Odo said. "But now that you mention it . . ."

"Not only have the Dominion made my people forget their own soul by *concealing* laws, they've also made them careless. Forty-seven at once. That *is* exceedingly rare."

"Then how did they escape the justice system unless . . ."

"Yes?"

"They weren't *in* the justice system."

Garak pointed at the padd. "But you see their names here. And I see that some were thieves, some were, oh, robbers. A blackmailer."

"And the other codes . . ."

"Of course, Constable." Garak pretended to study the display more carefully, then pointed at one of the entries. "This one? It means 'Incitement to political connivance.' And this one? He was not very popular with the neighbors for some reason. Oh, and here's one you didn't see very often even in my day—'Intellectual privateering.' "

"What the hell does that mean?"

"He wrote something that someone else didn't like. Or painted a picture or sang a song that caused offense. Who can say?"

The tumblers clicked into place. "Political prisoners," Odo muttered.

"Not *prisoners*," Garak said. "If they had been incarcerated, they never would have made it as far as the cargo pods on a Lurian ship. More likely, these charges were logged against them without their even knowing it. A convenience for when the day came that they should be rounded up."

Odo stared into the middle distance, his mind racing. "And somehow they got wind of it and made arrangements to leave."

"That has the ring of truth about it," Garak agreed. He scanned the list more carefully. "If it's any help, I've never met nor heard of any of them. None of them were known artists or intellectuals."

"And you would know that because . . . ?"

Garak attempted to wither Odo with an acid stare. "Constable, do I ask you how you know so much about what goes on here on the station?"

Grunting in acknowledgment, Odo relented. "So what you're saying is that none of these people was a threat."

Garak set the padd down on the table and passed it back to Odo. "The Dominion is notoriously disapproving of anyone they consider a dissident." Lifting his mug of tea, Garak sipped it and made a face. "It's gone cold," he said. "And I really have to open my shop. If you'll excuse me, Constable."

"Of course," Odo said. "Thank you for your help."

"Not at all," Garak said. "Always happy to assist an officer of the law . . . whichever law it happens to be today." He rose and headed toward the recycler with his cold tea, then paused and turned. "There was a time, Odo," he admitted, "when I would have been happy to shoot boxloads of such people into the sun without a second thought. But I've found my attitude about such things has changed over the past few years." He stared down into his cold tea and smiled a sad, ironic smile. "Personally," he said, "I think the Federation puts something in the water."

"How could they have been so . . . so . . . *thoughtless? So careless?*"

Kira didn't answer immediately, but picked up the *raktajino* mug on the corner of her desk, stared into its depths, winced at the cold, black sludge she saw there, and then took a sip of it anyway. Grimacing, she finally asked, "That's a peculiar choice of words, Odo. What do you mean by 'careless?' "

Odo stared at the list of names and now-meaningless statistics displayed on Kira's desktop terminal. He had called up the data to show to her because . . . well, he didn't know why precisely. Somehow, it had just seemed important. He was being irrational; he knew that, but he couldn't stop thinking about the men and women in the cold, dark cargo pods, some freezing to death and the rest dying of suffocation. There was no sense to it, no logic. And then there were the air and battery packs. Why go into space without them? "They obviously hadn't been thinking clearly," Odo said. "Why else would they have taken such a foolish chance? How could they have allowed themselves to become enmeshed in such a desperate situation?"

"You're talking about them like they had a choice," Kira said. "Maybe they felt like they didn't. During the Occupation, many Bajorans had to make similar or even more desperate choices. They did what they did—*we* did what we did—because we wanted to be free. As dangerous and as desperate as the choice must have seemed, they must have felt like this was their only option."

"But *you* didn't run away," Odo retorted, an anger he could barely comprehend creeping into his voice. *"You* stayed and fought. If they had stayed on Cardassia, maybe they could have made a difference. Now all they are is *dead."* He punched up the bio of an overweight middle-aged man with graying hair and drooping jowls. "Look at this," he said, pointing at a line of text Nerys couldn't possibly have seen from where she sat. "This man had two children." He flipped to another record. "And his wife died, too." Bringing up another pair of records, Odo said through gritted teeth, "This couple had *three."* He spun away from the monitor, raging. "And what do you suppose will happen to the children without their parents? What happens to orphans on a Dominion-controlled Cardassia? I'm not even sure I know!"

As it had the day before when he sat in his office opposite Thrax, Odo sensed his frustration building in his chest and flowing up his arm into his hand, hardening it into the shape of a wide, flat hammer. . . . *And why not?* he wondered, looking at the images on the monitor. *What else is there to do except lash out . . . ?*

Nerys held up her hand. "Children?" Nerys asked sharply. "How *many* of them had children?"

Odo stopped his fist in mid-swing and stared at her. He felt his face go blank and the extra mass in his arm flew back down into his torso. Reaching down, he began to flip through the biographical notations for the first ten records, and then the next ten. "Most of them," he said.

When he looked up at Nerys, she was staring into the middle distance, her mind obviously racing ahead, annoyed with herself for being able to ask only one question at a time. "And the married ones . . . are there any with a husband or wife who *wasn't* in a cargo pod?"

While not an expert with databases, Odo knew enough to quickly parse the records, construct a query and run a search. Tense moments later, he said, "Yes. One. A woman named Tarrant. She was the wife of Kizon." He skimmed through her biographical data searching for some telltale difference between Tarrant and the other dead refugees. The entry for occupation stopped him. Unlike most of the others—the vagrants, instigators, and writers—Tarrant had a job that did not require a euphemism: She was an EV specialist.

Odo read this aloud and Nerys asked, "How many cargo containers would a freighter of that type normally carry?"

Odo called up the schematics, fearing he already knew the answer and cursing himself for not checking earlier. When the information came up, it was exactly what he feared. "Eight," he said.

Kira slapped her combadge. "Kira to O'Brien."

"Go ahead."

"Prep the *Defiant,* Chief. We're taking her out immediately."

They found the cargo pod tumbling several million kilometers beyond the debris field. A quick scan with the *Defiant's* sensors showed weak life signs, but they also showed that the irradiated hull wasn't permitting a positive transporter lock. "If we're going to bring them aboard, we'll need to do it manually. A tractor beam would crush the pod," O'Brien said.

"Suit up and take an away team over, Chief," Kira said from the command chair. "We'll match velocities and move in as close as we can. . . ."

O'Brien rose. "I can be ready in ten minutes."

"No," Odo said suddenly. "I'll go. I'm ready now."

Kira half-spun around in her chair and met his eyes. She knew he could tolerate hard vacuum, at least for a while. And every minute would count now.

"Go," she told him.

The airlock door opened silently and Odo stepped through, willing his epidermal layer to thicken and thin membranes to form over his eyes. No sound now, no gravity. Only the pinpoint stars framed by the open hatch. With one end of a grappling cable in tow, Odo pushed off the side of the *Defiant* and floated toward the cargo pod.

There was no sense of movement, only the grayish-green box growing larger in his sight as he closed with it. When he was less than a meter away, a fine crack appeared on one side of the pod. While anyone else would have had to wait for the hatch to open, Odo latched the cable to the pod, pressed a finger into the crack, and poured himself through.

Reconstituting himself inside, Odo saw the interior of the pod was as black as pitch except for a dim oval of light in one corner. A hand moved through the light—a helmet beacon?—then fell limp. Moments later, he sensed rather than saw all around him a circle of forms, all of them touching him, pulling at him, dragging him toward the fading light.

As Odo watched, the oval of light faded into nothingness.

"They're hungry, of course," Bashir explained outside the infirmary. "And exhausted and dehydrated, and there's some tissue damage due to radiation, but we can treat that." He had large, dark circles under his eyes and wore a haunted expression that Odo had not seen on his face since the earliest days of the war. *Just when you think you've seen the worst thing you could ever see, the universe throws you a new one. . . .* "And, they're terrified, all thirteen of them. They've been asking for their parents." He rubbed the back of his ear, then closed his eyes. "And I don't know what to tell them, Constable. I don't have the words."

Odo didn't have an answer, so he asked another question. "What about Tarrant? What did she die from?"

"Asphixiation," he said. "Just like the other adults. She must have been monitoring their batteries right up to the end, swapping out the dead ones for the ones the children's parents left her. In the end, she must have had to choose between staying alive to continue working or giving one of the children her own battery." Bashir smiled wearily. "We might have been too late for one or two of them if you hadn't gone out for them, Odo. It was a matter of minutes for a couple. . . ." The doctor looked up at Odo like he was expecting a smile in response, something wan, heroic, and reassuring.

He would wait a very, very long time.

"Thrax."

Seated alone at a table on the balcony level of Quark's, the Cardassian looked up from his glass of *kanar*. His eyes, which before had struck Odo as bright, seemed dull now. "What is it, Constable? I'm very tired and I'm due to depart in less than an hour."

Odo sat down across from him. "You knew about the missing children," he said. "You laid out the clues deliberately, hoping we'd put them together and find them for you. That's why you were so interested in the details of the Militia's recovery operation."

"Of course I knew," Thrax said. "I helped get them into the containers. I made sure Tarrant was with them in case the worst happened. And it did. Once I learned what your people found, and what they *failed* to find, deducing what really happened was a simple matter."

Odo shook his head, still struggling to wrap his mind around the chain of events he had put together. "The freighter didn't blow up immediately. While the Lurians tried to stop the core breach, the parents put Tarrant and the children into a single pod, along with the suit batteries and the air packs, and launched them into space before the ship blew. Then the parents returned to their pods and waited. If the Lurians could save the ship, they could retrieve the children's pod later. If not, at least the children had a chance at being found before their air and heat were depleted."

"And Tarrant *was* their chance," Thrax told him. "She was a clever woman. Calm under duress . . ." He shook his head, eyes tightly shut. "No child should ever have to see their parents die. Not that way, at least."

Odo could see the man was exhausted, but he didn't care. Still putting the pieces together in his mind, he needed confirmation.

"The planet you contacted in nonaligned space—Lejonis, in the Celeth system—that was their destination, wasn't it? This whole body exchange program, it's a cover. To get people like them off Cardassia."

"Not that we don't also return Starfleet's fallen to the Federation. We do." A shadow of a smile played at the corner of Thrax's mouth. "Just not as many as the Dominion believes."

Unable to contain his anger any longer, Odo hissed, "How can you put people at risk like that?"

The light that had been missing from Thrax's eyes suddenly blazed. "Because some of us are that desperate. Because *this* is what your people have brought mine to."

"They aren't *my* people," he said, acutely aware it was the second time he had said it in the last day.

"No?" Thrax asked. "Then whose are they, Constable? Or should I ask, who are yours? Who do you belong to?"

"That's not the issue. . . ."

"Don't misunderstand me," the Cardassian said. "I'm not accusing you of anything. Just stating facts. And the fact here is that the Dominion *isn't* going to return Cardassia to any state of former glory. It's crushing us. Slowly. Inexorably. And the first to die will be those the Dominion considers unnecessary."

"The men and women in the cargo containers—not criminals?"

"The worst sort, Odo," Thrax said, smiling wanly. "Writers, artists, freethinkers. Never popular on Cardassia at the best of times. Even less tolerated now."

"So you set up your pipeline—the smugglers, the neutral planets."

"I can't take credit for the idea, but, yes. I've been working on this for months."

"And if something went wrong—like it did with the Lurian freighter—you'd be the logical person to deal with it."

"Exactly. I had to make sure the pipeline wasn't exposed. So I came to the station under the pretense of conducting a criminal investigation, hoping to defuse the situation here before the Dominion took notice of it." He paused, shaking his head slowly, shoulders sagging again. "And then when I realized not everyone was accounted for in the wreckage, I knew, I *knew* they'd taken steps to keep the children safe. I had to find them."

"You could have told me the truth. . . ."

"You really understand *nothing* about us, do you, Odo? All those years living with Cardassians and you learned *nothing*. I couldn't risk it. Finding the children was important, yes. But keeping the pipeline from the Dominion was even more imperative. It still is."

"I would never have—"

"This is war, Odo," Thrax said. "If your side took sufficient notice of something like this, that guarantees that Dominion would take notice too. *Unless* I could defuse the situation first by convincing you it was, at worst, an isolated scheme hatched by someone like Quark."

Odo's shook his head, astounded by the wild chances, the desperation being revealed to him. "You can't keep this up forever," he said.

"It doesn't need to be forever," Thrax told him. "Just long enough."

"Why haven't you fled Cardassia as well? Why do you stay?"

Thrax smiled. "Because someone has to."

Odo's voice softened. "Perhaps I can help."

"If you want to do something, Constable, then bury this incident. Make it disappear, and make sure the children get to Lejonis. There are other refugees already there who will take care of them."

"Done."

"Thank you." Thrax lifted the glass and threw back his *kanar* in one shot, then stood up. But before he left the table, he said, "And then, perhaps, you could practice the art of looking the other way. That freighter wasn't the first with such precious cargo to pass through here. And it won't be the last."

"He's gone?" Nerys asked. They were back in her quarters, she once again on the couch, feet under the blanket and Odo was once again stalking about the room, with no clear direction for the anger that surged through him.

"Yes," Odo said, and he heard the slight snarl in it. He paused in his pacing, standing behind the couch and looked at Nerys, who had half-turned to look at him, a trace of a sad smile at the corners of her mouth. She was, he realized, watching him, waiting to see what his mood was. While he was rarely what he would call introspective, Odo knew what the look meant. He had to stop now, try to still the many voices clamoring for attention inside him and listen for his own. Settling into a state somewhere between fluid and solid, he let himself go in order to understand what he was feeling. Finally, minutes later, he said, "I'm angry."

Nerys asked calmly, "At whom?"

"At those people. At Thrax. At *my* people for causing all of this."

"That's a lot of anger."

Odo grunted, neither agreeing nor disagreeing. It *was* a lot of anger . . . and something else, too.

Almost the moment the thought entered his mind, Kira said, "But there's more to it, isn't there?"

The corner of his mouth quirked upward and he stepped to the couch, reached down and touched her shoulders. "Have you been taking counseling lessons?"

Nerys smiled. "They make you do that when they put you in charge."

"Really?"

Laughing, she said, "No. But it doesn't take a counselor to understand this. All those kids floating out there in space, what else could that remind you of except *you?* Alone and afraid, not knowing why you were there or where you were going. You never talk about it, but you must remember it. Don't you?"

Almost against his will, he felt his gaze drawn to the cabin window that looked out into the depths of space. If he walked closer, he knew he would be able to see the sweeping arc of the station's pylons, but from where he stood all Odo could see were the inky depths of space punctuated by tiny pinpricks of white light.

Odo nodded, but did not speak.

"The difference this time," Nerys continued, "is that someone saved them. *You* saved them."

Odo touched her palm and felt the warmth of her skin. *"We* saved them."

"All right: We saved them. But who saved you? No one, really. And maybe you're still angry about that. Maybe you're even still a little afraid."

He considered her words and knew that while, yes, once that had been true, and maybe would be again, for now, for that one instant, it wasn't. In that moment, he was neither angry nor afraid. Reaching down, he wrapped his arms around his lover and bent his head so that his mouth was next to her ear. "You found me," he whispered. "You saved me."

Smiling softly, closing her eyes, Kira kissed his neck. "We found each other," she said. "We saved each other."

Chiaroscuro

Geoffrey Thorne

Historian's note: This story is set between the seventh-season episodes "Afterimage" and "Take Me Out to the Holosuite."

Geoffrey Thorne

Geoffrey Thorne lives in Los Angeles with his supernaturally patient (and apparently prescient) wife. He likes to draw and he likes to write. For most of his life he has very much liked *Star Trek*.

"Chiaroscuro" is his second official foray into the *Star Trek* universe, his first being his prize-winning story "The Soft Room," from the sixth volume of the *Star Trek: Strange New Worlds* anthology, edited by Dean Wesley Smith.

Chin on hands, hands on tabletop, Ezri Dax watched the ice dissolve. It was sort of beautiful; the tiny bubbles bleeding off the cubes dashing madly upward, only to be trapped again in the froth at the top of the glass.

Years and parsecs away, near the middle of her bottomless memory, Torias Dax, suffering through an otherwise tedious lecture on the fluidity of space-time, had gotten an image similar to this one wedged in his mind. Personally she didn't see the humor, but she remembered the smile it had brought to his lips as if it had been her own.

"Either drink it or marry it," said a voice behind her. "Anything else is a waste."

It was Quark. Again. The Ferengi bartender had been making excuses to hover around her table for the better part of an hour.

She actually liked Quark. In spite of the obvious surfeit of qualities that made him a good Ferengi—greed, cynicism, and a mind that not only played the angles but recombined them in ways undreamt of by even the best grifters—there was something about him that generally lifted her spirits.

Tonight, though, he wasn't selling anything she wanted, not even the drink she had purchased an hour ago.

When he realized she would not turn his way, Quark swiveled into the empty chair on the opposite side of the table. She thought he might dust off his patented grin—it had brightened the mood of more than a few gloomy sentients in its time, she knew—but, looking at her staring at the booze that way . . . no. He seemed to reconsider, opting instead for a genial smirk.

"One of those days, huh?" he said.

Still she didn't move, preferring to regard his features only as they were distorted by their trip through the glass of amber liquid.

"Ezri?" he said.

"Sorry," she said, her voice drifting out of her like wisps of steam. "Just thinking."

"So I see," he said, more gently than she might have expected. "Want to talk about it?"

Absolutely not, she thought. *I absolutely do not want to talk about anything with anyone right now. And, if I did, it wouldn't be you, it wouldn't be here and it wouldn't be this.*

It was a message Quark wasn't capable of receiving. Ferengi sympathy was as ephemeral as Ferengi altruism but, once awakened, damned hard to evade. Ezri knew from experience that the only way to make him go was to invite him in.

"Will it cost me?" she said.

"Well, normally, empathy is an extra," he quipped, happy that she had finally engaged. "But for friends . . ."

He let the sentence dangle from the edge of what she remembered was his version of a smile.

"Is that what we are?" she said softly, almost to herself.

She remembered laughing with him and drinking too. She remembered thrilling adventures and games of chance. She remembered the banter, the meaningless little innuendoes tossed back and forth. She remembered more about him than he had learned yet about her.

"Sure," said Quark, still not quite getting a fix on her mood. "Sure, we're friends. Why, I can't count the times Jadzia and I—"

He caught himself, but it was too late. Her eyes met his over the foam.

I'm not Jadzia, she wanted to say. *Jadzia is dead.*

Quark knew that, of course. All Jadzia's friends knew. Some of them had seen her die. But they also knew that Jadzia had been joined to the Dax symbiont that held all of her memories. Now

Ezri carried it and them as well. Jadzia had been Dax. Now Ezri was Dax. What none of them seemed to grasp, she believed, was that Ezri Dax and Jadzia Dax were not the same.

It had been weeks since she'd agreed to rejoin the station crew. At the time it seemed like the right move, fulfilling a longing within her that had been growing ever since her impromptu joining. Now it seemed like a mistake. Whatever Ezri did, whatever she said, whatever fleeting expression might bend her features, would put one of her *friends* in mind of Jadzia.

It was maddening and frustrating and very very sad. She was sick of it. She was sick of hurting them just by coming into a room. It had to stop. Whatever comfort she'd been able to provide as the receptacle of Jadzia's memories was totally offset by the fact that every day, she continued to not actually *be* Jadzia. She was like Jadzia's ghost, haunting them. Their grief was still so fresh, none of them could see that Jadzia haunted Ezri as well.

If there was ever justification for the rule against joined Trills reassociating with aspects of their past lives, this was it.

So why am I still here?

"I'm sorry," said Quark. "Really, I didn't mean—"

Ezri dredged up a smile to put him at ease.

"It's okay," she said. "You're right. I'm just having a bad day."

"Sounds like you could use a break," he said.

"Yes." She pounced on the understatement as if it were manna. "I just need a break." What she meant was, *I just need to get away from this place and these people and Jadzia's damned ghost.*

There was chirp from her combadge. *"Lieutenant Dax, please report to Captain Sisko,"* said the disembodied voice of the station's computer. *"Immediately."*

Ezri sighed. She stood up sharply, making a little show of checking to see if her uniform was presentable. As she started off, she apologized for making Quark worry.

"Not a problem," she heard him say as she departed. "That's what friends do."

★   ★   ★

He was in the wardroom as he almost always was these days, planning, debating, strategizing.

Captain Sisko. Benjamin.

Silhouetted there amongst the battle displays and starcharts, he looked nothing like the reedy ensign whom Curzon Dax had taken under his wing more than twenty years previous. Nor was he the puckish older brother Jadzia Dax had found waiting when she'd arrived on Deep Space 9. Current events, the war with the Dominion being chief among them, had recast her oldest friend into a shape that was both unfamiliar and a little unnerving.

He was harder now than at any point in her memory, hammered by his need to win this war and tempered by his fear of the consequences should he fail. He had scant time for much else and almost none for the little Trill girl who shouldn't even need his shoulder to cry on anyway.

He acknowledged her arrival with a slight inclination of his head and then finished the order he was giving to a nearby ensign who, his task now set, dashed off to complete it.

"Clear this room," said Sisko in that deep baritone of which she'd always been fond. "Dax, you stay."

The people disappeared so quickly it seemed they'd all been beamed away by personal transporters. The holographic images vanished; the myriad tactical displays, one by one, went dark. Well, not all of them. A single sector of wardroom screen remained active, hovering in the space beyond Sisko's massive shoulder like an unblinking and disembodied eye.

"Ezri," he said, gesturing for her to come nearer, "we have to talk."

A wave of panic went through her as she moved toward him.

He knows! she thought, suddenly frantic. *He's seen the effect I'm having on the crew and he's giving me my walking papers.*

"There's a situation, Lieutenant," said Sisko as she drew near.

I knew it! she thought. *Here it comes.*

"What do you know about Pandora?" he said.

Or, she thought. *He could just ask me something random, out of the blue.*

"Pandora," she said slowly, feeling the word on her tongue. "Human myth, I think. Something about monsters in a jar?"

The corner of his mouth twitched at that, and there was a sparkle of something behind his eyes, but it was gone too quickly for her to decipher.

"Pandora," he said, "is a research facility situated on an asteroid in the Ibarri system." There was an odd cadence to his speech, as if he were sorting and approving the words individually before use.

He's holding something back, she thought.

"What sort of research?" she said.

"Archeological," he said, still watching her closely. Ezri had the odd sensation that she was being scanned rather than spoken to. "With an emphasis on cryptography. Apparently, there are ancient ruins of a lost civilization on the surface."

He stopped, as if waiting for her to add something.

"So . . . the situation?" was the best she could do. Why was he acting so strangely, anyway?

There was a beep from the companel behind him. Sisko stepped aside, allowing Ezri her first unobstructed view of the display screen.

There were words there—PRIORITY COMMUNICATION—white on a black background—and the familiar Federation seal. There was a clock in the lower left corner beside the words, REESTABLISHING CONNECTION IN. . . . The numbers on the clock were ticking down. When they hit zero the emblem vanished and was replaced by the unfamiliar and static-broken image of a woman in a captain's uniform.

"Sorry about the loss of signal, Captain," said the woman. *"We're still having problems with our comm system."*

She was Selenean, Ezri guessed. It was a species she knew of but had never actually seen. Her skin was a deep golden brown and burnished to the point of seeming metallic. Her hair, if hair it was, hung in a hundred finger-thick ropes from her head. Her eyes, slightly more round than most humanoids', were like marbles of turquoise glass. While totally alien, even to Ezri's sensibilities, she found the face beautiful.

"I understand, Captain Medoxa," said Sisko. "What's your status?"

"Unchanged, Captain," said the golden woman. Then, seeing Ezri, *"Is this Dax?"*

"It is," said Sisko.

An unreadable emotion flickered across the woman's face. Ezri felt the bright light of Medoxa's attention on her even through the comm chaff. To her mind, there was something invasive about it, like the woman was looking not so much at her as into her.

"How much have you told her, Captain?" said Medoxa.

"I was just beginning," said Sisko. "Since you're on the scene, perhaps you should provide details."

Scene of what? Details of what? What was going on? If this was some sort of officer transfer procedure it was one of which Ezri had never heard.

"Three days ago, the researchers on Pandora found what they thought was a second Protean artifact," said Medoxa. *"They requested more sensitive analysis equipment from Starfleet and my ship the* Anansi *was sent to make the delivery."*

The image of Medoxa broke up completely for a moment but returned.

"Apologies," she said. Then, continuing, *"When we arrived to make delivery, Pandora's satellite defense array fired on us. We sustained heavy damage, which we are still repairing."*

"Have you been able to make contact with Pandora, Captain?" said Sisko.

Medoxa shook her head. *"All attempts at communication have been ignored,"* she said. *"Until now."*

Ezri looked up at Sisko, the expression on her face saying, *What's going on?*

His hand on her shoulder said, *Wait.*

"This," said Medoxa, *"is the transmission from Pandora we received sixty-two minutes ago."*

The screen went black for a moment and was replaced by— Ezri couldn't tell what. At first it seemed to be a field of darkness bisected neatly by a jagged swash of light. Within the swash she could sort of see a conical object rising out of what she was arbitrarily calling the floor.

Suddenly, on the right side of the screen, a piece of the darkness moved, and she realized that someone had been standing there the whole time. That single tiny movement gave her the necessary anchor to resolve the image into something she could understand.

It was a room, a very small room. There was a man standing to one side wearing what appeared to be some variant of a Starfleet uniform.

All at once, the man began to speak.

"It's closed," he said, and his voice had the sound of something left out in the cold for far too long, like the anatomy he used for speech was somehow unfamiliar. *"It's closed, and none of them knows how to open it."*

He moved again, a sort of lurching shamble, which brought the left side of his body into the light. He was holding something that looked disturbingly like a weapon.

"Two hundred and fifty people." The man was suddenly agitated, almost hysterical. *"Two hundred and fifty and not* one *of them knows* anything *and I'm going to kill every single one of them unless someone opens the gate."*

There was a long silence during which it seemed to Ezri that the man was struggling to maintain equilibrium. Then, *"I know it's you up there, Y'Lira Medoxa,"* he said. *"Watching. Listening. You know what I need. Bring it."* Then he was gone.

Medoxa's face returned. She looked worried. *"That was Axael Krinn. Until this incident he was one of fifty cryptolinguists stationed at the Pandora facility."*

"What happened to him?" said Ezri.

"We're still working on that, Lieutenant," said Medoxa.

"So Krinn hasn't got access to the Codex, then?" said Sisko, cutting in.

"My people haven't detected any spikes," said Medoxa. *"So my guess is the gate is holding."*

"Does he have any other way into the chamber?"

Medoxa shook her golden head, making her hair shimmer and glint in the light. *"No, Captain Sisko,"* she said. *"If it weren't for the hostages we could just wait him out. We need Dax to—"*

The screen went black. The notation in the lower left read, CONNECTION BROKEN BY SENDER. Ezri was, to say the very least, nonplussed.

"I'm sure you have some questions," said Sisko.

It wasn't much, but the little he did make clear—*Ancient ruins containing some sort of alien artifact*—The Codex . . . *Impossibly old, immensely powerful, hidden behind an exotic and sophisticated security device* . . . had her head spinning.

"Krinn can't be allowed to get the Codex, Ezri," Sisko had said. "Captain Medoxa thinks you can help defuse this situation, and I'm inclined to agree."

He knew more. He certainly knew more than he was saying but there was something, some—was it sadness?—preventing him from giving her much beyond the order to go.

Ezri found the whole business, particularly its effect on Sisko, to be more than a little unsettling.

"Medoxa will tell you anything else you need to know," he said as he hustled her off, "when you get there."

Why me? she thought as her runabout tore the distance between Deep Space 9 and the *Anansi* into unobservable shreds.

There were plenty of counselors with more experience as crisis negotiators. There had to be contingency plans for retaking the Pandora facility should something like this happen. Why should Ezri be the fulcrum on which this situation shifted?

True, she did have Curzon and Lela Dax's memories. Both of them had been gifted speakers. Maybe that's why her name had come up.

Well, she thought, *I said I wanted a break.*

★   ★   ★

Her runabout rendezvoused with the *Anansi* where it sat, licking its wounds, in the bosom of a phenomenon called the Fassig Drift. Two comets had intersected here once, millennia ago, and obliterated each other. The Drift was what remained.

The *Anansi* itself, while clearly a Starfleet vessel, was of one of the newer designs made specifically for use in the Dominion War. Smaller, with a blunted nose and more hard corners than the normal Starfleet issue, the *Anansi*'s designers had clearly sacrificed all aesthetic value in favor of martial function. Even the double warp nacelles, characteristic of all Starfleet vessels, seemed to Ezri like the paws of some great feral beast waiting to pounce.

Captain Medoxa was waiting when Ezri's runabout docked. Flanking her were two of her officers—a tall, dangerous-looking Andorian and a smaller, apparently human, female with dark, close-cropped hair and an expression that leaned toward wily.

"Welcome to the *Anansi,* Lieutenant Dax," said Medoxa.

The first thing that struck Ezri as she stepped out of the shuttle's confines was how dark the *Anansi* was.

The shuttlebay was one massive shadow broken only occasionally by bright patches of light. She caught the spark of some exposed circuitry in her periphery and thought, *Battle damage. Pandora's defense array caused this.*

As she followed Medoxa and the others out of the bay, the ship lurched violently around them. No one lost their footing, but it was a near thing.

"What was that?" said Ezri.

"We're under way, Lieutenant," said Medoxa. Then, to the female officer, "Casey, get down to E section and find out how Bors is doing with the warp drive."

"Aye, Skipper," said Casey and vanished down an adjacent corridor.

"All right, Lieutenant," said Medoxa, moving forward again herself. "Let's get you up to speed. What exactly did Sisko tell you was happening here?"

"Not much," said Ezri, her voice full of displeasure. "And less than I think he knew."

"Yes, well," said Medoxa. "Don't be too hard on him, Lieutenant. I just dumped all this in his lap. Most of what you're about to learn is classified."

"So," said Ezri. "This isn't about negotiating to save the hostages?"

"In a word, Lieutenant, no," said Medoxa as she led Ezri and the silent Andorian through the *Anansi*'s maze of tight utilitarian corridors. "Axael Krinn is not just a researcher at Pandora. He is—he *was*—their chief cryptolinguist."

"You said they'd found something recently," said Ezri. "Some kind of artifact."

"A Protean object," said Medoxa. "The second of two."

"This 'Codex' being the first," said Ezri. Medoxa nodded. "You seem to think that contact with this second object has something to do with Krinn's behavior."

"There are many theories," said Medoxa. "That is one."

"Why?" said Ezri. "What is it about these objects that leads you to even entertain something like that?"

"What do you know about the Proteans, Lieutenant?" said Medoxa.

"Nothing," said Ezri.

"Shavras," said Medoxa, meaning, Ezri guessed, the big Andorian.

"Protean," he began in a voice like autumn leaves scraping together. "is the Starfleet designation for an extinct civilization believed to have held sway over most of this galaxy about a billion years before anyone in the Federation learned to harness fire."

Ezri whistled and said, "What happened to them?"

"We have no idea," said Shavras, following his captain around yet another tight corner. "But eight years ago a starship stumbled upon some ruins of theirs in an asteroid belt encircling the Ibarri red dwarf."

"The ruins themselves offer amazing insights into the Protean civilization," said Medoxa, taking over again. "Starfleet could have studied them for decades and not cracked all their secrets. But there was something else there."

"The Codex," said Ezri.

"The Codex," said Medoxa somberly. "Yes."

"What is it, exactly?" said Ezri. "Captain Sisko wasn't very specific."

Medoxa fell silent briefly, causing Ezri to think the information must be classified. Then, "Our best guess, based upon available data," said Medoxa, "is that it's a model."

"A model? Of what?"

"Of everything, Lieutenant," said Medoxa. "The Codex is a model of what we call 'reality' as seen from the outside. As best we can tell, based on the observations made by the team that discovered it, we think it's plugged into the fundamental structure of space-time in ways we don't and perhaps can't understand."

"And now Krinn wants it?" said Ezri.

Medoxa nodded.

"Excuse me, Captain." An end was still loose in Ezri's mind. "If this thing's just a model, why's it so dangerous?"

"May I continue, Lieutenant?"

"Of course," said Ezri. "I'm sorry, sir."

"Axael Krinn was part of the away team that first discovered the Codex hidden in a chamber beneath the ruins," said Medoxa. "But, unlike the ruins on the rest of the asteroid, the Codex chamber was pristine, and the Codex itself was active."

"Active?"

Medoxa stopped and turned to Ezri. "It killed two of the team as soon as they came near it," she said. "It maimed two more, including Axael Krinn."

Yes, thought Ezri. *That's fairly active.*

"Only the team leader got out relatively unscathed," said Medoxa.

"Lucky one of them did," said Ezri.

"On the contrary," said Medoxa. "She considered herself to be the least fortunate of the five."

"You said she made it out relatively unscathed."

"Physically, yes."

Ezri pushed past Shavras to get nearer to Medoxa.

"I'm a counselor, Captain," she said, a little more sharply than she'd intended. The winding trip through the *Anansi*'s guts was taking its toll. "I've dealt with a lot of injured minds, especially since the war started. I've also seen the casualties that come through Deep Space 9 from the front."

"What's your point, Lieutenant?" asked Medoxa.

"Only that I have a pretty good understanding of the resilience of the average humanoid mind," said Ezri, herself a little surprised by the intensity of her emotion. "It's rare these days, even during wartime, to come across a psychological trauma that can't be treated by current methods—assuming the patient *wants* to get better."

Where was all this coming from? It was as if learning of these events had stirred up some deep reservoir of anger in her over which she had little control.

"A valid opinion," said Medoxa, apparently unfazed. "But one not shared by this particular officer."

"Well," said Ezri. "Who was this self-obsessed ingrate?"

"Her name was Jadzia Dax."

When the world stopped spinning, Ezri realized she was still standing in the same close little corridor with the same unfamiliar officers looking impassively her way.

"That's not possible," she said eventually.

"It's not only possible," said Medoxa. "It's true."

"No," said Ezri. "You don't understand. If Jadzia had been there, if she even *knew* about it, I'd remember."

Again that thing flashed behind Medoxa's eyes that Ezri was unable to place. Then, as if she had not interrupted her story, Medoxa continued.

"Jadzia Dax managed to drag out the two other surviving members of her team before succumbing to the Codex effect herself," she said. "She and they were beamed up to their ship and treated while Starfleet determined what to do next."

"Skipper," said a familiar voice over the *Anansi's* comm system. *"Bors says we'll have warp drive again in under an hour."*

"Thank you, Casey," said Medoxa.

"And internal comms are back up."

"I gathered that, Ensign," said Medoxa. "Let me know when we are approaching the Ibarri system."

"Aye, Skipper."

Medoxa seemed confused, as if she'd forgotten for a moment what she was about. "Where was I?" she said.

"You were about to tell Dax here about the gate," said Shavras.

"Yes," said Medoxa, firming up. "The gate."

"Look, Captain," said Ezri. "No disrespect but, really, this is all a crock. I don't remember any of this. There's no way that it could have—"

Medoxa held up a hand for quiet. "The reason that you have no memory of this," she said evenly, "is that Jadzia had those memories erased."

Ezri could feel something hammering behind her eyes and realized dimly that it was her own pulse. It was only with effort that she was able to find her voice again.

"I don't believe it," she said, trying to put words to the feelings ringing in her mind. "Jadzia was a Trill, a host. She was *Dax's* host. She would never—"

"Lieutenant." Medoxa looked as if she would reach out to the younger woman in some comforting way.

"No!" said Ezri, angry tears welling in her eyes. "She would never let anyone take her memory."

Ezri's mind was in retreat. She couldn't hear, couldn't think, couldn't feel anything but deep soul-numbing horror at the act of mutilation Medoxa described.

Yet it had happened before, hadn't it? For reasons they considered sound, the Trill Symbiosis Commission had itself forcibly repressed all knowledge of Joran, Dax's only unstable host, who had remained forgotten for close to a century before the memories began to surface in Jadzia just a few years ago.

Now Medoxa was telling her that years before, with Joran's memory still suppressed, Jadzia herself, without even consulting the Commission, had willingly allowed memories of her own to be stripped away. It was inconceivable.

"Jadzia saw the Codex kill two of her friends and nearly kill two more," said Medoxa. Her tone was soft, but the words had iron in them. "She would have done anything to prevent it from happening again."

"I can't . . ." Ezri cast about blindly for a nonexistent exit. "I can't listen to this."

"Lieutenant Dax!" said Medoxa sharply. "Compose yourself."

With difficulty Ezri did manage to come to something like attention. Medoxa moved close to her then and spoke in a tone too low for Shavras to hear.

"We need to be on the same page here, Dax," she said and pressed something into her hand. Ezri looked down at it through watery eyes. It was an isolinear datachip.

"What's this?" asked Ezri.

The *Anansi,* as stripped down to the bare essentials as it was, still had a holodeck. It was small, about three meters cubed, but for her purposes it would do.

"*It's a message,*" Captain Medoxa had said. "*From Jadzia to you.*"

The opportunity to speak with her predecessor face to face, even holographically, was startling enough to put the brakes on Ezri's skepticism. She agreed to take a look.

"Computer," she said. "Run program, Dax Infinitum."

"*This program is Read Only,*" said the computer. "*You will not be able to interact.*"

Suddenly Jadzia Dax was standing before her, but it was a Jadzia that Ezri found herself hard-pressed to recognize.

The image was younger than Ezri had expected, by almost a

decade. *Eight years ago,* Ezri thought. *That means it had to have been during the first year after Jadzia was joined. Two years before she was assigned to Deep Space 9.* Though she possessed Jadzia's memories, the self-image that went along with them was that of a mature Jadzia, complete in herself. This one was scattered, agitated, seemingly ready to jump at the slightest provocation.

"I guess introductions are unecessary," said Jadzia. "If you're seeing this it means that some time has passed and that, so far, we did the right thing." Jadzia forced herself to smile, briefly. Maybe it was something like bravery but all Ezri saw was rue. "Starfleet agreed with me, finally. That thing down there is too dangerous for anyone to get near it. They let me design the security system to make sure no one gets in there until we have some way of protecting ourselves from—" Her voice broke and she was overcome by some powerful feeling. When she recovered, she went on.

"There are engineers down there right now putting in the hardware. I made sure that none of them would be telepaths. I think—I think that's what happened to Etoli and Sovak and to the rest of us, too. It does something to your mind—" Again she broke off.

Ezri watched in horrified fascination Jadzia's struggle to keep herself together.

It was painful for her to see Jadzia this way; broken into pieces by the trauma she'd undergone. She longed to reach out, to give Jadzia some kind of solace, but this was all ancient history. Jadzia was dead. Even the memory of this was gone.

"They're setting up a permanent dig there," Jadzia went on. "That's the plan anyway. They want to translate the glyphs that are all over everything. So, someday, maybe, in a century or two, we'll be able to understand what it is, how it does what it—how to make it *stop.* Maybe."

Jadzia's eyes grew cold then, as if all of the emotions had drained out of her body. "Until then," she said. "That thing stays locked up behind my gate. It's the best way. Only Dax can open the gate, and only Dax can live long enough to know when it's time—if it ever is."

Jadzia's demeanor changed again suddenly. Ezri thought she looked almost ashamed.

"I'm letting them wipe the memory of this out of me," she said. "The only way to make sure the gate stays shut is to hide the key. *I'm* the key. And that means, so are you."

There it was, right from Jadzia's own mouth. What was the Codex that a single contact with it could so shatter Jadzia that she would go against thousands of years of Trill tradition this way?

"Right now you think I'm taking the easy way out," said Jadzia. "Or that I'm being selfish or something. Please, believe me, I don't deserve to forget this. I don't deserve to go away and live my life without some—*punishment.*"

Jadzia broke off again and seemed to be fighting a losing battle to maintain self-control. She was shivering slightly, and there were tears obvious in her eyes—eyes which refused to focus on anything for longer than a few moments. Ezri had seen enough soldiers in recent weeks to recognize battle trauma when she saw it.

With obvious difficulty, the image of Jadzia did manage to continue.

"You're wondering how I could do this to you—to *us.* I'm wondering it myself. Memory is sacred. I know that. If there were any other way . . ." she said. "But there isn't. There just isn't. That thing down there is too dangerous to be let out. It's just the most—"

Jadzia made a good show of pulling her spiraling emotions back in.

"I can't tell you the secret of opening the gate," she said softly. "But I can tell you what it is. It's a holographic maze. There are no safety protocols. If you can't beat the maze, it'll kill you. Another precaution against anyone but Dax being able to open it."

Ezri was stunned. A lethal maze designed by this woman who was obviously teetering on the brink of total mental collapse? What had her superiors been thinking? Or maybe this confession was the only time Jadzia had allowed herself to break down, to show the chaos she was fighting inside.

"If you're Dax, you can do it," Jadzia said. "And here's an added bonus: Complete the program, and you'll get your memories back. Posthypnotic trigger. Then you'll understand why all this was necessary, and hopefully, that knowledge will do some good when the gate comes down. But don't open the gate unless you're sure—absolutely sure—that the time is right. If it's not and that thing gets out . . . everyone loses. And I mean *everyone.*"

The hologram vanished, and Ezri was alone.

She found Medoxa waiting when she exited the holodeck, her face still the unreadable golden mask it had been before. She was alone, having dismissed her subordinates while Ezri was inside.

The expression on Ezri's own features made it clear to Medoxa that, whatever the contents of Jadzia's message, it had done the trick.

"Are we on the same page now, Lieutenant?" said Medoxa.

Ezri nodded slowly. "You need me to somehow help prevent Krinn from opening Jadzia's gate."

"No, Lieutenant," said Medoxa as she turned, heading for the nearby turbolift. "I need you to open it for him."

"This is insane," said Ezri as they went over it for the fourth time.

Medoxa had taken Ezri to the armory to meet with the ship's tactical officer, a human named Gabrielli, and had laid out the so-called plan on the way.

"You said that before," said Medoxa. Her attention was on Gabrielli as he triple-checked the modifications he'd made to Ezri's combadge.

"It's a good plan, Lieutenant Dax," said Gabrielli as he placed the altered chip back into the badge and resealed it. He handed it to her and stood by as she reattached it to her uniform.

"And it's the only one we have," said Medoxa. Then, to Gabrielli, "Is the weapon ready?"

The weapon was a modified hand phaser, reduced to the size of Ezri's little finger. Provided she wasn't searched or observed too closely, she might get a clear shot at Krinn.

"It's ready, Skipper," said Gabrielli.

Medoxa nodded, satisfied, and tapped her own cambadge. "Bridge."

"Bridge, Oktesh here," said an unfamiliar voice.

"Take us as close to Pandora as you can, Mr. Oktesh," said Medoxa. "Full impulse."

"Aye, aye, Captain," said the voice.

"Mr. Edmunds," said Medoxa. "Put me through to Pandora."

"Channel open," said another voice.

"Pandora facility, this is Captain Medoxa," she said to the air. "I have Dax with me, Axael. She can open the gate for you but I want you to let the hostages—"

Suddenly the room was filled with ear-splitting static. This was followed immediately by that same strangely hollow voice.

"Send Dax," it said.

"The hostages first," said Medoxa. "Let's negotiate a—"

"No negotiations," said the voice. *"Send her now, or people start dying."* There was another burst of static, then silence.

"We're being given transporter coordinates," said Edmunds's voice.

"Let me know when we're in range, bridge," said Medoxa. "And if Pandora's defense array even twitches I want to hear about it."

Ezri stood on the transporter platform waiting for the minutes to tick down. She had never been so nervous about anything in her life. Strange electric pinpricks attacked the insides of her fingertips. Her mouth was dry.

A few feet away, manning the transporter controls, was Medoxa. She'd dismissed the technician in order to have one last private moment with Ezri.

"This will work, Dax," she said, noting Ezri's agitation.

"Only because it has to," said Ezri.

"I can't think of a better reason," said Medoxa.

"Two minutes to transport range," came Edmunds's disembodied voice over the comm system.

"Before you go, I want you to know something" said Medoxa. "I was part of the away team that found the first Protean Relic."

"I guessed that, Captain," said Ezri. "I thought you seemed a little close to all this. And in Krinn's earlier transmission, he referred to you by name."

"Points for you, Lieutenant," said Medoxa.

"So, I guess you and Jadzia were the lucky ones," said Ezri. "I mean, to have come out of it alive. And intact."

"I was maimed in the encounter, Lieutenant," said Medoxa. "Permanently."

Ezri, while stunned by this confession, did her best to keep her face neutral.

"But," she managed. "I thought Krinn must have—"

"Krinn suffered extensive nerve damage," said Medoxa calmly. "But it was treatable. I wasn't so lucky."

By all appearances, Medoxa was one of the more formidable physical specimens Ezri had ever met. There wasn't a single visible blemish on the perfect golden skin. She had no obvious synthetic limbs.

"Selenean brains have five lobes," said Medoxa, perhaps sensing Ezri's confusion. "Mine has only four. I no longer dream. I can no longer procreate. Among my people I'm considered a ghost. That's what the Codex did to me."

"*Twenty-five seconds to transport range,*" said Edmunds's voice.

"I tell you this, Lieutenant, so that you will understand," said Medoxa. "I felt that thing scorching a hole in me—in my mind. I know what it means if it gets out. If this doesn't work, I will do whatever it takes to burn Pandora and everything on it out of the sky."

Delay. That's what Medoxa's plan boiled down to. Krinn wanted the gate open, so Dax, the only one who could, would do that for him. It would take time though. Time was the only weapon Krinn had left them.

"Take your time with the gate," Medoxa had said. "Draw it out as long as you can. Keep Krinn focused on you. You're buying us time to hack into Pandora's defense array and retake control."

Once that was done, Medoxa would own Pandora. She could beam

down thousands of rescue teams if she wished or, if she was lucky, beam one
Axael Krinn straight to the Anansi's *brig.*

　　Easy. Simple. All it had to do was work perfectly the first time through.

Ezri materialized inside a small dark space, which, to her, seemed
like some sort of shallow cave. She was thankful to find the space
empty. While, under normal circumstances, she enjoyed using the
matter transporter over more conventional means of travel, in this
case the idea of being beamed in blind to coordinates provided by
someone who was less than sane did not inspire a sense of security.

　　As per Medoxa's plan, Ezri tapped her combadge and began to
relay what she could see to the *Anansi*. They would not respond.
In modifying the device to boost its signal, Ensign Gabrielli had
sacrificed its two-way capabilities. Ezri was alone.

　　"I'm here," she said softly. "There's no sign of Krinn."

　　As her eyes adjusted to the dim light, she was able to pick out
the details of what she had thought to be a natural indentation in
the asteroid's surface. It was not. This space had been made by the
hands of sentients. Aside from the part of the wall that had crumbled away, all the visible surfaces were covered in strange raised
markings she recognized as glyphs.

　　There was a sort of circular pedestal in the center of the space
the top of which was the only thing in the room not covered by a
fine sheen of dust.

　　"There was something here," she said. "Whatever it was has
been moved."

　　He flexed her wrist to feel the modified phaser in her sleeve.
Still there.

　　"I'm going in," she said.

She found herself in an open courtyard with what appeared to be
naked sky above her. She knew that there was a massive force field
there, holding the breathable gases in, maintaining pressure. She
knew there were artificial grav generators scattered around to keep

the researchers from just floating away. She knew these things and still had to force herself to keep a normal breathing cycle.

Pandora was amazing.

Setting aside the massive red sun rolling slowly across the star-filled sky and the seemingly infinite number of asteroids stretched out in all directions like a blanket of floating stones, there were the Protean ruins themselves. Their mammoth crystalline spires towered above her. Their upper reaches, even broken as they were, seemed to stretch out into space indefinitely.

There were smaller structures, dwellings at one time perhaps, huddled in semicircular clusters around the base of each of the massive pillars. Though ancient there was still an aura of vitality about the place, as if its makers had only been gone moments and could return at any time.

The signs of Federation presence—the discarded ground buggies, the field generators, even the communications tower—seemed incongruous to her. They were rough-hewn things, primitive by comparison to these elegant ruins.

"No sign of the hostages," she said even as she noticed the odd device that had been welded to the base of the nearest field generator. She moved in for a closer look.

"Bad news, Captain," she said. "I think Krinn has attached some kind of incendiary to one of the forcefield projectors. The timer looks simple but the explosive could be thermium."

"You aren't Dax," said a now-familiar voice behind her.

On instinct she spun, snapping the phaser into her palm and bringing it up, but it was too late. In a lightning movement, a bit of heavy pipe smashed into her hand, forcing her to drop the weapon.

"Who are you?" said her attacker, who could only be Axael Krinn.

He was not what she'd expected. He was gaunt, for one thing, emaciated. His uniform hung off him like a shroud. His eyes were wild, animal things that glittered in the starlight and seemed governed by something other than intelligence. Was this his normal appearance or had this transformation had taken place in the last few days?

"I'm Dax," she said, clutching her bruised hand. "Ezri Dax."

"Jadzia is Dax," he said.

"Jadzia *was* Dax," she said firmly. "I'm Dax now."

There was some kind of weapon in the hand not holding the pipe. Krinn swiveled it up and pressed it to Ezri's temple.

"This is Medoxa trying some trick," he said. "Only Jadzia can open the gate."

"Only *Dax*," said Ezri, hoping there was enough lucidity left in him to understand. "But if you kill me, I can't open it."

The hand with the weapon wavered, stiffened, and finally dropped away.

"All right," said Krinn after a time. "But if this is a trick . . ."

He led her away from what was obviously the main part of the Pandora excavation and into a little maze of natural rock formations. He never spoke during the short walk though Ezri tried to engage him. He just kept prodding the small of her back with that hand weapon of his. Eventually they came to the opening of a cave.

A soft light spilled out at them from within and, Ezri noticed, there were sensor brackets imbedded in either side of the opening. Both had been smashed. Obviously Mr. Krinn had anger management problems.

A nudge from the gun told her to go inside.

It was a blast door, the kind used to seal off sections of starships which had been compromised by radiation leaks or hull breaches. It was blast-proof, phaser-proof, and apparently Krinn-proof. Ezri could see where some sort of high-intensity energy discharge had blackened small areas of the surface. The damage was entirely cosmetic.

"Open it," said Krinn.

Right, she thought. *This is it.*

Not really knowing where to begin, she stepped forward, meaning to touch the thing in hopes of finding some sort of hidden key pad or vox device. She needn't have bothered.

"No!" screamed Krinn behind her. Ezri had time to turn his way and see him leaping at her, his arms outstretched. Then Krinn and everything else in the cave was lost in a shimmering cascade of light.

That was a transporter effect, she thought when the moment of disorientation passed. She'd been scanned, apparently by some automated sysyem, accepted, and whisked away to—where?

She was on a rocky ledge near the summit of what appeared to be an impossibly tall mountain. All around her, great billows of crimson and black vapor swirled violently.

Behind her the ledge on which she stood became a sheer cliff descending until it vanished into the maelstrom below.

Before her, slung across the black maw of a cave, was a gigantic iron gate. An enormous latch held the thing closed but Ezri was sure she could open it if necessary. Below the gate she could see the hint of some sort of staircase extending down and down into the impenetrable dark.

Above it, carved into the living rock of the mountain, were the words ALL HOPE ABANDON, YE WHO ENTER HERE. Ezri had read and understood the words before realizing they were written in a language her conscious mind found unfamiliar.

I know this, she thought, though she couldn't yet say from where the knowledge came.

Suddenly the ground began to shake beneath her feet. Remembering Jadzia's admonition that this place, however virtual, would still kill her if it could, Ezri dived forward away from the edge of the crumbling precipice.

Even as she did so, the massive fragment of the mountainside fell away behind her. She had bare seconds to grab hold of the gate's rusted lower bars and save herself.

Corroded by time and the elements of this place, the jagged contours of the gate tore viciously at her fingers as she hauled herself up toward the ragged latch.

This is insane, she thought.

As she'd predicted, the latch proved easy enough to open. Though doing it one-handed and from below did present a bit of a challenge.

Her weight, now supported by only one half of the gate, caused that half to swing outward on its suddenly very flimsy-seeming hinges. Not for the first time Ezri thanked her memory of Emony Dax's gymnastic training. She swung her feet wide, shifting her center of gravity enough to halt the gate's outward momentum.

Then, catching the latch between her feet and holding it, she slowly pulled the gate closed. As soon as the edges came together Ezri dropped down into the opening of the cave.

The steps there extended that same impossible distance down into the inky depths.

All right, she thought. *Let's get this done.*

She took four steps down before the world around her began to run like a painted watercolor left out in the rain.

Suddenly she was tumbling down into the dark with no walls or stairs or even a rusty gate to stop her.

The fall hadn't killed her, and the stop at the end had not been sudden but a gentle slowing until she felt she was barely moving at all. She realized she'd closed her eyes sometime during her descent and opened them again.

She was surrounded by sheets of translucent mist. There was nothing under her feet, nothing in the air above. Unlike the chaotic motions of the clouds at the gate, this place seemed serene, almost soothing in its gentle ebb and flow.

She tried to move but it was like being adrift in space. With nothing to provide thrust or to push against, all she succeeded in doing was waggling her arms and legs.

After a time she felt she could see something darkening in the mists ahead of her. At first she thought it was just a trick of light, but soon it was clear that a small portion of the clouds in that region was thickening somehow, becoming more solid.

Soon the point of density became a shape, the shape became a figure and the figure became a woman dressed in a garment of iridescent white.

As the woman walked—not floated—toward her, Ezri was shocked to see the pattern of elegant markings, spots, framing her face on either side. The woman was a Trill. Moreover she was someone Ezri knew. This was Lela, the first person ever to join with the Dax symbiont.

"I have a question for you," said Lela, smiling. It was strange to see her this way, from the outside. Ezri had all her memories but, as it had been with Jadzia, the act of meeting one of the former hosts in any physical way was unnerving.

"What is the price?" said Lela.

The price? thought Ezri. *The price of what?* As riddles went, this one was pretty vague.

The breeze that had been gently supporting her began to pick up.

"What is the price?" said Lela again.

When Ezri failed to answer the second time, the breeze, now actually buffeting her, began to shove her violently from one position to the next. It was like being tossed back and forth by invisible giants.

"What is the price?" said Lela's voice over the now-screaming blow.

"Of what?" Ezri shouted back. "The price of what?"

The jolts were so powerful now, so abrupt, that Ezri swore she could feel her ribs cracking.

"The price," came Lela's words again, the first half of the question eaten by the gale.

Ezri almost shouted that she didn't know when suddenly, she thought she might.

It *wasn't* a riddle, not in the conventional sense. It was part of an aphorism Audrid Dax had created for her daughter, Neema.

Neema had been a headstrong girl, always wanting to know the whys and hows of things. Though Audrid had encouraged this curiousity she'd always hoped to instill a healthy respect for the consequences that getting the answers to some questions might bring.

"What is the price of knowledge?" she would say to Neema.

That was what Lela Dax was asking, Ezri was sure.

"The price of knowledge," she shouted over the wind, "is knowing."

Suddenly, as quickly as it had come, the cyclone vanished. Ezri was again held aloft by those first gentle zephyrs.

Lela's beautiful smile broadened. "That's true," she said. "But remember that it is also sometimes pain."

With that Lela Dax was gone, vanished again into the mists that had spawned her.

Then there was a rush of air, a spinning of light and sound, and Ezri was somewhere else.

She was hot, sweating, and submerged in something she couldn't quite see—something in perpetual motion. It was as if she'd been thrust into a universe composed entirely of writhing snakes.

She registered a dim glow above her and a thick, oily sort of darkness below.

Even as she decided to make a try for the light, something smashed into her face and was gone. She had only just realized that the taste of copper in her mouth was her own blood when she felt the fingers—she was sure they were fingers—taking hold of her limbs—tearing at her clothes.

In a panic of flailing limbs she half scrambled, half swam, upward toward the light and, she hoped, some measure of safety. Her progress was terrifically slow, and, with all that heat and motion undulating around her, she began to fear that she'd never make it up.

What is this? she thought, still struggling.

Her hand broke through to a patch of space unoccupied by the seething mass and she did her best to pull herself through. It was difficult. Everything she touched seemed to squirm in her hands.

Everything had the disturbing texture of flesh and bone. She was almost sick with the sensory overload.

Finally her flailing hand landed on something solid and blessedly unmoving—a rock. She forced her other hand up to join the first and pulled herself out.

Her perch, the rock, was only a lip of stone jutting out from what turned out to be an incredibly high and circular wall. It was the inverse of the moutain Ezri had stood on at the beginning of all this.

There seemed to be no break in the wall, no means of egress. For all intents and puposes she was sitting on the edge of an enormous stone bowl.

The whole place seemed designed to contain the turbulent sea of—were those *people?*

To her horror she realized they were.

The strange mass she'd just escaped was really just thousands—hundreds of thousands—of people writhing in apparent torment.

"Down, sinner!" bellowed a voice from behind.

Ezri turned in time to witness an enormous humanoid creature in black bearing down on her. Its massive, overmuscled arm flashed out, the three-fingered hand taking her wrist in a viselike grip.

She tried to pull free but it was useless. The creature, some sort of uniformed guard, dragged her back to the edge of the pit.

With one hand around her throat it held her out over the edge, giving her an unobstructed view of the tormented souls below. Only they weren't so tormented now that she saw them closely. If anything the naked writhing figures seemed to be engaged in activities from the opposite end of the spectrum.

"There is no escape, harlot," said the creature. "You have sinned, and you have been judged."

With a chill, Ezri realized it meant to throw her back into the pit, to cast her down into that seething hedonistic mass.

She'd never been particularly claustrophobic before but her short time in the pit had pushed her limits to the breaking point. She had no wish to endure a repeat performance.

Ezri kicked viciously at the creature but it was no use. She was flung screaming out into the center of the mass.

Immediately, she felt the hands on her, tearing at her clothes, trying again to drag her down. As before, she fought through to the surface only to be met by the boot of another of the massive guards.

Each time she fought her way to the edge of the mass of bodies, one of the black-robed brutes was there to force her back down. She was bruised, tired, and not a little frightened that there might not be a way out of this.

Even without the guards to prevent her escape, she took a terrible pummeling each time she tried for the pit's edge.

Most troubling was that Jadzia had promised that there was a solution and that any Dax should be able to find it.

She rifled through her near-endless store of memories in desperation. Lela Dax's life of bureaucratic intrigues offered nothing. Nor did Audrid's. Nor, even, Curzon's, whose pleasure-seeking tendencies were the stuff of legend. Tobin's engineering skills were meaningless in this situation, as was Joran Dax's talent for murder.

Torias, she thought even as she fought to keep herself aloft. *Test pilot.*

He'd flown more experimental vessels than any six Trill combined. Sometimes, even often, things went wrong.

What was it he always said?

"When nothing's working, trust the flow."

He'd coined the notion after a particularly awful moment with an engine burnout ten miles above the surface of Trill. Another pilot would have fought the planet's pull, burnt out his other engine in the process thereby killing himself and the ship he flew. Not Torias. Instead of fighting gravity, he let it take him, using retro jets to change his angle of entry.

A few seconds later he'd gained enough momentum that a simple refiring of the operational engine had been enough to skip his ship off Trill's atmosphere and save himself from fiery death in reentry.

Find the flow, Torias's voice seemed to whisper to her.

Everything about this place told her to fight to get out of the pit, to try to find a way past the brutal and implacable guards. What if that were the trick? She'd assumed the exit was somewhere away from all this. What if it wasn't? What if it had been beneath her all the time?

Ezri relaxed, let the fingers grasping at her feet take hold. She stifled the flash of panic as they drew her down and down into the sea of bodies.

I'll only get one shot at this, Torias, she thought. *You'd better be right.*

The dog lowered its middle head, growling as it prepared for another pounce. Ezri had avoided the teeth so far—no mean feat with that many heads to keep track of—but she was getting tired.

This third world was nothing more than one enormous abattoir. Bodies and bits of bodies lay strewn all over. The rough stone walls were soaked with something that had to be blood and from the shadows she could hear the sound of, well, *munching.*

Then there was the dog. Big as a runabout and sporting three heads, the dog stood directly between her and the only obvious exit from the place.

The most maddening aspect was that the whole thing was so damned familiar. Jadzia had been fascinated with the stories of other cultures, other worlds. Ezri knew this whole thing was culled from one of them, but there were so many with so many overlapping symbols that she couldn't lift one out of the mosaic.

And, of course, there was still the dog.

It pounced again. She dodged again, barely, the blood-slick floor forcing her to skid to the far side of the room. Worse, she had lost the broken length of chain she had been using to keep the thing at bay.

She was cornered, weaponless, tired, and the dog knew it. Its approach this time was deliberate, even blasé. She wasn't going anywhere.

Think, dammit, she told herself. *There's a solution to this. A Trill solution. A Dax—*

Tobin Dax had once become obsessed with a trinket from Earth called a finger trap. It was some sort of flexible tube. You stuck a finger in either end and then couldn't get them back out again. Not by pulling, at any rate. The secret was to give in to the trap and push. The flexible trap would then expand just enough for the fingers to be drawn slowly free.

Why would she think of that just now?

What about a giant holographic dog trying to make a meal of her was similar to . . .

She smiled and rose from the defensive crouch she'd fallen into.

"Come and get me, boys," she said, hoping it was the right answer. If it wasn't, the next few minutes were really going to hurt.

Dante.

The answer came to her as the dog's jaws closed harmlessly over her head. This whole scenario was culled from the work of an obscure human poet.

As a young woman Jadzia had been mad for his stuff for about a month. What was this one called?

The Inferno.

It was a travelogue of some sort of place of eternal punishment that humans had once believed reserved for the wicked after they died. Being a Trill, whose culture had no such views, Jadzia had found the piece both beautiful and amusing. Each of these holographic worlds corresponded to one of the Circles of Dante's supposed Hell . . . or, rather, Jadzia's unique reinterpretation of it.

You were right, Jadzia, she thought. *Only a Dax would come up with something like this.*

She'd survived the first three challenges on wit and memory. Now that she knew the pattern, she was ahead of Jadzia's game. If the rules held true she'd made it to the Fourth Circle, where the greedy found punishment.

Yes, she thought, taking in the tableau before her. *I expected something like this.*

Three people—a Romulan, a Cardassian, and someone in a Starfleet uniform—were ahead of her, seated at a table in the center of a large but otherwise featureless room. They were playing a game of cards for a massive pile of golden discs. There was one empty chair.

The players barely noted her as she approached the table.

"What are you playing for?" she said.

"Power," said the Romulan.

"Survival," said the Cardassian.

"Knowledge," said the Starfleet officer, who bore not a little resemblance to the younger Jadzia Dax.

"That's what I thought," said Ezri and kicked the table over. The chips went flying. The players, screaming, scrambled to collect what they could of their scattered loot. Ignoring them, Ezri proceeded to the suddenly visible door and passed through.

This isn't right, she thought as she took in the pack of Kytharri hunters that were taking her in. Only one had a blaster, thankfully, but the cleavers sported by the others weren't much comfort. And then there were their claws.

This should be the Fifth Circle, she thought. *The place of Wrath. They're just standing there.*

Then she remembered. Circles Five through Eight in Dante's poem all had to do with violence.

Jadzia had puzzled over Dante's separating them into different flavors. It had seemed incomprehensible to her Trill sensibilities. Violence was violence. It was useful sometimes, other times not. This human fascination with attaching binary moral formulae to every aspect of Life must have been very tiresome.

Still, for violence, one couldn't do better than Kytharri. They lived for it in a way that even the Klingons had never done. It was something in their brain chemistry. Their vaguely feline bodies seemed almost intentionally designed to inflict bloody death on an opponent. Their society, if it could be called that, consisted of packs of Kytharri ripping the throats out of each other on a fairly constant basis. The Kytharri were chaotic, vicious, and relentlessly hierarchical. Starfleet had deemed their world off limits for quite some time.

This was something for Curzon Dax, she thought. *Part brawl, part diplomacy.*

Curzon could talk his way through nearly anything and fight his way out of the rest. He'd always longed for the chance to meet the Kytharri himself and bring them into the civilized fold.

Ezri wasn't Curzon, though, not in size or inclination. She could never fight or talk her way past these brutes. Jadzia hadn't planned on someone like Ezri ever being Dax's host.

"There are many ways to skin a *targ,*" she remembered some nameless Klingon telling Jadzia.

Curzon had been fond of rule bending too—of finding the unaccounted for edges of things and using them to his own advantage. In that, it seemed to Ezri, they were very much alike.

Ezri might not be the host Jadzia had expected or planned for, but she was still a Dax.

She had the memory of Emony's gymnastic skills to help her, as well as decades of combat training as a member of Starfleet. Her current lack of mass made direct conflict almost certain suicide.

Joran Dax, the serial murderer, had been fond of violence, though he'd never have admitted it. He had been adept in fact. Jadzia hadn't known about him when she created this maze.

Creation is destruction, she remembered Joran thinking. *The world has a shape, a pattern. To change that shape, one has to see it and be willing to do what's necessary.*

Leafing through his ugly memories, Ezri formed a plan. Only one of the Kytharri had a blaster. He was also the only one with a leather thong around his neck. The thong denoted leadership status among the Kytharri. Ezri had other uses for it.

"You want me?" she said to the collection of brutes. Obviously they did. "Then I will go with whoever is strongest."

For a moment nothing much happened. If anything, the Kytharri looked confused. Then, all at once, they exploded into a fantastic orgy of cleavers, claws, and knives flashing like lightning as the hunters cut each other to bloody shreds.

Watching the carnage intently, Ezri inched toward the Kytharri with the blaster, who was in turn looking for a clear shot at one of his former comrades.

Ezri's hands had the ends of his leather collar drawn tight around his throat in an instant and her knee in the small of his back. A quick jerk, a sharp twist and the Kytharri's neck snapped like a dry stick. The blaster fell to the floor. Ezri managed to snatch it up even as the other Kytharri realized something bad was about to happen.

Seven shots later the Circle of Violence was gone.

Wherever she was, it was dark. There was nothing to see, nothing to hear and, aside from the floor on which she stood, nothing to touch.

Suddenly there was a bright light in her face.

"Lieutenant Dax," said a familiar voice. "You okay?"

The light withdrew a bit and, as her eyes readjusted, Ezri could make out several figures, all in Starfleet EVA suits, silhouetted in the halo of some sort of handheld lamp.

"Must have bumped her head," said one of the others.

"Is that you, Captain Medoxa?" said Ezri.

Someone snickered at that.

"Uh," said Medoxa. It sounded like Medoxa anyway. *"You're* the senior here, Lieutenant."

"I think she may be injured," said a placid masculine voice.

"I'm fine," said Ezri. It wasn't true. Her head was splitting all of a sudden.

"Good," said the one she thought was Medoxa. "Because we've found something."

Someone took Ezri's hand and led her away.

Her head hurt. Something was glowing in the distance and her head hurt.

"What is it?" Ezri managed. She wasn't sure what exactly was happening but figured the best thing to do was to play along.

"We have no idea," said Maybe-Medoxa.

"Getting some strange readings here," said one of the others.

"Should we get closer, Lieutenant?"

Were they talking to her? It was so hard to think with her head about to split in half.

"Lieutenant?"

"Sure," she managed. "Check it out."

Why had she said that? What was wrong with her?

"You heard her," said Medoxa or whoever. "Get in there and scan the hell out of that thing."

The others moved off toward the glow. Medoxa bent toward Ezri and had enough time to ask if she was really feeling all right before the screaming started.

"What the hell?" said Medoxa.

Ezri looked up to see the three figures closest to the glow screaming and clawing at their helmets. Two of them fell and didn't move again. The third lay where he fell, moaning piteously.

"Gods below," said Medoxa. "That thing is killing them."

Ezri couldn't think for the thunder in her brain. What was happening? Was this part of the maze? Who were these people?

"We've got to get them out of there," said Medoxa.

"No!" Through the haze of pain, Ezri clutched at her. It was too late. Medoxa's black shape sprinted toward her fallen friends. In mute horror Ezri watched as she too was caught in the grip of some unseen force and broken. Medoxa crumbled like the others before she'd taken five steps.

Then the space was silent again except for—was someone crying?

Ezri hauled herself to her feet and stumbled toward the sound. To her dismay she realized that the sound of weeping and that central point of light were in the same location.

It didn't matter. The pain in her head would kill her soon anyway. She might as well see what all the fuss was about.

One step, two, three and she reached the place were Medoxa lay.

Two more steps and she had passed the others. Four more steps and she was in sight of the origin of the glow.

There on her knees, weeping uncontrollably, was Jadzia Dax.

"I'm sorry," said the prostrate figure between sobs. "I'm so sorry."

Ezri, her own pain forgotten for the moment, knelt beside her and ran a gentle hand across her temple.

"I didn't know," said Jadzia. "How could I know?"

"It's all right," said Ezri. "It's all over now."

"NO!" said Jadzia, jerking away. "I betrayed them. They're dead because of me."

"Not all of them," said Ezri soothingly. "You saved Y'Lira and Axael."

"Y'Lira," said Jadzia, suddenly far away. "She was so happy, so beautiful. Look what I've done to her."

I no longer dream, said Captain Medoxa's voice in Ezri's memory.

"And Etoli," said Jadzia. "It was his first mission. Sovak was going to be married."

"Jadzia . . ."

"I have to be punished," said Jadzia softly, so softly.

There was a knife between them suddenly, a glittering curved thing of Syroccan design. There was no reason for it to be there, no way for it to have come.

I'm still in the maze, Ezri thought.

The pain in her skull and the shock of those deaths had disoriented her. She knew where she was now. This was the Ninth Circle of Dante's Hell; the one reserved for traitors.

Oh, Jadzia, she thought. *What did this place do to you?*

So. Was the answer to use the knife or to leave it? A human, knowing what Ezri knew of Jadzia, might choose the former. Even this stupid binary paradigm of Heaven and Hell had room for mercy. But Ezri was Trill. No human could ever know Jadzia Dax the way Ezri Dax could.

Ezri was Dax was Jadzia was Dax was Curzon was Dax was Joran was Dax was Torias was Dax was Audrid was Dax was

Emony was Dax was Tobin was Dax was Lela was Dax was Ezri. She knew the answer to this riddle as well as she knew her own soul.

I forgive you, Jadzia, she thought.

"Suffer," she said aloud.

Then the pain was an iron spike through her brain. This time, when the world went away, Ezri Dax went with it.

Ezri remembered . . .

. . . *Etoli saying something about a new cavern. He was excited, almost dancing with the desire to be the first to discover Something New. His boy-ish Deltan features radiating pleasure even through the polarized face plate of his EVA suit.*

. . . *Sovak, almost certainly as eager, but holding it inside under the weight of implacable logic.*

. . . *Axael clucking merrily over his tricorder, wondering aloud at the strange spikes in the violet wavelengths.*

. . . *Y'Lira asking what they should do, if they should check in with the ship before they went on.*

. . . *Jadzia thinking,* Now, Curzon. Now, I'm finally free of your damned ghost.

. . . *All of them moving toward*—something—*something beautiful and glowing and not quite present.*

. . . *Etoli reaching, crying out, dying.*

. . . *Sovak going down beside him.*

. . . *Axael twitching and writhing in the dust as his nerves were set on fire.*

. . . *Y'Lira screaming as the part of her that dreamed was ripped away.*

. . . *Something . . . something not quite there . . . something not quite alive . . . something that knew only longing . . . and searching . . . and a fear of the increasing cold . . . something alone . . . wanting and feeling, yes, feeling, its own incompleteness . . . trying with her, with all of them . . . to join . . . with their minds . . . to make itself whole . . . pouring more into them than their poor brains could ever hold . . . the first fire . . . the final ice . . . and everything between . . . trying and failing and killing them over and over and . . .*

She fell to the floor, only realizing she was crying from the drops of water that splashed against her hands.

Behind her the doors, open, and before her, mere meters away, the sidereal engine of her—no, of *Jadzia's*—friends' destruction.

The Codex.

"I think," she heard herself saying, "I think I know . . ."

She did know, not all of it—no one could know that—but enough.

The universe was winding down. It had begun with a single colossal outburst of energy but eventually all that energy would equalize. Time would stop; Life would stop; matter, energy, hot, cold, all of it would stop, replaced at the end by eternal, infinite gray.

The Proteans had created the Codex to fix all that, to reignite the fires that had fueled the universe, and give it a second chance.

The Codex, the asteroid belt, even the dying Ibarri star were all parts of the reignition mechanism. The Codex was the information source, the Why and Where. What it lacked was a driver, the When and How.

It had mistaken the minds of Jadzia's team for that driver, forcing upon them all its collected data in one terrible instant.

No wonder it had overwhelmed them all.

Even Ezri, even with the luxury of distance, was struggling to process the memory of all those images and feelings. Something brushed past her, toppling her into the dirt. It was Krinn. He was carrying—what *was* that? It was so familiar, like something gone so long that it could only be defined by its own absence.

Like a sleepwalker Krinn dragged the thing toward the Codex. Wild energies danced and spun around him, bathing him in ethereal light.

He raised the thing with effort over his head.

"No!"

It was Medoxa's voice and it was followed immediately by a phaser blast. The beam of energy caught Krinn just as he was to bring the thing in his hands down into the writhing coil of light that was the Codex. He faltered. A second beam cut across the room, striking him again. He fell.

Suddenly Medoxa's slender but powerful arm scooped Ezri up, hauling the disoriented Trill onto her shoulders.

"Y'Lira!" said Ezri, struggling. "No! What are you doing?"

"Saving your life," said Medoxa, still sprinting away from the Codex chamber.

"Wait," said Ezri, trying to regain focus. "What about the hostages?"

"We got them, Dax." said Medoxa. "All fine. You bought us the time we needed."

Medoxa had carried her nearly to the exit of the massive subterranean tunnel. Just as she was crossing the threshold, Ezri grabbed hold of a nearby outcropping and pulled herself free. The sudden wrenching motion caused Medoxa to stumble and fall. Both women hit the ground hard. Medoxa was up first, still moving toward the tunnel exit. She looked back and saw Ezri heading slowly the other way.

"Dax, no!" she said. "What are you doing?!"

". . . going back," said Ezri. ". . . have to help them finish."

"Dax, listen to me." Medoxa was desperate, torn between escape and completing her rescue of Ezri. "The Protean objects—as soon as the gate came down, they started reacting with each other. Resonating. The energy spikes are off the scale."

"Spikes . . . ?" said Ezri, her faculties returning.

"Edmunds says the entire asteroid belt is lighting up with the same energy. We have to get back to the *Anansi* and get out of here."

Ezri, fully lucid now, turned and said, "Captain, if those things are doing what I think they're doing, there won't be an *out of here* to get to."

Then, without waiting for a response, Ezri bolted back toward the Codex chamber.

Krinn lay where he'd fallen, the second Protean artifact centimeters from his fingers. Ezri took a breath and picked the thing up. Liquid tongues of unknown energy licked up her arms. The noise and wind in the chamber were fierce enough that she had to fight to keep her footing.

She moved toward the center of the chamber and, for the first time, looked directly at the Codex.

To her eyes it seemed like a coil of some kind, wrapping endlessly around itself. Bits of it kept disappearing, as if it were moving in and out of shadow. It couldn't have been, she realized, not with all that energy crackling around.

Something, some forgotten something at the bottom of her memory, resounded with the thing's vibrations, and Ezri found herself a little afraid.

"*Dammit!*" she yelled and slammed the two things together.

She was . . .

Elsewhere.

At first she thought it might be another holographic trick. She'd been through enough of them lately. This wasn't that though. Whatever the strange shapes and colors were, Ezri knew they were real.

Something's wrong, she thought. *There's still some kind of—distance— between [us.]*

She knew the problem in an instant. The Codex was afraid. After all that time alone in the dark, waiting to be joined with this Other, now that the moment had come it was—unsure?

Ezri knew that feeling. She'd felt it before she'd first joined with Dax, the sense that she was losing something, becoming Less. No wonder Jadzia had been so traumatized by contact with the thing. She had never experienced that fear. She'd never had to feel herself pulled in a thousand directions at once and none of them her own. But Ezri had. She'd had to navigate all those fears and gravities without help, on the fly. Just as the Codex would have to.

That's not how it will be, she felt at the Codex and the Other. *You will be more. Much more. And you'll be together.*

Two separate Somethings looked into her then and found the truth of her [thoughts]. Ezri was Dax. Dax was Ezri. Complete. Joined. It was enough. It was more than enough.

The two [intelligences] withdrew and completed their bonding.

[I/we are the Catalyst,] the new entity felt at her. [Are you the Maker?]

She was not. She was just a tiny thing that wanted to keep living for a little while longer.

[I/we are for Beginnings once the End has come. I/we are the Catalyst,] it felt.

Ezri's mind was flooded with gray, an endless formless uncold gray that she knew was the end of the Universe—entropy increased to maximum. It was the most frightening thing she had ever experienced.

It's not time, she felt at it. *You're too early. You have to stop.*

[There is no stopping once begun,] it felt back. [I/we are the Catalyst.]

But you'll kill everything, she felt frantically.

[No,] it felt back. [There can be modification. See.]

All at once she did see.

She saw that the Catalyst was not a being or an object at all, but rather it was a conscious symphony of boiling energies, which, once ignited, must expand. That expansion, meant to rekindle life in a moldering universe, could not be stopped, not even by the Catalyst itself. It could be checked, however. It could be bound to this place like lightning confined in a thin strand of copper.

It wanted her to go, she suddenly felt. She and the others were still close enough to be consumed by the Catalyst's energies, however restrained.

[Go,] it felt at her. [Go now.] It released her then, back into the familiar world of Form. Krinn was stirring. They had only a little time.

"Skipper," said Edmunds. "We're getting a hail from Pandora. It's Lieutenant Dax. She's got Krinn with her."

"Well, get them out of there, Ensign," said Medoxa. "What are you waiting for?"

It was a beautiful sight, the dying crimson star now surrounded by a stunning ring of light. It was unique. Hard to believe the ring had, just yesterday, been nothing more than one more belt of floating rocks.

"Good thing we got out of there," said Medoxa. "The shock wave when the asteroids ignited would have cut through us like butter."

"Good thing," agreed Ezri. "Do we have confirmation of what happened?"

Medoxa snorted. "I don't know if we ever will, but if your conclusions about that thing are right, and if our survival is any indication, the Catalyst has successfully bonded to space-time. Which means that, when the universe finally does run down, it'll be able to renew itself."

"So much grief," Ezri said. "So much lost, for something that won't happen for billions of years."

Medoxa shrugged. "Depends on your point of view. After all, whatever sentients are born in that next universe will owe their existence to what happened here today . . . even though they'll never know it."

Ezri found her thoughts unable to go there just yet. Maybe later. Maybe never. Some truths, she was beginning to believe, were simply too big for a mind to hold. For now, she'd stay focused on the here and now. "Axael is all right?"

"We think he will be," Medoxa said. "The artifact's influence is gone. He's back to being the old Krinn, but he remembers most of what happened, and it's weighing heavily on him."

"I understand the feeling," Ezri said. "I'll see if I can help him during the trip back to Deep Space 9."

"Thank you," said Medoxa.

They stood there for a little while, basking in the strange and wonderful brilliance.

"Jadzia loved you, you know," Ezri said softly. "All of you."

"Jadzia was good at that," said Medoxa.

"She just wanted to get out of someone's shadow," said Ezri. The admission was difficult even now—even after everything had come out right—but it was the least she owed Jadzia's friend. "Can you understand that?"

"I always understood it, Lieutenant," said Medoxa. "I wish Jadzia had been able to confide in me."

"She couldn't," said Ezri. "It was—it's a Trill thing. Too many ghosts. Too many shadows."

"Still."

"What would you have told her?" said Ezri, genuinely interested.

"That the shadows are part of the price," said Medoxa.

"The price?" said Ezri.

"For the chance to see this light."

Face Value

Una McCormack

Historian's note: This story is set primarily during the seventh-season episode "The Dogs of War," the penultimate episode of *Star Trek: Deep Space Nine.*

Una McCormack

Una McCormack discovered *Star Trek: Deep Space Nine* very late in its run, but loved it immediately for its politics, its wit, its ambiguity, and its tailor. She enjoys classic British television and going to the cinema, and she collects capital cities. She lives with her partner Matthew in Cambridge, England, where she reads, writes, and teaches. "Face Value" is her first professional piece of fiction writing.

Prologue

Each minute brought it closer and closer . . .

A long time ago, right after one of Kira's first missions, Trelar had a few quiet words with her. They were hiding out in the mountains—it was bare and cold, and he was struggling to get a fire to light in the steady winter rain. "That was brutal, what you did today," he had said to her, softly, and his eyes were dark and sharp as he looked up from his work. "There's no glory in it. Just kill them and be done with it."

Garak stepped up alongside her. "We'll be coming into orbit soon," he said, and she caught the tremor in his voice—excitement, anticipation . . .

Kira had been a pale and hungry child, running on rage and not much else. Earlier that day she had pulled back the head of an enemy and made him look at her before finishing him off with her knife. She was still exhilarated from the victory, still had the adrenaline rushing through her, and Trelar's words brought her back to miserable reality. He was a good man, a man she admired. She hated to think she had disappointed him, and she masked her shame with anger. "What the Cardassians do is brutal," she shot back. "I want them to know who it is that killed them. I want the last thing they see before they die to be the face of a Bajoran."

Damar paced back and forth, back and forth, every inch the soldier, every inch the Cardassian . . .

"Leave the kid alone, Trelar." Furel had come up behind them. He ran his big hand affectionately through Kira's damp hair. "We can't all be

philosophers, you know. She got the job done just fine." She had flushed in pride at this rough praise and he had grinned down at her.

Trelar had not answered, just turned back to his slow task, trying to coax a flame from his spoiled tinder. Kira watched the rain slide off his dark hair and down his thin cheeks. He was a quiet man who killed with precision. In another life, on another world, he would have been a teacher, or a scholar, or a priest.

"Sometimes I fear for our future," he murmured at last; and then the fire finally caught, and soon they were warmer and dryer and eating something hot, and glad of each other's company, glad they were all still alive. But Trelar did not speak again that evening. As the others traded their old stories and told their bad jokes, she felt his eye fall on her. The gaze was questioning, challenging—but she would not meet it. The next morning, as they trekked on eastward, he had given her half his breakfast—an apology typical of him. None of them ever left a disagreement standing for too long. You never knew if the chance to make your peace would suddenly be gone for good.

It was not long before Kira lost the taste for killing, but she did not lose her passion for justice. And she had promised the child she had been that she would never forget her, would never forget how she had made herself fierce so that she could face her fear.

Remember that, Nerys. Remember. You have never been afraid to look your enemies in the eye.

Still, right at this moment, she found herself offering up a silent prayer of thanks to the Prophets that these Jem'Hadar ships did not come equipped with viewscreens. For whatever she told herself to give herself courage, the truth was that the knowledge of their destination was quite enough, and that she had no real desire to find herself face to face with . . .

"Cardassia," murmured Garak, his voice low and reverential, as if saying his own prayer of thanks. "It's as beautiful as I remember." Behind the headset, his eyes had lit up, as if he were looking once more upon the face of a long-lost friend.

Damar started speaking then—or perhaps declaiming would be a better way to describe it. Something about how the planet would not be beautiful to him until it was free. She tuned him out. *Cardassians,* she thought. *They really* can't *do anything without making a speech about it first.*

But even though she had not listened, Kira was irritated by Damar's display of self-importance, and she found herself snapping back at him, reminding him of the risk they were all taking on his behalf, coming to Cardassia to meet Gul Revok. No matter how many men Revok had promised to bring to the fight against the Dominion, Damar was still a wanted man, and his face was well known. Fighting a guerrilla war depended on secrecy, and having Damar around was as good as firing off a flare.

Then, to her own disgust, she found herself saying to Damar that perhaps it would be better if she stayed on the ship. What could a Bajoran do amongst Cardassians other than arouse hostility? Damar's answer was short and contemptuous, and Kira was honest enough with herself to know that she deserved it. She was not there as a Bajoran, after all—she was there to represent the Federation. But she doubted that there was a Cardassian on the planet who would look past the ridges on her face and see instead the Starfleet uniform she wore. Cardassians and Bajorans. They had long been enemies, they were still enemies, they would always be enemies. It was as simple as that. Some things would never—*could* never—change.

And you've always looked your enemies in the eye, Nerys . . .

They were cleared for orbit now, and the transporter room was ready to beam them to the rendezvous with Revok. Kira left the bridge with Garak and Damar, and prepared to face Cardassia.

One

Night fell quickly on Cardassia Prime. The daylight was stark and harsh, and all the ways of the city were laid bare beneath it. Then, suddenly—almost as if a switch had been hit—it would be gone. There was a moment of total darkness, and then the street lights came on, bright and searching, and once again all the wide boulevards and the narrow alleys were exposed. It was indeed a city for the watchful. But it was not a city in which you could easily hide.

Kira flexed a stiff arm carefully, trying to keep her movements to a minimum, and sighed very softly as she looked out toward the river. Only a week had passed since they had become stranded on Cardassia Prime—a week since Revok had betrayed them. From an organization equipped with ships and soldiers spread out across the empire, the Cardassian resistance was now down to three people hiding in a cellar. *The future of Cardassia,* Kira thought bitterly. *A drunk, a tailor, and a Bajoran. Someone, somewhere, is having a long, hard laugh at me.*

She leaned her head back against the wall, resisting the temptation to put a hand to her forehead to wipe at the sweat. Nightfall brought little real change in temperature, and the air was hot and dusty. Now and again a dry breath of breeze would rub across her face and fill her eyes with grit. Even the view she had, out across the river, brought no relief. The water was brown and sluggish, and even the barges seemed listless, drifting with the tide. Memories of Bajor, of cool green valleys and ice-cold streams, of the scent of moba blossom, flooded into her mind. . . .

Come on, Nerys! Focus! This is hardly the time or place to be daydreaming!

She looked out again, trying to stay alert. A dirty, disheveled part of the city, down by the docks. A thread of lamps set along the embankment traced the curve of the river, heading down toward the distant glow of the port, and casting a cold white light on the bridge that was the focus of this vigil. Tomorrow she and Garak would be there meeting a man who could sell them weapons, a friend of hers from the old days. She knew he'd been here on Cardassia Prime before the Dominion arrived, but had not really believed he would be here still. She'd made the contact expecting nothing to come of it—and found herself listening to a friendly voice for the first time in what seemed like an age. She smiled to herself, remembering how relaxed he had sounded over the communicator, as if they were making a date for dinner. He'd always been so easygoing. *Anything you need, Nerys. No problem, Nerys. You just come along and we'll fix it, Nerys.*

She had brought the news to Garak and Damar in triumph. *Weapons? You want weapons? I can conjure up weapons with a snap of my fingers!*

Garak, however, had been less than satisfied with the arrangement.

"Forgive me, Commander," he murmured delicately, "but one thing that tailoring taught me was that you should never conduct a business transaction without proper . . . preparation."

She had not much liked the implication that her friend—and, perhaps too, her judgment—could not be trusted, but she knew he was right. They had to be sure the meeting place was not being watched. So here they both were, a day in advance, squashed into a narrow space between two abandoned warehouses, watching the bridge and—in Kira's case—sweltering.

Garak had seemed to know the spot well, and had settled down almost comfortably. Kira glanced sideways at him. He had not moved or spoken for over an hour now, had just sat beside her, knees drawn up and arms folded, watching the river and the bridge ahead, watching all that went on before him with cool, lizard patience.

You could just go back . . . She dismissed that thought as quickly as it had arisen. It would be cooler down in their hideaway, but going back there without Garak meant she would be left alone with Damar. And the fact was that she would rather sit out here and suffer the heat. She looked up at the sky, heavy blue with unfamiliar constellations, and sweated.

"I don't know why you're taking so long over this," she said at last, keeping her voice low.

Garak did not answer.

"I've known Estal Vilar for years, we grew up together in Singha." *Even managed to play together,* she thought, although Prophets knew the camp had been hard for children.

Still no answer, although he did flick her a cool look.

"He supplied weapons to the Shakaar cell regularly. He never once let us down. He'd never betray me, Garak."

At that, Garak uncoiled a little, stretching his arms out for a languid moment, then letting them come back to rest.

"I must ask you to indulge me just a little longer, Commander," he murmured. "There are few things I refuse to do as a matter of principle, but trusting myself to an arms dealer I've never met is one of them. If you prefer," he added, and this was with a sly, sideways look, "you could always go back and leave me to satisfy my paranoia alone. I'm sure Damar would welcome your company."

"No thanks," she shot back quickly—and then cursed herself for being so transparent. She stared ahead again with sudden interest, watching the reflection of the moon's light as it flickered and broke on the ripples of the river. Her words hung between them, heavy as the night air.

Garak tapped a finger against his arm. "Sometimes, Commander," he said eventually, his tone measured and unrevealing, "as I am quite sure you are already aware, it is necessary to set aside personal animosity to get a job done."

She swung her head round to look at him, but he just kept on staring out patiently toward the river.

"I hardly think I need a lecture about the greater good from *you* of all people—!"

"You might not need a lecture, but you certainly need a reminder." He was still looking out across the water. "You're not the only one who could hold a grudge against our beloved leader, Commander. But right at this moment such things have to take second place."

Ziyal. He's talking about Ziyal. . . .

She stared back at the river herself, and did not see it. She could not talk about Ziyal—not here, not now. Not if she wanted to go back and be able even to look at Damar, rather than launch herself at him, finally bring him to justice for the murder of that poor girl, her friend . . .

She stretched out decisively and stood up. "I think we're done here."

"Not *quite*—"

"Enough, Garak," she said, cutting him off before he could push any further. He raised an eye ridge. She drew in a deep breath of the thick air and then rubbed away the sweat on her forehead, her face, the back of her neck. The gesture calmed her, a little. "The curfew will be starting soon," she said, pulling her hood over her face. "Do you want us to be even more obvious than we already are?"

He shrugged as if the matter were not of importance to him and stood up. "Very well. Let's go, then." He walked on ahead of her, and she followed him as he slipped into the shadows.

"And you needn't worry too much for your safety, Commander," he added silkily. He did not turn, and she could not see his face. "I've been dodging curfews in this city since before you were born."

Two

Legate Damar—Hero, Legend, and the Man They Couldn't Kill—sat by himself in a dark cellar and spun the empty bottle resting on the table before him.

Damar was not a man much given to introspection—as he himself would be the first to admit. As his wife had often told him. He preferred action—preferred being faced with a plain choice, making his decision, and carrying that decision through, without second guesses or much in the way of regret. It was not the subtlest of philosophies, but it was one that had stood him in good stead throughout much of his life. It seemed, however, not to be working too well anymore.

He rested his elbow on the table and his chin on his hand, and gave the bottle another spin. It came to a halt pointing to his right.

A plain choice. These days—when they did come—they came with consequences he'd never imagined, had never wanted to be his responsibility. There'd been a plain choice before him just a few weeks ago, when there'd still been a resistance to speak of, and they'd gone to steal that Dominion ship for Starfleet. That choice had unfolded before him, out of his control before he could stop it, when Rusot had aimed his disruptor at Kira, and Garak had aimed his at Rusot. Choices didn't come more straightforward than that, Damar thought bitterly. Perfectly plain—kill Garak, or kill Rusot. Choose the future, uncertain and unsafe; or choose the past, the Union he and Rusot had loved and served, and would have died for . . . And Rusot had died for it, Damar thought now, died instead of Garak, and Odo—and Kira . . . Rusot had died at Damar's hands, telling Damar how much he trusted him.

He spun the bottle again.

Trusting Revok had seemed like a good choice. Half a million men. All his problems solved. He should have known it was too good to be true.

The bottle pointed left.

Kira had warned him about Revok, but he had not listened. And, in his heart—since Damar was not a dishonest man—he knew that it was not just because he had wanted the simple solution Revok's offer gave him that he had ignored Kira's warnings. It was because he had not wanted a free Cardassia delivered by a Bajoran in a Starfleet uniform. And now—thanks to his choices—he would not get a free Cardassia any other way. The insanity of this struck him once again.

What was I ever thinking of? What possessed me to choose her? Rusot and I served together all our adult life. And I shot him to save her.

Introspection did not come easily to Damar—but neither did dishonesty. And he knew too in his heart that he owed Kira; not just because she would—even if it killed her—do her utmost to deliver his free Cardassia, but because of another choice he had once made. Another choice that, at the time, had seemed like duty and now, with distance and—maybe—a little more wisdom, seemed like madness. The choice to shoot Tora Ziyal.

With an abrupt, dismissive movement, he reached out again and gave the bottle another twist. At least the fact that the bottle was empty wasn't his fault.

A clatter at the top of the steps interrupted his thoughts. He looked up, reaching to his side instinctively for his disruptor, but relaxed when he saw that it was only Mila. Then he caught the look on her face.

"Now where've you hidden the medical supplies?" she scolded.

He gestured toward them, starting on a question—then more noise on the steps made him look up again, to see Kira and Garak coming down slowly toward him.

"What's happened?" he said, standing up to meet them.

"Garak's been shot," Kira replied, raising an eyebrow at him.

He didn't seem to be too badly hurt, Damar thought, appraising him anxiously, although he was leaning on Kira slightly and holding his left arm close to himself. Probably more to do with shock.

"We found ourselves facing a wall that we weren't expecting," Kira added as she maneuvered Garak toward a chair.

"I did find a way around it, Commander," Garak murmured, his expression taut as he looked down at his upper arm. "Eventually." He sat down heavily, and Mila set to work, berating him for his carelessness. Damar looked over her shoulder and winced a little at what he saw, but Garak had been very lucky—it was superficial. He would have had much worse in the past in the line of duty, Damar suspected—but it still looked painful.

"I thought you knew the city like the back of your hand," he said.

Garak looked up at him sharply. "I did—eight years ago. It seems it's rather difficult to keep track of town planning when you're in exile," he said bitterly. "So you'll have to excuse me the lapse . . . Mila, that *hurt!* Will you *please* be careful!" She carried on with her work thoroughly unabashed, and keeping up her stream of reproaches.

Damar looked over their heads at Kira, and she gave him a faint, wry smile. "We got a bit lost on the way back, down by the docks.

There was a new building there that Garak didn't know about—it blocked our access across the river."

"The new factory," Mila said, shaking her head and tutting. "I could have told you about that, if you'd asked!"

"Remind me in future to run all my plans past you first," Garak shot back.

"Seems to me you'd be better off if you did—"

Damar ignored their bickering and kept on looking at Kira. "And?"

"So we had to come back another way, but it was patrolled and the curfew had started. We ran into a couple of Jem'Hadar. We spotted them right away, but one of them got off a shot at us." She grinned down at Garak. "He didn't get a second one out though, did he, Garak?"

"And I believe I've thanked you for that once already."

Careless . . . Damar thought. He ignored—since it made little sense to him—his irritation at their display of camaraderie. *We can't afford these kinds of mistakes.*

"I take it you weren't followed back?" he snapped.

She looked up at him scornfully. "Of course we weren't."

"And the rendezvous?" He glared back at her, but she kept her eyes leveled on his. "You're both satisfied?"

"I'm happy on that score at least," Garak said.

Kira lowered her eyes first. Damar did not feel it was a victory.

"Done," said Mila brightly, patting Garak's arm with just a touch of malice, and he grimaced and scowled at her. "You'll live. You won't be going anywhere for a couple of days, though."

"I'll be going out tomorrow—"

Kira rubbed her back, working at the muscles, and sighed. "You'd just be a liability, Garak. I can't make allowances for an injured man. I'll have to go and meet Vilar alone."

"You need someone to watch your back," he said, looking up at her. "I can still do that."

"Why are we even talking about this?" Damar cut through. "I'll go with her."

She hesitated. A split second, but Damar caught it. "You're too conspicuous," she said, turning away from him to busy herself by helping Mila clear up the medical supplies. "Your face is too well known. I'll try to contact Vilar and fix another meeting."

"They can trace the transmission. We can't risk it, Commander," Garak reminded her softly. "Go with Damar, or don't go at all." He leaned back in the chair wearily and closed his eyes. Kira gazed down at him thoughtfully.

"Well, Commander?" It came out sounding more like a challenge than Damar had intended.

When she turned her eyes back up to him she too was giving no quarter. "It'll work, I guess. It'll have to."

"Well, thank the Prophets for that," Garak muttered. Kira and Damar both looked down at him, but his eyes were still shut.

Three

Kira strode up the steps of the bridge two at a time, just behind Damar, but matching him stride for stride. Reaching the top, she saw that the bridge was lined with statues, tall gray figures of men. They went and stood in the deeper shadows beneath one of these, out of sight, but still able to watch the steps up which they had come, and the length of the bridge heading toward the north bank. Dim lamps between the statues cast a little light. Damar leaned back against the crumbling stone, his face hidden from Kira's view. The silence deepened between them, and Kira struggled to think of something to say.

"Who are all these statues of?" she said at last.

"Legates," he replied, and then seemed to decide she merited a less abrupt answer. "This is the Veterans' Bridge," he continued. "Commemorates men who had great victories in battle. It's a good spot, a quiet part of town. Gives a clear view of the city. I can see why Garak picked it."

"Garak seemed to know this part of town pretty well," she said, trying to keep him talking, and picking the only subject on which she thought they might agree.

He snorted. "Garak *would* know the disreputable bits," he muttered, and Kira risked a smile. He jerked his thumb to his left. "The north side—where we came in from tonight—is better. In fact, Tain's house is in one of best parts of the city. You're staying at a very exclusive address, Commander." He leaned forward slightly so that a little light caught his face and she could see his expression, dry, and with a slight smile of his own.

She did laugh then, thinking of the hot, dirty cellar into which they were crammed.

He pointed ahead, to where the river bent toward the south. "I had a house over there."

And a wife and son, she remembered, and bit her lip.

"What's that?" she said, to change the subject. She gestured a little further east, where a tall black ziggurat rose above the low levels of the buildings around it, all sharp angles and points, forcing the eye upward to the single bright light at its peak.

"That? That's the Tozhat Memorial."

"*Tozhat* Memorial?" Why, she wondered, would there be a monument in the Cardassian capital named after a province on Bajor?

He turned his head to look her full in the face. "During the withdrawal. Twenty Cardassian women and children and nine soldiers were killed by a bomb left in a barracks." He went back to keeping watch on the steps.

Tozhat . . . They told a different story about Tozhat on Bajor, about how the base was being used to store—what was the phrase the Cardassians used for them?—that was it: soil declamators. Part of the scorched earth policy of the withdrawal. Planning to poison Tozhat province as they abandoned it, just like they'd done in Rakantha. Two cases of explosives had put a stop to it, but no one had known that only a few hours earlier the base commander had brought the little group of settlers still living in the area inside the compound. They said later in the resistance that he'd probably been ordered to use them as shields while the declamators were brought online, but Cardassian Central Command denied it, of course.

So that monolith was how the Cardassians remembered the tragedies of the Occupation? She cast her eyes again over it. There was a memorial in every town or village on Bajor, too, no matter how small or remote. Some of them were imposing, with gracious domes and curves, but none were so ostentatious as this one. She'd seen a memorial out in Amantha raised from the rubble of an ancient monastery that the Cardassians had burned to the ground. It was not much more than a cairn, a few feet high, but it had a subdued solemnity. Bajorans remembered their dead with reverence, she thought; they didn't need show. *Prophets, our whole planet's a memorial to what the Occupation cost us. . . .*

Carried on the night air she heard the unmistakable sound of someone approaching, coming up the steps. Damar stirred beside her, pushing himself up from the wall. Kira turned her head quickly.

"Vilar, is that you?" she whispered, peering at the figure emerging from the darkness. A small man, hurrying toward them. As he came closer, out of the shadows, she gasped.

"Vilar, what have they *done* to you?"

"What?" Sharp familiar eyes blinked at her from an unfamiliar face.

"Your *face* . . . !"

"Oh!" He put a finger up to the spoon-shaped ridge on his forehead.

Damar had set his hand very obviously on his disruptor. "I thought you were supposed to be Bajoran," he said bluntly.

"I was! I mean, I am . . . is that a disruptor?"

Damar turned to Kira, his anger held in check but plain to see. "Is it him, Kira?" His hand had tightened on the weapon.

"Yes, yes!" she said quickly. "I'd recognize him anywhere." She turned back to her friend. "Vilar, what happened? Who *did* this to you?"

"Nothing happened! No one's done anything!" He looked anxiously at Damar, whose hand was still clenched around the disruptor. "I didn't think you were bringing your minder with you, Nerys. Any chance you could you call him off?"

Kira glared at Damar. "Take it easy, will you? Vilar's a friend. He's put himself in danger coming here. There's no need for threats." She saw his shoulders relax just a little. His hand, however, stayed firmly in place on the disruptor.

She looked back at Vilar, and gestured at his face. "What did you do it for?"

"I was here . . ." he hesitated, "well, on business. Then the Dominion arrived. Not the best place for a Bajoran to get stuck. So I took . . ." he gave a short laugh, "evasive action! Quick snip here and there, and I was safe again."

Kira's gut twisted. How could he be so offhand about it? She remembered with revulsion seeing her own features warped into those of a Cardassian. And Vilar had *chosen* to have this done to him . . . ?

"Nerys," he said, patting at her arm nervously, "it's good to see you again, but we've got to make this quick. Not a good idea to be out after the curfew. The Jem'Hadar squads are far more efficient than the Cardassians ever were." He looked Damar up and down. "Well, you know what they're like. Brawn and no brain."

Kira snorted despite herself. Damar didn't move a muscle.

"So—what d'you need?" Vilar said.

"What have you got?" Kira answered frankly.

He fired off a list of equipment he could supply, and she nodded as he spoke. "And people, Nerys," he concluded. "I can get you in touch with people who want to help . . . influential, important. Just let me put out some feelers. Meet here again in two days, yes?"

"All right." She took his hand, ignoring the rasp of the strange skin against her own. "You always manage to fix things, Vilar. *Thank you,*" she said, pressing his hand tight.

"Pleasure!" He shot a quick look at Damar. "Nice to meet you," he said. "I think." Then he grinned at Kira, and she could see his old face through the new one. She grinned back. It was good to be with a friend again—no matter what he looked like. "See you soon, Nerys!" He squeezed her hand back, let go, and then went off back the way he had come, with a wave.

"Take care," she murmured, watching him disappear into the darkness and waiting for him to be out of earshot. Then she turned to Damar. He was staring down the bridge in the direction in which Vilar had just gone.

"Perhaps if you'd been a little more obvious about it, he might have realized you didn't trust him."

"I *don't* trust him."

"Well, I never would have guessed that!"

He released his hold on the disruptor. "It seems to me we're being handed exactly what we need at exactly the moment we need it. I don't believe in luck like that, Commander. So—no. I don't trust him."

"Well, Damar, I really don't know that you're in a position to make judgments like that. You hardly read Revok right, did you?"

He took a single step toward her. She tensed.

So this is it. I knew we'd come to blows one day. Perhaps we should just get it over and done with . . .

But he was just standing still and staring at her. "No," he said simply. "No, I did not." He looked out across the river again for a moment. "I think we should leave now, Commander." He did not wait for her answer, and strode off. She followed, but the silence between them was deeper than ever.

Four

Damar stalked down the steps, across the cellar, and threw his disruptor onto the table. It landed with a clatter, waking Garak, who was stretched out on one of the beds.

"Sorry," Damar muttered. He sat down at the table, folded his arms and frowned. Kira took the seat just to his right. She seemed to be inspecting her phaser with an unusually high degree of interest. He turned his head slightly so that he could not see her, watching instead as Garak pulled himself off the bed and came to sit beside him.

"So," Garak said, a little bleary-eyed, looking at each of them in turn. "A productive day?"

Damar shrugged. Kira didn't respond either, just kept on making a show of checking the settings on her phaser.

"Much as it lends itself to thrilling narrative, I'm afraid that in my everyday life I find suspense rather tiresome. Would one of you consider enlightening me as to how the meeting went?"

Damar raised his eyes upward. *Obsidian Order. Fifteen words when one would do. Why not just ask us what happened?* With an effort, he put his irritation aside. "I don't trust him," he replied, just as Kira said, "It went well."

Garak leaned an elbow on the table. "I sense some disagreement amongst us," he said. "Perhaps some more clarification would help me . . . ?"

"As I said, I don't trust him—"

"You weren't even prepared to trust him—!"

"I really am beginning to lose my sense of humor about this," Garak murmured, then raised his voice over theirs. "Commander, Legate—might I remind you of the precariousness of our situation? We are hiding in a cellar, and the hounds are almost at the door. This little feud of yours is getting out of hand. And it's . . ." he frowned, "unprofessional."

"'*Unprofessional*'?" Kira looked over at him, eyes blazing. "Who's the one who got himself shot?"

"She does have a point there," Damar said, feeling a smile curl across his lips.

"Well, at least you're now agreeing on something." Garak fell back in his chair. "Will one of you tell me how the meeting went? Damar?"

Damar shifted forward in his chair. "We got there safely, we got back safely. He's offered us equipment—"

"And contacts," Kira cut in.

"—and I have some very serious doubts about him."

"Which are?" Garak prompted.

"He's now Cardassian."

Kira threw her phaser on the table. "And this *worries* you somehow? Isn't it better than him being Bajoran?"

Damar turned to her slowly, feeling his hold on his temper begin to slip. "And what do you mean by that?"

"You know *exactly* what I mean—"

"I think that you should just come straight out and say it, Commander—"

"Well, maybe I just will—"

"Commander, Legate, will you *please* control yourselves—!"

"Shut *up,* Garak!"

With a crash, something landed on the table before them, stopping their quarreling dead. It was a large serving pot.

"Supper," said Mila.

Garak composed himself first. "Thank you, Mila," he said in a low voice. He rubbed his hand across his eyes, and then reached to take the bowl that she was offering him.

They sat in silence as she served out the *tojal* stew. Damar took a mouthful, and then swallowed quickly. Mila was quite right—she wasn't much of a cook. He smothered it in *yamok* sauce. Out of the corner of his eye, he saw Kira try a little, sigh, and reach for the water bottle.

"What do you mean," Garak said eventually, and quietly, "that he's now Cardassian?"

"He's had some kind of cosmetic or genetic modifications," Kira explained. "I don't mind admitting it was a shock to me at first too. But underneath he's still the same old Vilar." She smiled a little.

"I'm assuming," Garak said, "he got it done when the Dominion took over."

"And this is what worries me," Damar said, leaning forward. "Why did he stay here? Why didn't he just leave when they arrived? Do they know about him and, if they do, why have they done nothing about him? And why is it he's appeared just now, just when we need him, and with almost all that we need?"

Garak looked back at him thoughtfully.

"He got stuck here!" Kira's exasperation was clear. "It wasn't safe for him!"

Garak waved a hand to quiet her. "Let me think for a moment, Commander . . ." he murmured. Mila piled another serving of stew into his bowl and he stirred it absently with his spoon.

Damar watched him closely. *Why,* he wondered, *am I suddenly so concerned to get Garak's backing in this?* He risked a sideways look at Kira. She was leaning forward, eyes intent on Garak. Looked like she felt the same way. *It's as if we've turned him into some kind of referee. And he doesn't look happy about it.*

"It's hard to judge . . ." Garak said at last, slowly. "I wish I'd met him face to face . . . Still, there's something that's troubling me . . ." He rubbed at his arm. "I think you've put your finger on it, Legate," he said at last, nodding his head and with more conviction in his voice. "Why now? Why all this?"

"That's what your father used to say," Mila agreed. "Beware arms dealers bearing gifts."

Garak pursed his lips and tapped a finger on the table. He didn't, Damar thought, look very happy about that either.

And then there was another loud crash. Damar swung his head round.

Kira had slammed her fist down hard on the table before her. Her bowl had gone flying. She was glaring around her.

"You really do all stick together, don't you?" She stood up. "This is just a *waste* of my time!" She turned on her heel and strode toward the stairs, and up into the house.

"Well," said Mila, after a moment, looking down at the table. "I guess I'd better fetch a cloth for that. It's not going to clean itself, and I don't think she'll be doing it."

"I wonder," Garak murmured, watching Mila leave, "whether it might be wiser simply to accept the commander's judgment in this."

"I won't trust this man just to make *her* feel better!" Damar jabbed an angry finger toward the stairs.

Garak scowled. "Don't be ridiculous, Damar! I'm not saying we should take him at face value. But Kira has known him for years, after all. Surely that should carry some weight?" Garak sighed deeply. "I should go and speak to her. Make her feel better." He gave a short laugh and stood up.

Damar cleared his throat. "Before you go . . . I want to thank you, Garak."

Garak looked down at him. *"Thank* me?"

"For your loyalty."

A smile passed across Garak's face. It was not a pleasant smile. He set one hand upon the table, leaned forward and fixed his eyes on Damar's. A slow chill crept up Damar's spine. With all of Garak's dissembling, it was just too easy to forget that this was a man who had tortured and murdered routinely.

"Take great care, Legate, not to misunderstand me," Garak said softly. "My loyalty has always and only ever been to Cardassia, and I have never liked entrusting her to anyone other than myself." He stood up straight again. "You have a long way to go before you prove yourself worthy of Cardassia in my eyes, Damar." Then he sighed, and he seemed to fade a little; an older man, injured and rather tired. "A long way to redeem yourself."

He continued looking at Damar for just a little longer, leaving Damar feeling that his worth was somehow being measured, and then he turned away and made slowly for the stairs. "You must excuse me, Legate. I have a Bajoran to placate."

A long way to redeem yourself . . .

Damar watched him go upstairs, and was left sitting in a cellar with only the specter of a dead girl for company.

Five

Kira stood still, arms stretched out before her, clutching the mantelpiece and staring ahead.

The frame of the mirror was dark, almost black, wood, the carving skillful and ornate. Up close, it was easy to become lost in the detail, and then her eyes adjusted and the pattern resolved itself into the trefoil so beloved, it seemed, of Cardassian artists. Ziyal, she remembered, had painted this symbol over and over again, but in bleached colors, and softening the lines . . .

She looked up, into the glass.

The last time Kira Nerys had paid a visit to Cardassia Prime, she had looked into a mirror and a Cardassian had stared back. Only the eyes had been familiar in that twisted face, and they had been filled with shock and revulsion. In the days immediately afterwards, when she had been held captive here, the soft words of the Obsidian Order agent assigned to her had almost persuaded her that there was not—and never really had been—a Bajoran face there at all.

There was one there now, but it was tired and hot, and flushed with anger. Kira closed her eyes, only to see herself besieged again by Garak, Mila, and Damar, staring at her after her outburst. She raised a finger to touch soft skin, smooth forehead, the bridge of her nose, and tried to remember how it felt to be cool. The heat seemed to overwhelm her. And the stink of *yamok* sauce made her feel sick.

She heard the door click, and opened her eyes quickly. Someone came in, closing the door again quietly a moment later. A few footsteps as he approached her, then stopped, and waited. She did not speak.

"This was Tain's . . ." he paused, "library," he said at last, and then laughed a little. "As if you couldn't tell from all the books."

She had not, in fact, in her rage even noticed the books when she had come in, being too busy kicking the door shut and then striding across the room.

"First editions of Preloc and Iloja . . . Nothing offworld, of course, that would have been unpatriotic. Tain was very proud of his book collection, thought it gave him an air of erudition. I doubt he'd read most of them. Clever, but hardly what one would call a literary man."

He took a few more steps toward her and she stiffened instinctively, although she doubted he would be foolish enough to try to touch her.

"He used to stand there just like you're doing now, staring into nothing while I talked and he was silent. Eventually I would start to babble. I gather I do that sometimes." He gave a slight, self-deprecating laugh. "Tain taught me all I know about interrogation," he concluded genially.

Kira swung round. A comparison to Enabran Tain was not exactly to be welcomed.

Garak was standing a few steps away. He had picked up one of the books, a slim pale-blue volume, and was running a finger along the cover.

What must it have been like, she thought suddenly, *to have Tain as a father?* And why had this never crossed her mind before?

It was this place, she thought, looking about her at the somber room, dark browns and yellows, heavy colors, and the press of all the books, signifying no more than their owner's desire for power, not insight. For a moment it seemed to Kira as if she stood alone at the very heart of Cardassia, and the weight of it threatened to crush her.

But is that really because I'm a stranger here—or is this how it feels to be Cardassian?

She shook her head, trying to clear it, and then something else came to mind, the memory of her own father, quiet and undemanding, and whom she had left behind as he lay dying . . . And then she recalled what Ziyal had told her about Garak, and how far he had gone to be with Tain at the end. She met his eye, uncertainly.

"Well," Garak said smoothly. "At least I've gotten you to look at me."

The moment of sympathy passed as quickly as it had arisen. He had just been trying to get her to calm down. Manipulating her. Of course.

Her anger flared up again; she felt her cheeks go red with it. *This damn heat . . . !*

"How can you bear it?" she said, and although her voice was soft it carried her rage. "How can you stand being near him—after Ziyal?"

His fingers tightened around the book he held. For a second that stretched on, Ziyal's ghost loomed large between them.

Kira could picture her so easily, as if she had seen her only yesterday—laughing as she listened to Garak and Bashir bickering over lunch . . . her forehead creasing in concentration as she worked on her newest painting . . . the twist of her lips that meant she was not going to change her mind, no matter how good your arguments were . . . the curves and angles of her face, at once familiar but alien, and uniquely hers . . . In recent months, the fact of Ziyal's death had deadened to a dull ache, but now Kira felt her grief sharpen into focus again—and then saw it reflected on Garak's face. Just for a moment, and then it was covered.

When he spoke, his voice was completely controlled. "Commander, Ziyal was a lovely, generous-spirited girl who for totally inexplicable reasons decided that she was in love with me." It bore, Kira thought, all the hallmarks of a prepared speech. He cleared his throat and tapped his fingers against the cover of the book. "Life goes on."

"That's it? That's *all* you can say? Life goes on? She *loved* you, Garak, and *he* killed her!" She pointed her finger angrily in the direction of the cellar. "Does that mean nothing to you?"

His face remained completely unreadable.

Is it even possible *to get a reaction from you, Garak? Is there anything going on in there at all?*

"This conversation, Commander," he said eventually, with effort, and she caught the warning in his voice, "is not about me."

Kira took a deep breath. The heat seemed to subside a little.

"I'm sorry," she said.

He tilted his head in acknowledgment.

"I shouldn't have lost my temper."

He nodded his head in agreement.

"But you've got to start being honest with me—both of you."

He looked at her inquiringly. "I'm not sure I quite follow you, Commander—"

"Come off it, Garak! The reason you and Damar don't trust Vilar has nothing to do with his line of business. It's because he's Bajoran."

He laughed, once more at his ease. "Now, there you do me an injustice! As if I would be concerned with something so arbitrary! I don't trust your friend because I don't trust anyone."

"Well, then we'll leave *you* aside as a paranoid exception, but it's certainly true of Damar!"

Garak frowned. "There might well be something to what you say," he conceded. "But it cuts both ways," he added sharply. "He's lost both wife and child to this rebellion. He killed Rusot to save *your* life, Commander, and Odo's. And despite those sacrifices, you still refuse to trust him. And why is that? Because he's Cardassian."

It was no more than the truth.

"You don't need to be friends, Kira. You just need not to be enemies." He sighed. "For a little while, at least." He gazed down at the book for a moment, and then raised his eyes to look at her directly. "And what *I* need to know is that you *really* believe we can trust this man. That you're not just trying to prove Damar wrong."

She looked him straight in the eye. "We can trust him, Garak. I'd stake my life on it."

"Staking your life on it is exactly what you are doing. And mine, and Damar's—and Mila's."

She nodded. "I know."

"Then I'm prepared to take you at your word." He slipped the book into his pocket. "Will you come back downstairs now? It really isn't safe for us up here."

She pushed her hands through her hair, hesitated.

"Kira?"

"All right."

She followed him to the door. As they walked down the hallway, she tapped him gently on the arm. He looked down at her hand in complete surprise.

"If it makes you feel any better, Garak," she said, "it's not because you're Cardassian that I don't trust you." She smiled. "It's because you're untrustworthy."

Garak beamed at her approvingly, rather as a parent might at a small child who has just said something extremely clever.

"You're learning, Commander! You're learning."

Six

There was a plaque beneath the statue of Legate Rantok. It listed his greatest campaigns and conquests. He had once kept a city on Bajor under siege. For four months, they held out against him, until he won the nearby dam and cut off their water supply. Still they lasted: another eight weeks. Not long after the surrender, the rest of the region fell to Cardassian control. It was a turning point at the start of the occupation, and had ensured Rantok's name would go down in history. He had been a legend.

The metal of the plaque was tarnished, and the stone around it was weak. Damar crumbled it industriously with his forefinger. Like his father before him, he'd brought his son to the Veterans' Bridge, to see the great men from the stories that were read to him at school. The boy hadn't liked it here much, he recalled. The gray, looming figures had upset him.

He looked up abruptly at Kira. She was frowning down at his hand.

"I'm sorry," he said. "I didn't mean to annoy you."

"What?" She looked up at him and blinked. "Oh! No, it's all right." She wiped a hand across her face, then set it back to rest upon her phaser.

"The heat really gets to you, doesn't it?"

She sighed. "I'm sure I'll get used to it soon."

"I'm sorry it makes you so uncomfortable."

She came to stand beside him, leaning both arms on the bridge. "And I'm sorry—"

He raised a slow hand to check her. "I'm afraid I have to say, Commander," he intoned, deadpan, "that we might have to stop apologizing to each other all the time. I'm almost certain it will irritate Garak more than if we were arguing."

She laughed. "I guess we shouldn't try his patience too much."

"And certainly not once his arm is better."

The silence between them was a little more companionable now. More than it had been for the last couple of days, that was for sure, when they had both been looking past each other, embarrassed by what they had said and done.

"So," he said, after a moment or two, "you wish that you were cooler. And I wish . . ." he thought for a moment, "for a full night's sleep. Or, failing that, a decent meal."

She grinned. "It isn't just me, then?"

"No," he said, smiling down at the stone, "it isn't just you."

Out of the corner of his eye, he saw her start slightly, and her hand shift back down to her side.

"Ah," said Damar calmly, without looking up. "There you are."

Vilar shuffled forward as he spoke, his feet making little valleys in the gravel. "I thought I was being quiet . . . Er, no disruptor this time, I see, that's good, I suppose . . ."

"Vilar," Kira scolded, "you're late."

He was still staring at Damar. "Does he ever move? I mean, I've heard him speak, but I don't think I've seen him move. Not that I'm complaining, mind you, if he wants to stand there and not move that's fine by me . . . it's certainly better than having him go for that disruptor . . . but still it's a little bit unnerving that he doesn't ever seem to, well, you know, *move*—"

"Vilar, shut *up!*"

"Eh? What? Oh yes. Sorry, Nerys." He sidled closer to the

bridge, looking past Damar, toward Kira and relative safety. Damar shifted his weight, just a little, advising no further progress in that direction.

Kira leaned forward. "Well, Vilar?"

"Oh yes. Well, I've done a bit of poking around since we met, spoken to a few people here and there . . . nothing too obvious, of course, you can't be too careful these days . . . well, *you* can't be too careful anyway . . ."

Damar was not certain whether he was about to like him or about to end his life. "Agreed," he said.

"Er, where was I? Oh yes! I've found someone who can get me a supply of some of those, what do you call them, pulse grenades . . . they're not terribly nice, I gather . . ."

Damar shook his head.

"But I suppose that's the point, isn't it? . . . Oh, and someone *else* I was talking to just last night—he said he could get his hands on seven of these new plasma rifles . . . oh, hang on, they won't be much use, there's only three of you . . . Did I *really* just say that . . . ?"

Kira started to laugh.

Damar fixed him with an amused stare, and was just about *not* to smile—and then he heard footsteps behind them. Kira ducked her head, hiding her face within the shadow of the hood. Damar raised his hand to shield his face and looked back over his shoulder.

It was a young couple, walking arm in arm. Damar watched them as they came to a halt on the other side of the bridge, only a few feet away. The young man turned round, frowned when he saw the three of them standing there, and glared hard at Damar. Looked like he'd thought it would be quiet here too. And then, before Damar could turn away again, before he could say it was time for them to get out of here, he saw it pass over the young man's face—he saw that he'd been recognized. His response was automatic.

The young woman screamed. She was dead too a moment later,

but it seemed to Damar that the noise was echoing around him, out across the flat expanse of the city.

"So you can move after all," he heard Vilar say.

He didn't reply.

"I knew I had to worry about that disruptor."

Damar straightened himself up. "Come on," he said. "We can't stay here." He started to walk quickly down the bridge.

"Yeah, I think you're right . . ." Vilar fell into step beside him, and Kira had hurried on ahead. He followed her.

"Where are we going?" Vilar said.

"I don't know. Somewhere else. Somewhere safe."

"Oh, well, *that's* all right then."

Seven

Later, when Kira cast her mind back to this strange interlude in her life, it was not the casual death or the considered treachery, but the heat that she would always remember first—its heavy weight dulling her mind and her spirits, and the haze that hovered in the air, blurring her vision and her thoughts.

"You were impossible," Garak told her, later, "for the whole of that first week. Half the time you were exhausted, and then you'd flare up like *that.*" He snapped his fingers.

"It was so damn *hot* . . ."

He looked out at the black rain lashing down on a ruined land.

"That won't be an issue on Cardassia anymore," he said.

What she would most often remember next was a sunset, the only one that she saw on Cardassia Prime. They were slipping along the north bank, Kira a few steps ahead, on the lookout, and a golden light had suffused the whole city. It had turned the river from brown to a lazy, liquid amber, and all the edges of the buildings were blurred by a soft glow. The wide, flat sky, which had until now felt oppressive, embraced her. For a moment it seemed to Kira that she was back again on Bajor, hiding with her friends in the hills, talking about their future and how they were making it real. Then she saw the city stretched out all around her; and they struck north, into a side street, where it was more covered, but the golden haze still lingered.

They took the short cut that Garak had taught them, coming into Tain's house the back way. As they came down the steps into the cellar, Kira saw that Garak was waiting for them, and he had his disruptor in his hand.

"I'm afraid," he said, "that we may have something of a problem."

"What is it?" she said, stepping toward him, willfully ignoring where the disruptor was pointing.

"Commander, I'm sorry," he said, and then she saw a flash of anger cross his face, before he could suppress it. "You shouldn't have brought him back here."

"That was my fault," Damar said from behind her. "The patrols forced us here. Where else in the city is safe?" He looked pointedly at Garak's arm.

"Not one of your better ideas, Legate."

"What's going on?" Vilar's voice came out almost like a squeak.

"Still," Garak said calmly, not answering, "it does at least save me the effort of having to track him down."

Kira roused herself at that. "Garak, we've been through all this once already. What are you talking about?"

He kept the weapon fixed on its target. "While you were out, I took the time to do a little investigating, Commander, and I found out some things that rather disturbed me." He gestured at the table nearby, toward a padd that was lying on it. "We're not the only ones he's been talking to, Kira." He looked straight at Vilar. "Are we?"

"I've got no idea what you're talking about! Nerys, what's going on here?"

"You'd better have a good explanation for this, Garak—"

"And so had *he,* Commander." He jerked his head at the table. "Take a read through that. Some . . . transactions that can be attributed to your friend here."

Kira grabbed the padd and started scrolling through the information. Something about system-2 disruptors, details of purchasing and supply. She glanced at the dates. "This was ages ago, just after the Dominion arrived—"

"That's it!" Vilar cut in, "that's right! Look," he said, speaking directly to Garak, "it was when they first got here. They were rounding up aliens—they were going to *shoot* me! I had to give them something. You know what it's like!" He took a step forward, put his hands out in a placatory gesture. Garak stayed still, although Kira saw his grip tighten slightly around the weapon he was holding. Vilar backed away from him—straight into Damar, who placed a hand upon his shoulder.

"Surely there's nothing here we need to be worried about?" Kira said. "Supplying weapons is what Vilar does. That's why we're working with him, isn't it?"

"Except that your friend here has been working with our *enemies,* Commander. Are you quite sure he won't do it again?"

She looked up at Garak quickly, but he was still staring past her.

"You *shouldn't* have brought him back here." His fingers had tightened a little more, and his anger was barely concealed now.

"It's done, Garak," Damar said firmly, from behind her. "Now we have to deal with the consequences."

"What consequences?" Kira shot him a quick, almost frantic look.

"I haven't *done* anything!" Vilar's voice had gone up another notch.

"Garak!" Kira said urgently, taking a step toward him. He didn't move. "You know this business at least as well as I do . . . Wouldn't you be more surprised if he *hadn't* been dealing with the opposition? That's what this game is like, you know that! Surely what matters is that he isn't doing it now?"

She looked back toward Vilar. Beneath Damar's hand, he had started to shake with fear. He was staring at Garak. "What do you want?" he was saying. "I can get you whatever you want—"

"Don't you see, Commander?" Garak said. "He breaks under

pressure. They had him once—and he gave them what they wanted." When he spoke again, it was very softly. "Do you know what they can do to him, Kira? Do you know how many ways there are to make a man tell you *everything* that he knows?" His voice began to rise, and she watched Vilar's terror grow with it. Behind him, Damar stood silent and watchful. "He's done it once already, Kira," Garak said. "You *shouldn't* have brought him back here."

Kira turned back to look at Garak. He flicked his eyes at her for just a moment, away from Vilar, asking her the question she did not want to answer. She dropped her head.

"Kira!" he said violently.

She drew in a deep breath of the hot, heavy air. And then she looked up at Garak again, nodded her head slowly, and passed sentence.

"You're right," she whispered. "He would break."

"Nerys, no!"

In a daze, Kira reached to her side, fumbling for her phaser, and then suddenly found that she had been stopped. She looked down. Damar's hand was clamped around her own, restraining her. His skin, she thought, seemed to scrape against her.

"Let Garak deal with this," he said, almost gently. She didn't move, just kept on staring down as she listened to the footsteps heading up the stairs, to Vilar's pleas, and Garak's silence.

Then she lifted her eyes to look at Damar.

"Take your hand off me."

He did not move; and they just stood there, closer than they had ever been, face to face at last. She realized that his hand had begun to shake. And then she saw in his face the effort it took for him to speak.

"I think I'm sorry," he whispered, "sorry that I killed Tora Ziyal."

And that was something else that Kira would remember, later.

Eight

The sun was setting in splendor over the capital of the Cardassian Union. It was a rare sight. Elim Garak lowered his arm and raised his head to watch it as it died, blood red against a bruised sky.

Cardassian memory was constant; it endured both change of circumstance and the passage of time. In the first years of his exile, Garak had found the weight of memory crushing—the sharp angles of the station had acted as persistent reminders of all he had lost, crudely approximating the more graceful contours of home. Bulkheads had stood in for architecture, corridors for avenues, artificial lighting for the heat and the vigor of the sun.

Cardassians were constant in memory, and so he had set it aside, suppressed it ruthlessly as he had much else across the years, only to find it could be quickly triggered—by a warm draft of air, the smell of spices drifting from a shop front, the touch of Ziyal's hand upon his own. Then, set free by these sudden reminders, a flood of images would cascade through his mind—summer evenings by the river watching a terra-cotta sky; sheltering from the late-afternoon sun under the dark-green leaves and scented shade of trees in a city square; raising his face to feel the scarce and precious rain falling to freshen the dusty, shabby streets. And then there were the other memories—summoned in their turn too easily by Sisko's simmering mistrust or Kira's sour contempt—memories of the cries of men in fear or pain, or of the coldness of metal in the hand.

Garak put away his disruptor. The sun was almost gone now, the crimson fading into shadow. He watched the darkness settle on his home, and rubbed absently at his aching arm. What was it Damar had said, just after he'd killed Rusot?

His Cardassia's gone. And it won't be coming back.

It was full dark. Then the city lights came on.

"Well," said Garak, to no one in particular, there no longer being anyone else there. "Another day, another death."

His words passed away into the night, and then he heard a soft footfall in the yard behind him. He did not turn to look, but he did close his eyes for a moment. The footsteps halted.

"Don't say it, Mila," he murmured, with more than a touch of weariness.

"I will say it," she answered fiercely. "I have to say it, because it seems to me you need the reminder. It's like you've forgotten everything you ever learned." He listened to her come a little closer. "And don't stand there making me look at your back! That was your father's trick, and I never liked it from him either."

There were some comparisons that were insupportable. He turned to face her.

"You shouldn't be mixed up in all of this—" she began again, shaking her head, and he cut her off straightaway, raising a finger to silence her, but speaking gently.

"But I am—and I *should.*"

"Your father—"

"Is dead and gone. And so is all he stood for."

They looked at each other for a while, she unsure and he quite certain, and then she lifted her hands as if to acknowledge defeat. She looked at him fondly and gave a snort of laughter.

"Are you becoming an idealist in your old age, Elim?"

"Better late than never, I suppose." He smiled at her, sadly, but affectionately. "And you know me, Mila. I always preferred to set fashion, rather than follow it." Then he looked down at the ground at his day's work, and gestured with his good arm. "Would you . . . ?"

It was her turn to hold up her hand to silence him. "It wouldn't be the first time. Go back inside and forget about it, Elim."

And he did part of what he was told, and left her to her task.

He passed quickly through the house and went down the steps into the cellar. The other two were sitting there in silence, waiting for him. Damar sat with his arms folded, straight-backed and eyes fixed on the wall opposite. Kira was slumped with elbows on her knees, head resting in her hands, staring at the ground.

Garak walked straight past without giving them a second glance.

His arm was aching abominably now. He hunted around in their medical supplies until he found the painkillers, then measured out a dose in a hypospray and pressed it against his skin with practiced ease. Its numbing effects took hold pleasingly quickly, but his mouth was still sour and dry. There was a full flask of water on the table, and he drained it. By the time he turned to face the others, he had schooled his expression back to its customary blankness.

He pulled up a chair, sat down, and then looked at the other two in turn, expectantly, wondering when they were going to ask what they plainly wanted to know, and wishing that they would do it sooner rather than later.

Damar spoke first.

"Is it done?"

"Done? Yes."

Damar opened his mouth as if to speak again. Garak narrowed his eyes.

I swear, Damar, if you thank me, I'll shoot you on the spot.

Damar hesitated for a fraction of a second, then shut his mouth. He looked directly at Garak, and then gave one firm nod of the head, closing the matter between them. Garak felt a grudging respect for the man. You had to hand it to Damar—he never flinched away from looking you straight in the eye. Such directness from another Cardassian was not only unusual—it was almost . . . refreshing.

Kira took a little more time to ask her own quiet question, and when she spoke, she was still staring down at the space before her feet.

"What about . . . what about the body?" She was trying hard, he could tell, but she could not quite keep the distaste out of her voice. Garak forgave her, since he knew she was making an effort and, anyway, he felt much the same way. For although he had throughout the years never lost sight of necessity, or expediency, it was a very long time since Garak had had a taste for killing.

"Mila will take care of it," he said gently. She nodded slowly, and then all three of them lapsed back into silence.

Garak thought for a little while about the sunset, and then pondered his arm. The pain, at least, had subsided. "Well," he said at last, and the other two looked up at him quickly, startled out of their thoughts, "at least the past few days have proven we really do all have something in common."

"Which is?" asked Damar, and something close to a smile touched his eyes.

Garak smiled back unreservedly, and lifted up his arm. "All three of us are perfectly capable of making some really stupid mistakes."

He watched as Kira and Damar exchanged a long and searching look. They made a curious picture, he reflected—the terrorist who seemed to him more and more like a freedom fighter, the soldier who seemed more and more like a savior. . . .

"I think," said Kira, slowly but deliberately, her eyes still on Damar's face, "that that's not all we have in common."

Epilogue

They buried Trelar at dawn, in the shade of a moba tree that was just beginning to come into blossom. They each spoke a few awkward words, and even Furel had been in tears, but Kira had remained dry-eyed. A disruptor blast had taken Trelar full in the face, but he had lingered on for the rest of the day and into the night, until his soft pleas had at last become too much, and Shakaar took him by the hand and finished it.

"The last thing he saw was a friend," Shakaar had said to Kira afterward, but at the time it had not been a consolation.

Now, seeing Damar lie dead in Garak's arms, she understood.

She glanced up at Garak. The mask had finally slipped. His eyes were wide, his jaw slack; he looked as if he had just watched the death of the future, or of hope.

We have no time for this, no time, she thought, listening to the disruptor fire closing in around them, raging inwardly at the injustice. Damar had become—had *been*—a good man. He did not deserve to die such a squalid death. *But we have no time. . . . We can*

end this war now! Later we can grieve, but now we have work to do—his
work to do.

"Remember his orders," she said firmly. "We stop for *nothing.*"

She watched as Garak took his shock and turned it into rage. *"For Cardassia!"* he cried.

"For Cardassia!" Kira shouted back—and meant it.

The Calling

Andrew J. Robinson

Historian's note: This story is set after the events of the novel *A Stitch in Time* and the stage play "The Dream Box," both of which follow the story of Garak beyond the events of the television series.

Andrew J. Robinson

Andrew J. Robinson comes by his knowledge of Garak from having played him on the series *Star Trek: Deep Space Nine* for seven years. In 2000, Pocket Books published his novel about Garak, *A Stitch in Time*. He was born in New York City where he received his B.A. from The New School For Social Research and a Fulbright Scholarship to study in England at the London Academy of Dramatic Art. He has written poetry and his plays have been produced here and in Europe. As an actor and director he has worked in theaters all over the country as well as in film and television. He is curently at work on *Masks*, a memoir chronicling his life in theater and film, and he and his wife, Irene, divide their time between Los Angeles and Paris.

Prologue

My dear Doctor:

I have had to send this communication through a rather circuitous route to prevent it from being exposed to anyone but you. If some unfortunate soul does manage to get his hands on this, it will be the last thing he'll ever hold. All this sounds extreme, I know, but I assure you, I'm not sending a poison-pen letter because I got up on the wrong side of the bed this morning. Actually, I count myself fortunate to have gotten out of bed at all, but more about that later.

Despite the fact that you have disappeared without a word, I'm hopeful you're still alive and have a good reason for breaking off all contact. Yet, while I'm aware that you are swimming in murky waters these days, my friend, you'll forgive me if I say that I am somewhat piqued. My request for a rendezvous in the Vinculum many months ago was urgent, and when you didn't appear . . . well, let's just say that my life has changed radically, and in light of our agreement when we last met, I think it only fair that I let you know where this change has led me.

And it's not a question of blame, Doctor. Such a childish word. No, it's more an issue of responsibility, wouldn't you agree? If one is encouraged by a dear friend to undertake a dangerous, indeed, life-changing course of action, and is promised support for this action (without which, success is surely unattainable), how is one to react when that dear friend and his promised support disappear? No, we can only be responsible for our own choices, not for the actions of others.

There are those who have argued that our encounter in the Vinculum was a dream, or that your image was a projection of my own overactive imagination. But if one has never been in the Vinculum, how can one understand a place where past, present, and future, each with several layered and intertwined veils, dance with the imagery of life in its total and terrifying expression? You and I know that it's a shadow world that exists beneath and behind every manifestation of this world; and in that shadow world all those neat distinctions that we make between dream and reality, truth and fabrication, the living and the dead have no more meaning than spices in a karalian stew. I believe it was you I encountered in that place, and that's why, once again, I'm writing to you.

When I was unexpectedly reunited with you in the Vinculum, I was a man on an errand. I needed to bring back a cure that would stem the plague that was destroying Cardassia. You provided me with that cure . . . and with something else. When I left the Vinculum, I was a man on a mission, a mission I embraced the way a lost traveler hurries toward a distant light in the darkness. I was determined to step out of the shadows, leave the ranks of the "night people," an identity that had been imposed upon me since I was a child, and guide Cardassia back to the fold of civilized community.

But that light disappeared, and I needed your help. The reality of trying to bring order out of Cardassian chaos brought me back to the Vinculum on two subsequent occasions, but I found nothing that suggested a vision of healing or relief. No Federation support . . . and no Dr. Bashir. Perhaps the constant travails of our planet and its never-ending degradation became tiresome to you and unworthy of your effort. Well, you wouldn't be the first to feel that way. Or, perhaps, making a rendezvous in such a place is not as simple as entering the coordinates of a destination on a shuttle flight. Dr. Parmak cobbled together a way to get there and return, but he'd be the first to admit that it's not an exact technology. But whatever has happened to you, my friend, my mission has changed, and I hope you won't be offended when I tell you that the agreement we made has been superceded by another.

I've had to go underground for a period ("silence, exile, and cunning"), but here I am, popping up again, like an irrepressible protagonist (Punch?)

in one of those puppet shows for children I saw in Paris. Please bear with me as I attempt to describe what has happened in the intervening months since we last met. My fervent hope is that this communication finds its way to you.

1

They came from all over Cardassia. The Sabutahim, callused and sturdy farmers from the southern provinces; the gaunt and ghost-like Kasmoc, herders and breeders from the north; renegade soldiers and mercenaries who have formed primitive tribes in the Mekar and Morfan provinces; ragged, half-mad fundamentalists from Lakarian City, rebuilding among the Hebitian ruins in a desperate effort to return to simpler times; and, of course, those die-hard Imperialists (the base support of the Directorate) from their protected enclaves in Rogarin and Brakk. All survivors: most exhausted by the destruction and disease of the civil wars, looking for some kind of resolution; many demented and haunted by loss and grief, looking for a scapegoat to direct their rage. Cardassia is now divided among countless tribes, each one ferociously defending the borders of its pathetic realm. Our Reunion Project to establish a Cardassian democracy is like making a suit of clothes from grains of sand.

I stood on the dais crudely erected from the rubble of the Assembly building that once dominated the Tarlok Sector, the seat of Cardassian power. I watched as thousands streamed into the clearing that was once the majestic and elegant Imperial Parade Grounds. This was the place that commemorated the heroes and triumphs of the Union with martial music underscoring great rhetoric as it echoed throughout the monuments. Now it serves as the gathering place for the volatile remnants of Cardassian civilization.

"No! No! He's blind!" a woman's voice screamed. I looked to my right toward the rubble of what was once the Hall of Records and saw two men beating another as a woman feebly attempted to deter them.

"He fought against us at Begata," one of the attackers growled.

"And I'm proud of it!" gasped the blind man between blows.

Dr. Parmak dispatched two of the dozen or so men providing a thin line of defense around the dais to stop the beating. Thin indeed. Conflicts flared up throughout the crowd, and if any one of them expanded and connected to any of the other conflicts, nothing would be able to stop the chaos from engulfing the city.

Spontaneous combustion.

Violence has a mysterious life that feeds on our despair and desire for revenge, and destruction is its legacy. The desperation of each of these tribes makes it a calculated risk to bring them together in this open forum. So many people in one place looking for the cause, the source of their despair and rage. Their grudges seem to energize them and keep them alive. Of all the emotions, revenge is the one that rules the Cardassian psyche. An eye for an eye, I thought as I watched the blind man being tended to by the woman.

"I wonder . . ." I spoke aloud, my words amplified throughout the Grounds by the crude sound system Dr. Parmak had devised. "I wonder what would happen if we all went blind." The words hung in the dry, hot air as the crowd roar subsided to a rolling murmur.

"What?"

"What did he say?"

"Quiet!"

A shoving match broke out to my left at the place where the entrance to the Obsidian Order had once stood.

"How do they exact revenge in the land of the blind?" I asked. "What do they take next?"

"You take until there's nothing left!" a deep voice bellowed.

" 'Until there's nothing left,' " I repeated. "Then let me ask you all this. How do they exact revenge in the land of the dead?"

The question was greeted with the first silence of the morning.

The shrill and mocking call of the narawak could be heard over-head.

"Because if there's nothing left, how do we go on?" I asked. The narawak's shriek faded and the silence was now complete. I moved to the front of the dais and scanned the faces in front of me. I imagined what I must look like to them. A graying man, trying to stand tall against exhaustion and the gravity of the situation. My eyes, however, were still strong enough to hold their collective gaze, and at the same time, study individual faces, the way I had learned in the Vinculum when I was being urged to take on the mantle of leadership. But that was another time and another reality. In this place, the pain and the sorrow of the lives of these people standing in front of me began to bleed through their rage as my last question came to ground. How, indeed, do we go on?

It was nearly a year since Alon Ghemor, the democratically elected leader of the Reunion Project, was assassinated, and since then nearly as many people had died in the civil war and plague as during the Dominion occupation. Cardassia was so degraded it was nearly uninhabitable, and most survivors already had "nothing left." In order to find some kind of protection, each person pledged his or her support to a collective and surrendered their autonomy to that group and its leader. Even the devoutly religious Neo-Hebitians had to surrender to the military discipline of the Lakarian City collective to protect themselves against the maraud-ing predators of other collectives. The democratic order that Ghe-mor and the Reunion Project had attempted to institute had dissolved into anarchy and cruel self-interest. Cardassia had lost its civilization . . . and its soul was now up for grabs.

I had always believed that the planet could be rebuilt and re-structured, that the survivors could identify the underlying causes that had brought them to the brink of annihilation, that a just and open society could be created. I had not fully reckoned with the tenacious strength of those who would not let go of the old struc-ture, no matter how discredited and degraded it had become.

The Reunion Project had won the elections by a two-to-one

margin, but soon after the new group of leaders attempted to re-align governance along more democratic lines, the resistance led by the Directorate and its so-called Restoration Cadres dug in. The battles were fierce and cruel, and the needless loss of life sapped the strength of both sides. The young, democratically elected political structure was mortally wounded. Those who be-lieved that power was their hereditary entitlement saw the will of the people as something to be destroyed; and those who were will-ing to submit to the will of the people did whatever was necessary to survive.

Ghemor adamantly refused the offer of Federation help that was made to me by Julian Bashir during our meeting in the Vinculum. He believed that any outside interference would be construed by many in the Project as a Federation ploy and an attempt by Ghe-mor to grab power. What would prevent the Directorate, he asked, from making a similar alliance with the Klingons and Romulans? *What's to prevent them from doing it now?* I countered. In the end, Ghemor came around to my way of thinking, but sadly, the argu-ment had splintered the Reunion Project . . . and Ghemor was the one who paid the ultimate price. The cruel joke was that we had become the *Dis*union Project because many believe that Ghemor was assassinated by one of his own followers and not by some Di-rectorate thug.

As I scanned the crowd, I noticed members of another tribe; hooded figures off to the side and isolated from the others by empty space. These were the survivors of the plague hiding their disfigurement under full-length robes. How brave of these people to come here today. The others in the crowd resented their pres-ence, but pretended that they didn't exist. We had never anticipated the plague and its virulence. One day it appeared, a virus as myste-rious as the evil that had enveloped the planet, and one out of every three Cardassians died in agony. The plague brought us to the edge of oblivion, and yet it was the reason I was standing in front of this ragged and motley assembly.

When I returned from my first visit to the Vinculum with the plague cure Dr. Bashir had provided, I knew that my trip to that place was no dream. Dr. Parmak was eager to hear of my adventures, but it took me days before I could make sense of it. Not that we had much time to chat. We worked tirelessly to disseminate the curative substance that quickly stemmed any further mutations of the virus, as well as the preventative techniques Dr. Bashir had wisely included. When it was later confirmed that Palandine was indeed among the dead, I went into an emotional tailspin. I tried to believe that her disfigured appearance in the Vinculum was some kind of hallucination, a hoax my mind was perpetrating in the heat of the moment, but I couldn't deny the fact that she was not the only dead soul I had encountered in that place. Nor could I deny the truth of Palandine's statement, once I had returned to this world and made an investigation, that her daughter, Kel, was missing without a trace. Ironically, this bit of news rallied my spirits, and I dedicated whatever time and energy I could spare from my plague work to finding her.

"Ereket, what do you think you're doing?"

"Excuse me, Docent?" The young man preparing to administer the plague antidote to his patient was as surprised by the sharpness of my tone as I was. Behind them, a long line of people waited in the late afternoon shadows of the old Imperial Parade Grounds of Lakarian City. We had been working since early morning and the pace of the work had slowed considerably.

"These people need your help, they don't need to be impressed by your wisdom and expertise."

"But, Docent, I was just trying to explain . . ."

"Ereket, just administer the protocol as you've been taught to do. We have to finish this group before we lose the light. Do you understand?"

"Yes, Docent," he replied, hiding the hurt and shame he felt at being called out in front of all these people. The old man receiving the injection maintained his stoic demeanor, but his eyes thoroughly studied me. He was clearly more interested in me than in

Ereket's childish abuse of authority. I nodded to him and moved away to supervise the other probes.

On the surface, my reaction appeared extreme and unjust, but Ereket liked to demonstrate his authority with pedantic behavior and there was no time for that. Ever since I returned from the Vinculum after the first meeting with Dr. Bashir, I felt like someone who had awakened from a deep sleep after an evening of too much *kanar.* But it was more than just disorientation; my perception of people and the motives that drive their actions now had a clarity that often made me wince. I had to take more care with my reactions. This new perception, and the obligation to back it up with action, could be a problem if I let it get out of hand. To correct the behavior of a probe like Ereket, especially if I'm his docent and we're working day and night to defeat this plague, is clearly an acceptable situation. But if my peers and those in positions of real power need correction . . .

"Excuse me. Elim Garak?" It was the old man, Ereket's patient from earlier in the day. Something about his look alerted me.

"Yes."

"My name is Cronal Gys. I want to thank you for the good work you've been doing here and elsewhere."

"Thank you. And I apologize for the behavior of—"

"No, not at all. He's young, he has to learn how to work. Unfortunately, our schools these days are real life, and the lessons tend to be harsh ones."

"You're very kind," I replied. Cronal Gys held my attention with those gray eyes that never stopped studying me.

"Your work, Elim Garak, has particular significance for some of us here in Lakarian City." Bells began to toll, an old Lakarian tradition that marked the end of the day. I was gratified to notice that the line of people had dwindled since my reprimand. This was our third day in the city and it was vital that we maintain the scheduled quotas.

"My work?" I knew he wasn't just referring to what we were doing in the field.

"I think I can help you find the person you're looking for."

"Kel. Is she safe?"

"When it's convenient for you, you can meet me in the grounds adjacent to the Citadel. I'm sure I don't have to tell you how delicate the situation is." Cronal began to walk away.

"It won't take me long to finish up here," I said after him.

"I'll be there."

Only when he was gone did I wonder how he knew I was looking for Kel. I hadn't had the opportunity to inquire about her in Lakarian City. When I returned from the Vinculum, I took what time I could to look for her, as I had promised Palandine I would. The Oralian temple in Cardassia City where she had performed her duties had disappeared without a trace, however, and there was no one else I could really ask. I was certain their disappearance had something to do with the danger that faced Kel. Palandine had warned me in the Vinculum that my enemies were planning to discredit me and the Reunion Project by arranging Kel's death to appear like my act of revenge against her family. Pythas and the Obsidian Order couldn't help me; their resources were already exhausted. Because it was a stronghold of what was left of the Oralian Way, I purposely volunteered for the mission to Lakarian City so that I could make some inquiries when I had the time to spare from my work. Somehow this Cronal Gys anticipated my intention.

Before Cardassia City was created to be a more appropriate seat of power for the empire, Lakarian served the purpose of centralizing planetary government in a more subtle and aesthetic manner. Many of the buildings dated back to the early days of the Republic, and there were even Hebitian ruins that had somehow survived the almost total eradication of that culture. One of these ruined structures was in the neglected grounds next to the old Republican Citadel that was itself partly constructed from the ancient volcanic rock the Hebitians used to build with.

As I warily approached what was once, perhaps, a watchtower, the soft evening air of the Lakarian climate assuaged the stress and intensity of the day's work. My thoughts went back to other evenings, other meetings in grounds more cultivated and maintained. I put my hand on the rock; it had a spiky, but pliable solidity.

"The first people also touched that," Cronal's voice came out of the dark. Despite my vigilance, I was barely able to make out his shadowy presence standing beneath a wild *ocran* bush that only grows in the Lower Hemisphere. How long had he been standing there?

"There's almost a plasmic quality about it," I said as I moved my hand over a surface that perceptibly responded.

"We'll never find a better building material," he said.

"Why wasn't it used for everything?" I asked.

Cronal laughed. "It's not as imperial-looking as the obsidian stone from the Toran mountains."

"But that's on the other side of the planet," I said.

"Yes, but they had plenty of . . . expendable labor." Cronal shrugged. He referred to the sad truth, expunged from official histories, of how the invaders had subjugated and enslaved the Hebitians to create a Cardassian Empire that would last forever. "Please, Elim Garak, come with me."

As we walked through the grounds, the gardener in me wanted to stop and study what was left of the old plantings. It would take some time to restore the soil and bring back the original integrity, but well worth the effort. We crossed a wide and empty promenade and came to an older, more congested section where the dwellings were jammed together in a bizarre hivelike organization. From the outside, the entrances appeared to be placed in a chaotic and random manner, but this placement assured the most efficient use of the inside living space. This was an area created to house a dense population . . . but no one was in the streets.

"The plague was especially cruel here," Cronal explained. "Almost no one remains, except, of course, those who have no choice." He treated me with an easy familiarity I found unsettling.

"What do you know about me, Cronal?"

"That you travel, but you always come back to the same place," he answered.

"Isn't that true of almost anyone who travels?"

"Some of us stay where we've gone."

"The dead."

"Not just the dead, Elim Garak." We had stopped in front of what first looked like any of the other dwellings with multiple entrances. "And some of us don't come back to the same place in *this* life. Even if we come back to the same neighborhood." I was feeling some irritation with his oblique manner.

As we passed through a simple gate there was a palpable charge of energy flowing up from the ground and into my body. We'd entered some kind of energy field that seemed to "contain" this particular dwelling. Cronal didn't react to the change as he led me to the only true entrance—the others, as I looked carefully, were false, designed to confuse unwelcome visitors. I heard a faint electronic, almost choral sound coming from inside. I suddenly became afraid that this was all an elaborate trap that I had willingly walked into.

The door opened and the blood drained down to my feet. It wasn't Palandine—Kel definitely had her own look, a strong face and jaw, as much her father as her mother—but it was the energy that I recognized . . . and loved. Expansive, embracing . . . that amused and inquisitive expression asking, "Who are you, really?"

"Hello, Kel."

"Elim Garak." She took me in with a frankness and total lack of judgment. "Please come in. We've been waiting." Other than four padded, backless seats, the room was empty. The walls were covered with some kind of plain material. I wondered if the frieze celebrating the Hebitian cycles of life I had once seen when Palandine and I had visited an Oralian temple was on the other side of the material. The floor seemed to have the texture and give of the volcanic rock. I became aware of a barely discernible pattern that would form on the ceiling and then fade. Each emerging shape was similar but different, and the rhythm of the sequence was connected to the pulsing energy that continued to flow through me.

"So you've become an Oralian Guide," I said to Kel after a long silence.

"When it's not a danger to others. It's difficult for people to gather and celebrate the Mysteries," she replied.

"That's my fault, isn't it? You're being caught up in a strategem that's directed against me. I regret—"

"What a funny man you are, Elim Garak," Kel interrupted. "I assure you, you don't have to take responsibility for our problems—you have plenty of your own."

"But I was under the impression . . ."

"I know. But if you never existed, those people who hunt us now would still be threatened by the Oralian Way," she gently explained. "But certainly Cardassian efficiency would dearly love to destroy both of us at the same time." The idea made her laugh.

"You have so much of both your mother and your father. I feel so . . ." I trailed off, suddenly unable to breathe.

"You loved my father, didn't you?"

"Yes." With this admission I began to breathe again. For the first time, I allowed myself to feel the deep shame and sickness I have lived with ever since I murdered her father.

"Did it ever occur to you, Cronal, that sometimes we seek out that person . . . how do I say this . . . who gives us our death?"

"There are precedents in nature. The *balteen,* at the end of its cycle, offers itself at the lair of its most dangerous antagonist. Even Garak's *regnar* tries to choose its death." Cronal looked at me.

"Mila!" Kel cried out with pleasure at remembering the name. Those intelligent gray eyes, surrounded by a boundless, childlike enthusiasm, triggered another memory of Mila, the *regnar* that guided me and alleviated my loneliness during my first days at the Bamarren School. Until I met Kel's mother, Mila was my sole companion.

"What *don't* you know about me?" I asked with open admiration.

"It's only information," Cronal said.

"My father would have disagreed with you," I replied.

"But he waited for you before he died," Kel said.

The breath went out of me again. I had secretly harbored that thought, but never shared it with anyone.

"My father had been looking for the person who would give him his death," Kel said with an intensity that obliterated the young girl of moments before. "He also chose you for that moment."

We lapsed into another long silence. Until that moment, I had never made the connection between Kel's father, Barkan, and my father.

"Men who want to lead are often conflicted," Cronal broke the silence. "Does one have a calling? Or is it merely an appetite for power? Is it to nurture life? Or to devastate a planet? And if it *is* a calling, how does one answer?" His look challenged me with the last question.

"Perhaps it's simply about helping people to die," I muttered. I was not only thinking of my last moments with both men (men who had elevated me and then betrayed me), but of my "calling" since returning from the Vinculum, where it often felt as if I were presiding over a dying planet.

"That, too. Certainly." Cronal nodded. "But I repeat my question, Elim Garak: How does one answer the call?" In his gentle manner, the old man was issuing a direct challenge.

"You know about the Vinculum," I said.

"Of course we do," Kel replied. "Before an ancient Hebitian could be anointed as a leader, he or she had to make a pilgrimage. The Vinculum is a place where the living and the dead find common ground. Unless you've made your peace with the dead, how can you guide the living?"

"If that's the case, then why would a human, Julian Bashir, be the one to encourage me to return to Cardassia and lead the Reunion Project? Shouldn't that message, that 'call,' have come from one of our own?"

"Are you sure it was him?" Cronal asked.

The question stopped me. "But why——?"

"Elim, you're an extraordinary person," Kel interrupted gently. "You're also a stubborn one. Perhaps you received the information from someone who appeared to be Julian Bashir because you wouldn't have taken it from anyone else."

"Then who was it?"

"Only you can answer that," Kel replied. "All I can tell you is that you went to the Vinculum because you desperately needed to find a cure for the plague. Dr. Parmak, in his exhaustive search to find this cure, discovered an ancient Hebitian medical text that describes a metadimensional nexus that contains all wisdom, knowledge and resources, a nexus that slices through creation and connects with everything that ever was, is, or will be. The text calls this place the Vinculum. When Parmak took this information to Mindur Timot . . ."

". . . Timot determined that this Vinculum could be accessed through the same technology that enables us to reconfigure our subatomic structures from matter to pure energy in order to be transported from one place to another at near-warp," I finished.

"At warp, and beyond. But the real trick, dear Elim, as you well know, is to be able to locate that place where imagination, intuition, and creativity intersect. Much harder—and more dangerous—than being transported into the next room." Kel placed her soft hand on my head. "The coordinates of an inner journey," she almost whispered.

I became aware that her touch was alleviating a terrible headache. "When I was in the Vinculum, your mother . . . or someone who 'appeared' to be Palandine, told me that I had to save you."

"Am I in danger?"

"I think we all are," I replied.

"Then you have to save all of us," she said with a smile.

"I'm afraid there are many who don't want to be saved," I said.

"Then they must seek their death." The smile disappeared. "It's delicate, isn't it?" Kel said to both of us. "Just because you've been called, doesn't mean you don't have choice."

"The Hebitians taught that first we learn how to rule ourselves," Cronal said. "Coexistence depends on each of us maintaining our own boundaries."

"If we can't do that, Cronal, how can we possibly guide others?" Kel asked, relishing the absurdity.

"I'm afraid that's a lesson that didn't survive the Hebitians," I observed.

"No, Elim Garak! It's surviving right now. In this room!" she said with an energy that made the pattern on the ceiling blaze. "Why do you think we're here?" As she gestured, she referred to far more than the three of us. "Why do you think *you* are here? You must know by now why you were sent to the Vinculum."

A part of me didn't want to know. I continued to hang on to the answers, the certitude I had felt when I returned from my first visit to that mysterious place. I had come back with the charge of political leadership, and I was determined not to waver. But Kel's words were beginning to open up another, more frightening dimension.

"You've been called, Elim. We need you. However you choose to share the wisdom of the Vinculum, just remember, your choice comes from your need, your integrity . . . and whatever vision you return with. If you lead no one else but yourself, and live according to whatever vision you've received, that will be enough."

"So I will return to the Vinculum," I said.

"It appears so," Kel replied. "It's a great gift, Elim. A source of wisdom few are allowed to experience . . . and then be able to return . . . and share."

"The traveler who returns to the same place," I repeated.

"And finds it terribly changed because *he* has changed," Cronal added.

I nodded my acceptance. To what, I wasn't altogether sure. When Dr. Bashir informed me that the Federation had "anointed" me as the Cardassian leader of their choice, of course my lingering suspicion was that they needed a suitable puppet. But Kel and Cronal were making me understand that for whatever reason, I was being "called," and I was facing another "choiceless" choice.

The room suddenly began to pulse with a dark red urgency that obviously served as a warning. Immediately, the three of us stood up and I looked to the others for instruction.

"Just leave the way you entered and make your way back to the Citadel without drawing attention," Cronal instructed.

"He knows how to do that very well," Kel said with that familiar playfulness. She seemed untouched by the imminent danger.

"What about you?" I asked, remembering Palandine's warning.

"We'll be fine. No one has more protection than I do," she said, looking at Cronal.

"Will I see you again?" The question surprised, even embarrassed, me.

"Don't you know?" Kel laughed. "You're one of us, Elim Garak. Now go."

Before they disappeared, Cronal gently, but firmly guided me to the door. Like a dream, I found myself outside, moving through the grounds toward the main thoroughfare. The neighborhood seemed as quiet and uninhabited as before, but the energy darkened with a threat I began to perceive on the periphery. I wondered how wise it was for me to have left like this. Certainly, the forces threatening Kel and Cronal were also a danger to me, and I felt the need to withdraw my presence. Even though I knew this action was taken for self-protection, it brought back all those feelings of shame that had originally motivated my desire to perfect this facility for passing through much of my early life unnoticed. A facility that Enabran Tain had cultivated and encouraged.

"My fellow Cardassians," I began my prepared speech to reconcile the scattered tribes of our planet. I so desperately wanted to put all these thoughts, these memories behind me, to move forward. But as I began to deliver my speech, thanking the assembled groups for coming and urging them to lay aside their differences, the faces and images of the past intruded even more. In the Obsidian Order we were taught to operate on two or more levels of conscious intent at the same time. It's a basic technique; as you're putting someone at ease, you're manipulating, even dismantling him, and at the same time, you're devising a way to reassemble him in a way that suits your purpose. The mind has a master plan and complete control over each level. I had no control over the imagery now flooding my mind. The speech I had wanted to give, the words of reconciliation, of healing and hope, wouldn't come.

"We've all gone mad," I found myself saying. "Or we've reached that final evolutionary stage where we've outlived our reason for being here. Perhaps now all that's left is the final implosion from within."

I was shocked at what was coming out of my mouth. Judging from the faces in front of me, this was not the speech they had expected either. Some voices started to protest.

"No no no no no no!" I shouted over them. "Not your fault! No, you were only reacting to the circumstances that he . . ." I pointed to a random spectator ". . . created, and the insults and injuries that she . . ." pointing to another ". . . committed. And every one of us is so wronged and dishonored and inflicted with the deaths of those nearest and dearest to us that we righteously believe that we have the right to strike the last blow!"

"Yes, we do!" cried a voice.

"Alright," I answered the voice. "But let me ask you a serious question, my fellow long-suffering Cardassian; have you thought about what this world is going to look like if you *do* strike the last blow?"

Complete silence. Stillness. They stood looking at me like stunned animals. Suddenly I hated them. I hated us all. I hated what we had become. The empathy, the connective tissue between us had rotted away along with any lingering desire for reconciliation. The best of us had already been sacrificed—the sooner the end came for the rest of us, the better.

"Think about it. It's very simple. Whichever one of you does strike that last blow, imagine the satisfaction as you stand all alone in a wasteland of dead bodies. The cruelty and barbarity and madness of our civilization devolves on you. And at that point, all I can wish for you is that you have enough strength and live long enough so you can bury the rest of us . . . that is, if there's even a shred of decency left in you."

Behind me I heard Dr. Parmak murmur, "Elim." Indeed, this was not the speech I had imagined giving when Dr. Bashir and I had our reunion in the Vinculum. This was not the "calling" I had heard in Kel's words to me. Perhaps it was exhaustion . . . or some suicidal desire . . . but what I was facing on this rubbled dais was a reality that defied all political idealism, and that had finally driven me mad. Perhaps my calling was to preside over the final death rattle of our civilization.

The crowd, like some great organism, began to respond, first in a rolling murmur as each faction calculated what my words meant to them. Only the hooded people appeared not to react. Instantly the murmur became a roar of competing opinions and passion. There was a slight surge forward. Some truly wanted a dialogue, to follow through on the promise of a reconciliation. Many of these people actually were in agreement with my sentiments. Unfortunately, they had to deal with the outrage of the Directorate reactionaries who raised their protest to a howl and began to chant, "Death to Garak! Death to the traitors!" The traitors, or course, being the Reunion Project.

The surge of the crowd became stronger as it was pushed from behind. Our undermanned line of defense was losing the battle of keeping them from the dais. Just before Parmak grabbed me, I noticed that the hooded people had disappeared. Whoever they were, they had suffered enough.

Parmak had devised a contingency plan in case the rally ended badly. The reason we had located the dais where we did was because it was accessible to an old Obsidian Order underground passage. The others held the crowd back just long enough for the two of us to make our way behind the dais and disappear around a corner where a wall that was once part of the Assembly Building remained miraculously intact. We opened a ventilation grille large enough for us to slip through. The grille closed behind us and we opened a hatch on an exposed section of the ground floor and scrambled down a ladder built into the side of a hole just large enough for my body. The hatch lock clicked shut above us and we climbed down in total darkness. Parmak preceded me and opened the door to the familiar underground passageway that connected several clandestine escape routes to what remained of the Obsidian Order labyrinth. Much of it was intact because Enabran Tain, the former head of the once-omnipotent internal security organization, had reinforced the underground structure to withstand severe attack.

"What was that all about, Elim?" Because of his facial disfigurement and the voice control he always exercised, it was difficult to discern Pythas Lok's attitude. He was sitting at Tain's old desk, and Limor Prang, our old mentor who never seemed to age, stood to the side. These two men had survived and made the Order's infrastructure functional again, this time in the service of the Reunion Project. Without the revitalized Order it was doubtful that we would have been able to resist the Directorate reaction. But the house that Tain had built was now supporting a very different Order.

"I couldn't give the speech," I replied.

"Obviously." Was Pythas smiling?

"I'm tired of them. They behave like children," I said.

"They're afraid. Did you think that scolding would bring them together?" No, Pythas wasn't smiling.

"I'm sorry. I couldn't control myself."

Now Pythas smiled at the irony of hearing those words spoken in Tain's old office. Prang, the most controlled man on Cardassia, just looked at me.

"It's gotten worse," a voice said behind me. I turned as Nal Dejar entered the room. Her stern, handsome face frowned as she listened to a report on her comm chip to what was going on outside. Ever since she had nursed Pythas back from the edge of death when he'd nearly been incinerated in a Dominion ambush, Nal had been his constant companion and near silent partner. It was always a bit of a shock to hear her speak.

"A battle is raging through the Tarlak Sector. It seems that the Directorate had planned to break up the rally in any event. Garak just made their task easier." Nal spoke as if I weren't in the room. I was too weary to defend myself.

"Send in the Paldar and Akleen units," Pythas ordered.

"That just about exhausts our reserves," Nal warned.

"What can we do, Nal?" Pythas asked. "Give them the coordinates and stay in touch." Nal left the room issuing orders into her comm chip.

No one said a word, but we all shared the same thought. Every time there was a truce, an attempt at reconciliation, inevitably an act of violence destroyed the momentary peace. Usually it was the Directorate and their so-called Restoration Cadres under the leadership of Korbath Mondrig. His demagoguery fueled the passions of those who were convinced that Cardassia's woes were directly related to a rumored Federation plan to assimilate the planet without its inhabitants. There had to be a reason why so many had died, and Federation genocide made as much sense as anything else. But every group, no matter what they believed to be the cause of the present horror, reacted with a paranoid ferocity to the slightest provocation. No one was saying out loud what was painfully obvious.

"How many more fires can we put out, Pythas?" I asked. He shrugged. He knew the answer better than anyone. When I returned from the Vinculum the first time, encouraged by Dr. Bashir's promise of Federation support, and after the Lakarian encounter with Kel and Cronal, I became a more visible presence and advocate for greater ties with the Federation. Parmak and I traveled all over Cardassia combining our task of plague alleviation with a presentation of what the Reunion Project meant. It was a strange, almost schizophrenic experience, because wherever we went we would gain new adherents to our cause, and at the same time harden the opposition against us. After Alon Ghemor had been assassinated and the civil war entered its most intense phase, the Reunion Project had to be reorganized, with Pythas as the head of the military section. Dr. Parmak and I continued to guide political strategy, but I became the primary spokesman and the magnetic point for all reaction to the Project, good and bad.

"It's a stalemate, Pythas. There's no productivity, our resources are at a critical low—"

"Yes, I know this, Elim," Pythas interrupted. "And the fact that you know it as well makes me wonder all the more why you weren't able to 'control' yourself and follow through with our plan of reconciling those groups out there."

"Because it's futile. All you had to do was look into their eyes. They want revenge, someone to blame. The thugs were just looking for the opening to attack us. Nal said so herself. The only people who want reconciliation are the plague victims, and who's going to listen to them?"

"Then what, Elim? What? You must have had *something* in mind when you delivered your lecture today." This was a tone I had never heard from Pythas before. The stalemate was getting to all of us. I took a deep breath.

"We have to contact the Federation," I said. No one in the room expected this. After a moment Pythas cleared his throat.

"I quote you, Elim. 'It's futile.' "

"It's futile to return to the Vinculum," I replied. "For whatever reason, Dr. Bashir was not able to maintain our contact in that place." And contrary to what I had expected after my meeting with Kel, nothing more was revealed in those visits to the Vinculum.

"If Bashir was ever there," Nal Dejar said as she came back into the room.

"What do you mean, Nal?" I asked sharply. I was sure that she hadn't meant it the same way Kel did.

Nal just looked at me. "The Directorate's cadres are pinned down," she informed Pythas. "They want to negotiate a truce that would allow them to return home."

"A truce," Pythas snorted.

"Kill them," Limor Prang stated quietly.

"No," Pythas responded immediately. "We don't need any more martyrs to their cause. No," he sighed. "Keep them isolated. I want to speak to their commanders." If Prang disapproved of this tactic, he didn't show it. "What about the other groups?" he asked.

"They've either left or they're scattered throughout the city," Nal replied.

"Maybe Bashir was never in the Vinculum," I persisted. "Maybe it *was* a dream. But the curative formula I came back with wasn't a dream. Parmak and I were able to stem the plague."

"It's true, Pythas," Parmak concurred.

"And the Federation approved our receiving that formula. If I can somehow explain to them what our present needs—"

"May I remind you, Elim, why Ghemor was assassinated." Pythas was losing patience. So was I.

"He was assassinated because he refused to protect himself."

"No!" Pythas countered. "When Ghemor agreed with your proposal that the Federation broker a settlement to the civil war, it activated the divisions within our own group. To many, Ghemor was a traitor for even speaking to the Federation, and for all we know it was one of *our* people who killed him. And what are you going to do, Elim? Announce your departure for Earth with the stated intention of presenting yourself before the Federation Council and leave us here to face the reaction to your apparent treachery? Because the reaction will come, and those of us who are left behind will feel its full force."

"No one will know I've gone," I said quietly. Pythas's scarred, immobile face was like a mask that made his eyes so powerfully direct and open.

"You're serious," he finally said.

"Yes."

"Fine. But when you show up in Paris, who is *not* going to know that you're there? You're no longer some anonymous operative in the Order. You've become the face of the Reunion Project."

"No one will know," I repeated. Pythas leaned back in his chair, searching me for the answer to this riddle. Only Limor Prang understood what I was getting at. He held my look.

"How's Timot's health?" I asked. Besides giving us access to the Vinculum, Mindur Timot, the Order's technical wizard, had also devised the "wire" that Dr. Bashir had skillfully removed from my brain when I became addicted to its endorphin-producing capability.

"He's well enough," Prang replied. "But I'm not so sure about you, Garak."

"What's this about?" Pythas demanded. Prang and I continued to look at each other.

"I believe Garak wants to go to Earth as a hew-mon." It always amused me that old Prang pronounced the word exactly as Quark did.

"That's impossible!" cried Parmak.

"No, it's not," I replied. "Pythas, do you remember when Entek abducted the Bajoran, Kira Nerys, and had her transformed into a Cardassian to make Ghemor's uncle believe that it was his long-lost daughter?" Pythas looked back at me with a blank expression.

"Very few people know about Entek's misadventure," Prang explained. "Mindur Timot devised a procedure whereby a member of one species can appear as another. A Bajoran to look like a Cardassian . . . a Cardassian to look like a hew-mon."

"Was this common practice?" Pythas asked.

"No, it was too dangerous," Prang answered. "It involves adjusting the genetic code, and the procedure lacked . . . precision."

"I'll tell Kira that the next time I see her," I said.

"Why would you want to take the chance?" Parmak asked me.

"Because we've run out of solutions, Doctor. Because if we don't find one soon, you'll be able to add Cardassians to the interplanetary list of extinct species. And because I was made a promise by a friend."

"So you would go to Earth as a human."

"Yes, Pythas."

"How would we explain your absence?"

"After my behavior today? Easily."

The room became still. I could sense Pythas weighing this idea against the solutions that had been offered to halt Cardassia's slide into oblivion. Dr. Parmak's concern was evident while Nal and Prang typically showed nothing as they waited in silence. Pythas let out a long sigh and looked at Prang and Nal. Prang returned the look with a barely discernible nod.

"How would you present yourself?" Pythas finally asked.

"How else, Pythas? As a plain and simple tailor."

2

The description of Earth as the third planet in the Sol system, a class-M world located in Sector 001, doesn't do justice to what the planet actually looks like from the shuttle. Dr. Bashir often rhapsodized about his Earth. While we were on Deep Space 9, I think he missed Earth almost as much as I missed Cardassia. As the shuttle approached Earth's atmosphere, I could see the attraction it held for him.

Marbled blue, green, and snow white whirling patterns fixed by the deep and dark blue of the oceans gave the planet an organic liveliness that provoked a yearning and sadness within me. I could only compare it to the gray pallor of stress and decay of my own planet.

"Faded, hasn't it?" the voice of the flight attendant said. "According to the accounts of the first astronauts, the intensity of the blue was almost too much to bear." I smiled and nodded knowingly as he looked past me to the approaching planet. "We'll be landing at Charles de Gaulle in a few minutes, M. Tranger," he pleasantly informed me and moved up the aisle.

I returned my attention to the Earth guidebook padd Julian had once given me. As the shuttle entered the atmosphere I tried to expand my limited knowledge of this planet as best I could before we disembarked at Paris where the Federation was headquartered. But my eyes kept wandering back to the window and the faint reflection of my human face superimposed over the approaching world.

The operation was short and relatively uneventful. The most difficult part was getting up the courage to look at my new facial identity. Mindur Timot was his usual affable and talkative self as he earnestly tried to reassure me.

"Now, Elim, everything has worked out just fine. There's nothing to be worried about. But before you look at yourself, just remember that humans have an entirely different sense of . . . how shall we say? Beauty? Physical attraction? Being a different species, of course, they have their own standard of what appeals to them. Now I've taken as a model someone I've been assured is a perfectly acceptable representative of the human male."

"But what am I? There are so many types?"

"Elim, with these humans, there's no such thing as a pure racial type. This gentleman's genetic disposition is native to the Mediterranean basin. He has—I should say, you have—family from both French Europe and Arabic Africa. Now regardless of how repellent the idea of mixing races is to us, on Earth any given mixture is possible within the human species, especially with the French. But being a mixture—hybrid, if you like—gives one certain advantages."

"Like what?" I was grateful for his chatter since it delayed the inevitable first look.

"Well, for one thing your particular hybrid has greater resistance to the deleterious effects of their sun. On your previous trip, I believe, you found the solar intensity somewhat discomfiting." While Timot rattled on he was setting up the image reflector.

"There. Now you can look at yourself, if you like, Elim." I hesitated. "Sooner or later, my boy, you're going to have to face your new identity. Come now." He thumped me on the back as he moved me toward the reflector. "I'm eager to know what you think of my handiwork."

I allowed myself to be maneuvered into place . . . and I looked. "Oh, Mindur," I whispered, the breath having gone out of my body.

"Yes, my boy?" he answered eagerly.

"Where am I?"

"Why, you're right here, Elim. But you look like *Emile Tranger* of Paris, France, and Earth. Extraordinary, wouldn't you say? I've ironed out some of the wrinkles in the process since that Bajoran woman."

"But at least Kira made a comely Cardassian. I look like . . ." Words escaped me.

"You look like a comely human, Elim. Absolutely first rate, believe me."

"And you've transformed my entire body!" I cried, noticing for the first time the missing shoulder ridges and the smooth skin.

"Yes, of course. You have to be able to live a normal human life, Elim. What if you should become . . . intimate with someone? Or if someone were to walk in on you when you were '*deshabille,*' as they say *en français*. I'd like to see you explain your way out of that!" He positively cackled at the thought. "You look marvelous, my boy!"

"Emile Tranger?" the customs official asked as he looked at the picture on my *carte d'identité*.

"Yes."

"You've been away quite a while, M. Tranger. What kind of business did you have on Borlan III?" he asked. Borlan III is a neutral planet that was "programmed" into my travel documents and itinerary. As in the good old days of the Order, I was smuggled on to the planet with my new identity and history intact. I was amazed at the resources Mindur and Prang still had at their disposal. I knew that the Order had always prepared for the worst, but I hadn't realized just *how* well until this moment.

"I run a small export business, mainly arranging shipments of Borlan's bloodworm silk," I explained to the official.

"Very expensive stuff," he noted, carefully studying me as he consulted his padd, which he skillfully blocked from my sight.

"I have a particular *clientèle,* monsieur, willing to pay for only the highest quality material," I replied with an appropriate Gallic hauteur that seemed to come naturally.

"Welcome home, monsieur." He stamped my *carte* and motioned me on. As I passed through the gate that led to the main terminal, a group of people stood with small boards flashing different names. I saw one flashing my new name in a garish green light and approached the young woman who held it.

"M. Tranger?" she asked. I nodded. "Please follow me." She swiftly led the way through the crowd that was a mixture of just about every racial type . . . except Cardassian. As it had struck me on my previous visit to Earth, it was reminiscent of another place where I was the sole Cardassian. But here, I was the only one who knew it. Or was I?

"I hope you don't mind, monsieur, but the fastest way into town is the *Métro,*" my guide informed me as she gracefully wove her way through the crowd. "I've arranged for your baggage to be picked up and delivered to your apartment."

"What is your name?" I asked.

"Mila."

I involuntarily stopped, not knowing what to say.

"Are you alright, monsieur?" Mila asked.

"Yes. For a moment . . . I thought . . . I'd forgotten . . ." She watched me as I pretended to look for something in my vest. "No, it's fine. I have it." I patted my pocket and we started walking again. Of course it was only a bizarre coincidence, but the fact that this young woman had the same name as my mother . . . and my pet *regnar* who was perhaps my first guide . . . unsettled me.

"We haven't met before, have we?" I regretted the question as soon as it came out of my mouth. She gave me a sideways look without responding or slowing down. "Perhaps it's just that you remind me of someone," I hastily added. "It's been a while since I've made this trip." I couldn't believe how clumsy I was. It was like I'd never been on an assignment before where something unexpected had happened. Political life had made me obvious and stupid.

We spoke very little during the brief journey into the central city of Paris and the *Gare du Nord,* an old and stunningly filthy terminal filled with what looked like the refuse of the human race. I was appalled at the chaos and the rude jostling of bodies rushing in every direction. The gravitational heaviness of Earth's atmosphere had already made me feel as if I were carrying twice my weight, but the damp heat of the day and the smells and the undisciplined behavior of the crowd brought on a wave of nausea. I was determined, however, to follow Mila closely as she calmly sliced a passage through this seemingly impenetrable mass of flesh and noise. She was quite short and I marveled at how she could even see where she was going.

Suddenly, I was nearly knocked off my feet by a man who returned my outraged look with an insult in Arabic, something to the effect that if God gave me eyes, why wasn't I using them to look where I was going? My blood was boiling as I answered, in flawless Arabic, that if God gave him a life, he had best value it more dearly. The man laughed at my threat and actually waved good-bye to me as the crowd swallowed him. Was this a common Parisian interaction?

"I see you're a man of the world, monsieur," Mila observed with a wry smile. Before I could answer I was hit from the other side by some kind of basket on wheels that contained a human baby. The woman pushing the basket didn't even bother to look at me. I realized how dangerous it was to stand in one place; people resented any stoppage to their flowing chaos. I was sweating profusely and breathing in desperate gulps. Ah yes, being a human didn't alleviate the claustrophobia.

When we got outside to the "taxi stand," the sight that greeted me was unlike any I could ever have imagined. The stand was connected to a magnetic power grid that pulsed in a faintly discernible blue light above the street level. Hundreds of these small taxis moved in all directions along the pulsing grid like blue and black insects.

As above, so below where a mass of people and conveyances again somehow moved in several directions without colliding or even obstructing each other. It seems that as long as everyone agrees to move, this mysterious and sluggish flow is maintained. If anyone stops suddenly, as I had done inside the terminal, they are bumped and cursed without mercy until they rejoin the flow. I knew that Earth was a heavily populated planet, but I hadn't known that everyone lived in Paris. If Cardassians lived this tightly packed, we would have self-destructed long before now. The thought filled me with an unbearable sadness. Mila noticed my reaction to the intense activity of the city.

"It'll be alright, monsieur. It's the beginning of a holiday and everyone wants to get away."

Mila finally secured a taxi, an odd, cramped conveyance that I had to squeeze my body into. Once the doors were shut and the "driver" had programmed our destination into the taxi's computer, fresher air filled the interior and I began to breathe again. Except for the driver's occasional complaints about the *circulation,* the traffic, and the government that, according to him, no one seemed to like, we rode in silence within this network of pulsing blue lines.

From my narrow seat behind the driver I watched this strange world pass by; a motley collection of old stone buildings and modern designs of floating glass and metal. Streets, or *boulevards,* straight and seemingly organized according to a rational plan, suddenly broke off into branches of directional chaos (that word again). Even the smallest *rues* were crowded with people, some of whom were walking four-legged beasts that left their urine and feces for others to step in. Yet somehow, the slanting sunlight of the late afternoon, a filtered and roseate hue I had never seen before, cleansed the city of its filth, and these seemingly disparate and dissonant elements came together in a way that both attracted and saddened me, and awakened in me a mysterious yearning for something or someone. I could sense Mila discreetly watching me.

"It's not the same as you remember it?" she asked.

"Yes. For the most part," I answered. "I'm always surprised at how different it is from . . . other places."

"The Americans and the Germans think we're recalcitrant. They call Paris the 'museum city' because we won't make the changes they've made in their cities." She was looking out the window.

"But they keep coming here, don't they?" the driver snorted. "And do you know why?" He was looking directly at me.

"Uh . . . because they like a museum?" I ventured.

"Au contraire, monsieur!" he snorted again. "The Americans and Germans live in sterile boxes, but they don't want to forget what real life is like. So they come and eat our real food and walk our real streets with their guidebooks and begin to feel real feelings again. They remember what it is to be a human being. Why do you think the Federation chose us to build their headquarters?"

"Uh . . . because they want to be in a real city?"

"Voila!" I passed his test and he went back to his "driving." Mila continued to look out the window with a faint smile. It was clear that I was being introduced to a part of Earth, a diehard culture that wasn't featured in Federation propaganda. I vaguely remembered something Julian had said about the French being "different."

The "apartment" was not far from the *Gare du Nord* in an even older section called *Menilmontant* in the city's *"20th Arrondissement."* It was a small and cramped space with sleeping quarters and windows that opened onto a courtyard, a central and shared open space the apartment house was built around and that gave tenants access to the air outside before the building was retrofitted with climate control. It also gave tenants access to what was going on in their neighbors' apartments. Even with modern climate control, most tenants' windows were open, and the noises and smells of their lives drifted out onto the courtyard and up to my top floor. The building was long overdue for demolition, but because of the "historical" value of this section of the city, demolition was a legally complicated process. I was to find that my taxi driver wasn't the only person in Paris who wanted to keep it "real."

As I stood in the main room, the *salon,* and listened to the echoing conversations of my lower neighbors, and smelled their pungent food preparation, I wondered how long I had to stay in this relic. My understanding was that this would be a temporary lodging until I found accommodations that would include space for a tailor shop.

"Who arranged for these living quarters?" I asked Mila after she had explained the domestic details. She looked at me with a puzzled expression. Again, I felt like a fool.

"M. Sharib. I thought—" she began to ask.

"I know who my contact is," I interrupted, a bit too brusquely. "I just want to know who he used as an intermediary."

"Ah, an estate agent, you mean."

"Yes. Whatever you call him." I was losing my control; I had to be more careful. I could see Mila was somewhat confused by my confusion.

"I only know about M. Sharib. His information is on the apartment's data padd. He told me to tell you welcome, and he'll be in touch," she calmly explained. I nodded understanding, trying to repress my anger at being so inept. I knew that Mila was picking up everything—she was too good to just be a "tourist guide"— and she was too careful to reveal any kind of reaction to my ridiculous behavior.

"Well, if there's anything else, monsieur?" I could see that she wanted to leave.

"No. Thank you, Mila. You've been very kind." She nodded and went to the door. "How do I find you . . . if I need you for some reason?" I asked, again feeling clumsy. She stopped at the door and looked at me with her dark and steady eyes. The more time I spent with her, the more I was impressed by her grace and control.

"That information is also on the padd." She pointed to the table. She was about to say something else, I'm certain, but she just smiled and quietly left, shutting the door behind her.

I continued to stand, my feet rooted to the worn floor covering, and listened to the faint sounds of Parisian apartment life drifting up to my new home. Mila said that the building was nearly 500 years old. A conservative estimate, I think. Never in my life did I imagine I would be living in an alien culture's ancient history. The dreamlike circumstances surrounding me ever since I arrived collided with the sensory realness of it all, and I wondered if I hadn't died and been transported to some bizarre afterlife.

And then a more frightening question took shape: What if I had come to this place to die? I shivered, uprooted myself from these thoughts, and walked over to the padd on the table. Sharib. Why was the name familiar? I had to get busy and find out who this M. Sharib was before my disorientation turned my ancient Parisian apartment into something worse.

I picked up the padd and this is when the bottom literally began to fall out from under me. As I punched in the code Timot gave me, my hands and the padd began to liquefy. Everything—the apartment, the furnishings, the atmosphere—was flowing in a counterclockwise direction and being swallowed by a single black point. The code had activated the dissolution of my body and the surrounding space, and my consciousness, crystal clear and totally aware of what was going on, immediately surrendered to this unraveling of my Parisian reality. Rivers of energy, like great tributaries suddenly emerging from hidden sources, broke through the façade, joined the flow and swirled and roared around me flashing familiar images that dissolved before I could identify them. The whirling wormhole engulfed everything, and my dissolution into noncorporeal consciousness was complete; the "I" experienced an unattached lightness and equilibrium that was able to witness this furious process of matter returning to energy from a still, calm center.

"I" was pure feeling, and the feeling was an ecstasy of loving and knowing acceptance. The yearning that I felt in the Parisian taxi was somehow being fulfilled. I saw who "he" was: Elim Garak, a Cardassian creation of such narrow and meager dimensions it was a wonder he could even sustain himself on the most primitive level. Yes, "he," a starved cave dweller groping in the dark with

countless other cave dwellers, all reacting fearfully to the occasional shaft of light that briefly illuminates and blinds.

The ecstasy was Light. Every shadow dissolved, every dark corner revealed, every secret flushed out and exposed as an agent of
the death and decay the cave dwellers worshipped. A fleeting
thought connects this experience to death, but as the center ex-
pands and the Light becomes more familiar, the I understands that
the concept of death is as narrow as the three-dimensional concept
of life the cave dwellers have accepted. Yes, the I remembers that
there were promises, intimations of this Lighted Reality; the
blending hues of the Mekar Wilderness at twilight, the gentle healing light that cleansed and unified a filthy Paris, the moonlight that
contained Palandine in the Bamarren grounds. Where did he end
and she begin? Yes, there were premonitions, a foresight and fore-
taste of this journey to . . . ?

A structure assembles . . . elements of color, line, and texture
make shapes that begin to move like . . . Yes, the first shadows
pierce the light, and the center contracts into a box that presents a
vision of life from the other place where Elim Garak lives. It still
exists! The vision plays out and a shudder rocks the center as Elim
Garak walks out of Pythas Lok's office with Dr. Parmak. I am now
a Witness.

*"What do we do with him?" Nal Dejar asks Pythas. The answer is clearly
in the question.*

"He can never come back," Pythas agrees.

*"I'll arrange it," Prang says, completing the agreement, but before he can
leave, Pythas stops him.*

"I want him to live."

"I don't understand." Prang understands and is annoyed.

*"Let him live, Limor. Just as long as he never comes back," Pythas ex-
plains carefully to reinforce the decision.*

"Where is this possible?" Prang asks. His face has turned to stone.

"The Vinculum."

"Listen to me, Pythas Lok. Garak has many enemies. It would be a

422 Andrew J. Robinson

simple matter to just kill him. To spare his life is no solution. And it's not mercy. His life has run its course!"

Yes, we (I am not the only Witness) can even hear Pythas thinking: For Limor this is an oration, and he's right. Elim is exhausted, he no longer has any resources to draw upon. The inability to give the speech shows how depleted his morale is. Perhaps it is a kindness to kill him.

And Prang thinks: This is the sentimentality that Enabran allowed to come into the Order, and that nearly destroyed us. I taught Pythas to be harder. But the chain of command must be preserved, and Pythas is our only chance. So be it.

But the weakness galls Prang. Nal is so devoted to Pythas that she meshes in every way to the contours of his thinking. The harmony between them is powerful and Prang accepts the decision.

"Arrange it with Timot Mindur so that Elim will go to the Vinculum and never return," Pythas orders. "Parmak assures me that the controls are on this side."

"Should we worry about Parmak?" Nal Dejar asks.

"He'll never find out, Nal," Pythas replies. We're going to send Elim to Earth, he'll disappear, and it will be revealed that he was assassinated as he was attempting to make some kind of deal with the Federation. I don't think I have to explain to you how this will work to our advantage."

"I'll arrange it with Mindur." Prang's mind has gone blank. The Elim Garak problem has now been resolved, and there's nothing more to be said or thought on the matter.

Without thought the scene fades. The being called Elim Garak is disposed of in his father's former office by his oldest and closest friend, but he continues to exist in some dimensional fold as long as I keep him in my thoughts. I live in a paradox of motion and stillness. I can think, I can let go of my thinking. It makes no difference here. In the narrow, dimensional world of Elim Garak, the fear of death is the motivation for action and reaction; in the ecstatic world, the death of the ego is the starting point for all creative thought. But that doesn't mean that the ego can't be reborn. Anything is possible if creative thinking is supported by desire.

3

My dreams receded to that delicate area between sleeping and waking, and as I tried to assemble the remaining jumble of faint imagery into a coherent order, they disappeared completely. I opened my eyes and a soft, bluish light and utter calm greeted me. My first thought was that only death could be so peaceful. I couldn't remember where I was. Perhaps it was still a dream. I lifted myself up from the pallet into a sitting position, but the effort made me momentarily nauseated. I had to put my head down between my knees and breathe deeply to stem the anxiety. When I looked back up, there was a full-length mirror on the wall in front of me. Was it there before? And why was I relieved to see the image of myself looking back?

In the mirror, I saw a door slide open behind me. Somehow I knew I had to walk through the door and into the corridor beyond. I got to my feet and moved to the door, my head feeling light-years away from my feet. I stopped at the threshold and stared down the long corridor that receded into a blackness that brought back the memory of the blackness that had swallowed me. It was not fear that prevented me from crossing the threshold, but the uncertainty of what was real and what was a dream. I couldn't tell.

"Does it make any difference, Elim Garak?"

"Palandine?"

"Because if you're going to get out of here, my little *regnar*, you're going to have to learn to live in both places."

Shards of light swarmed out from the blackness and collected at a single point to create the radiant image of . . . Kel.

Before I could even form a question in my mind, I was crossing the threshold without any physical effort and following Kel, who was moving down the corridor toward a brightly lit opening. There was still no effort involved, and judging from how quickly we were nearing the now-lighted end of the corridor, it was almost as if we were riding on some kind of lightspeed conveyance. As we approached the end, the light engulfed us with such intensity that I couldn't keep my eyes open. I sensed the presence of shadowy figures all around me and the murmur of several conversations.

Gradually, and with great difficulty, my eyes adjusted and I found myself standing in the middle of an immense glass atrium filled with exotic plants and flowers, surrounded by countless groups of people engaged in earnest conversation. The openness of the space, the different levels, the soft, diffused light was a welcome relief after my confined and dark journey. The sight of artfully arranged Edosian orchids in the middle of the room lifted my heart and almost made me cry. The people were attractive and animated; I wanted to hear what they were saying.

"Go ahead, Elim. Feel free." Kel was standing next to me. Had I voiced my desire to mingle and be a part of this pleasant, civilized gathering? As I scanned the room, looking for a group to join, a thin figure caught my attention in an alcove bordered with vines. His back was turned to me and he was laughing at something someone in his group has said. At the exact moment of my recognition, he turned and looked directly at me. Julian! He nodded to me and indicated that I should join him and his group. He's not a Cardassian, I thought, what's he doing here? I immediately began to make my way through the crowd, but my progress was impeded by the thick groupings. I desperately tried to keep Dr. Bashir in my sightline, but the increasing number of people made it almost impossible.

"Julian!" I cried, but my voice couldn't rise above the din of the room. I found myself wedged in between several groups and unable to move. All requests to pass through were ignored, and I began to feel that I was invisible to these people. No one reacted or paid the slightest bit of attention to me. My breath came in shorter gasps and the familiar panic was constricting me with its icy grip. The room was becoming darker and the bright, intelligent people fading to shadows. My head was spinning and I suddenly wondered why I had come to this place to die.

"Elim. What a pleasure to see you again."

The voice shot through me like an electric charge. I turned and a shadowy, shimmering Tolan Garak was standing in front of me. He was dressed in an archaic robe worn by people engaged in Oralian ceremonies, and his appearance, although incomplete, suggested a man in his prime. Kel was standing behind him, her solid figure in contrast to his wavering shadow. Everyone had disappeared and we were standing in a smaller space that resembled the Lakarian City room where I had encountered Kel and Cronal Gys.

"Father," I whispered. The sight of him transported me to a simpler time, when I believed that Tolan *was* my father and that I would follow in his footsteps and become a gardener. "I've missed you."

Tolan studied me with his appraising kindness, and as he was about to say something, his body began to break up and fade like a faulty transmission. I looked at Kel, who was studying the walls of the room. The Hebitian frieze, celebrating the cycles of life, that I had first seen with her mother, Palandine, so long ago was beginning to appear at the bottom of one corner and move continuously around the walls, higher and higher on a diagonal, until the beginning began to disappear at the top of the same corner. The frieze was growing into a proud processional of ancient Hebitians displaying their prowess in every activity that sustains life. One of the dominant figures was Tolan, dressed in the same robe and cultivating a field of his beloved Edosian orchids.

"If they are able to understand how connected they are . . ." I realized that Tolan was speaking to me. ". . . if they can accept the connection, then the tribes can come together, they can celebrate . . ." His words wavered and faded with his body, but the frieze was now fully energized and moving more rapidly along the walls. New figures entered from the bottom and joined the half-naked Hebitians engaged in their traditional arts, trades, and crafts. These new arrivals were the survivors of modern Cardassia; the same farmers and herders, soldiers and mercenaries, fundamentalists and imperialists—even the surviving plague victims—that gathered in the Imperial Parade Grounds of the Tarlak Sector to hear me speak. They all joined in the procession that now filled the walls with metadimensional activity.

To accommodate this explosion of life, representing the entire history of Cardassia, the walls of the room expanded to the point where the three of us were dwarfed by the immensity and fullness of the spectacle. Nothing was left out. Creation was balanced by destruction, compassion by greed, love by hate. All acts were depicted, sublime and depraved. Heroes and sages appeared with despots and murderers. Nothing was left out.

The people who had filled the room when I first entered this place with Kel began to appear and join this stream of life. These charming and attractive people were the souls of the dead, I realized, who had been waiting for their place in the processional. And was it for my benefit that certain individuals were thrown into sharp relief? At first I experienced a great heaviness when I recognized Maladek and flashed to when we were probes on Tohvun III . . . then Toran and Entek, men I had murdered after I was exiled to Terok Nor . . . Barkan, who I once worshipped . . . and many more Cardassian souls I had dispatched to this place. But they marched in the procession with such pride of place, in the fullness of their youth and power, and with a dignity that's traveled far beyond my murderous acts.

My heart lightened when I saw Alon Ghemor, a great patriot and founder of the Reunion Project; Damar, the enemy who became my friend; Ziyal, the daughter of another enemy, who touched me in a way I didn't think was possible again. My feelings were more mixed when I saw Tain, my real father (even in death he seemed so sure of himself and his legacy), and Mila, the mother who pushed me to follow Tain's path. And while the path was lonely and painful, somehow she possessed the magic, and the will, to appear in many forms and to guide me at crucial moments.

And Palandine . . . so open and alive. The great empty place in my heart. Even now, I want to join you and walk together. Even now . . .

I can't hear Tolan's words, but I can see them in the unity of the frieze. Everyone is included, everyone is connected in the "great summing up" that Hebitians speak of as part of their daily life. Everyone is connected to his or her action and to each other. Cardassians—and I suddenly looked at my hands and my arms and felt my chest and groin and remembered that I was a Cardassian again—moving ahead, accepting the summing up, and at the same time returning to a desire to be awake and responsible for the choices that collect and form a civilization. There are no separations here, no breaks in the continuity.

In the minds of the living, we think we can interrupt the flow of life with acts of alienation that we justify and rationalize. War is a logical extension of diplomacy, someone once suggested. One can argue that murder is a moral act, even an extreme form of friendship. After all, I killed a person I loved. But here, in this Vinculum, as I watch all the souls who have gone before, it's clear that this separation, this alienation from the continuum, is our greatest illusion. It's simply a choice: We can live and die as separate beings, pain and suffering guaranteed—or we can merge and unify. Either way, it's all part of the procession, the living and the dead flowing together, collapsing time and unifying experience. Spiraling up, we move inexorably to recycle on another level.

"Are you still working with the orchids, Elim?" Tolan's apparition is barely visible.

"Not for a long time," I reply. He nods and smiles.

"Cultivate what's left. And teach someone else the method."

"I will," I say.

"Do you still have the mask?" he asks. Tolan means the recitation mask he gave me just before he died. Hebitian poets wore these masks at the festivals that celebrated Oralius, the spiritual entity that guided their community.

"Yes," I answer.

"Wear it the next time you speak, Elim. It will help remind them." Tolan reaches out his hand and holds it over my forehead. Slowly, he disappears completely. A suffusing glow radiates from directly overhead. The winged creature is suspended above us in a

great domed space and is turned toward a sun disc from which the
light emanates. Extending down from the creature's body are
countless tendrils that enter all the bodies of the now-halted processional as well as Kel's body and mine. My last image is Tolan and
Tain standing together with all the others spiraling up into infinity,
contemplating the sun disc and the creature whose face is covered
by the recitation mask.

"Are you alright, Elim?" Dr. Parmak's concerned eyes are peering
into mine. "Elim? Can you hear me?"

"Yes, Doctor, no need to shout." I'm stretched out on a pallet in
a room I don't recognize. "Where am I?"

"An old family home. What happened to you, Elim? And how
did they know to bring you here?" Parmak is relieved by my response, but his confusion remains.

" 'They'?" I ask.

"What?"

"Who brought me here?" As I raised myself from the pallet, I
felt a stabbing pain between my eyes.

"I have no idea. A person I had never seen before told me that
there was a . . . a situation involving you, and somehow he knew
that the house was uninhabited." Parmak cocks his head to his left
shoulder when he doesn't know something. "He made it very clear
that I wasn't to tell anyone about your return. What happened on
Earth, Elim?"

"Yes, Earth," I murmured, and I recalled how Dr. Bashir had
once spoken those words. It was another lifetime. Another mission.
Parmak studied me as I stood up and stretched my tight and
aching body—somehow it had returned to its Cardassian form.
And I'm not upset that it's older than I remember. "But I'm here
now, Doctor. At long last. And there's much work to do."

"Indeed, there is," he agreed.

I looked at him, wondering how I could ever explain. Parmak
was a scientist; he believed that we can reconstruct a society based
solely on a rational model. He had no idea that before he could

even get to that point, we had to surrender everything. Only then could we begin to move toward the unified vision Tolan unfolded for me in the Vinculum.

". . . where the pain of one is felt by all," I spoke aloud. Parmak was clearly unnerved by my behavior.

"All very mysterious, I must say. Perhaps I should contact Pythas."

"No!" I responded immediately. "Don't tell anyone that I'm here. Not even your Federation contact."

Parmak is shocked. His mouth opens, but words won't follow.

"Yes, I know," I replied gently. "Dr. Bashir told me during our first meeting in the Vinculum."

"You understand . . ." he stammered. "I meant no . . ."

"I do understand, Doctor. When you sent me to the Vinculum to find a plague cure, you also meant for me to encounter Dr. Bashir so that I would make an accommodation with the Federation."

"Did you find him?" Parmak asked.

"On that first trip, yes. Since then, we've lost all contact. But now it's vital that you tell no one that I've returned."

"But surely Pythas—"

"No one," I interrupted. "It is also vital that I find a way of getting to Lakarian City as soon as possible."

"Lakarian City," Parmak repeats. I knew how desperately he wants to ask why.

"There's much work to do, yes. But more important, it's work that we've never done before . . . or, not for a long time," I corrected myself.

Parmak nodded. *He's a good man,* I thought. I just didn't know if he was strong enough to take the next step of this journey.

I didn't know if I was.

Epilogue

You see, my dear Julian, the ancient Hebitians not only had access to the Vinculum, but the Vinculum was an integral part of their living reality. Everything was connected . . . and it still is, despite the fact that many of us deny it.

If you have any need to contact me, you know how. In the meantime, I send you my warmest regards.

Elim

Revisited
Part Two

Anonymous

Daylight poured through the window, casting shadows that moved restlessly across the rug—a dance of leaves caught in the morning breeze.

Melanie looked up at Jake, her eyes moist. "Thank you," she whispered.

Jake smiled. "You're a good listener. That's important in a writer."

She looked away. "I'm not a writer *yet.*"

"Sounds like you're waiting for something to happen that's going to turn you into one," Jake observed.

"I'm not waiting," she protested, then shrugged. "I'm doing a lot of reading. You know, to see how it's done. And . . . I'm still trying to figure out what I want to write about."

"I see," Jake said. He watched her for a moment, then made a decision. "I want you to see something. Go over to my desk."

Melanie hesitated, but then did as he instructed. When she saw what was on top of the desk, she looked up at him.

"Go ahead," he encouraged. "It's a collection of new stories."

Melanie picked up the manuscript and looked at the title page. *"Prophecy and Change.* Is this . . . is this about . . . ?"

"The people I knew on Deep Space 9," Jake confirmed. "Some of them anyway. I guess you could say it's part of the 'unofficial record.' I've been trying to decide whether or not to publish it. Now I think perhaps I will, after all. I want you to have a copy. Let me get you one . . ." Jake rose from the couch.

"Can I have these instead?"

Jake stopped and shrugged. "If you want, but they have hand-written notes all over them."

"I know," Melanie said. "I want to study them. So I can see the changes you made . . ."

"Because you want to be a writer someday," Jake said with a smile. "Thank you, Melanie."

She looked surprised. "For what?"

"For helping me to remember that the last page isn't necessarily the end of a story, and that there's still a lot that can happen in between, and before, and after."

"Because every chapter of our lives is formative," Melanie quoted. "And every moment is crucial."

"Keep that in mind until your next visit."

"Next visit?" Melanie repeated. "You're inviting me back?"

"Of course. And next time, I'll want to read *your* stories."

Tears streaked down Melanie's cheeks. Clutching Jake's stories to her breast, she went to him, kissed his cheek, and then was gone.

Jake stared at the door for a long time after she departed. He was still smiling when he finally moved to his desk and sat, resting his hands on the smooth wood surface. Almost without thinking, he reached for the baseball, gnarled fingers brushing its old worn hide, tracing the path of its stitching before his hand closed around it. It felt good against his palm. As it always did.

You really should get some sleep, he told himself. *You're too old to be staying up all night, much less all night and the following day.*

Jake returned the baseball to its pedestal.

Then he opened his desk, took out pen and paper, and began to write.